PENGUIN

The Summer of the Barshinskeys

Diane Pearson has worked in the publishing industry in London since she was sixteen, when she started as a junior production assistant at Jonathan Cape.

The Summer of the Barshinskeys is her first novel since the 1975 best-selling *Csardas* and arose from her interest in the relief work done by Quakers in Russia during the First World War.

The Summer of the Barshinskeys

DIANE PEARSON

Penguin Books

Penguin Books Canada Ltd., 2801 John Street, Markham, Ontario, Canada L3R 1B4
Penguin Books Ltd., Harmondsworth, Middlesex, England
Penguin Books, 40 West 23rd Street, New York, New York 10010 U.S.A.
Penguin Books Australia Ltd., Ringwood, Victoria, Australia
Penguin Books (N.Z.) Ltd., Private Bag, Takapuna, Auckland 9, New Zealand

First published in Canada by Penguin Books Canada Ltd., 1984
First published in the United States of America by Crown Publishers, Inc., 1984

Published in this edition by Penguin Books, 1985

Copyright © 1984 Diane Pearson

Manufactured in Canada

Canadian Cataloguing in Publication Data

Pearson, Diane.
  The summer of the Barshinskeys

ISBN 0-14-007456-2

I. Title.

PR6066.E18S85 1985   823'.914   C85-098639-7

TO RICHARD,
With my love

My thanks and acknowledgments are due to the following people, who helped me with a wide variety of subjects that I could not find in reference books: Mr. Albert Smith of Little Horwood; Mrs. Donald Robb of Connemara; Capt. Henry Howard of Midhurst, Sussex; Mr. M. Hyder of British Rail; Mr. David Spon of the Isle of Wight; Mr. J. Liston of the Ben Line, Edinburgh; the staff of the Library of the Society of Friends; and the Imperial War Museum.

Author's Note

Of course this book is fiction, most of it. But when I began to research the background I realized—so incredible were the stories I heard—that it could well and truly have happened. Indeed, some of the personal experiences that were related to me were far stranger than my tale. And so I decided to keep some of the real events that happened and include them in my story. Captain Patterson and Chief Engineer Bathgate were real people, the S.S. *Moscow II* was a real ship, and all the events pertaining to them are true (allowing for a little poetic license here and there). For those readers who are interested, Captain Patterson and Chief Engineer Bathgate did get home all right.

My little group of Quakers traveling to Buzuluk in 1916 is fictitious, but groups of Quakers *were* arriving there during the summer and autumn of that year. Flora D'Ete, Elizabeth Stubbs, Mr. Foulgar, and Mr. Goode are my people, but Robert Tatlock, Dr. Manning, and Nurse Morgan were real. If I have misrepresented any of the real people in this book I can only apologize. The entire episode of the Friends' Unit in Buzuluk was a remarkable one, both in courage and in endurance. The full story is told with scrupulous accuracy in Richenda Scott's *Quakers in Russia*.

The Summer of the Barshinskeys

Part One

—✧—

Sophie's Tale

1 THE FIRST TIME I SAW MR. BARSHINSKEY HE WAS strolling across Tyler's meadow with a fiddle under his arm. He was singing at the top of his voice in a language none of us could understand, and around the crown of his black hat was a garland of buttercups.

Behind him, pushing a handcart on which were an iron bedstead, a chest, and two kitchen chairs, came Mrs. Barshinskey. And behind her, carrying a variety of smaller household goods, were the Barshinskey children, two girls and a boy, the same as us. It was summer when the Barshinskeys came, and although the story of the Barshinskeys, which became our story, too, stretched over many summers and winters, that golden time of 1902 was when our strange, involved relationship began, when our youthful longing for the exotic, for the fulfillment of dreams not even dreamed, took a solid and restless hold upon us.

I still do not really understand what drew the Barshinskeys to us and, even stranger, what drew us to the Barshinskeys. They were little better than tinkers, we were "peasant gentry." They were poor, dirty, but free; we were well fed, comfortable, but confined tightly within our barriers of respectability. Sometimes I think our fascination for one another began because of *that* particular summer—I look back and remember everything bathed in a golden haze, and it is not just the magic memory of childhood that makes it so. I have spoken to old men and women about that summer of 1902, and it *was* a good summer, a strange one, when wild geese flew across the skies every evening, when there were bumper crops of wild strawberries, when haymaking finished two weeks earlier than usual. They remember and can date it because it was King Edward's coronation and the end of the war with the Boers and so they remember all the good things that happened, the record harvests of apples and plums and apri-

3

cots, the yield of honey and the number of swarms and the strength of the mead that was made that year.

I was eleven years old and I remember best the way the hedgerows were smothered in white blossom. When you walked to school along the lanes it was almost too much to bear.

That summer engrossed us all. Every day there was some new phenomenon, some new excitement to see and remark upon. And in May it was the evening flight of the swifts—thousands and thousands of them, screaming and whirling up into the air. No one could remember flights like it before, the circling and plummeting and then the final disappearance into the darkening sky. Every evening, just before tea, we ran to the top of the garden, pushed our way through a copse of elderflower and sycamore, and stood by the stile that led into Tyler's meadow to watch the miracle of the swifts. And there we were when the Barshinskeys came.

Edwin and I were shortish, so we were at the front, our arms and legs hooked all around the stile. Lillian stood behind us, tall, fair, her right hand stretched forward a little to lean on the post. Lillian had beautiful hands. I once heard Mother saying to Mrs. King, "Lillian's beautiful hands came from her Grandmother Cobham." I think Lillian heard it, too, because I noticed since that time she made a point of displaying her hands at every opportunity. They were indeed beautiful—slender, white, with long oval nails of rosy pink. Mine, in contrast, were short, stubby, and the nails were bitten down to the quicks. I took after my Grandfather Willoughby, although I suppose I couldn't blame him for the fact that they were chewed. Whenever I saw Lillian waving Grandmother Cobham's hands about in the air I would resolve to stop biting my nails, but it was difficult, and especially that summer it was difficult when the hedges were white and the swifts flew in the evening sky.

We didn't notice them much that evening because almost at once we saw the Barshinskeys. *He* was wonderful—big, with a thick curly black beard and eyes set deep and slanting in his brown face. He saw us watching and he waved his fiddle at us. It was a gesture of love, of welcoming warmth. You could feel, see him smiling. His beard and eyes moved, the brown face crinkled, and he shook his head at us in a way that suggested we shared some wonderful knowledge about how good life was.

Mrs. Barshinskey just looked faded and worn, but I suppose that was because of pushing the cart. The children were ragged and dirty, like tinkers' children, and they had no shoes. At once the gulf of social distinction was defined between us. Shoes more than anything else were the measure of living conditions in our village. Children with shoes were respectable, children without were not. Those who had no shoes had to undergo the gentle but humiliating experience of Miss Thurston, the schoolmistress, asking them to wait behind after class. She used to pretend that she wanted to talk about a lesson, but we all knew that as soon as everyone had gone she would open the cupboard and pull out the box of charity clothes. The next day would see the child hobbling to school in boots either too large or too small. Miss Thurston always provided thick stockings if the boots were too large. When they were too small she recommended that the laces be left undone. I only once saw her upset, and that was when someone had had the temerity to cut slits in the toes of too-small boots. Miss Thurston forgot her rule of never mentioning the charity clothes in front of the rest of the class and explained, sadly and earnestly, that mutilating good boots meant they were unlikely to survive another owner. Whenever I saw children in the charity boots I felt guilty. I felt guilty now and I pulled my legs back through the stile just in case the tinker's children should think I was flaunting my feet at them.

The boy saw us, and he turned his head and gave a kind of half-grin, a reflection of his father's smile, but not having quite the same effect. He didn't have the size or presence or warmth of his father. Still, it was a friendly sign—sort of—and I smiled back, but not too much. He stepped out of his way and came toward me, just close enough to call out, "I saw your knickers when you got off the stile." And he grinned again, nastily, and followed his mother with the cart.

"Well!"

I wanted to shout back something rude (if only *he* had been carrying the chamber pot, but no, it was the smaller girl who bore that), but I couldn't think of anything quick enough. Rage and mortification struggled for supremacy, and mortification won. It didn't help when I heard Lillian give a little snigger.

"I shall go and collect the eggs," I said with dignity. Both Lillian and Edwin ignored me.

"Are you coming?"

"I'll bet that's Mr. Hayward's new cowman," said Edwin without taking his eyes from them. "Dad said he was coming today, and he said he had three children. It must be the new cowman. . . ."

We stared afresh, in horror and in wonder. No cowman had ever looked like this one. Cowmen were respectable, responsible folk. They didn't wander into the village with fiddles under their arms, leaving their wives to push the furniture on a handcart.

"Dad's not going to be very pleased," Edwin continued thoughtfully.

Our father was head stockman at Hayward's farm and he wasn't very pleased anyway about the taking on of the new cowman. Mr. Hayward was what you would call "experimental" if you were feeling kind, or a "new-fangled idiot" if you weren't. He had a pedigree herd of shorthorns that took prizes every year at the county show. For the past two years he'd been experimenting, crossing breeds, trying different feeding tricks. Dad, who'd been patient but disapproving to begin with, had seen the herd grow, the milk yield increase. It had been decided that come Michaelmas a new man would be taken on; a man carefully selected by Father and Mr. Hayward at the Michaelmas Fair. And at the end of April Mr. Hayward had had one of his impetuous impulses and had told Dad that he'd seen a man at Sevenoaks market who "looked all right" and he'd taken him on. Dad, who never trusted farm workers who were out of work between the

Michaelmas hirings, was filled with suspicion and affronted dignity. The appearance of this black-bearded stranger was not going to allay the suspicion or mend the dignity.

I stared again at the little procession moving across the meadow. The woman was having trouble with the cart. One of the wheels kept veering to the left and she was constantly trying to push it out of dips and ruts in the ground. I saw the boy run up and heave on the handle with her, and suddenly the mortification I felt for myself changed into something deeper and more hurtful. I was ashamed—ashamed for the woman, not the man, and that I didn't understand. I felt she was wrong to let herself be used like that. It hadn't mattered when I'd thought they were tinkers. That was the way tinkers lived and the women expected to push the carts and do the work. But if he was a cowman it was humiliating for her, and now that I looked again she obviously wasn't a tinker. She was just a tired, ill-looking country woman who should have had more dignity and pride. I felt I couldn't bear to look at her anymore.

"Come on. We've still to collect the eggs. We'll be late for our tea."

Again they didn't answer or move, and then I saw that Edwin was staring at one of the girls, not the little one carrying the chamber pot, but the taller one, dark like her father, who carried a laundry basket full of kitchen things on her head.

At that time I was too young to recognize her sensual quality. I have seen it in one or two others since and now, because I know what that quality can do, I try to avoid the girls and women who possess it. Then, that first evening, I only knew she was different from any other girl in the village. She was wearing a gray dress, no pinafore, just the dress, and the bottom of it was uneven where the hem had come down. Her feet and ankles were brown and slim. A thick, glossy dark braid hung over one shoulder, and all around her face the hair sprang into curls, just like her father's. Her eyes were set into her face at a slant, like a cat's eyes, and her coloring seemed to be all black or olive or red. There was a brilliance about her, a lightness in the way she walked, a gaiety that made you feel she was going to burst out laughing at any moment.

"What are you thinking, Eddy?" I asked jealously. He was still looking at her, but you could never tell with Edwin just what he was thinking.

"What a very big nose that girl has," he said.

Somehow I felt happier. I looked at her and indeed she did have a big nose. It made her look even more like a cat. All she needed was whiskers standing out from each side of the nose.

"Come on. Let's get the eggs."

But still they didn't move, so I walked away and left them, staring at the retreating figures of the Barshinskeys, while the swifts screamed and disappeared up into the sky.

When you are young you believe that you will change beyond all recognition when you grow up. From the chrysalis that is me, now, will emerge at least a white cabbage butterfly, and if I am lucky a splendid dragonfly. It is not so, although sometimes there is what appears to be a drastic metamorphosis. What we are when we are young is what we remain all our lives. The selfish, greedy child grows into a selfish, greedy adult, although clever manners may conceal the greed and the selfishness for a while. Similarly, the patterns of our future are laid down within us, cast by our very natures, our likes and dislikes. Now, when I look back to that summer I see that the way we were, and the way the Barshinskeys were, set the pattern for the rest of our lives. Everything that happened that summer was a microcosm of the years that followed.

I collected the eggs and I thought about the man with buttercups around his hat, and the woman pushing the handcart. I thought about Grandfather Willoughby's hands, all bitten and nasty, and I thought about growing up into a world where white hedges and swifts were only the tip of wonderful things that were going to happen. And by the time I thought about all these things and dawdled over the eggs I realized I was going to be late for tea. When I got in, Lillian and Edwin, neatly washed and combed, were sitting in their places. Mother was very particular about cleanliness at mealtimes.

"Where have you been, Sophie? And look at your hands—go and wash them at once."

"I've been collecting the eggs."

"Well, you should have begun earlier and left time to wash your hands."

I glared at the other two, who sat there looking smug and righteous. One look at my mother's face had convinced me that indignant self-justification would be unwise. It was hot, it was baking day, and she was harassed and tired. The best thing to do was keep quiet. I went out to the scullery, washed my hands, and kicked hard at a sack of meal on my way back. I imagined the meal was Edwin's head and it made me feel a bit better.

"For what we are about to receive, may the Lord make us truly thankful," said Dad, and Mother, only just restraining herself for the Amen, fell upon the teapot.

I had divided feelings about baking day. On the one hand the bread was new, warm, and crusty. The smell of it made you happy and you couldn't really spread your butter unless you had the outside crust. You had to daub it on in lumps and watch it melt.

"Don't put your butter on like that, Sophie. If Lillian can spread hers then so can you."

"Lillian's got the crust."

"Don't argue with me."

That was why I had mixed feelings about baking day. The bread was good, but mother's temper was bad. She didn't really like cooking. She had been head parlor maid at the White House before she had married Dad, and although she set high household standards she had never really come to terms with having to cook for a family. It was worse in summer when the range had to be kept hot all day. Considering that she hated it so much it was surprising how good at it she was. Bread, sponge cakes, gingerbread, and pastries, all came out of the black range at their correct degrees of lightness or crispness. And with every risen loaf, every batch of buns, Mother's temper got worse.

"Don't slurp your tea, Sophie. And sit up straight. Your chin is practically on the table." I began to feel persecuted, a not unfamiliar feeling on baking day. Nervously I reached out my hand for another slice of bread. It was particularly *good* bread on that day when the Barshinskeys came.

"Just look at your fingernails, Sophie! When will you stop biting them? I'm going to put bitter aloes on again and see if that will cure you . . . and *ask* Lillian for the butter . . . don't push across like that. . . ."

Just when it was becoming too much Edwin gave me a little kick under the table and, when I looked up, he gave me a half-wink that Mother, fortunately, didn't see. She had just opened her mouth to say something more when Edwin hurriedly cut in.

"I think we saw the new cowman, Dad. Coming across Tyler's with a handcart and all the stuff piled on it."

"I've no doubt you did, son."

"Where are they going to live, Dad?"

Dad didn't answer at once. He sliced and buttered and drank, and we waited. That was Dad's way. There was always a reason for his slow responses; sometimes he was thinking, sometimes he wanted to prepare us for a surprise—or a shock. But whereas we never bothered to listen to anything Mother said, we always waited with full attention all through Dad's long pauses.

"They're going to live right next door. In the old Owl House."

A stunned silence fell over the table. Mother stared at him. Lillian's rosebud mouth rounded into a little "ooh!" of horror.

"Mr. Hayward won't have a cottage free till Michaelmas," Dad continued stolidly. "Told the chap that when he hired him. Chap said it didn't matter so long as Mr. Hayward could find him something to live in. Mr. Hayward told him there was Dent's old cottage up on the green—four shilling a week—or he could have the Owl House for nothing. Chap chose the Owl House."

The shocked pause continued. Mother, I think, felt her sense of decency outraged. That anyone should live in the Owl House was bad enough, but when in addition it was right next door to her, then her reverence for respectability was doubly assaulted. Lillian was obviously tingling with pleasurable horror, and Edwin and I were faintly resentful that our favorite hiding place should be legitimately occupied. Mother finally found words to break the silence.

"*Nobody* can live in the Owl House," she snapped, "least of all a woman with children. Has this man *seen* the house? Has his wife seen it?"

"I don't know, Maud," said Dad mildly. "But if it ain't right, then the cottage on the green is still empty—if he likes to pay four shilling a week."

Mother clattered the teapot lid, banged the kettle, pushed a cake plate a few inches to the left, then back to the right. "No doors between the rooms. No privy. Dirt floors. No proper stove. The nearest pump at the top of Tyler's meadow . . ."

"Unless they use ours, Maud."

"I'd want to know what kind of people they are before I let them make free with my scullery."

"They were tinkers, Ma," said Lillian. She had recovered from her shock and was beginning to enjoy the excitement of it all. "The children didn't have any shoes, and their furniture was old and shabby. We could see everything. They didn't even have the cart covered up." She cut her bread and butter into quarters and ate them daintily with Grandmother Cobham's hands.

"They weren't tinkers," I said, suddenly angry with Lillian. "The woman wasn't a tinker anyway. She was just . . . ordinary."

"She was pushing the cart like a tinker's woman," Lillian flared back.

Mother straightened her back and firmed her mouth into a line. "Well, whatever they are, we want nothing to do with them. Being neighborly is all very well, but there's enough poor folk in the village needing help without encouraging a lot of shoeless thieves who'll no doubt be at the chickens just as quick as they can climb over the hedge."

"I'd like a piece of seedy cake, Maud, when you're ready."

Mother, two spots of color in her cheeks, cut and passed. Everyone was silent, thinking of people living in the Owl House. I could never remember anyone living there, but Dad said that when he was a boy an old woman who bred ferrets had lived there. It was derelict, deserted except for owls and grass snakes, and surrounded by an enormous orchard of nettles and old apple trees. Edwin and I used to play there on wet baking and washing days. It was a wonderful place to play in—from the outside a mass of roofs, chimneys, and windows all at different levels. The roofs (there were nine of them) were made of red tiles covered in moss. Most of the windows were broken, but they were all unusual shapes. Some were arched like church windows, some were square and latticed. Inside it was just as weird. There were, as Mother had pointed out, no doors between the rooms, each opened directly into the next. Furthermore, no two rooms were on the same level. The first room one entered had a brick staircase rising out of it and this led to a tiny, very high room with two windows set one above the other. A flight of steps led down to a kitchen, another step down into a damp basement washroom (no water, but a huge stone trough along one side) and so it went on. It was like a rabbit warren—a marvelous house in which to play ghosts or murder. You never knew who was going to spring out at you behind an open doorway or down a steep staircase.

"Well now," said Dad, pushing his plate away. "That was a very good tea, Maud. I'd like to think that everyone in this village had such a good tea."

Mother didn't answer. She began to clatter plates together.

"I don't like to think of a woman with children going to bed hungry—not even someone to tell her where the nearest pump is." Mother clattered a bit more. "We've been very blessed in our family," Dad continued, his mild blue eyes blinking slightly, "and I wouldn't like it thought that we've set ourselves up above others less fortunate."

He rose from the table then, put his cap on, and left to return to the farm. Edwin went into the scullery, lifted the bucket of pig's swill from the floor and went to boil it on the outside stove.

I followed Mother out into the scullery. I vaguely knew what would happen next.

"Sophie," she said, "as soon as you've washed up you can go over next door and tell that woman where the pump is. You can tell her that for tonight she can draw water here. You can ask if you can be of help in any way—but there's no need to be too pressing. Just ask for politeness. And you can take this. I'll put a few things up." While she was talking she had filled her shopping basket; there were a loaf, a dozen eggs, butter in a cup without a handle ("For I don't suppose I'll get it back, not that I would fancy it if it did come back"), a jar of last year's crabapple jelly, a twist of tea and one of sugar, and a pail of milk.

"You're not to stay too long. I know what you are for talking to people. And you're to empty the basket there and then and bring it back."

"Can I go, too, Ma?" asked Lillian. Mother hesitated. To have clean, smooth, elegant Lillian visiting the Owl House was almost as bad as going herself.

"Please, Ma. You know what Sophie is—she'll end up spending the evening there and she'll come back without the basket. And she won't tell you the truth about what they're really like. She'll be full of some old nonsense about the color of their eyes or how long they can stand on their heads or rubbish of that sort."

"All right, then. You're to finish your evening jobs first, both of you."

Mine was the washing up, and filling the big kettles for the morning. On account of its being baking day there was a lot of washing up. Lillian's job was the mending. She was excused rough work because of her "aptitude with her needle." She was fourteen and would be leaving school in July and then, to the envy of every girl in the class, she was going to be apprenticed to Miss Clark, the dressmaker. Mother had been saving the premium for years out of her egg money and Miss Clark's acceptance of Lillian was the crowning achievement of Mother's life. One of us was going up in the world. In a small village like ours there weren't a lot of opportunities for "going up." If you were a girl there was only the jam and pickle factory if you were common, and service if you weren't. Lillian had transcended the fate of most village maidens. One had to admit that Lillian was elegant. She was tall, like Mother and like Grandmother Cobham. And she always considered her appearance, even when she was doing something ordinary like going to fetch the milk. She finished her sewing and by the time we were ready to go she had taken off her pinafore and wound her braids around her head in a thick flaxen crown. She was suddenly very grown up. Miss Lillian Willoughby, elder daughter of the house, on her way to pay a kindly call.

"I shall take the basket," she said. "You may carry the pail of milk."

There were two ways to the Owl House. The way Edwin and I used was through the gap in the box hedge and across the wild overgrown garden. The long way was from our back door, through our yard, down the brick path past the front door (never opened) to the road, turn right, thirty yards along the road, then into the Owl House gate, through the shadowy garden to the Owl House door.

"We'll go the long way, as we're visiting," said Lillian.

I huffed along behind her trying to hold the pail so that it didn't bang against my knees and slop. When I'd seen how nice Lillian looked I'd been tempted to take my pinafore off, too, but by the time we got to the Owl House gate I was glad I hadn't. My pinafore and my shoes were soaked with spilled milk.

We knocked on what was supposed to be the front door, although with the Owl House you could never really tell, and weren't a bit surprised when no one came. That was another curious thing about the Owl House—even though there were no doors, the sound hardly carried at all. One could scream and scream and never be heard. Finally we opened the door, climbed the brick steps to the high room, then went on down to the kitchen. I call it kitchen because it had two shelves that were really ledges in the wall, and a duck's nest fireplace. That was all, no larder and no range.

The woman was there, sitting on one of the chairs with her head leaning back against the wall. Her face was gray and little beads of sweat stood out on her forehead. The boy who had been so rude to me was lighting a fire in the duck's nest fireplace and the small girl, the one who had carried the chamber pot, was unpacking china and pans from a basket and putting them on one of the shelves. The big, black, exciting man and the girl who looked like a cat were missing.

Lillian put her hand up to her mouth and coughed delicately. "Excuse me," she said, in her pretty, good-mannered voice. "We're from next door. I'm Lillian Willoughby and this is my little sister, Sophie."

The woman opened her eyes. The boy and the girl spun around from their tasks.

"Mother has sent a few things, not knowing how you were placed and all." Lillian's eyes were darting all over the place, taking in the quality of their china and the degree of cleanliness over everything. "She thought you might not be able to find the pump," she continued sweetly. "It's at the top of the meadow. You can get to it by going to the top of the garden and climbing through the hedge."

"But you can use our pump right next door," I added quickly. "Just for tonight."

The woman stood up and tried to push strands of faded fair hair back behind her ears. She flushed a little and said, rather stiffly, "That's very kind of you. But we can manage. . . ."

Her voice, surprisingly, was gentle and ladylike. She had a Kentish burr like the rest of us but she spoke . . . nicely, as Mother would say. It was the voice of a respectable country girl who had been to school and then into service in a big house. It was rather startling to hear such a voice coming from a woman who looked like a tinker. She rubbed her hands down the side of her mud-colored dress.

"I'm Mrs. Barshinskey," she said. "And this is Ivan, and this is Daisy May."

Barshinskey! What a name! Never, never had we had a name like that in the village. And Ivan too. No Ivans at all. Plenty of

Daisys and Mays of course but even so, Daisy May Barshin-skey . . .

Daisy May took the basket from Lillian's hand very quickly, as though she thought Lillian might change her mind.

"We want the basket back," said Lillian, slightly nettled.

Daisy May began to take out the things. The attention of the three Barshinskeys was riveted on the basket. They were absolutely silent and their eyes moved back and forth with Daisy May's hands. The last item to come out was the loaf, still warm and smelling of yeast. The air suddenly became charged.

"How very kind of your mother," said Mrs. Barshinskey at last. "Please thank her. Most thoughtful . . . most thoughtful . . ." Her voice faltered and faded.

"Mother baked the bread today—it does cut so badly when it's fresh, doesn't it? And, oh dear, the handle of the cup is missing. How remiss of Mother. She couldn't have noticed otherwise it would have been thrown away, but the butter was churned yesterday and the eggs are fresh. We collected them just before tea."

"No, you didn't. I did."

She pretended not to hear but the back of her neck went pink. I slapped the pail of milk down on the floor, what was left of it.

"Would you like to come over to our house for some water?" asked Lillian graciously.

The boy stopped looking at the bread and looked at Lillian instead. He was a good bit shorter than she was but the way he looked at her made me almost forgive him for calling out about my knickers. "No, thank you. We can find our way to the pump." He stared and stared at Lillian and finally she went very red and turned to Mrs. Barshinskey, who was easier meat.

"Please do come over and ask if you need any help. Perhaps Mother could loan you a few extra things. . . ." Her eyes wandered over the few pots and bits of china, then rested on a sacking mattress cover that was half filled with grass. "We've got all Grandmother Willoughby's things stored in the shed. I'm sure Mother would help if you needed some bedding."

16

My back was crawling with embarrassment, but I didn't know how to put it right. I just wanted to get out of there.

"We don't need anything, thank you," said the boy. "The rest of our stuff is coming later. We've just brought what we could manage. Isn't that right, Daisy?"

"That's right." They stood side by side, a solid barrier between us and their mother. I tugged on Lillian's dress and backed toward the steps.

"Oh well," said Lillian coldly. "I must be going. I still have my harmonium practice to do. Come, Sophie." She swept past me and up the steps. She was out of the house before I'd even left the room. At the top of the steps I turned back, trying to think of something nice to say, something to show that we were no better than they were, but I wished I hadn't because Mrs. Barshinskey was holding a big brown egg in her hand and was looking at it as though it were a guinea piece. "Oh, Daisy," she was murmuring, "just look at all this food—all the eggs and butter and milk. . . ."

"No better than tinkers," said Lillian angrily as we walked back through the nettles. "That child, so rude, and the boy, did you see the way he looked at me, him without shoes and his backside hanging out from his trousers."

"I'll tell Mother you said backside," I said spitefully, and Lillian gave a little toss of her head and hurried on. I let her go, and then looked back at the Owl House through the growing dusk. There were sprigs of blossom on the ancient apple trees, not that they would fruit, they never did. But they were pretty and beyond them was another of the huge streaked skies that were so prevalent that summer. It had never struck me before how mysterious the Owl House looked. One could imagine a magician living there. The sky changed, scarlet to purple, and I wondered what I would do if a magician, or a black knight with his visor down, suddenly came around from the back of the house. No knight or wizard did come, but Ivan Barshinskey did, with a bucket. He paused, then turned up toward the top of the garden.

"Shall I come with you?"

17

"No, thank you. I can find it."

He had a sallowish skin and a funny snub nose. His hair was black, like his father's and like the cat girl, and his eyes, too, were set at a slant.

"It's getting dark. You might miss it." He didn't answer so I took it to mean it was all right if I went with him. We pushed through the gap in the hedge, and then walked up the meadow to the top stile. It was dark by the time we got there and we could only just see the pump.

"It comes out with a gush unless you're careful. You hold the bucket and I'll do it."

He didn't answer, but he held the bucket under the spout and I began to pump. Whether it was because it was dark, or because I was nervous I don't know, but I did it too hard and suddenly the water did spout in a fierce jet all over him. He dropped the bucket and jumped back shouting at me, "You dirty pig! You did that on purpose!"

My first reaction was one of shock, to think that *anyone*, even a shoeless lout like Ivan Barshinskey, could be so rude. But shock didn't last long and almost immediately I felt a deep and scratching fury. Ever since Lillian had played Lady Bountiful to Mrs. Barshinskey I had felt uncomfortable, and that same discomfort needed to be relieved.

"Serve you right for shouting out about my drawers, you dirty tinker!"

In spite of the spouting pump some of the water, quite a lot, had gone into the bucket. Ivan Barshinskey picked it up and threw it over me.

Most of it went in my face, caught me on an in breath and made me cough and splutter. Usually I wasn't a very aggressive person. Anyone who liked to threaten me with physical violence found that Sophie Willoughby was a weak, cringing, crawling coward. But the Barshinskeys had changed me. There was a sore abrasive spot somewhere in my middle that was making me unhappy. When I tried to think why, I couldn't. It was something to do with baking day and my bitten nails. It was Mrs. Barshinskey pushing the cart when she wasn't a tinker. It was Lillian being beautiful and at the same time so nasty. And it was none of these things. It was a soft May evening and a sense of longing for I didn't know what. The deep fury welled to the surface, and then Ivan Barshinskey scooped the last few drops of water from the bucket and threw them in my face.

"Yah!" he sneered, and I lowered my head and charged.

I caught him in the middle of his chest and although he was bigger than me I took him off balance and we crashed to the ground where we rolled and pummeled and punched. If we had been able to put our fight into words we would have realized that neither of us was fighting the other. We just needed a punchbag.

I was no match for him. He was thirteen, tough, and wiry. I was eleven and small for my age. I also had long braids which I have always considered an unfair female handicap in a fight. It wasn't long before I lay flat on my stomach, Ivan Barshinskey's knee in my back, and my head pulled back by my hair. It was agony and made my eyes smart. I hated Ivan Barshinskey with a burning hatred that was all the worse because I couldn't move. I wriggled and called him a hog, a maggot, a crow, and anything else I could think of. All he did was jerk my braids even harder and grind his knee into the small of my back.

"Say feignits!"

"No." A harder tug.

"Say feignits!"

I really thought I was going to have to say feignits, the pain was so bad. But I was saved. Never had I been so pleased to hear my dad's voice before.

"Well, Sophie. I don't know what your mother's going to say when she sees the state you're in. I've a feeling she's not going to be best pleased."

The pressure on my back suddenly stopped and my braids were released. When I managed to roll over and climb to my feet, Ivan Barshinskey had sprung away and was glaring at both me and my dad.

"What are you doing up here this late anyway?" he asked mildly.

"Showing *him* where the pump is."

"Oh . . . um . . ." Dad pursed his lips together, nodded his head, and then stared up into the sky. "You're the cowman's lad, aren't you? The Barshinskey boy?"

Ivan didn't answer. His face, in the dim light, looked like that of a trapped fox. I could even see the whites of his eyes moving from side to side. I stood there with my dad, and even though I knew I was going to be in real trouble when I got in, I was suddenly much sorrier for him. He looked wild, and frightened. His clothes, such as they were, were as wet as mine, and he didn't have a nice clean feather bed with sheets and blankets to go to. Behind my misery was the comfort of home, and Dad, and warmth with everything predictable and familiar, even the clumps around the ears and the scolds by Mother on baking days. I'd seen what lay behind him.

"We fell over, Dad," I said sullenly. "The pump spouted and we fell in the mud."

"I'm pleased to hear it, Sophie," said Dad solemnly. "Now you two hold the bucket steady between you while I fill it, then no one will get wet or slip in the mud."

Side by side, not speaking, we held the bucket while Dad filled it. Then he came around, lifted it, and set off in the direction of the Barshinskey hedge.

"I can carry it," said Ivan Barshinskey stubbornly.

Dad didn't hesitate for an instant. He passed it straight over with a "Right-o" and then strode off into the night. "Now don't you be long, Sophie."

Ivan and I walked back in silence, the way we had walked out. When we got to the hedge I held it back so he could get through without spilling any water.

"Thanks," he said distantly, and as though the sound of his voice broke the icy silence and gave him another chance to be rude he continued, "When I saw you all standing gawping at us from the stile, I thought you looked a stuck-up lot. And you are. You think you're better than anyone else, don't you? Your sister's a stuck-up cow, and you showed your drawers when you got off the stile."

It was quite a lot to swallow, but I did. For I carried the memory of him standing trapped and frightened by the pump—frightened of my dad because he was grown up and on my side and represented order and rules. I understood that Ivan Barshinskey had no one to fight on his side with those kinds of weapons; order, rules, respectability were threats to him. I understood as well that the basket of food, which was in one sense so very necessary, had hurt him. So had my offer to show him where the pump was. So had the fact that my dad had not threatened him, but helped him. He owed us favors on all sides, and he hated it.

"Lillian is a stuck-up cow," I said weakly, wondering if the sky would open and the Lord strike me dead for such family disloyalty. I often didn't like her much, but it was one thing sharing critical notes with my brother Edwin and another thing altogether calling her a cow to placate this strange boy. "She's the eldest, and the prettiest. She takes after the Cobham side of the family and she's very neat and elegant and also has an aptitude with her needle. She's Mother's favorite and I'm afraid she suffers from *folie de grandeur*." I had read that phrase in a book at the beginning of term, and had asked Miss Thurston what it meant. Her explanation delighted me because it meant just the way it sounded. For several weeks I had used it on every occasion, about Lillian, Mother, Mrs. King, even Lady Audley, who was the prize cow in Mr. Hayward's herd. Everyone was tired of hearing me say it and Dad had finally banned the expression from the house. But here was a virgin ear, and never had the circumstances for its use been so right.

"Ay must be goin'," mimicked Ivan Barshinskey. "Ay still 'ave my 'armonium practice to do."

That I didn't like much. There is something especially offensive about ridiculing people's speech and to mock Lillian's manner of speaking was to mock mine.

"Ha ha! Very funny," I snarled, and Ivan Barshinskey looked pleased.

At the door of the Owl House, Daisy May was waiting. "You've been a time. Mother wants the water to boil for tea."

She took in the condition of us—wet, muddy, hair tangled, faces red with anger.

"My," she said, staring at my dress and pinafore. "You look awful. Won't you get into trouble looking like that?"

The balance of privilege suddenly swung over to Ivan Barshinskey. I looked at him, then down at my clothes. It was obvious that no one would give one jot for his appearance, but I was going to be in terrible trouble. The drying milk stains were bad enough, but now I was soaking wet, covered in mud (which was also well caked into my hair) and, oh horror, I had a warm sticky feeling in my nose.

"Is my nose bleeding?" I asked, and "Yes" they chorused in such quick unison that I knew I was shortly going to add blood to my collection of stains.

"That's it, then. I'll be for it. She'll know I've been fighting . . . that's the one thing she won't have. The milk and the mud are bad enough, but if I've got nosebleed . . ." The brief passage of pity, of insight into Ivan Barshinskey, vanished in my own desperation. Somehow I had to walk across that garden, push through the hedge, and walk into our kitchen. I closed my eyes and saw Mother's face change from astonishment to disgusted fury. I quickly opened my eyes, not wanting to imagine the rest. The panic began to give way to apathetic despair. "I wish I hadn't come," I said hollowly.

"Wait here." Daisy May darted back into the house and emerged a few minutes later with the chamber pot. "Put some of that water into here," she instructed her brother. "Not too much, we can't spare it if the pump is that far away." He poured out a few inches of water and she held out a piece of rag. "Wash your face," she said, "and see, I've brought my comb. If you rebraid your hair, and wash your face, you won't look nearly so bad. It will only seem as though you've fallen over."

I'd never washed in a chamber pot before and for a moment my stomach turned at the thought that it was most unlikely the Barshinskeys ever scoured out their chamber pots as we did.

"Hurry," said Daisy May. "The blood's going to drip on your pinafore any minute now."

Grandmother Cobham turned in her grave, and I dipped the rag in the chamber pot and wiped my face. The blood began to come faster from my nose and I held the rag over it. "*Please* stop bleeding, nose," I prayed, for Daisy May had been quite right. If I went in looking as though I had slipped at the pump it would be no more than a slap and an everlasting scold. If I went in covered in blood and with my hair pulled out and tangled, Mother would know it was more than a fall.

As I knelt over the pot, dripping blood, I felt Daisy May undo one of my braids. Her movements were very gentle, neat and quick, rather like Lillian's. Then, to my astonishment, I felt someone undoing the other braid, just as neatly, just as quickly.

"Comb your side first, Dais, then I'll have a go at this one," said Ivan Barshinskey. Like a plow team, or like my dad and Mr. Hayward when they were milking forty cows on their own, they unbraided, combed, and braided again.

"Has it stopped bleeding yet?" asked Daisy May with interest.

"Doh."

Ivan pushed me back on the ground. For an instant I thought he was about to pummel into me again, but he was just trying to stop the bleeding. He held the wet cloth jammed up hard against my nostrils so that the blood could not run onto my clothes. Finally he put the rag around two of his fingers and stuck them up my nose like plugs, and there we sat, the three of us, surrounded by nettles and old bramleys, lit by a thin sliver of moon, and silent except for my breath heaving noisily through my mouth.

"I'd best take the water in," said Daisy May, and she vanished into the house with the bucket and the chamber pot, while Ivan and I remained in disjointed intimacy.

With his fingers jammed up my bloody nose, he stared disdainfully out into the darkness. "You're not very pretty," he said, resuming some far distant conversation, "but at least you're not a stuck-up cow."

"Thangs."

"I think it's stopped now." Gingerly he removed his fingers

and wiped the rag across my mouth. I stood up, very carefully, and he brushed the back of me down and pulled bits of grass from my neatly combed hair. Later I was to think how strange it was that these two ragged, shoeless, dirty, undisciplined children should take such care about returning me home in mint condition. It was as though they were observing the customs of a foreign and favored tribe, wanting to show that they knew the rules and could execute them just as efficiently whenever they had the chance.

When I stepped into the scullery the blast descended upon me. There was a moment while she made certain that I was all right, for she was a good mother even to me, the most irritating of her children, and then the wrath of baking day exploded. I didn't get a slap around the ear (which was just as well considering the delicate condition of my nose), but I was wrenched forward to the sink, pinafore ripped off and thrown into a bucket, frock pulled roughly over my head with a shouted, "Father! Edwin! Keep out of the scullery. This child is filthy! Dad, pass me in the big kettle . . . this is what comes of having riffraff move in next door . . . look at you! Just look at the state of you . . . mud all around your petticoats! Stockings!"

Off came the flannelette petticoat, then the flannel (ne'er cast a clout till May be out) and finally when I was down to my liberty bodice and drawers Mother was satisfied that the contaminated garments had all been removed. Dad's hand came modestly around the door with the kettle.

"Right. You get yourself washed down, my girl, and then you get up to bed."

"But Edwin and Lillian are still up . . ."

Oh, why hadn't I the sense to be quiet? I got the slap then, several of them across the legs and another across the shoulders, and a nonstop tirade which was Mother's way of getting baking day out of her system. As a background to the incessant voice was the noise of Lillian creaking away on the old harmonium. When Mother's temper was finally exhausted I was left with the kettle, family washing flannel, and carbolic soap to wash—and feeling sorry for myself. At one point the door opened and my nightgown was thrown in.

When I finally went into the kitchen it was to find Dad sitting reading his Bible, and Ma, with a face like an old prune, cleaning the silver. Usually at this time of night she stopped working and would read alongside Dad, or just sit by the stove and drink tea. But tonight it was as though she wanted to drive herself even further, to demonstrate by work that we were going to be better than anyone else, in spite of ourselves.

"Goodnight, Dad."

"Goodnight, lass."

I paused and went over to Mother. "Goodnight, Ma."

Mother held out a stiff, disapproving cheek for me to kiss. "Goodnight, Sophie."

I knew it would be better if I just went silently to my bed, but I couldn't, for I was worried about my friends, the Barshinskeys. My way of telling things wasn't always the truth, but neither was Lillian's and I couldn't help wondering what kind of tale she had come back with.

"They were ever so grateful for all the things, Ma. Mrs. Barshinskey nearly cried she was so grateful."

Mother gave a disbelieving—or maybe it was disapproving—sniff.

"They're not riffraff . . . or tinkers. Mrs. Barshinskey looked ill, and the little girl is called Daisy May and she was very nice. And although they didn't have many good things . . . well, the rest of their stuff is coming."

She sniffed again, and rubbed at the silver as though it represented every tinker or piece of dirt in the world.

"Mrs. Barshinskey was . . . well, *respectable*, Ma. She spoke just like you do." I realized at once that I shouldn't have said that. Mother's mouth practically disappeared back into her face. "And she didn't *presume*," I went on hurriedly. "I mean, we told her she could use our tap for tonight but she said no, thank you, they could manage all right. That shows she's respectable, doesn't it?" And as Mother showed no sign of unbending, or even acknowl-

25

edging my comments, I flung in my last card. "And she really did look terribly ill. When we went in she was leaning back against the wall and her face was all covered in sweat."

"Don't use that word, Sophie."

"Perspiration."

"I should go to bed now, lassie. It won't be long before the others are up."

"Goodnight, then." I lingered, swinging on the door, but Mother didn't answer and so I stumped my way gloomily up the stairs. Lillian and I shared the small room at the back of the house. Edwin had the big middle one all to himself, which wasn't really sensible except that you had to go through Edwin's room to get to ours. And Mother was adamant about girls' rooms being private.

I thought idly about making him an apple-pie bed to pay him back for not helping me with the eggs, but the heart had gone out of me, and apple-pie beds seemed rather childish when I thought about the Barshinskeys and their mattresses filled with grass.

I said my prayers, and included the Barshinskeys in those who were in need of care and protection. If Ma was going to take against them they would need God on their side. When Lillian came up I pretended to be asleep. I had a lot of scores to settle against Lillian on that particular day, not least introducing me to the Barshinskeys as her "little sister, Sophie." She knew I wasn't asleep, and I knew that she knew, but we lay there and watched the moon over the May trees, and after a while I felt her side of the bed shaking.

"Don't you dare laugh at me," I snarled.

The bed went on shaking, and I reached out my hand and touched her. She was all curled up with her hands knotted against her chest and the pillow all wet. Lillian was crying! Immediately I felt horrible because I hated her so much.

"Oh! Don't cry, Lil. I never told Ma you said backside."

"Don't call me Lil," she sobbed.

I stared out at the moon and listened to her crying, not really knowing what to do. She was fourteen and grown up, and I was conscious enough of the developing years to know that I was still

26

a child. I had never seen her cry before and I didn't know what kind of things made grownups cry. I thought hard. I had cried when my rabbit died, and even more when Grandfather Willoughby died for he was a dear old man and I was his favorite grandchild. I'd cried when my finger was broken in the hen house door, and again when the doctor set it. I'd *wanted* to cry when I'd seen Mrs. Barshinskey holding the egg.

"Lil," I whispered. "Lillian, is it something to do with the Barshinskeys?"

"I only wanted them to like me," she sobbed. "And that boy stared at me as though I were dirt. He didn't even say thank you —not for all those lovely things I gave them. They weren't a bit grateful, not any of them, not after I'd taken all that trouble."

I was too young then to explain to Lillian how hard it is to be grateful. To describe how awful it must be to have boots out of the charity box or be offered bedding from the woodshed. And I think that even if I had been old enough to explain these things to Lillian it wouldn't have done any good. Lillian had a bit missing out of her. She was the only person I ever knew who was entirely lacking in empathy. She never could understand what went on in other people's heads.

From the ineffectualness of eleven years old, the groping for words to put instincts and feeling into practical terms, I could only pat her on the shoulders and say miserably, "Don't cry, sis. It'll be all right in the morning."

Her sobs died slowly away and by the time the moon moved above the top of the window she had gone to sleep. But I couldn't sleep, and after a while I realized I could hear something strange and alien out there in the darkness, something other than owls and the barking of the old dog fox who ran across Tyler's meadow every night. I lay rigid, and then my bedroom door opened and the noise was louder. I heard Edwin whisper, "Sophie, are you awake? Come and look out of my window."

The window of his bedroom looked right out on to the Owl House garden (and how glad I was that Mum and Dad's room was at the front of the house). We stood, riveted against the window, for there in the nettles and undergrowth of the Owl

House garden was a huge fire, flames red and golden, leaping up to light the weird shapes of the old trees. Silhouetted against the flames was Mr. Barshinskey in his funny black coat and wide-brimmed hat. His fiddle was tucked under his chin and from it came the most exciting music I had ever heard. We'd all heard fiddles before and they played tunes like "Gathering Peascods" and "Stripping the Willow." And at school we sang hymns, and "Linden Lea," and "Old Meg She Was a Gypsy." But this music was different. It was wailing and melancholy and it made you want to reach out your arms and scream, and then it would change and there would be such a wild strong beat that I felt the whole village must get up and dance. As we watched, and listened, a figure stood up on the other side of the fire. It was the girl with the big nose who looked like a cat. She raised her hands over her head and began to clap them in time with the music. Edwin and I, unconsciously, were tapping our feet. The music got faster and the girl began to whirl and twirl around the fire, ragged skirts flying out, just missing the flames. Then she flopped down flat on her back, stretching her arms and legs out in pleasure, just the way an animal did. The fiddle wailed again. Edwin's hand reached for mine and our fingers clasped. For the first time I was aware that somewhere in the world there was more than just growing up and having children and being respectable. There were huge things and terrible undefined longing, dreams that had no visible shapes but that you still had to reach up for. I felt I would never be satisfied with anything in my life again.

We stood there for hours, or so it seemed, until Mr. Barshinskey finally put his fiddle down and the fire turned into a controlled flickering. Then, when we saw Mr. Barshinskey roll himself into a blanket, and the girl on the other side doing the same, we realized we were cold and tired.

"Get into bed with me, Soph," Edwin said, his body shaking, and I did. And as we clung together I knew it was more than just the cold making us shake. We had had a foretaste of that heady potion called life.

2 FRIDAY WAS BEDROOMS. AS SOON AS EDWIN HAD FIN-
ished washing in the scullery Mother came up with
the clean bed linen.

"Up now, you girls. Edwin's finished, and there's
these beds to be done before you go to school."

In a household of two men and three women, modesty was
the product of strictly observed rules. Dad was up first, at half-
past four. In the winter and on baking days he lit the range and
got the kettles boiling. Then he went off for early milking.
Mother rose, washed in the privacy of the scullery with her half-
kettle of hot water, roused Edwin, whose turn it then was for the
scullery. When Edwin went to feed the pigs, it was our turn.
Scullery door locked, curtains pulled across the window, half a
kettle of water each. Dad and Edwin were men and had to make
do with cold water. That was one of the advantages of Mother's
eleven years at the White House. There she had acquired the
manners and philosophy of her betters, among which was the
belief that women were frailer than men and needed a little more
cosseting. The rule was broken in winter when the water had ice
on it. Dad and Edwin were each allowed a trickle of hot in the
basin then.

After we'd washed we went back upstairs and made the beds.
But Friday was Bedrooms and we had to change the linen of
Edwin's bed and on ours. Lillian and I always quarrelled when
we did this. She liked to fold the dirty sheets into tidy packed
piles. I liked to throw them all over the floor so that it looked like
an Eastern harem. (I had a red Bible with pictures in it and one
of them showed the court of King Solomon. There were sheets
draped all over the place, only they were satin and colored.)
Lillian liked the covers turned down low so that when she was in
bed her shoulders were exposed. I liked them high so that I could
burrow right down into a smelly old cave. This morning she was

29

particularly bossy, and I was particularly wild. The Barshinskeys had something to do with it.

With a screech of what I hoped was horror, I flung the dirty sheets high into the air and let them fall over Lillian's neatly coiffed head. She fought manfully to get out and it really looked very funny as the sheets bumped and heaved in fury.

> *"There stands the ghost of Lillian Willoughby,*
> *Died,*
> *A bride,*
> *At the age of fourteen."*

She emerged from the sheets red-faced, her braided hair fraying a little.

"You're a nasty, loathsome little girl! I'm not going to make beds with you. I shall leave you to do them on your own." She pushed me out of the room and closed the door. I heard her put a chair under the handle so that I couldn't get in again. What she meant was that she would do our bed just the way she liked it with the covers down, and leave me to do Edwin's. I began to strip his bed and then I looked out of the window.

We hadn't dreamed it. There was a circle of black on the ground and a few charred embers. It had all been exactly as we'd seen it, but for some reason I didn't want to think about it and I knew Edwin didn't either.

Lillian finally came out of the bedroom. She'd rebraided her hair which was exactly the kind of thing she would do. Down the stairs, the smell of porridge cooking on the range, and a warning, "Only a few moments now, Sophie."

"Can I have some milk for Tibby?"

The enamel bowl was filled. I went to let Tibby out of the woodshed, and then stopped. Ivan Barshinskey was waiting outside.

"Hello."

" 'Lo."

He scuffed his toes on the ground and looked sulky. "You all right?"

"Yes."

Tibby, released from smelly captivity, bounded out from the woodshed, raced three times around the yard, jumped on top of the dog's kennel, then into the hedge, then came back to drink her milk.

"What d'you lock her up for? She don't like it."

"So as the fox don't get her."

Tibby looked up, her face and whiskers smothered in milk, sneezed, and Ivan Barshinskey smiled.

I never saw a smile make so much difference to someone. It totally changed him. He turned from a sallow-faced, worried, sulky-looking boy into a shy and welcoming young man. The brown eyes seemed to lighten and warm and there was a look about him that suggested he thought everything was tremendously funny. I couldn't *believe* it was the same person. *This* Ivan Barshinskey was a wonderful person and when you looked at him you forgot all about his snub nose and his dirty feet and his backside hanging out of his trousers.

"Sophie! I told you . . . only a few moments . . ."

The smile was switched off. "I've come to ask if you'll take Daisy May to school. My mother's ill."

"Sophie, do I have to tell you again . . ." Mother came out of the scullery and when she saw Ivan Barshinskey she stopped.

"Ivan wants me and Lillian to take Daisy May to school, Ma."

"Lillian and me," said Mother automatically. She looked at Ivan's torn trousers and dirty shirt. He really did resemble one of the pictures in my Sunday School prize book, the pictures that illustrated stories about slum children dying of consumption in attics. He looked down at the ground and mumbled something that ended with "Mrs. Willoughby . . ."

"I beg your pardon," said Mother forbiddingly. "I didn't hear you."

He lifted his head a little. "My mother's ill."

"That will be all right," said Mother coldly. "Sophie will take

31

your sister to school. And I'll come over later and see how your mother is."

"Thanks, Mrs. Willoughby." He looked even snubber and paler and more harassed and, oh horror, his nose was running. Mother would never forgive that. If only he would smile, just let Mother see a glimpse of how he *could* look and it would be all right. I knew that it didn't matter how dirty and poor they were if Mother's sympathy could only be aroused, if she could feel, somewhat patronizingly, "poor creatures, we must do what we can." And I knew that Ivan's smile would do the trick because it showed just what a nice person he could have been. But Ivan didn't smile. Instead, he sniffed.

"Wait here," she said distastefully. She disappeared into the scullery, then emerged with a piece of old pillowcase which she handed to Ivan. He took it without a word, blew his nose, then turned and vanished through the gap in the hedge.

"You're not to get too near those children," said Mother. "They've probably got lice."

Was she cruel? I look back now and see her with different eyes, eyes that understand how hard it was to attain and preserve the standards of cleanliness, godliness, and a place near the top of our particular stratum of society. In our village we were considered wealthy, cultured, and respectable among the farm workers and laboring class. Above us were those who farmed their own land, or farmed rented land, and above them were the gentry. But we were at the very top of the laboring class. Dad was a skilled stockman. Mother had been a head parlor maid. We had a high standard of living, partly because there were only three children, but also because Mother and Dad never stopped working. We had good food and some to spare for others. Our home was spotlessly clean. Our larder had more preserves and pickles and hams than anyone else. Our bed linen was monogrammed and edged by Grandmother Cobham, our antimacassars and tablecloths were hand crocheted. Lillian and I had harmonium lessons and we had clean pinafores and petticoats twice a week instead of once. We wore ribbons on our braids instead of string, and our boots were cleaned every day (Dad and Edwin's job). We

32

were respectable. And now I look back and realize how Mother fought and worked for that respectability, and she wasn't about to have it damaged because a family of tinkers had moved in next door.

She was silent at breakfast, doling out porridge and tea with her slim back even straighter than usual. Only when Dad came in was the silence broken.

"Well? How did he do? The new cowman . . ."

"He'll do."

I waited, agonized. It was terribly important that Mr. Barshinskey should be a good cowman. If he wasn't, then the Barshinskeys had nothing.

"Did you put him to milk Lady Audley, Dad?"

Lady Audley was the prize cow of the herd. Her milk yield was always good and when she dropped a calf it was always the pick of the herd. But she was a difficult cow, temperamental and slow to let down the milk when she was in a bad mood. Dad could manage her all right, although even with him she sometimes put her foot into the pail just after it was full. Both Mr. Hayward and the boy had been butted across the milking sheds when she was in one of her tempers.

Dad smiled. "No, lassie, we'll let him work up to Lady Audley. But the others like him well enough. Poppy, Charity, he had a nice gentle way with them. He'll do, for all he's a strange, foreign kind of chap."

My heart swelled. My dad was the most wonderful stockman in the world, and the fairest. No one could have blamed him if he had resented Mr. Barshinskey and certainly, from first appearances, the man was strange and unconventional. But my father, with all his slow and deliberate ways, was totally without prejudice or grudge. I felt a warm, overflowing relief that extended to Poppy and Charity and the rest of Mr. Hayward's pedigree herd. Ma couldn't dismiss them as tinkers if Mr. Barshinskey was a first-class cowman.

Lillian always left for school before Edwin and me. She said it was because she liked to practice the hymn and the march before school assembled for prayers, but I knew it was because

33

she was ashamed of being seen with us. I didn't always behave too well. Off she went, all cream and roses and white starched pinafore. Edwin, smelling faintly of pigs, hovered at the door while mother retied my pinafore strings and put a clean handkerchief in the pocket.

"Now mind," she said coolly. "You're to take that child to school and hand her over to Miss Thurston. But you're not to sit next to her in the classroom, and you're not to play with her at playtime. Be polite—manners don't cost anything—and if she asks you where to put things or what to do, you're to tell her. But there's no need to do more than that."

Poor Mother. It was one of those times when her Christian duty was in direct conflict with her quest for respectability.

Daisy May was waiting outside the gate of the Owl House, and when I saw her my heart sank. It was apparent that an effort had been made to get Daisy ready for school so that she looked as much like the rest of us as possible. It would have been so much better if no one had tried. It wasn't the bare feet or the string-tied braids. I'd expected that. I'd expected that she'd be wearing the same frock. It was the pinafore that was so damning, that said tinker, beggar child, sloven. It wasn't a pinafore at all. It was a man's old shirt, blue and white stripes, with the sleeves cut out and the curved tails hanging down around Daisy May's skirt. It was patched down the front in the place where shirts always go first, just beneath the collar. A strip, cut presumably from a worn sleeve, had been carefully hemmed and formed a tie around the waist. It was dreadful.

Daisy May's gray eyes stared hard at me, glanced quickly at Edwin, then back to me. "I'm ready for school," she said brightly, and I swallowed and managed to give her a feeble smile.

"This is Edwin."

I don't think the awfulness of it, the stigma of social outcast, even registered with Edwin. He was thirteen and nearly a man. He was in the top class and he didn't notice, or if he noticed he didn't understand, the implications of "one of the small girls" going to school in a man's old shirt instead of a pinafore.

34

"Hello," he said, without really looking at her.

Daisy May's eyes traveled slowly from Edwin's neat brown head down to his woolen socks and polished boots. Then she looked at my white pinafore, starched, frilled. Over her face came an expression of tightened misery. Then she smiled.

"Over Marden, where we've just come from, *nobody* wears white pinafores anymore. Everyone wears the new sort, with buttons up the front like this."

I couldn't answer, and Edwin was bored. To my chagrin he began to walk up the lane ahead of us. In a mood of agonized embarrassment and a friendship as yet uncemented and therefore unable to take the strain of a situation like this, we wandered after him.

"There was one girl who had to wear her old white pinafore out and it was *awful* for her. She cried when she saw everyone in their blue-and-white striped ones with the curved hems. She felt so dreadful at being . . . old-fashioned. Of course we all said it didn't matter, but it did. *Nobody* wears pinafores like that anymore."

"It's very nice," I said, not looking at her.

"Over Marden way it's the very latest thing."

I thought about walking into the playground with Daisy May. The little girls wouldn't notice. But Brenda Jefford and her set would notice. They noticed everything, and once they'd noticed they'd move in on Daisy May. And if I was with her they would move in on me too.

"I just kept asking Mother if I could have one of the blue-and-white striped pinafores like everyone else, and in the end she said I could. They're not easy to get. But over Marden way you can buy them. Sometimes people came all the way from Ashford to buy them."

Brenda Jefford had three in her set, but the three were weak and when Brenda wasn't there they disintegrated into isolated pockets of unpleasantness. They weren't actually dangerous when she wasn't there.

"Have you noticed the buttons? They're very special, the

buttons. You can't get buttons like this on pinafores, only over Marden way."

No. You couldn't get buttons like that on pinafores. Only on men's shirts. As soon as Daisy May walked into that playground, Brenda Jefford would notice her. She would notice the patches where the collar had worn holes in the shirt—when it had been a shirt—and she would notice the special buttons you could only get over Marden way.

"I don't suppose anyone else at this school has the latest pinafore, do they?"

Edwin had forsaken us and was out of sight. We were hurrying through the churchyard, the school playground only a few moments away. Daisy May's face was an explosive red and she had a dreadful fixed smile on her face. For one moment I considered abandoning her but the moment passed. What I did was nearly as bad.

"Look, Daisy May. I think it would be better if you took your shir—pinafore off and went to school in your frock."

The smile collapsed, but her face went even redder. "I can't do that. Everyone wears pinafores. They do, don't they? I bet there's no one in your class who doesn't wear a pinafore."

She was absolutely right. Even the poorest wore them. They were a symbol of respectable servitude and, as such, were passed down through the village from the charity box and from Mrs. Fawcett at the White House who organized a "pinafores and stockings fund for poor children."

"I can't go to school on my first day without a pinafore," she cried, all the pretense and pride suddenly gone. "I don't mind not having boots." Her voice began to tremble as though she was about to cry. "I do mind really, but as it's summer there's others that won't have them. But my dress is patched under the arm in a different color and I can't go without a pinafore. If we stay in this village that's the way they'll remember me, by my first day. That's the way it always is. That's how it was at Marden, and at Tonbridge, and at . . ." She reeled off a list of names, many of them places I had never heard of. She didn't cry. I thought she was going to but somehow that last shred of pride remained.

"It wasn't true what I said about everyone at Marden wearing blue-and-white pinafores," she choked. "It's a shirt, you see. Mum and I made it last night—so that I would look like everyone else!" Her scrubbed round face was filled with panic and a picture of Brenda Jefford came into my mind, fat and terrible, moving toward Daisy May with finger and voice ready to release scorn on the deficiency of a man's old shirt worn as a pinafore. There was only one thing I could do.

"Come on." I stopped by the yew tree at the end of the churchyard. "Take it off and hide it in here. I'll take mine off too. They'll be safe in the tree and we'll get them on the way home. If there's two of us it'll be different."

A look of total relief swam over her features. I had to look away it was so embarrassing. The hated shirt was removed and bundled up beside my mass of starched frills. I stared down at them and something curious began to happen to me. There they were, snowy folds, symbol of Willoughby preeminence in the village, all crushed and tumbled in the yew and suddenly I didn't care anymore. There was a great and splendid bursting of disciplinary bonds within me, a shaking free, a feeling of wild elation that was something to do with the young hot summer but even more to do with the music I had heard the night before. I, Sophie Willoughby, eleven years of age, was suddenly in control of my life. I could do anything. I would do anything. The world was waiting for me to come and conquer. No one could touch me or diminish my strength. I was about to soar unerringly through the pygmies that surrounded me. I heard the school bell ringing in the playground. I would go to school although I could just as easily have decided not to. But why should I not go and begin my revolution there?

I looked down upon the pinafore—childhood bonds cast away forever—and it was not enough.

"I shall take off my boots and stockings as well," I said to Daisy May. "Then we shall look exactly alike."

Boots and stockings were placed in the yew tree, and then we turned and hurried through the passage that connected the churchyard and the playground. The monitor was giving her last ring on the bell and the classes had formed into their double lines. Daisy May and I tacked onto the end of Class Five. I saw the stupefied stares of my classmates but, godlike, I was above them.

The door to the hall opened and from inside came the sound of Lillian banging out the preliminary chords of "The Haymaker." She always played "The Haymaker" on Fridays. Class by class we marched in, the little ones first, going to their places at the front of assembly.

Class Four moved up the two steps into the hall and we followed. "The Haymaker" suddenly became a triumphant fanfare of freedom and, as we marched past the piano, I gave Lillian a lofty and exultant smile. "The Haymaker" was interrupted—a jangle of chords tumbled over each other. There was a long break and I looked back over my shoulder at Lillian. Her eyes were dilated and staring, her mouth open. I gave her a cheery little wave to reassure her, and then her face assembled itself into an expression I knew only too well: tightened lips, bright spots of color on the cheeks like Mother, eyes that blazed blue fury in righteous indignation at me. She fumbled, found the keys again, and "The Haymaker" was resumed, but with what deafening military anger . . . !

And looking down at my bare feet the elation drained away from me. Miss Thurston was staring at me from the side of the hall with pained bafflement on her face. Was she going to have to offer one of the Willoughbys a pair of boots from the charity box? Brenda Jefford and her set were sniggering. The rest of the class was smiling, or looking away, embarrassed. Oh, I wished I hadn't done it! My feet were dusty already, and I realized that the concrete playground was rougher than I'd thought. "The Haymaker" stopped, prayers began, and I could feel Lillian's eyes boring into my back. Why had I done it?

Daisy May stood beside me, frightened, but determined not to show it. She felt me looking at her and she turned her head and gave me a small grateful smile. The elation, the wild burst of freedom that had assailed me, might have gone, but the misery and protectiveness for my new friends remained. Mother, Lillian, and to a lesser degree Edwin, had all turned away from the Barshinskeys. But Dad and I were of different salt. We were Willoughbys. We didn't have nice hands but we stuck by our friends.

Two things stand clear in my memory about Daisy May's first morning at school. (I cannot speak for the afternoon as I spent it in bed, in disgrace, and without tea.) The first was her name, and the second was what happened with Brenda Jefford.

As soon as assembly was over I took Daisy May up to Miss Thurston's desk and explained who she was. At first Miss Thurston didn't seem to be taking it in. She kept staring at my feet and finally she said, "Sophie . . . is there, er . . ." and then she pressed her lips together, gave a little blink, and pulled the register toward her.

While she called out the names Daisy May waited humbly by her desk, and when Miss Thurston had finished she began to write Daisy May's name at the bottom of the page.

"We'll put you at the foot of the register for the rest of this term, dear. Now then, it's Daisy May, isn't it?"

"Yes, miss."

"Yes, Miss *Thurston*, Daisy May."

"Yes, Miss Thurston."

Miss Thurston finished writing, then paused. "Daisy May . . . ?"

"Barshinskey, Miss Thurston."

Miss Thurston moved her upper lip over her dentures. Miss Thurston's dentures didn't fit very well and when she laughed they had a habit of dropping.

"Yes . . . Barshinskey. B-a-r-s-h-i . . ."

"No, Miss Thurston, after 's' comes 'c'."

Miss Thurston coughed and crossed out in the register. "C-i."

"H" came back the answer from Daisy May. The class began to titter. Miss Thurston went a faintly tinged shade of pink. "I think you had better write it on the blackboard, dear," she said nervously.

Daisy May took the chalk and wrote a jumble of letters that

began with B-a-r and went on with "c's" and "h's" and "s's" and "z's." The class tittered again. Daisy May looked resigned, and Miss Thurston rather cross.

"There's no need to be silly, Daisy May. Rub that out at once and go and sit down. You can sit next to Sophie as you seem to be such close friends already." It was said with a faint note of asperity which was the nearest Miss Thurston ever came to chastisement. She was really a gentle and kindly teacher, not very well educated and frightened of ridicule, corporal punishment, and Mr. Deacon, the headmaster.

Daisy May sat next to me, and Miss Thurston wrote a name firmly in the register. Then she passed Daisy May her class exercise book and on it was written DAISY MAY BARSHINSKEY, which was the way I would have spelled it and which was the way everyone in the village spelled it from then on.

During scripture Daisy May was given her Scripture Progress Card, and her first Text. All the children had their first Text given to them, after that you had to earn them. They were highly coveted, partly because he who had the greatest number at the end of the year got a prize, but also because they were very attractive in themselves: stiff cards printed with the Text, and a glossy multicolored picture. Occasionally one was fortunate enough to receive a "sparkler," a Text that in addition to the words and picture had a sprinkling of silver dust glued over it. Daisy May didn't have a sparkler, but she had "Give, and It Shall Be Given Unto You," in rose and blue lettering, and underneath was a little girl in rags giving her last crust to a very fat dog. Behind the little girl was an open door and a hand was beckoning her to a table laden with grapes and apples and oranges. Daisy May was very taken with her Text.

When playtime came we went outside to the playground, and at once Brenda Jefford, fat and menacing, began to move toward us. I waited, swallowing hard and trying to appear nonchalant. On what was Brenda Jefford going to pinpoint her attack? No pinafores? Hardly. It wasn't worthy of her scorn for even she knew that I, Sophie Willoughby, had cleaner and better pinafores than anyone else if I wanted them.

"Give us yer Text," said Brenda Jefford.

The other three closed around us in a half-circle. In desperation I looked around for Lillian, not that she would take part in a brawl with the Jefford set, but her mere presence, scornful and disdainful, reduced the Jeffords to scrubby eleven-year-olds instead of well-organized bullies. But Lillian wasn't there. Senior girls, just about to leave school, were permitted to stay in the classroom at playtime and indulge in adult conversation and crochet.

"You 'eard what I said. Give us yer Text."

"Why?" said Daisy May coolly. Brenda Jefford was disconcerted for a moment. No one had ever asked why before. It was sufficient to show strength and demand. No one else expected an explanation.

"Because I says so," she growled.

"Why do you say so?" continued Daisy May.

"Because . . ." she floundered, and for one blessed second I thought she might give best and go away. It was a vain hope. "Because no one with a name like yours should 'ave a Text. Give it 'ere . . ."

"No," said Daisy May, clutching "Give, and It Shall Be Given Unto You" tightly to her chest. The mob moved closer.

"Let her keep it," I said in a feeble wavering kind of voice. I felt it was about the bravest thing I had ever done in my life. "I'll give you mine the next time I get one."

Brenda Jefford looked at me with contempt. "We'll 'ave yours anyway," she said, and just for good measure gave me a push up against the wall. "Now"—she turned back to Daisy May—"are you going to give us yer Text?"

"No," said Daisy May.

It is hard to describe the terror that the Jefford mob could strike into the hearts of Class Five (and indeed all the classes below Class Five). There were only four of them, so why did the rest of us not band together and stand firm? Hard to explain, but I believe that bullying and organized force comes naturally only to bullies. Unless the aggressive instinct is the greatest single component in someone's character, it is almost impossible to initiate force and fight. The temperate man is nearly always intimidated by the aggressive man, even if the temperate man is a genius and the aggressive one a fool. Only when the temperate man is inspired by high endeavor or a strong moral code will he stand firm against the bully. I had no divine light burning in me. I'd been chased and punched too many times by the Jefford set.

And also, on a less elevated scale, there was the *appearance* of Brenda Jefford to strike terror into our hearts. She was very fat and she towered over the rest of us. In the winter she wore a mustard coat that made one think of cow pats. It was very unnerving to see a large cow pat moving in on one.

"All right," said Jefford threateningly. "We're gonna 'ave it anyway."

They pushed Daisy May up beside me, and for a beginning pulled the string from her braids and tugged at her hair. Brenda punched her in the chest and then tried to wrench the Text from her hand.

"I'll tell Miss Thurston." It was the second bravest thing I had ever done in my life. I might have saved myself the trouble.

"Shut up, you," said Jefford, and gave me another push.

"All right, then. We'll hold her down and take it from her." They reached out their hands to claw Daisy May to the ground and then, to my amazement, I saw Daisy stuff her Text down the neck of her dress, and then lash out with hands and feet. She was like a small, controlled tornado, arms punching and her right foot kicking into Brenda Jefford's shin. It might have done some good if only she had worn boots. As it was it just made the mob lose their tempers and in a moment Daisy May was on the ground. But even then she didn't give up. Before they could get the Text she had rolled over onto her stomach, protecting "Give and It Shall Be Given Unto You" with her body.

"Give it to us!" screeched Brenda Jefford, her fat face the color of overripe strawberries, and "No!" was the muffled reply from the ground.

I was just getting ready to do the third bravest thing in my life (namely, hitting the Jefford) when out from Senior Boys' Lavatories strolled Edwin. He took one look at me and then

42

surveyed the heap of bodies on the ground.

"Oh, do help, Edwin!" I cried. "That's Daisy May under there."

Edwin wasn't an aggressive person either, but he always became almost speechless with rage whenever he encountered cruelty or bullying. He was once in serious trouble when he discovered one of the Kelly boys playing "hangings" with a mongrel dog. Edwin, usually so stoical and slow, had leaped upon Kelly like a madman and had beaten him so badly that he'd lost two of his front teeth and had to have a stitch in his gum. Mrs. Kelly had come screaming up to my mother and there'd been a terrific shemozzle. Dad had had to pay the doctor's bill and had tried to explain to Edwin that although it was wrong to torture the dog, it was also wrong to beat another boy so badly. But Edwin, in spite of everything, would not say he was sorry and now Mrs. Kelly referred to him as "that murdering Willoughby boy."

Now, as he looked at the heap of squirming bodies, I saw his face change and his temper let rip. He got hold of the Jefford's pigtail and literally threw her across the playground. She crashed into the railings around the playground and crumpled into a heap. He picked two of the others up by the scruff of their necks and banged their heads together, and before he could get hold of the third she was up and away, casting a frightened look over her shoulder to make sure he wasn't coming after her. I was suddenly afraid that he might do what he had done with the Kelly boy but suddenly he stopped. He still looked angry and he shook the two bullies he was still hanging onto, but I could see he wasn't mad anymore.

"Right," he said. "Into Mr. Deacon with you."

A loud wail burst from two pairs of lips, and also from Brenda Jefford leaning against the railings. The balance of power had tipped. Edwin was a senior boy and a monitor and had the right to report things to Mr. Deacon. (He never did. The results were terrible and unnerving for everyone.) Brenda Jefford began to cry. It was the most wonderful thing I had ever seen in my life.

"Don't report us," she wailed. "Please don't report us . . . pleeeeease!"

The color in Edwin's face faded slowly away and he let go of the two cohorts. "Oh, get away," he said crossly. "Nasty little girls." I could tell he'd suddenly lost interest and they must have divined it, too, for they all ran, up and away and into the safety of the girls' lavatories.

"Are you all right, Daisy May?" said my brother kindly, staring down at the flattened form of Daisy. It was obvious that Daisy May was anything but all right. Her shoulders were shaking and a series of nervous sobs broke from her.

"You do something, Soph," he whispered. "I'll go and get Miss Thurston in case she's hurt."

"Not hurt . . ." came from the ground. She sat up, her face grimy and wet, and in her hand was the Text, cracked down the middle, covered in dirt, and with one corner broken right off.

"It was so pretty and . . . *new*," she sobbed. "And I'll never get anymore. I never do. I'm so behind with my lessons I never get anymore. . . ."

"I'll give you some of mine."

"It's not the same." And of course she was quite right. However neat and new mine looked (and after a few days in my possession they didn't really look all that nice), they were still secondhand. The thrill, the first delight of a brand-new, shiny, unsolicited Text could never be repeated.

Edwin stared down at her. In his uncomfortable, unformed boy's face was a kind of desperate pity. He turned suddenly and walked away.

"Thank you very much," Daisy May called tearfully after him. "Thank you very much indeed."

The back of his neck went red and he waved his hand carelessly in the air without turning around. I think he was pleased.

Lillian of course was home before I was, and I walked in to a stormy silence. But after the traumatic crisis of playtime I have to admit it didn't worry me too much. That morning I had looked into the pit and survived. I knew I was in extra special disgrace as Mother didn't nag.

"You're to eat your dinner, and then get up to bed," she said icily. "Your father will deal with you this evening." That did upset me a bit. I hated it when Dad was cross with me—he always seemed so unhappy.

There was bacon and onion pudding with parsley sauce for dinner, and I ate a lot because I knew it was the last meal I would get that day. No one spoke to me, not even Dad, and the only reference that was made to my presence at all was when I held up my plate for a second helping and Lillian nearly choked. "Just look at her," she said bitterly. "Eating and eating and eating, as though nothing had happened!" She hadn't touched her dinner, and on her cheeks were the red spots of mortification that had first appeared during "The Haymaker." I considered answering her, but thought better of it and continued to shovel my bacon pudding into my mouth. It was very filling but, come seven o'clock, I was going to be hungry.

"She's utterly disgusting!" spat Lillian. "I wish she wasn't my sister."

"That's enough, Lillian," said Dad, and, "Go and make a pot of tea, dear," said Mother. That was virtually a vote of approval from Mother as the tea was always made after we had gone back to school. It looked as though Lillian really was grown up now, if she was going to take part in the postdinner teapot. At any other time I might have felt envious and outcast, but my mind was too full of Daisy May's courage and the vanquishing of the Jefford set.

There was a long silence, then as we were eating our stewed rhubarb and custard, Dad asked quietly, "Did you visit Mrs. Barshinskey, Maud?" and Mother said very coldly, "Yes. I've sent over some aspirin. It's no wonder she's sick the way they're living, no proper bedding or food or . . ."

"That's very good, Maud, that you called on her. If anyone can keep a kindly eye on a sick woman, then I know you can."

Mother, prevented from giving voice to a tirade against the

Barshinskeys, flushed and firmed her mouth. It was not always easy for her living with a good man like my father.

I was in bed when I heard Edwin coming up the stairs, and then the noise of him rummaging in his box of railway books. The only thing Edwin had ever wanted to be was an engine driver. It seems funny now, because of course every small boy wants to be an engine driver. But Edwin had stuck to it. He haunted the village railway station and was sometimes allowed to clean the brasses in the waiting room and to sweep out the ticket office. He had a notebook with all the times of the trains written down, and he and Mr. Watkins would have long discussions about why the 6:10 from Grinstead was two minutes late. He'd walked along all the lines as far as he was able through the fields and woods, and he could tell you where all the signals were placed and who was on duty there. Mr. Watkins had once given him an old rule book, and Edwin knew it by heart. I think Dad had hoped he would be a stockman. Certainly there would have been no trouble in finding "George Willoughby's lad" a place on a dairy farm. But Edwin's diligence and devotion had made Dad admit that he ought to try to get him into the railways, even though it meant he would have to leave home.

Under Edwin's bed was a box with all his books in, every one about the railways because that was all he spent his pocket money on.

"Edwin," I whispered, and he came to the door of my room, holding a book in his hand. "Will you walk to school with Daisy, just for this one afternoon so that she doesn't have to face the playground on her own? And tell her why I'm not coming."

"All right." He hesitated, then held out the book. It was nearly new and had a picture of a locomotive on the cover. "I knew I had two of these," he said. "Uncle Herbert gave me one for Christmas and I'd already bought it. It's not a very good book anyway so I don't mind giving it away. It hasn't got the latest locomotives in it."

"Oh . . ."

"I thought I'd give it to Daisy May. They don't seem to have very many things, do they? Not like us."

46

Dear, dear Edwin. It was the very best he could do (short of giving away one of the books he really valued) and I hoped Daisy wouldn't be too disappointed with such a gift. A similar doubt must have crossed his mind.

"Do you think it's a good idea?" he asked. "I mean, she's such a poorly little thing, ain't she?" That was Mother's expression when someone was to be pitied, but helped. I just wished *she* would use it about the Barshinskeys.

"It's very generous of you, Edwin. Are you sure you can spare it?"

He paused and reconsidered, looking hard at the book. "Well, I could give her the other copy, the older copy. It doesn't look as nice as this, but I really don't mind. It isn't a very good book. . . ."

Off he went, and I climbed back into bed, prepared to suffer the frustration and boredom of a long, sunny, May afternoon spent indoors, and a lecture from Dad in the evening. But the bacon pudding proved a useful soporific and I drifted into a pleasantish daydream about growing up and turning into a beauty like Lillian. Sometimes enforced meditation can be most agreeable.

I had a Saturday job: scrubbing out the dairy at Hayward's and helping to scald the pans. For this I received what was really a very generous sum of money—sixpence (threepence of this was paid straight to Dad, who put it into the Penny Savings Bank; one penny was for the Sunday collection; another was put into my money box for "saving to spend," and the remaining coin was gorged at Miss Penfold's sweet shop). I didn't mind my Saturday job at all. For one thing it got me out of Mother's way on another big cooking day. Saturday was when she cooked the joint and puddings for Sunday so that the Sabbath should not be profaned by work.

I liked the Hayward farm too. Mr. Hayward was a bit erratic and impetuous for a farmer (taking on a cowman without references was fairly typical of him) but Mrs. Hayward was everything a farmer's wife should be, calm, sensible, hardworking, and generous. They had a son, Peter, who was sixteen, worked on

47

the farm, and always gave me something when I left. Sometimes it was only an apple or a handful of hazel nuts but once it was a stamp album. Whenever the subject of my future was being discussed at home I always hoped someone would suggest I could go into service as a "general" up at Hayward's. I'd have liked that. But Mother was counting on getting me into the White House. I don't think she considered the Haywards quite good enough to be prospective employers for a Willoughby daughter.

As soon as I'd eaten breakfast and washed up I was off. Up the garden, through the copse, and over the stile into Tyler's fields. And there, pushing through the gap in the Owl House hedge was Mr. Barshinskey.

It was a shock, a surprise all over again to see him, he was so large, so . . . different. He had a leather strap around his waist that gave his coat a fitted look and his trousers were tucked into the tops of his boots. He wore his flat black hat at an angle and today, instead of buttercups, he had a piece of blackthorn blossom tucked into the band. I was suddenly too shy to speak to him but I needn't have worried. Mr. Barshinskey came straight up to me and smiled. The smile was exactly like Ivan's.

"So! Hello, *kroshka*."

"Hello, Mr. Barshinskey."

"Ha!" He shook his head from side to side, like a great dog. He was absolutely fascinating. "You know who it is I am then, *kroshka?*"

"You're working with my dad, Mr. Barshinskey. We live next door to you."

"Of course. Yes. You are the child of Willoughby, and you will play with my Galina and with Daisy May." The way he said Daisy May made it sound exotic and foreign. It blurred into one word, something like DaiZEEmay.

"I can't play on Saturdays," I explained. "I go to work at Hayward's, same as you."

"Good. So we shall go together." And with that he held out a huge hand, a hand that looked absolutely incapable of playing a fiddle or milking a cow, and when I hesitated he reached right down and took my reluctant fingers in his.

"And, so, what is your name, *kroshka?*"

"Sophie, Mr. Barshinskey."

"Sophie . . . ho hum." He looked down at me, smiling again, and his face was what I can only describe in memory as "sparkling." When you were close to him his eyes weren't as dark as they at first appeared. They were a warm, golden brown and they smiled and studied me, and offered all kinds of strange and interesting expressions. He began to hum a little tune and then he put words to it, foreign words, and among them I recognized "Sophie." We walked up the meadow, he singing and I in nervous silence. He was wonderful. Huge and warm and his hands were so strong you began to realize why he *could* play a fiddle and milk a cow. I stole another sideward glance at him. His hair and beard, all black and glossy and curly, seemed to glow with a life of their own. Every movement of his mouth, every stride of his huge legs, the sound of his deep voice rumbling up from deep in his chest, suggested bursting, pulsing energy. He looked down at me, stopped his song, and smiled again.

"What a small *kroshka* you are, Sophie Willoughby. But then" —he stared all about him—"everything in England is small, little. This wood now." He waved his hand around the thicket that separated Tyler's meadow from the lane. "Little woods, little fields, little girls." When he said the word "little" his voice went up several notes and it turned into a little word.

"Where I come from," he said, the voice dropping several octaves into a melancholy bass, "everything is big, great!" He shook his head from side to side again. "You must see the forests from where I come. Big trees, very dark. If you are there at night, then wolves and bears come. In daytime too."

"Where do you come from, Mr. Barshinskey?"

"Russia," he said sadly, and added, "Very big country, Russia."

I couldn't remember where Russia was and now I would have to wait until the evening before I could go into the parlor and look at the atlas. But everyone had *heard* of Russia and knew what a strange wild place it was. And here was Mr. Barshinskey, a real flesh-and-blood Russian, going to milk the cows on Mr. Hayward's farm. And he was holding my hand.

"In Russia," continued Mr. Barshinskey in tones of gentle memory, "are eagles that swoop down on little things. And if the eagles drop them, the bears and wolves will eat them." And suddenly I was lifted high onto Mr. Barshinskey's shoulder, sitting there, looking out over the lane and the thicket and, in the distance, Mr. Hayward's field full of cows.

He turned his head to look at me. He was laughing, a big deep laugh that showed white teeth and when he saw I was laughing, too, he nudged his head lightly into my side. His hat tilted rakishly and one merry brown eye blanked out as he winked.

As I sat on his shoulder, watching the ground vanish beneath the strides of his great legs, a feeling of warmth and helplessness began to pervade my body. It stemmed from his shoulder, the heat and energy flowed upward, making me happy, contented, but at the same time sapping everything that was me, Sophie Willoughby. I put my arm around his head, partially to hold myself steady but truly because I could do nothing else. He was like a magnet. To be close to him was to be conscious only of the need to touch him. He was singing again, the same melancholy music he had played at night by the bonfire. When the song ended he turned his head again and said, "Perhaps I shall make a little song for you, *kroshka*. A song that is special for Sophie Willoughby. This you would like?"

"Oh yes, Mr. Barshinskey!"

A surge of envy for Ivan and Daisy May passed through me. Imagine having a father like this.

"Will you play my song on your fiddle, Mr. Barshinskey?"

"Perhaps I shall. Perhaps I shall not."

"Could I learn to play the fiddle, Mr. Barshinskey?"

"No."

"Oh."

"The English do not have the soul to play the fiddle. They are too little."

"I can play the harmonium," I said dreamily, swaying on my shoulder seat. Mr. Barshinskey made a "poof" noise that summed up exactly what he thought of people who played the harmonium. We came out of the lane into the fields where Mr. Hayward's cows were grazing and we stopped, Mr. Barshinskey looking around at the field and the cows. He lifted me from his shoulder and set me on the ground and I felt cold, as though I had been severed from something that was mine.

As we moved across the field the cows began to move toward us and Mr. Barshinskey called to them in his beautiful foreign voice. "Poppee . . . Daizee . . . Victoreeea . . ." and they just kept on coming and finally they were up close, nuzzling into his side, walking along close to him, tossing their heads a little and butting him gently from time to time. It doesn't sound like much, but to anyone who knows cows it was incredible. They are gently inquisitive creatures. When they see people they come part of the way to stare, but if you walk toward them they will turn timidly away. Mr. Barshinskey had been one day on that farm and he had charmed them like the Pied Piper of Hamelin.

He touched a soft nose here, a flank there, and then he paused and stared hard at one of the herd. He "ticked ticked" the others out of the way, and stooped down over this one cow, gently putting his hands on her udders. "Not good," he muttered. "This one is not good," and he "ticked ticked" at her again and patted her ahead of him, away from the herd and up toward the gate at the end of the field.

"This one I shall take to your papa," he said to me. "This one is ill." He went through the gate and then vanished around into the sheds at the back of the farm, leaving me confused, fascinated, and feeling that I was somehow no different from the cows that had followed him through the fields. I was still standing there staring after him when Mr. Hayward came out and told me to get along to the dairy like a good girl as Mrs. Hayward had a lot to do that day.

I liked Mrs. Hayward. She was strict but not erratic like Mother. She also cooked on Saturday (being Christian like us) which was why she needed help in the dairy. She had just finished separating the cream and was about to churn when I arrived.

"You'll never guess, Mrs. Hayward!" I said, because I had to talk to someone about Mr. Barshinskey. "The new cowman can make the cows follow him! And he picked out Tansy right away as not being very well. And he separated her off from the herd, just like that. And did you know he's *Russian?*"

"You put this skim in the small dairy, Sophie, and then start on the pans. There's a lot to do this morning." Her brow wrinkled. "What's wrong with Tansy?"

"I don't know. But Mr. Barshinskey just looked at her and knew at once that she was ill."

"You can take a turn churning before you clean the pans. Are your hands clean?"

"Yes, Mrs. Hayward." I held them out for inspection. It was a great honor to be allowed to churn (I cannot think why as now I am older I just find it tedious and tiring) and it wasn't often Mrs. Hayward allowed me to do it. I huffed and puffed and turned the paddle and finally the butter came, little golden flecks floating in blue skim. Mrs. Hayward had gone out to talk to Mr. Hayward and she came back looking worried.

"Tansy's not too good," she said. "Your dad's looking at her now. Better give me that butter, Sophie, and I'll wash it. You get on with the pans, then scrub the floor."

I passed the morning in a dream of hero worship for Mr. Barshinskey. That there were anomalies in his life I did not see, or if I saw them I did not connect them with him, that figure of heroic proportions. That his wife pushed a handcart and his children were hungry I knew, but it had nothing to do with Mr. Barshinskey, who was going to write a song for me.

When it was time to go home I hung about, hoping that Mr. Barshinskey would be going home too. But there was no sign of him, nor of Peter Hayward. I suppose they were all busy with

Tansy and finally I set off on my own, through the "little" wood where no bears or wolves or eagles lived. Ivan was there though, picking up wood and putting it into a sack.

" 'Lo," he said, scuffling a bit, and then, "Thanks . . . you know . . . for yesterday. Looking after Daisy May at school. She told me."

"Ivan! Why didn't you tell me you came from Russia!"

He became very still. His hands grasping the neck of the sack tightened and he stood upright, glaring at me with a sullen, resentful expression on his face.

"I don't come from Russia," he said distinctly. "I am English. My mother comes from Dover and I was born in Wateringbury."

"But your father . . . he's Russian."

"He's Russian," said Ivan tonelessly, and then he turned away and began to fill his sack again.

"Oh, Ivan. You are lucky. All the stories he can tell you! And the tunes he can play. And he can practically talk to the cows. Not even my dad can do that and he's worked with them all his life. Your father's so different, Ivan. Oh, I just wish my dad was different like that!"

"Don't be so stupid! You don't know anything about it so shut up!"

He stood tall and very straight with a white face and eyes that suddenly seemed even more slanting and brilliant. We'd quarreled before, but this was different. He spoke to me as though I were a child, and he an adult. I was aware that in some way I had hurt him badly but I didn't know how.

"What's the matter, Ivan?"

He just walked away. From the back he suddenly looked like Mr. Barshinskey. He wasn't big, but it was the way he walked, a long swinging hard stride that was slightly intimidating and made you forget about his ragged trousers and thin body. The magic of Mr. Barshinskey left me and I was angry with Ivan. Everything had been wonderful until then, but he had destroyed it. And for what? Because I had admired his father?

There was a lovely dinner when I got in, roast lamb with mint sauce, new potatoes and spring cabbage, but the heart had gone out of me and it didn't taste as nice as Saturday roast usually did. Dad was late and Mother had to keep his plate hot. When he did come in he was full of Mr. Barshinskey, Tansy, and mastitis.

"I never saw anything like it, Maud," he said with an animation unusual in my dad. "He picked her out almost before there was anything wrong with her! Took me and Mr. Hayward some time to feel the mastitis coming and by the time we did feel it he'd got a fomentation ready and slapped on. I'm fairly sure she's going to be all right. He's going right through the herd this afternoon. Where there's any danger at all we'll milk 'em out dry. He's a rum chap though. Sings to them, he does, while he's milking, and in his own language too. But he's good. Oh yes, I've to hand it to Mr. Hayward—he picked a good 'un!"

"It's a pity he's not as good with his children as he is with his cows," said Mother coldly. "That girl was around here this morning asking for cake and a twist of tea."

I froze. Surely Daisy May, who pretended a man's shirt was a special pinafore and fought the terrible Jefford for a Text, wouldn't have come cadging from Mother. "Which girl?" I asked.

"The dark one. A dirty torn dress and a sly way of asking."

"Did you give her the cake and tea?" asked Dad.

"No. I said I'd come over and see her mother for myself." Mother's lip curled. "She practically swore at me, only I couldn't understand because it was in some foreign words. Then she scowled and ran off." She glared around the table at Lillian, Edwin, and me. "I know what I'd do if she was my daughter."

Well yes, and we knew too. But later, scrubbing down the red-brick yard ready for Sunday (my Saturday afternoon job), I reflected how depressing it was that everything the Barshinskeys did made another black mark with Mother. They were my friends, especially Mr. Barshinskey and Daisy May, and every moment I spent with them that summer would have to be excused to Mother.

I saw Daisy May once that afternoon, up at the village shop. Edwin had broken the chimney on the kitchen lamp (a clout around the ear for him) and I'd gone up to get one quick before

54

the shop closed. And there was Daisy May, a flushed face and a handful of money, and I remembered that Dad had said Mr. Barshinskey had asked for his two days' pay at dinner time. She was standing there staring at the tins of biscuits and the sacks of sultanas and figs, and the walls of tinned peaches and apricots on the shelves behind Mr. Sitford. And then she asked for oats, margarine, and a packet of candles. When Mr. Sitford had reckoned up what that cost, Daisy May looked at her money and then asked if he had a "yesterday's" loaf.

I stepped outside the shop while she bought it, and pretended I had only just arrived. No one would want to be seen asking for a yesterday's loaf.

" 'Lo, Daisy May."

" 'Lo, Sophie." She was holding a shopping bag which as well as her purchases had something flat and hard in it. When I looked it was Edwin's railway book.

"It's not really very interesting," I apologized. "But Edwin only thinks about railways. He doesn't understand that other people might not like a book about trains."

"It's a beautiful book," she said fervently, clutching the bag to her. "I think it's a beautiful book."

"Wait for me until I get the lamp chimney."

When I came out she was still hugging the bag to her, the way she had hugged her Text.

"Why are you carrying it around?"

She hesitated. "I don't know where to leave it," she said. "I don't want Galina—or anyone—to know I've got it."

I thought I understood what she was saying—one liked to have some things that were private, even from one's family. But of course I didn't understand at all, not then. Only later did I realize why she always carried her especially prized possessions with her.

As we drew nearer home Saturday night loomed over my head. As far as I was concerned it was the worst evening of the week.

"I hate Saturday evenings," I said suddenly, feeling that one confidence deserved another.

She eyed me curiously and said, "Why? What's different about Saturdays?"

"Oh . . . it's baths, and hair washing, and the scullery soaking wet and Mother bad-tempered again, and Dad all sad if we haven't learned our Bible passage for the week. And Lillian's awful . . . she plays the hymns for the morning service now and she spends all Saturday evening practicing. That way she gets out of helping with the copper and the scullery floor."

Daisy May was fascinated. "What do you do on Sundays, then?" she asked.

"We don't do anything much," I answered, bored. "Except go to meeting and sit around in our best clothes and have meals. Tea is nice though, and Mother's always in a good temper. And we have hymns in the evening, and extra cake and cocoa at bedtime."

Daisy May swallowed. "Why is tea nice?" she asked. "What's special?"

"There's always something extra, you know, lettuce or celery or something like that. And Mother always opens a new pot of jam. And there's all the cakes she made on Thursday. And bloater paste of course, and jelly and fruit and . . ."

I stopped, realizing how thoughtless I was being. I was as bad as Lillian showing off about our Sunday tea when the Barshinskeys were going to have yesterday's bread and margarine.

"Would you like to come to tea tomorrow?" I asked.

"Oh . . . no, thank you . . ."

"I can have someone to tea if I like. Mother says I can have a friend on Sundays if I ask. So please come." Yes, Mother did say I could have a friend but I had to name the friend first for maternal inspection, and if that friend passed muster Mother would ask *her* mother and it would all be understood that in a couple of weeks' time the compliment would be returned. So what was I doing asking Daisy May to tea? Not just asking her . . . *pressing* her to come.

"Are you sure it would be all right? Hadn't you better ask your ma first?"

"Not at all," I said grandly. "You'll be very welcome. We have our tea at half-past five."

"If you're sure." Her eyes were all open and bright, the way they had been when Miss Thurston gave her the Text. She stood there holding Edwin's boring train book to her chest, and breathing thanks at me for inviting her to tea. When we got to her gate she turned and said impulsively, "I think you're the *nicest* family I've ever known. You're really nice, all of you. Ivan and me both think so . . . well, not Lillian of course. Ivan don't like her. But the rest of you. You're . . . you're . . . wondrous!" And with that she vanished, embarrassed, into the Owl House garden.

Nice we were, I reflected gloomily. But would she think us so nice when either I had to retract my invitation, or she came to tea and got Mother's cold treatment? I stumped along the path, hating myself. Why did I do it? Would I never learn? What was I going to say to Mother? I'd been told not to play with the Barshinskeys and here I was inviting them to tea. And it was Saturday night, and she was in a bad temper, and the scullery would be hot with the copper alight and . . . just as I got to the back door I dropped the chimney and broke it.

"Thank you, God," I breathed fervently that night, lying, bathed, in my once-a-week clean nightdress with my hair still damp from the wash. "Thank you, God, from whomst all miracles cometh. Who has listened to Thy humble but grateful servant, Sophia Emily Willoughby, and hast answered her prayers a hundredfold, nay, a thousandfold. Thank you, O Lord, and I promise from heretoforafter I shall learn my Bible lesson swiftly, even as swift as the firstborn of Egypt were smited down, and I shall not think wandering thoughts in the meeting, nor shall I bite my fingernails. I will not annoy Mother and I will try to love my sister Lillian. I will give the contents of my money box to the next mission for lepers and I will practice harder at the harmonium so that I too can play the hymns at the meeting. I shall never forget what you've done, God, and I want you to know I am truly grateful, Amen."

For a miracle, so incredible it could be nothing less than a miracle, had happened.

As I stood by the back door, transfixed with horror, staring down at the broken glass, the door had opened and Mother, carrying a feather mattress, had pushed past.

"Out of my way, Sophie."

"The chimney's broken," I blurted, and Mother, instead of looking angry, had looked irritated. "Well, I wasn't to know you'd be there just as I came out. You should have got out of the way quickly. Never mind, we'll make do with candles for now. I want you to bring that kettle of hot water over to the Barshin-skeys. Mind you don't spill it and scald yourself, and then you can get back and restoke the copper."

Incredulous, I watched her bustle away, pushing through the hedge with the mattress (it was an old one but even so . . .) and vanish. There was just a brief flash of conscience that I had let her think she had broken the chimney by walking into me, but the flash was over instantly, drowned in a sea of relief.

I carried the kettle over to the Barshinskeys but Mother took it from me at the door and sent me back. I didn't get a glimpse of what was going on inside.

Details of the miracle emerged slowly during a succession of monologues throughout the evening while she was bathing, wash-ing hair, topping up the zinc bath with fresh hot water for the next one in, and mopping up the floor.

While I was at the shop, Mother had gone in to investigate Galina's request for cake and a twist of tea. And there she had discovered Mrs. Barshinskey lying on the iron bedstead with only a sacking mattress. And the thin veil of pride that had held Mrs. Barshinskey together on that first night when Lillian and I had taken the things over had crumbled. Crumbled between illness and the discovery that Galina had gone begging for herself, not at the behest of her family. And Mrs. Barshinskey, pride gone, had broken down and told Mother everything and that she couldn't cope anymore and was so ashamed and what was to become of them all.

And suddenly it was all right with Mother because now they

58

were a poor destitute family who needed help and would be grateful and look up to her. Now there was no danger of us being thought equal. Now we could be graciously superior.

If they really had been tinkers' children it wouldn't have worked. But as the story emerged it was apparent they were not tinkers' children and we wouldn't be contaminated by mixing with them. On the contrary, we would be improved because we would be busy setting examples all the time. They had to know their place, of course. Once let them speak or behave as though they thought they were our equals and Mother would freeze. But Mrs. Barshinskey, at least, appeared to have realized her true status and now Mother was firmly on her side.

Mrs. Barshinskey, it appeared, had been a member of the Friends over Dover way. She'd been in service—housemaid—in a house just outside Dover. And there she had met Mr. Barshinskey and, against the advice of the Friends, married him. Mr. Barshinskey had come from Russia and he worked on a farm and that was all Mother knew about him. Indeed, she wasn't really interested in him, other than that he was a Bad Husband who never kept a job very long and never had any money. Here Mother grew tight-lipped and would say no more in front of us. Mrs. Barshinskey, following her husband from village to village, farm to farm, getting poorer and less respectable with every move, had refused to go to the Friends for help. She was too ashamed, she said. And now here she was . . . ill (Mother gave Dad a meaning look which signified that the nature of the illness was not to be discussed in front of us) without a proper roof over her head or a decent mattress to lie upon. And there were her children, whom she'd tried to raise respectably, and Galina was already turning out a bad lot, begging at doors and sleeping outside by the fire with her father, and what was to become of the other two she didn't know, but their schooling had got behind what with moving about so much and she couldn't even feed them properly, let alone clothe them, and if it wasn't for Daisy May being such a good helpful little girl she didn't know what she'd have done this last move with feeling so ill.

"Can I have Daisy May to tea tomorrow, Ma?"

"Yes," said Mother, without a pause, and I could take some old clothes over in the morning so that the poor child had something respectable to wear, and would Dad look out that old duck-shaped boiler that would fit over their fireplace for goodness knows how the poor creature was expected to feed a family without a stove when she hadn't even got the right boiler to fit the fireplace.

And so it went on, and because it was Mother telling it, the sad, pathetic little story became a lament for lost respectability instead of a woman's personal tragedy. It didn't matter providing she was going to help them, but remembering Daisy May's pride over the man's shirt I hoped she wouldn't altogether forget their feelings.

Dad sat there, reading his Bible, and there was, now and again, a little quirk to the corner of his mouth. Only once did he answer Mother, and that was when she began to vilify Mr. Barshinskey—such a man should be horsewhipped, thrown in the village pond, etc., etc. Yes, she said, she had told Mrs. Barshinskey what she ought to say to her husband and what she ought to do and Dad looked up from his Bible and said slowly, "I hope you're not stirring up trouble between man and wife, Maud. It's right you should help them, but you must leave the man alone. 'Tis not your place to tell a woman how to behave with her husband. A man must run his own life and what he does with his family is not the concern of another woman."

It stopped her for only a few moments, then she was back again, talking about fitting out Ivan with Edwin's old clothes, and trying to get the eldest girl in a position somewhere so that she stopped roaming about like a gypsy.

Later, when Dad was drying my hair in front of the fire (the one nice thing about Saturday nights), I whispered to him, "Dad, I don't believe Mr. Barshinskey is a bad man. I like him." And Dad smiled and said very softly, "He's a very good cowman, Sophie, so let's just remember that."

The next afternoon, at exactly half-past five, Daisy May, attired in one of my old frocks and with a pair of charity boots on her feet, knocked at the back door. Mother looked at her critically, then approvingly.

"You look very nice, dear," she said graciously. "Your hair is nice and neat. I'll give you one of Sophie's hair ribbons and you can cut it in two and keep it for Sundays."

"Thank you, Mrs. Willoughby."

Daisy May, even in the man's shirt-pinafore and with bare feet, had looked neat. She was a neat, clean little person and so she remained all her life. She was never pretty. She looked a bit like me, in fact, with hair that was fairish and eyes that were grayish. She wasn't tall or short. There was nothing to distinguish her from me and nothing to distinguish either of us from a dozen other fair-skinned ordinary-looking Kentish girls. But she was always neat.

She sidled into the kitchen and stared at the tea table. Her eyes rounded slightly, then she looked quickly away with a slow flush spreading up from her neck.

Mother was always at her best on Sundays. It was her favorite day of the week. No cooking, and all the best tea things set out on the embroidered linen tea cloth. And the cake stand and cut-glass fruit dish that Mrs. Fawcett had given her when she left the White House to get married. And her family all dressed in their best, looking healthy and respectable and properly kept in order. It was her reward for a week of unremitting toil. To see the product of her labors, ranging from a lemon curd sponge to Dad in his best blue, all displayed and assembled together.

And she enjoyed the meetings too. Three times a day was too much for us, but Mother loved getting dressed in her best hat and coat, marching into the Mission Hall, knowing she looked smart and elegant, and then standing around afterward having a gossip with everyone else. And *what* a gossip she had had on this particular Sunday! The full story of "that pathetic creature next door to me" had been told to the full. The reactions had varied from a shocked and avid delight to a gratifying "Well, and at least you're doing your Christian duty by them, Mrs. Willoughby," and Mother had smiled, not just because she was being praised but because she loved the excitement and drama of the occasion.

I never forgot that first tea with Daisy May. Part of me was happy because she was having such a glorious feed, but at the same time I wanted to cry. Daisy May behaved as though she were in church. She stared long and awfully at her embroidered table napkin, and when she saw us tucking ours into our collars she did the same, but as though it were a piece of expensive lace. She watched to see what everyone else did, how many pieces of bread and butter we had, the way we spread our bloater paste, the right way to eat lettuce. When Mother came to cutting up the cakes and offering them around I thought she was going to refuse the lot because she couldn't make up her mind which she should have. It wasn't until Dad said, "On Sundays, everyone is allowed a piece of *each* cake," that her composure returned.

Mother smiled and was kind to her. Edwin put jelly on her plate (which was nearly the end of her) and even Lillian said that, if she liked, she could listen to Lillian playing the harmonium in the parlor.

I thought she would rather come out into the yard and look at Tibby with me. But no, she sat in the parlor, perched reverently on the edge of the sofa, her hands folded together in her lap, and listened and watched, staring around at the overmantel filled with Mother's elegant china, at Grandmother Cobham's antimacassars, at the biscuit barrel on the sideboard, at the polished linoleum and the rag rug in front of the fireplace. I think she would have sat there all night if, at seven o'clock, just as we were getting ready for evening meeting, Mr. Barshinskey hadn't knocked on the back door to collect her.

When Mother came in, mouth set rather disapprovingly, and said, "Your father is at the door to collect you, Daisy May. Apparently your mother wants you," my heart gave a sort of double lurch, and I got up and said, "I'll go and tell him you'll just be out, Dais."

He was waiting in our yard, big, shiny, filling the yard with Russianness and muscle and music. But after that first throb of pleasure at seeing him, disappointment set in. For by his side—his arm resting around her shoulders—was the elder girl, Galina. Some few paces behind stood Ivan. I realized suddenly that it

62

was the first time since their arrival that I'd seen Mr. Barshinskey with his children. It was obvious, from the way the girl nestled into his side, and from the way Ivan stood behind, sullen and resentful, who was his favorite child.

"Hello, Papa," said Daisy May, trancelike. "Do I have to come home now?"

"Your mama wants you, *kroshka*." (And I had thought *kroshka* was his name for me.)

"Yes, Papa," said Daisy dreamily, and she wandered across the yard and disappeared through the gap in the hedge. Mr. Barshinskey turned to my frosty mama.

"She has been good, yes? My little Daizeemay has been a good child?"

"Very good, thank you, Mr. Barshinskey," said Mother tonelessly.

"And how is this one?" said Mr. Barshinskey, putting his hand under my chin and tilting up my face. "How is the little Sophie? You like to be good friends with Daizeemay? Also with my Galina, yes?"

I looked at his Galina, and she looked at me. And what we saw we did not like. Her eyes, for a moment, held a certain hesitancy, a diffidence, then they narrowed, just the way a cat's eyes narrow. She looked from me to somewhere over my shoulder and her face lit into a smile, exactly that same smile that I had seen on Ivan's face and on Mr. Barshinskey's.

"Hello," she whispered shyly, and from behind me I heard my dad and Edwin answer her.

"She is beautiful, no? My Galina, is she not beautiful? Everywhere I go I look at the fathers and I look at the daughters, and I ask myself, how is it that I, Nikolai Igorovitch Barshinskey, have the most beautiful daughter in the world!"

"That's as may be," said Mother, bristling. "My own daughter Lillian is considered to be extremely pretty but the last thing we would do is say such things in front of her. If a girl keeps herself clean and decent then that's quite enough for me. And"— she bridled a little—"I'm happy to say that Lillian, as well as being pretty, has excellent manners."

Galina drooped. Her long creamy neck bent and lowered itself and the long eyelashes fell sadly over her cat eyes.

"But of course!" Mr. Barshinskey laughed. "To a papa, and to a mama, too, every daughter is a beauty, and every son a hero, no?" And with that he burst into a great bellow of laughter and reached forward to cuff Edwin under the chin. "A good boy, no?" he chuckled at Dad, and Dad just smiled and nodded.

"Now," he said with the air of a showman, "you have given the hospitality of your house to my little Daizeemay. So you are all invited to a party at the house of Nikolai Igorovitch Barshinskey. We have not much food, but what we have we shall share. But we have music, much music, and Galina will sing and dance for you and we shall have a fire to sit around. This evening, yes, you will come?"

Oh, how glorious it sounded! I stole a glance at Edwin and Lillian. Lillian was disapproving and a little frightened, but Edwin was grinning. He wanted to be over that hedge just as quickly as me.

"On the Sabbath!" reeled Mother, and before she could draw breath Dad waded in with, "That's kind of you, Mr. Barshinskey. But we go to meeting on Sunday evenings, and then after that we make our own music. My two girls have a go at the harmonium, and we sing a few hymns. Another time perhaps."

Mr. Barshinskey wasn't a bit offended. He waved a hand in the air.

"Another time for sure!" he sang in that lovely rich voice, and then he chucked me under the chin again, winked, and rolled his body around and away. The sun went out in the yard.

"Well!" said Mother.

Ivan remained, a thin figure leaning against the dog kennel. He managed to look wistful and proud and resentful all at the same time. I pulled on Mother's arm and whispered to her and, because it was Sunday, she forgot her indignation and stared at Ivan.

"We've finished our tea, Ivan. But you can come into the scullery and have a piece of cake."

64

He wanted that piece of cake. I knew what they'd eaten that day—porridge, stale bread and margarine—and Mum's crabapple jelly if any was left from the last two days. But, "No, thanks, Mrs. Willoughby," he said stiffly. He didn't say it the right way. He wasn't being humbly polite, he was being proud and Ivan Barshinskey had no right to be proud.

"As you wish," said Mother, and she turned back into the scullery with Edwin and Dad.

I walked over to Ivan and tried to think of something to say. It was no use talking about the thing I really wanted to talk about—his father. We'd tried that and he'd hated it. And I couldn't talk about Daisy May coming to tea in case he thought she had accepted charity. What was left?

"How's your ma?"

"Better, thank you."

A long pause.

"Daisy May is my friend now."

"Good."

If he didn't want to talk, why did he just stand there by the dog kennel? Why didn't he go home? And then . . .

"Do you think your dad would help me get a job? I'll do anything—I've worked quite a bit on farms, haymaking, harvesting, fruit picking, cows. I can do most things, and I've been two times down to the hops."

"Aren't you going to school?"

"No."

He was thirteen and officially he should be at school for another year. But where a family was poor Mr. Deacon often turned a blind eye on those kinds of rules. And in any case it would take too long to pin down all the right information about the schools and ages of the wandering Barshinskeys.

"Well . . . I expect he could ask Mr. Hayward if there's anything . . ."

"Not the Hayward farm," said Ivan quickly. "I don't want to work there."

"All right . . . well, I'll ask him, then."

65

He paused. "Ask him, but not in front of your ma." Some inner turmoil took place and he said waspishly, "We don't want your mother's charity. If I can get a job we can pay our own way."

"All right, Ivan."

He paused again. He seemed to feel I was owed some kind of explanation.

"It's different for Daisy May. She's too young to understand, and anyway she's a girl. And Ma's too ill to know what she's doing. And Galina gets what she wants any way she can and doesn't care. But me, I care. We're not tinkers, you know."

I didn't answer. I was too embarrassed. We kept talking about them as though they were tinkers.

"I'll ask my dad."

"Right." Then again came that brilliant smile, breathtaking, the more so now because it reminded me of his father. He was just about to go when the scullery door opened and Lillian came out with the remainder of the fruitcake resting on a paper doily.

"This is for you."

He stared at it and looked away. "No, thank you."

Lillian looked most odd, very unsure of herself and nervous. "Take it," she said sharply.

"No."

"Please take it, Ivan," I cried, and was then suddenly inspired. "Take it for your mother. If you make some tea I'm sure she'll enjoy it."

He still dithered and I snatched the cake from Lillian's hand and shoved it at him.

"Goodbye," I said, and bundled Lillian in through the door.

It was very strange. I'd thought Mother had instigated the offering, but later in the evening I heard her asking where the rest of the fruitcake had gone.

3 THE NEXT MORNING, IN SPITE OF ITS BEING WASH DAY, Mother went into action. Over to Mrs. Barshinskey's went the duck-shaped boiler, a pair of old but beautifully patched sheets, an armchair that had belonged to Grandmother Willoughby, two camping beds and two brown blankets, a sack of potatoes, and a large spring cabbage that Dad had cut from the garden.

When Daisy May and I got back from school at dinner time, Mrs. Barshinskey was up, wearing one of Mother's summer dresses and setting out spoons and forks on a table that I recognized as being the one from our woodshed. Scrubbed and scalded, and covered with a piece of old check cloth, it gave the Owl House kitchen a curious resemblance to ours.

Sometimes I think it was boredom that made Mother so irritable, not just the hard work. The boredom of drudgery that was dull rather than exciting. Certainly that Monday, in spite of everything she was doing, she was cheerful and excited, full of plans about how she was going to reshape the Barshinskeys' lives.

Mrs. Barshinskey was easily made over, quickly and gratefully subdued into a faded and pale imitation of Mother herself, even to doing bedrooms on Fridays. But it worked only as long as Mother was there to prop her up.

The next crusade was Galina, and here Mother's task was far more complicated for no one, understandably enough, wanted to take Galina into service.

The news of the Barshinskeys had quickly sped around the village, first at low level, and then into the big houses. It was all very well for Mr. Hayward to take chances with his new cowman. That was his affair. But who wanted a girl like Galina working in the house? It was further complicated by the fact that Galina wasn't all that taken with the idea of going out to work. Mother had her over to "give her a good talking to." Galina sat at our kitchen table, staring down at the cloth with her cat eyes and managing to look both demure and impertinent, all at the same time.

"I'm going to ask if Mrs. Hayward will have you," said Mother bluntly. "It's the best I'll be able to do, not like going in to a big house, of course, but you've no one to give you a character and Mrs. Hayward is a good Christian soul who'll pay a fair wage, if you're prepared to work hard and mind your tongue."

The girl flushed, and then suddenly looked frightened. "I don't get on with women," she said. "They don't like me." She had a most curious voice. Both Ivan and Daisy May spoke exactly as we did, but Galina's was a mixture of Kent and her father. She was the only one of the three children who ever spoke to her father in Russian too. Whenever Mr. Barshinskey spoke to Ivan or Daisy May in his own language, although obviously understanding, they answered him in English. But Galina spoke to him in Russian and sometimes they had very long conversations, even when other people were present. Mother said it was very rude.

"Well, my girl, I'm afraid you'll jolly well have to get on with women because they're the ones who run things, and if you want a job, you'll do as you're told."

"I don't think I do want a job."

Mother bridled and put on her prune expression. "And what do you think you're going to do with yourself, young woman? Go on living off your mother and father? A great lump of a girl like you should be bringing a bit of money into the house, not lounging around like a gypsy all day."

Galina's face went white, then red. She looked up at Mother and her eyes were brilliant with temper.

"Don't you call me a great lump of a girl," she spat, and pushed herself up and away from the table. She had reckoned without Mother, however, who had something of a temper herself and who, moreover, had several years of experience in how to use it to her advantage. Mother pushed her back into the chair quite roughly.

"You'll get up when I've finished with you and not before.

Your mother's asked me to do what I can for you, and that's what I'm going to do."

"My father and me, we manage all right." She was sullen again, the temper gone as quickly as it had come. "We don't want no one interfering with us. We manage all right."

"Very well, if that's what you want. But I'm not sending food over for you to eat. You can make do on the berries like tinkers do. And you'll not use my soap for washing your hair. You can smell like a tinker, too, and look like one. If you're happy to wear a dirty torn frock as though you're something from the Union, that's all right by me. Just don't mix with the others. Go out and live in the woods like a mad creature if you want. But I'll not have you mixing with decent men and women."

Insecurity and doubt flashed across Galina's face. Part of her wanted to slap Mother's offer aside, but she was young and not sure she *could* live on her wits. Not when there were people like my mother around. And the picture Mother had painted—of a dirty, smelly vagrant—was not the way she wanted to be. Her vanity was assaulted. To my utter astonishment her eyes suddenly filled with tears and she sort of crumpled down into a little heap on the table. I thought for a moment she was pretending, but no, real tears ran down her cheeks and splashed onto the table. Mother looked disconcerted. She stared hard for a moment, obviously thinking, as I had done, that the girl was playacting, and then she said, in a slightly less abrasive voice, "Now it's no use crying. The choice is up to you. You can go off and live in the woods like your father, or begin to improve yourself and take a job."

"If I'm going to work I'd want a new dress. I couldn't go out like this."

"You'll be fitted out wherever you go" was the crisp reply.

"If I go to Hayward's will I have to sleep in?"

Mother hesitated. "No, probably not at Hayward's. I expect you could go daily."

Galina suddenly looked away. She raised a hand to her thick glossy hair and stroked it. It was a self-caress, unpleasant; it showed the creamy skin of her under arm and, at the same time, she tilted her head back so that the eyes, still swimming in tears, appeared even more slanted and the shadows beneath her cheek-bones more pronounced.

"I'd like to sleep in," she said dreamily. "Sleep nice, in a bed with feathers, and sheets all soft against my body."

Mother flushed. The way Galina said it was immoral.

"You won't have any choice. If we can get you into Hayward's they'll decide whether you sleep in or out."

"All right then, I'll go." Another of those swift transformations. She gave a sudden smile, transient and sweet. She glanced up at Mother from beneath her long glossy lashes, then pouted a little.

"Thank you, Mrs. Willoughby," she said in a little, kittenish voice. "I know what you're doing for us all, and we're grateful." Another smile, warm and pleading, but Mother obviously didn't believe it. There was something feline about both of them.

In the event, Hayward's wouldn't take her. "I'm sorry, Mrs. Willoughby. I'd like to help the poor creature if I could, the mother I mean. But not that girl, not with Peter in the house. He's sixteen and I don't want any trouble with a girl of *that* background."

"Her mother was a Quaker, Mrs. Hayward. Came from the Friends at Dover."

Mrs. Hayward shook her sensible head. "It's not the mother we're talking about, and well you know it. If it was the little one now, that'd be different. If they're still around when she leaves school she'd do nicely for the dairy, but not the elder. She's trouble . . ."

Tyler's wouldn't have her, nor Borer's, nor the old Misses Tunes, nor Sitfords. It looked as though it was going to be the jam and pickle factory, but Mother had taken this crusade upon herself and to put Galina in the factory would, by this time, be nearly as bad as putting one of us there.

And finally she said she was going to speak to Mr. Hope-Browne the next time he called, "For the Church of England

70

always say they're ready to help their poor brethren, so now let them."

We had an uneasy passing acquaintance with the Church of England in our village. We, the Brethren, needed them because we got married there and got buried in their churchyard. We had to apply to them for Parish Relief and certain things like the coronation party which was coming up in June were held in the Parish Hall under the jurisdiction of the vicar. The Church of England was *official*. The King was Church of England and so were all the people in the big houses, and the doctor, and the vicar, and the school.

But they needed us, too, because nearly all the working families were Brethren (or they weren't anything at all or, even worse, they were Catholics like the Kellys, who lived down by the railway lines and didn't wear knickers). And my dad was a preacher, and Mother was the self-appointed leader of Brethren society, and so whenever a good reliable lad was needed to train as under-gardener, or a respectable girl required to live in, it was more often than not they came to us. A girl who had been recommended by Mrs. Willoughby was almost certain to be honest, hardworking, and one who "knew her place."

Mr. Hope-Browne, the curate, was the liaison officer, as it were. The vicar didn't usually condescend to approach us himself, and whenever we wanted to borrow the Parish Hall, or get married or buried, we asked to see Mr. Hope-Browne. He used to come into school on three mornings a week and take prayers and when it was Christmas and Easter he and Mother had long discussions about who should be the recipients of the Fortescue boxes—edibles bequeathed in trust in 1856 by the Hon. Mr. Simon Fortescue for the "poor of the parish taking no regard to their sex, social condition, or religious denomination."

I always felt sorry for Mr. Hope-Browne. I think everyone did. He was young and terribly shy, and he had the most dreadful acne I have ever seen on a young man either before or since. It was made worse by the fact that he had hair so fair it was virtually white, and that very light kind of skin that goes with it.

Every blotch and pimple shone out in varying shades of festering pink and scarred purple. And he blushed—oh, how he blushed—and that made it bad, too, because the colors of his spots were always changing. The one nice thing about Mr. Hope-Browne was his voice. It was a nice manly tenor and he spoke beautifully, not like us but at the same time not like the vicar or Mr. Fawcett who both said "end" instead of "and" and the "Lor-ud" instead of the "Lord." Mr. Hope-Browne said every word exactly the way you felt it should be said, and Peter Hayward (the Haywards were Church) had told me that when he sang "Come Into the Garden, Maud" at the church concerts you almost forgot about his terrible complexion.

I was sent up to the vicarage with a note asking when it would be convenient for Mother to see Mr. Hope-Browne, and the next afternoon there he was, propping his bicycle up against the woodshed at just about tea time. That was another thing about him. Although Mother asked very respectfully every time if he would like her to call at the vicarage, Mr. Hope-Browne always got on his bicycle and arrived at our house at tea time. Then he would apologize and blush for causing an inconvenience, and finally sit down at the table and make his way through bread and butter and lettuce, and salmon and tomato paste, and as many pieces of cake as Mother offered him.

The pattern of conversation was always the same. Mother put on her la-de-da voice (she didn't quite say "end" instead of "and" but almost) and asked after Mrs. Lovelace, the vicar's wife. She felt she was entitled to do this as she had waited on Mrs. Lovelace in her days of serving afternoon tea at the White House. Then Mr. Hope-Browne asked Dad how the milk yield was at Hayward's and Dad asked Mr. Hope-Browne how the vicar was. Then they talked about the poor who had had the Fortescue boxes, and about the King, and about anything else that was nice and nondenominational.

Recently I'd noticed there had been a change in the atmosphere when Mr. Hope-Browne came to call, and it was caused by Lillian. She didn't exactly join in the conversation (as children we were bidden into respectful silence and our contributions were no more than please and thank you) but she made her presence known in small ways, as though announcing that she was just about to enter the lists of the adult world.

On this particular afternoon she passed him a plate of fairy cakes with a "Do try one of these, Mr. Hope-Browne. They really are delicious."

I waited for Mother to freeze her with a Look (only Mother superintended the passing of cakes) but nothing happened. Mother smiled sweetly at Lillian. Mr. Hope-Browne blushed and took a cake, and Lillian set the plate down with a slight flutter of her eyelashes.

I couldn't believe it. Was Lillian setting her cap at Mr. Hope-Browne? Indignation burned within me. How dare she be allowed to pass whatever cakes she chose when I had to wait until bidden? How dare she flutter her eyelashes at him when he was Church and we were Brethren? I looked at her and I looked at him. Mr. Hope-Browne did not appear to be noticing the fluttering. He was too busy with his fairy cake. But Lillian was simpering at him like a silly rabbit—she couldn't really *like* him, could she? I stared hard at Mr. Hope-Browne's face and wondered what it would be like to be married to that terrible complexion. I suppose that's what was meant by "for better or worse" in the marriage ceremony. Mr. Hope-Browne suddenly felt me staring at him, looked up, and was disconcerted into a miserable spluttering of his tea. I suppose he knew what I was staring at.

"You've heard, of course, Mr. Hope-Browne, about the poor family who have moved into the Owl House?"

The curate nodded, still too discomfited to speak.

"I'm at my wit's end, Mr. Hope-Browne, and I'll be quite frank with you. I'd like to do my best for the poor creatures— certainly it's no fault of the woman, the condition they're in, but I can only do so much and now, I'm afraid, I've got to call on others to give a hand." Mother spoke in a bossy, self-righteous way that annoyed me all the more because there was an implication that the "condition they were in" was Mr. Barshinskey's fault.

"I see," said Mr. Hope-Browne.

73

"It's about the girl . . ." said Mother, and then stared around the table, suddenly noticing us. "You get on and feed the pigs now, Edwin, and—if you've finished, Mr. Hope-Browne—there's this table to be cleared and the washing up done. . . ."

We dispersed to our various tasks, and even with the scullery door shut I could hear odd words: "difficult girl" . . . "discipline" . . . "good Christian household," and so on. And I could hear, less frequently, Mr. Hope-Browne's strong melodious tones: "cannot promise" . . . "very difficult situation" . . . "something for Mrs. Lovelace to handle," and then a lot of coughing and scraping of chairs and Mr. Hope-Browne came into the scullery, fixed his bicycle clips on, and departed.

"Poor young man," said Mother, coming into the kitchen, and although she never said what it was that made him a poor young man (it would have been far too vulgar to talk about his spots), we all knew what she meant.

The next day came a message from Mrs. Lovelace, and Galina was bidden to the vicarage. It involved her coming into our scullery first of all, locked in with a kettle of hot water and instructions to "have a good wash-down."

I thought Galina would resent it. She didn't like orders that reflected that her person wasn't as perfect as it could be, but this time she didn't seem to mind. She looked at the clean towel and the carbolic soap, and at the clean underclothes that Mother had set out for her, and she said in a rather interested way, "Shall I wash my hair too?"

"It won't dry in time. You can wet the front if you like."

And after half an hour Galina emerged with a clean face and her braids wound around her head like Lillian's, and smelling of carbolic.

"This soap makes my face sting."

"When you're earning your own money you can buy your own soap," said Mother tartly, pulling an old frock of Lillian's over Galina's head and turning her around rather roughly to fasten the back. Galina stroked the folds of the skirt and that alluring Barshinskey smile spread over her face.

"When I've got my own money I'll have a dress of satin trimmed with fur. My father says in our country everyone has fur, even poor people have it. I'll have a velvet cloak and more fur on the hood, and shoes, not boots." She glared down disdainfully to where a booted toe projected from the hem of the dress.

She had her hair done the same way as Lillian, and she was wearing one of Lillian's old frocks, and she didn't look one little bit like my sister. Mother jerked her around again and stared at the dress.

"It's too tight," she said primly. "But there's not time to do anything about it now. And in any case, Mrs. Lovelace knows what the situation is. If she takes you on at the vicarage she'll find working clothes for you. Don't hold your shoulders back and the dress won't strain across the bodice so much."

She rammed her hat on her head, thrust a hat pin through it, tweaked Galina's dress forward in the hope of making it bigger, and sailed out of the door. Galina followed. The boots were clumsy, the dress too short and too tight, and yet she was more . . . noticeable than Lillian.

When they returned an hour later Mother was triumphant.

"She'll take her kitchen and general housemaid. Twelve pounds a year and living in. And mind," she said, turning to Galina, "that some of that money comes home to your poor mother. Your uniform will be provided, so you'll only need enough for stockings and shoes. And mind you listen to what Mrs. Lovelace says and learn your manners while you're there. She's a good Christian woman to take you, in spite of her being Church."

"I don't like her."

For once I sympathized with Galina. I didn't like Mrs. Lovelace either. And as for being kitchen and general housemaid, I knew what that meant. At the vicarage there was a cook-general and a woman who came in to do the laundry. That was all, and there were fourteen rooms.

But the next morning she went and I was pleased. Now I could have Mr. Barshinskey all to myself.

WHY DID IT TAKE ME SO LONG TO UNDERSTAND ABOUT Mr. Barshinskey? A mixture of reasons—some practical, like the fact that I was always in bed and asleep when he reeled home from the Fox, and some not practical at all, like the fact that I didn't want to know anything about him that destroyed his glory.

There was a morning when Daisy May came to school with a bruise down one side of her face, and another time when Mrs. Barshinskey had the same. And I never asked what was wrong. Daisy May was my best friend but some terror of what I might hear made me pretend the bruise wasn't there.

Once I was woken in the night by the sound of someone shouting, and then there was a crash and a woman screamed. It came from the Owl House, and I buried my head under the pillow and tried not to hear Dad hurrying down the stairs and opening the back door. It hadn't happened.

All I knew was that every time I saw him he had time for me, time to lift me on his shoulder and smile, and tell me a story about *his* country. And he *looked* at me, looked at me as though I was a person. When you are young and ordinary it is surprising how rarely people look at you as though you are special and interesting and real. They look to see if your face is clean and your boot laces tied, they look to see if you are telling the truth or to register disapproval of you. But no one actually lights up when they see you. No one makes you feel that just because you are there you are the most wonderful person in the world. That was what Mr. Barshinskey did for me. He was exciting and mysterious and grand, and he made me feel I was the one *kroshka* in the whole world that he wanted to see.

That is how I explain it to myself now, years after. But even then it was more than that. He had some great surging quality in him that drew weaker creatures and especially women. Whatever it was that had made the timid, respectable little housemaid at Dover leave her job, her family, and friends to marry a terrifying, near-illiterate foreigner, it worked its magic on me also. There was something raw and pagan about him, and when I saw him with his daughter Galina this quality was so stressed I could not bear to look.

It was Mr. Barshinskey himself who first mentioned his drunkenness, and it was told with such panache, was such a small part of an exciting story that even though I had to accept it, it seemed just another facet of the overlarge spectacle of the man, just something else that was violent and exciting and foreign about him.

I got to know the times he went to and from the Hayward farm, and I became expert at waiting so that we had a walk together through the "little wood" that was devoid of bears and wolves and eagles. And whatever I asked him about Russia he would tell me, of his childhood in the country around Novgorod, and the long, dark snowy winters, and the bursting of the rivers in spring. Everything he told me about Russia seemed magical, as though some mythical land from the *Brothers Grimm Fairy Tales* or *Pilgrim's Progress* had come to life. He told me about vast fields of sunflowers, acres and acres of them, and how in the winter you had to travel everywhere by a sleigh drawn by horses. He said that in every house was a big stove and the family slept on the top and kept warm all through the night. It seemed incredible that anyone would leave such a wonderful land as he described and come to work on Hayward's farm, and so I asked him why he had come.

"Why? Ha, *kroshka*, because fate willed it so. Because there am I, Nikolai Igorovitch, working on the estate of Boris Piotrovitch Morozov, seeing to his horses and cows and pigs, and one day I am head stockman—like your papa, you understand, only the estate of Morozov—pah! it makes the farm of Mr. Hayward look like farmyard of a flea—and the next day I am exile."

"Why are you exile, Mr. Barshinskey?"

"It is not me—no—it is my master, or at least the son of my

master. He is student, you understand, in Moscow, and one day comes government police to say he is revolutionary and has killed a man, not an ordinary man but one who is important. They have not caught him, they say, but they will, and they warn us that if he comes home we must report this matter. And so, of course, he does come home, and we see it is worse than even they said. He is like . . . like madman . . . shouting, and he has a big hole in his chest where a knife has gone. And we hide him, with me in the stables, and the police come again. Somehow he knows the police are there. He is like a wounded bear who will kill his captors and I cannot hold him quiet. The police come to the stables and he tears from me and it is terrible . . . terrible . . ."

For the first time since I had known him Mr. Barshinskey had forgotten I was there, even though he was talking to me. We had stopped walking. He stood with his arms hanging loose by his side and his head up, staring away at something in the distance. And his voice wasn't big and vibrant anymore, it was just filled with a terrible sadness.

"They start to beat him and he fights and then they begin to kill him and something explodes in my head. It is strange because this young man is not my family nor is he loved by me. But I explode and when I see things again they are lying on the floor, the two policemen, not dead but not alive either. And the young master is quiet and sane suddenly and he goes to his father and says we must run, both of us, for he is still sick and cannot go alone and now it is wise that I should go also. And so"—he shrugged and shook his head a little—"I am exile."

"But where is your master?"

"Him?" He grinned suddenly. "Who knows? We have enough money, for old Morozov gives his son plenty. Travel, he says, and while you are gone I will ask my friends in St. Petersburg to plead for you. With enough money and a little time you can come home again. So we go. First to Germany, then to Denmark— that is very little country—and then we get on ship and come to England. When you are rich, you must understand, always there is someplace to go. Someone who knows your uncle or your grandfather and who will make you welcome in his house. And so it was, here, in England. There is a house—an estate—near to the coast, and young Morozov has a letter from a friend who knows a friend—that is how it is when one is rich. And so"—he grinned again—"here we are in this great house, very grand, and there is shooting—not policemen but birds, you understand— and parties and all is very pleasant.

"And then young Morozov begins to go mad again. He wants to leave. He quarrels with his host. He insults a young lady." Mr. Barshinskey paused and said reflectively, "If I am truthful I say that I did not like young Morozov too much, even though I stopped the police from killing him. He says we shall go back to Russia, even though it is not safe. I am not too sure if this is good and so I drink a little to help make up my mind. I am not sure, but I am sick for my own country. I want to go home. I do not like it here for in this country there is no love between people. But in Russia the police may wait for me. I drink, and all the time I am thinking, thinking, thinking. I leave the house and I go to the village and I am drinking some more. And then I am fighting and quarreling. I wake up in a ditch, very cold, and still I have not made up my mind what to do, so I go to another village and drink some more. I had much money then, for old man Morozov had given me much because I was looking after his son."

He suddenly began walking again. He reached down his hand and smiled and pulled me close into his side as though he loved me.

"And finally, when I make up my mind to go it is five days later, and young Morozov has already left, and at the house they find me work, but it don't last for too long. I drink again a little and then I move away, to a farm, and so it has been ever since."

So there it was. Mr. Barshinskey was an exile because he had gone on a five-day binge and had missed his boat. But there was something magnificent about a man who drank like that. Someone who threw his whole future and fate into a whisky glass was not the same as an ordinary drunkard.

What must his life have been like then? Alone in a strange

country, knowing very little of the language, without friends and probably not even the right to be there at all, drifting from farm to farm, drinking, playing his sad homesick tunes.

"When did you meet Mrs. Barshinskey?"

"Eh? . . . Oh, sometime, when I am working on a farm. She is up at the big house and she is little and neat and she followed me around like a small and pretty dog." He nudged my chin gently with his fist. "She is like you, *kroshka*, and there is not a man in the world who can resist a woman like that."

What a wonderful thing to say. For nights afterward I lived a dream where I was Mrs. Barshinskey and she was me. I didn't see her as she was now, faded and tired, but I saw her/me being wooed and courted by Mr. Barshinskey, lifting her into the air, pulling her into his side, walking with her in the woods, being with her all the time.

I began to live a double life, which is I suppose what happens to everyone at that age. One life was taken up with my new friends Daisy May and Ivan, drawing them into my environment, teaching them how to live in our village and be part of the pattern that the Willoughbys created. And the other life was me and Mr. Barshinskey, a fantasy life where no one else existed at all.

School had broken up in July and Lillian had cast aside her pinafore forever. In a brand-new frock of flowered print (it wasn't really new but had been made over from one of Mother's) she had gone off to Miss Clark to learn how to be a dressmaker. Almost at once she became unbearable and very distant. She and Mother used to spend evenings up in Mother's room going through the wardrobe. I could hear fragments coming down the stairs while I was washing up: "Now if a new modesty vest was put into *this*, Mother, you could wear it with the blue skirt," and I would bubble and steam with resentment. In the summer holidays we were all supposed to get holiday jobs. Edwin went straight to the station and helped Mr. Watkins. Sometimes he was allowed to collect the tickets but for the rest of the time, so far as I could see, he made tea for Mr. Watkins, cleaned out the lavatories, polished the windows, and studied the timetables. Mr. Watkins gave him two shillings a week.

I did an extra morning a week at Hayward's, and was available for anyone who wanted "a clean reliable girl" to help with fruit picking and jam making. That summer, because it was such a good year, there was a superabundance of soft fruits in all the gardens and a second rich crop in August. I must have picked mountains of strawberries, red- and blackcurrants, raspberries and gooseberries. Every kitchen, including ours, turned into a furnace of spitting jam and, thank goodness, there was so much fruit about that Daisy May's services were required as well.

Ivan was a sad and sorry misfit that summer. My dad had tried to get him a job, but though they used him a bit for harvesting, no one was prepared to take him on permanently. The trouble was he still looked like a tinker. His hair was overlong and wild and his clothes ragged. If only he had taken advantage of Mother's charity he might have got something, but he had sent all the clothes meant for him back with a message that he didn't need them, thank you. He looked funny, and he spoke funny. He began to collect and chop firewood, then carry it in sacks around the village selling it in bundles. It was the wrong time of year to try to sell firewood and he didn't make a very good living. Mr. Hayward would have taken him on. He was the only farmer in the village who didn't mind about the Barshinskeys being foreign and dirty and peculiar, but Ivan refused to go there, even for harvest work.

When the vicarage garden party came around I was bidden, as every year, to the vicarage garden to pick fruit for the dessert. Mrs. Lovelace didn't pay me but I could eat what fruit I liked and in fact it was worth it just to see inside the vicarage garden. It was really the best garden in the village, very large and full of sweeping lawns and shrubberies with statues. The kitchen garden was vast—rows of soft fruit bushes and cherry trees covered in nets to stop the birds eating the fruit. I asked if Daisy May could come, too, and after her hands and face had been inspected she was in there with me.

That day it was hot and the kitchen door had been left open. When we handed the first baskets in we could see Galina in the kitchen cutting up bread and butter. Behind her was Mr. Hope-

Browne just about to lift a hamper of cups and saucers out of the other door.

"Off you go now," said Mrs. Lovelace's cook-general, handing us the empty baskets. "I shall need a lot more than that."

We went back to the currants and disappeared below the bush line. Bees hovered in and out among the fruit and the sun brought out the sickly sweet smell of blackcurrants.

"Have you noticed," said Daisy May, "how Mr. Hope-Browne's spots are getting better?"

I hadn't but was determined to study him before I left the vicarage garden.

"When we've done this lot," I said, "we'll move across to the raspberries. That way we can watch him putting the things out on the lawn."

Mr. Hope-Browne trotted in and out, fixing up trestles and setting up the hoopla. He heard us giggling in the raspberries and came over in quite a bouncy way.

"That's right," he said kindly. "Having a nice time there, are you?" He didn't blush at all, and Daisy May was quite right. His spots were getting better.

"Yes, thank you, Mr. Hope-Browne."

"Good, good. And who's this . . . oh yes . . . it's Galina's sister . . ." And he blushed badly again and then turned around and hurried back to the hoopla.

"Here comes my sister," said Daisy May tonelessly.

She came out through the French windows with an armful of white tablecloths. And if my sister Lillian thought that she looked grown up now that she was out at work, then she should have seen Galina. Her morning dress was blue and white stripes and the apron didn't look like an apron, it looked like a very tight sash that held her tiny waist in. Her sleeves were rolled up showing smooth round arms and beneath the white cap her knot of hair appeared to be so heavy you wondered how her neck could bear the weight.

"She looks . . . different . . ."

"It's because she's clean and wearing proper clothes," said Daisy.

But it wasn't that. There was something else about her, something about the way she spread the tablecloths, leaning right across the trestles so that one leg came off the ground and her hips swelled up rounded in the air. She smoothed her arms over the cloths, and then looked around, over her shoulder, at Mr. Hope-Browne.

He wasn't making any attempt to get on with the hoopla. He was standing quite still, holding the rings in his hand and staring at Galina. His face, extraordinarily enough, was very white.

"Come away," said Daisy May. "Don't watch. I hate it when Galina does that to people. Please come away."

But I couldn't. Daisy May crashed away through the bushes with something like a sob coming from her throat, and I stood there, agonizing for Mr. Hope-Browne, who was white and frightened, fixed in his place at the hoopla by something I didn't begin to understand but which frightened me too.

Galina turned and walked toward him, very slowly. It was like a dance. I couldn't see her face but I could see his, and suddenly the color broke, flooded, and receded a dozen times and his mouth opened a little and his eyes looked up and down her swaying body. She stood still, right in front of him, so close I wasn't sure whether they were touching or not, and Mr. Hope-Browne didn't move but I heard him give a little guttural cry and then Galina slowly lifted her arms and smoothed her cap down, stretching back and moving her shoulders as though they were stiff. And Mr. Hope-Browne raised his hands toward her, then gave another groan and turned and ran. The hoopla rings fell all over the grass and he stumbled over the step of the French window. Galina waited a moment, then she came back to the tables. She was smiling that Barshinskey smile and she seemed to be bubbling with a kind of suppressed excitement. She saw me almost at once and the smile faded as she ran toward me. I realized that she had lost her temper and I turned and tried to run, suddenly frightened by the brilliance in her face. But she caught me, grabbed my shoulder, and shook me hard.

"What are you doing, you nasty little cat!" she cried.

"Nothing."

She shook me again. "Yes, you were! You were spying. I can't do anything in this village without people spying on me!"

"I didn't see anything!"

She let go of me and turned swiftly away. "I just hate it here," she said angrily. "I hate it." She tore at a branch of a raspberry cane. Her face was sullen, resentful. Her hand caught on the branch and blood came to her fingers. She gazed at it as though fascinated.

"Your interfering old cat of a mother put me here, and I hate it!"

"You don't have to stay here," I shouted indignantly. Family pride had been assaulted, the Willoughbys attacked. "You can go back to what you did before, live like a tinker, stealing and begging, sleeping by a fire in the open. If you don't like it here you don't have to stay."

Suddenly she quieted, smiled again, slowly and nastily, and ran her hands over her dress.

"It suits me to stay for the time being," she said softly. "I'm learning things here. I'm not going to be poor all my life. When I'm ready I'll leave. I can put up with it until then. . . . I think I can. . . . Sometimes I feel I could never stop crying, I hate it so much. If it wasn't for him I couldn't stand it . . . he's kind, and nice." She glared at me again. "He doesn't treat me as though I'm dirt. He talks to me as though I'm a human being. And I'm nice to him too." Her mood changed yet again. I never did get used to the speed at which she changed from anger to a kind of dreamy serenity. Now she gazed over the vegetable garden and said softly, "I like being nice to people. . . ."

I didn't altogether understand what she was saying, but I sensed it was all related to what she had been doing to poor Mr. Hope-Browne.

"You leave Mr. Hope-Browne alone," I blurted. "You leave him alone, that's all."

"Why . . . I like him. Have you noticed his spots are getting better? I help people, you see. . . ." And she smiled, red lips stretching voluptuously over even white teeth. "And you've no right to talk. . . . I know how you wait for my father in the woods every day."

"Stop it!"

I put my hands over my ears and ran, and I could hear her laughing. I didn't understand, not any of it, but she was dirty and horrible.

"You all right, Sophie?"

"Leave me alone!" I pushed past Daisy May and ran out of the garden, away and up into Tyler's meadow. Everything was dirty and that evening I didn't wait for Mr. Barshinskey in the little wood.

I kept out of his way after that, unable to see him without thinking of Galina moving toward Mr. Hope-Browne. I didn't want to talk about him, or about Galina up at the vicarage. I went out of the room every time Mother began on that subject.

The summer had turned sour on me. I didn't enjoy doing any of the things I had before, not reading or working at Hayward's, not playing with the animals or digging in the little garden that Dad had given me for my very own. It wasn't Mr. Barshinskey's fault. It was mine. He was just the same but now I had thoughts about him that were impure. I felt I must try not to like him so much.

He helped me, but the effect it had on me was to make me even more confused and unhappy. For the first time I saw him drunk.

I realized later, after I had seen him really bad, that he wasn't very drunk, not that first time. It was Saturday dinner time and, for some reason he had gone straight to the Fox after leaving Hayward's. Usually there was a pattern to his drinking, never in the day, and mostly on Friday, Saturday, and Sunday nights. But as I walked down the road from Hayward's (I walked the long way by the road in order to avoid him) I saw him lurch out of the hedge and then stagger off in front of me. One time he fell over into the ditch and lay there for a moment. When I tried to hurry past he called to me in Russian, called and beckoned and laughed, then heaved himself up and began to come after me. I wasn't frightened. I sensed he wasn't drunk enough to hurt me, but he kept shouting and waving his arms and then he leaned over and a stream of whisky-colored vomit spewed out of his mouth.

How could I have thought him wonderful! How could Galina have said those things! I ran and ran and behind me I could hear him. "*Kroshka!* Come back! Little Sophie! Don't be afraid . . . not of me . . . not of Nikolai Igorovitch! Come back, *kroshka!* Come back."

"What's the matter, Sophie?"

"Nothing."

But Mother knew, and knew that this time it wasn't just sulks or me being impertinent and answering back. She took one look at my face, then hurried out into the lane and came back with her lip curled in distaste.

"Foul," she muttered. "How long do we have to put up with this." That was wrong too. I didn't want her to say that about him, even though . . .

"He ought to be horsewhipped," she hissed, "horsewhipped and thrown in the pond."

"No!"

Mother stared at me. "Don't you speak to me like that, my girl."

I wonder she didn't box me around the ears, but she didn't. Just sent me up to my room, very quietly, and there I lay on my bed, not crying but oh so unhappy I wished I was dead.

That night Mother dosed me with licorice powder and said that on the Monday Edwin and I could turn out the woodshed which hadn't been done for about three years. She wasn't sensitive, my mother, just sensible.

The memory faded, the humiliation was buried a little, and I was able to go out and look at people again without feeling ashamed. But still I couldn't face Mr. Barshinskey and whenever I saw him in the distance I would hide or run away.

And then, one day, when I was coming back from Hayward's along the road, he stepped straight out in front of me, right through the hedge he came, and he didn't speak. He just looked at me very seriously, then bowed, and handed me a little posy of dog roses and white daisies bound around the stems with a strand of hay. When I didn't take it he pushed it further toward me and shook it slightly.

"Please," he said in a deep sorrowing voice, and because he was so huge I had to take it.

"I don't see you anymore, little Sophie."

"I . . . I've been very busy."

"Ah-ha . . . I think it is not that. I think you are angry with me."

"Oh no! No . . . not at all . . . I've been busy. . . ."

"I have missed you, *kroshka*. Who else will listen to my tales?" And then he crouched down on his haunches beside me and took my hand in his great paw. His face was so close his beard was tickling my chin. "Sometimes, Sophie, I am silly stupid man. I am thinking, and then I am drinking, and this seems the only way to stop the thinking. Today I am very sad because I realize that Sophie Willoughby does not wish to see me anymore. And I do not know why."

"I've been . . ."

He put his hand over my mouth. "I do not want to know, *kroshka*. I am just filled with sorrow because in my heart I know you do not love me."

"Oh no, Mr. Barshinskey! That's not true!"

"Ha!" He rose to his feet suddenly, taking me with him, lifting me up in his arms and that wonderful warm Barshinskey smile lit his face, making his eyes glow with warmth and fun and happiness. He burst out laughing and then rubbed his forehead against my face. Then he crashed back through the hedge, taking me with him and began to walk up to "our" wood.

And the old magic of him began to work, the nearness, the pulsing strength, the safety of his great body. Oh, what did it matter what Galina said, or if he got drunk sometimes. This was real . . . my own special friend who smiled at me and loved to see me.

"Now I show you," he said, and he lifted from an old fallen tree a small wooden box with a hole no bigger than a penny in the lid. "See . . ." He raised it very, very gently, and as he did so there came into view the round, composed little body and beady eye of a blue tit. She had made a neat little square of moss that exactly fitted the base of the box, and she didn't move from her eggs, just fixed us with her bright little eye. Mr. Barshinskey let the box down just as gently.

"I do it every year," he said, amused. "Make a little box with a hole, and always the tiny birds come and sit in it. One year a wren . . . I know the names of your English birds, you see . . . a wren . . . I would do it at home, just the same. And always the little birds come."

I said nothing, just squeezed his hand very hard.

"Now I go milking. And tomorrow I shall see you here in the wood."

And everything was nearly the same as it had been. Nearly, but not quite, because questions unwittingly raised themselves in my mind. Why did he have so much time for me when he practically ignored Ivan, and was just tolerably affectionate toward Daisy May? How could he provide a home for a family of tits but make Mrs. Barshinskey live in the Owl House? The questions were driven quickly away by my own passionate devotion, but the crack in my worship was there, a fine hair thread that would not mend.

Mother's reclamation of the Barshinskeys continued, and the great triumph of her life came one Sunday when Mrs. Barshinskey and Daisy May followed the long line of Willoughbys into the Mission Hall.

Daisy had already been coming to afternoon Bible classes with me. I really couldn't understand anyone *wanting* to come when they didn't have to, but Daisy May used to stand wistfully swinging on the Owl House gate as I clumped past in my muslin dress and straw hat, and one Sunday I said disbelievingly, "Look here, Dais, you don't actually *want* to come to Bible class, do you?"

Her ordinary round little face had buttoned up tight, the way it always did when she wanted desperately to do something but didn't know how to ask.

"I don't have a Sunday dress," she said.

"That's all right. Not everyone does. And your poplin one's all right."

"And I don't have a hat."

"I expect Mother's got one."

She didn't come that week because the hat took a bit of organizing, but the next week she had everything, including a pair of gloves that had been Lillian's and looked quite good from the back where the darns didn't show. Daisy May embarrassed me with those gloves. She kept taking them on and off, pulling them carefully from the tips of the fingers and then drawing them slowly into the air. Then she would fold them on her lap, leave them for a few moments, and begin to put them on again. It was very distracting and Mr. King kept glaring at her.

When we had the closing hymn I hissed at her, "Do leave the gloves alone, Daisy May. It looks as though you've never had a pair before," and felt terrible immediately. Daisy May's composure collapsed, the composure that had sent her drifting up to the Mission Hall in a lofty dream, dressed in a hat and gloves and carrying a large old-fashioned black Bible. She had listened and watched and copied (Mr. King, thank goodness, didn't ask her to read a text, for which I was grateful—Daisy May's reading was really very bad) and on the whole hadn't behaved too badly, except for the gloves.

Now she just disintegrated, sort of crumpled into half her size and looked like a ridiculous, scrubby little girl in my old dress and hat and Lillian's darned gloves.

As soon as the hymn and prayer were over she raced out of the hall and began to run home.

"Daisy, wait for me . . . oh, bother!"

How irritating and tiresome they all were, those Barshinskeys, so prickly and proud and erratic. But I felt bad and so I ran harder and caught her up.

"I'm sorry, Dais . . . but really there's no need to get in such a state. It's not as though it's anything special, for goodness' sake. It's only dreary old Bible class."

"You don't understand."

I suppose I didn't, but I thought I did. After all, it was Daisy May's first pair of gloves and everything that was first was important.

"You looked very nice in them, Dais. I expect I was jealous because you've got such nice hands."

I was rather proud of that, and proud of the fact that I could say it and not mind too much. Daisy May did have nice hands, not as nice as Grandmother Cobham's but not as nasty as mine.

"It's not the gloves! You don't understand."

"What don't I understand, Daisy?" I asked feebly. She paused and stuttered a bit, searching for the words.

"You don't understand what it's like not to belong to anything. Always to be *outside* . . . outside school, and going out to tea and Bible class and everything. I don't belong anywhere."

She began to sob. She'd only cried once before and that was when Brenda Jefford had broken her Text. It embarrassed me terribly when Daisy May cried. And although I usually did understand her—and Ivan—quite well, this time I didn't.

"But you do belong, Dais," I said slowly. "Oh, not to Bible class and things like that. But you belong to your dad." I thought of him belonging to me and me to him, of having the right to see him all the time instead of sneaking off and waiting until he came back from milking.

"You can have your dad whenever you want. When he plays his fiddle you can listen, and he can tell you all about Russia and where he comes from. You're Daisy May Barshinskey, and you're different from anyone else in the village."

"I'm tired of being different!" she screamed. "Don't you understand? I don't want to be different!"

90

"But your dad . . ."

"My dad's *nobody*. He's nobody at all!" She ran away again, and this time I didn't try to follow her. There was no point. I liked Daisy May but she wasn't part of that secret world I shared with her father. If I had to choose between them I would have to choose him.

I thought a long time about what to do, and finally I asked Dad if I could have a sheet of writing paper from the desk. As it was expensive we weren't allowed to use it very often, only for writing our thank-you letters after birthdays and Christmas. But I explained that I wanted to write a letter to Daisy May Barshinskey and that it was important that it should be a proper letter.

I printed it, because Daisy was so far behind with her letters I don't think she would have understood writing.

Dear Daisy May,

    I am writing to say that you do belong somewhere because you are my best friend. Also your mother told mine that she didn't know what she would do without you.

    My dad who has been a cowman since he was twelve years old says your dad has the best way with cows he has ever seen. He said he could be head stockman like he was in Russia on any farm if he wanted to.

                  Yours faithfully,
                  Sophia Emily Willoughby

I put the letter in a proper envelope and glued it down, then put it through the letter box of the Owl House door.

It had been quite difficult to think of things to boost Daisy May's confidence. At school she was bad at nearly everything. She wasn't particularly pretty. She didn't have any possessions that could be envied and admired. Her family were all disastrous except for Mr. Barshinskey and she didn't appear to value him at all. But at least the things I had said were true, and the nicest part of all was that Mr. Barshinskey *was* the best cowman my dad had ever seen.

It was quite extraordinary, and his reputation was beginning to spread around the farms. Mr. Hayward, who had been criticized for employing a man so irresponsibly, was very cock-a-hoop. Dad told me a lot about it, but much I heard when working in the dairy.

All the cows liked him. It's very important on a dairy farm that the cows like the dairy men otherwise the milk yield drops. Even temperamental Lady Audley, who as a rule only let my dad come near her, was happy to let Mr. Barshinskey milk her.

And he knew exactly how to dry a cow out when she got near to dropping her calf. There's always a very difficult stage with cows about six weeks before calving. You have to stop taking milk from them and let them go dry so that they're strong and the calf will be healthy. You stop gradually, by not milking them right out every time and by sometimes missing a milking altogether. But if you leave too much milk behind they might get mastitis and so it's a hairbreadth line between taking enough to stop infection and at the same time dry them out. Mr. Barshinskey, so Dad said, seemed to sense exactly how much to take and when. Sometimes, in the middle of the morning, he would suddenly go back to a cow and milk her dry because "he could feel trouble coming." And when trouble was coming, like with Tansy, he had a fomentation on almost before the lump that meant mastitis appeared. And every time the fomentation worked. There hadn't been a single cow with a damaged teat since he had arrived.

It seemed very strange that someone as clever as he wasn't head cowman on a big farm. Then Daisy May could have lived in a nice cottage and belonged.

The letter must have made things all right, because the next time we met she was ordinary old Dais again, and although she didn't make any reference to the letter I guessed that it was tucked away with the gloves and Edwin's railway book and all the other things that she valued because they were hers.

Anyway, Daisy May became a regular member of Mr. King's Bible class, and Mother, inspired by this sign of religious progress, began to beaver away at Mrs. Barshinskey about "going somewhere on Lord's Day." Mrs. Barshinskey said she couldn't face going back to the Friends, she was that ashamed, and anyway there wasn't a Meeting House nearer than Redhill and she couldn't possibly afford the time nor the rail fare. And Mother went on and on about the Mission Hall, and about setting a good example to the children, and finally Mrs. Barshinskey agreed that if it was a choice between Church or Brethren, she would rather go with Mother to the Mission Hall.

When that special Sunday evening came, Mother accompanied me into the Owl House to collect Mrs. Barshinskey. I think she knew her neighbor's frail spirit might defect at the last moment without Mother to put iron in her soul. And because Mother came, so did Edwin and Lillian (Dad always went to the Mission Hall early when he was preaching to prepare himself with silent prayer).

We knocked on the door but as usual nobody answered, and then from out of the trees at the side of the house came Galina and her father. I felt Mother stiffen.

"Ah! All of you! You come to visit?"

"No," said Mother frostily. "We've come to take your wife and Daisy May to hear the Lord's word." She stared hard at Galina. "And how are you getting on at the vicarage, Galina?"

Galina kept her eyes modestly cast down. "All right, thank you, Mrs. Willoughby," she whispered in a little-girl voice.

Whenever you saw those two together they were in direct physical contact with each other. He had his arm around her shoulder and she was leaning right into him, her head resting back against his chest.

"My Galina, she has this day for her afternoon with her papa —but now, she must go back and to the church." He screwed his face up into a whimsical but also derisive expression. "The church—ouf!—in this country it is cold and dull like everything else. Not like Russia. But"—he turned his face down toward her

93

glossy black head and smiled with such sweetness my heart twisted with jealousy—"but, this church, it is the price she must pay for her soft bed and her pretty clothes." Mother's hat quivered.

"We are not Church, as you know, Mr. Barshinskey, but if Galina goes in the right spirit the Lord will speak to her. It is not given to each to worship in the same way."

Which was really very big of Mother as what she really thought was that Church wasn't proper worshiping at all—it was all standing up and sitting down and reading things from the Prayer Book which had been written by man and not God. Her success at getting Galina into service at the vicarage had indeed been marred by the fact that she had lost a soul to the church. Mrs. Lovelace had been adamant about that. If an act of charity toward a wayward gypsy girl was to be perpetrated, the soul of that girl belonged to the church, not the Brethren.

"My Galina worships me," said Mr. Barshinskey simply, and Mother and Lillian had both given little indrawn hisses of shock at such blasphemy.

"But come . . . now I take you inside," and with a crash of his foot he kicked open the door and led us into the house.

Daisy May was ready and waiting—my hat, Lillian's gloves, and the Bible clasped between her hands. She had an air of suppressed superiority about her. For once she wasn't the new girl. She'd been to the Mission Hall before and knew the ropes. Her mother was the new girl.

And Mrs. Barshinskey, flustered and nervous, was pushing more pins into her hair which was, as usual, fraying out at the sides. "Nearly ready," she fluttered, "just my hat to put on . . . where's my hat? Daisy, get my hat for me, will you, in the bedroom. Sit down . . . Ivan . . . get up and let Lillian sit down . . ."

There were only three chairs in the Barshinskey kitchen. Mr. Barshinskey with Galina on his lap had promptly sat on one, and Mother on another. Ivan, who had been finishing his tea, scowled and stood up to let the ladylike Miss Lillian Willoughby sit down.

As he pushed past her Lillian wrinkled her nose and sniffed. My stomach, already in turmoil because of Galina and her father, turned afresh with more disturbance. Poor Ivan did smell a bit. Mrs. Barshinskey and Daisy May, at Mother's instigation, had organized some system of "all-over washing" for themselves, but Ivan was too wild and rebellious to be trained, and Mrs. Barshinskey too feeble to insist. And his clothes weren't washed often enough either, again his fault, not theirs. But it was a cruel and wicked thing to sniff at him. If I could put up with it, so could Lillian. She stood there, all crisp and pink, and then raised her clean handkerchief smelling of Hungary water delicately to her lips and coughed.

I was angry with her, and frightened, too, for I knew what Ivan's temper was like and he was just as likely to hit her or shout something abusive or, at the very least, run out of the house and make everyone embarrassed.

To my astonishment he did none of these things. A slow grin spread over his face and he began to stare at Lillian. Then he raised the ragged end of his sleeve to his mouth and coughed, just as she had. A slow flush began to spread up from the neckline of Lillian's pink dress.

"I haven't finished my tea," he said gruffly, and he pulled himself up to the table and sat there, right in front of her, chewing a piece of bread and margarine. All the while he chewed he stared at her, letting his eyes roam over her straw hat covered in rosebuds, down her face to her rosebud-covered print frock. He chewed with his mouth open, too, showing the food inside, and I knew he was doing that deliberately. All the Barshinskeys had nice table manners, even Galina. It was one of the very few things their mother seemed to have bequeathed to them.

And finally Lillian could bear it no more. "I'll wait outside," she squeaked, and she got to her feet and rushed through the crowded kitchen into the washroom and thence to the back door. Ivan turned and gave me a radiant grin, but I was too disturbed and unhappy for both of them to answer him.

For the first time I began to see how that family upset us—

how *much* they upset us. Oh, Mother was only superficially annoyed when they didn't do exactly as she told them, but Mr. Barshinskey, his drunkenness, his gypsy behavior, his lack of responsibility to his family, flouted some deep core of feminism inside her. It was made worse by the fact that Dad would never condemn him, only praise his prowess as a cowman. I knew there was a part of Mother that would have delighted to see Mr. Barshinskey being whipped through the village at a cart tail, the way adulteresses were punished in olden time.

And Galina had exactly the same effect upon me. Only to see her made me jealous, and to see her with him was agony beyond endurance. Why did he always ignore me when she was around?

Now I began to see that Ivan had the gift of rousing some deep disturbance in Lillian. He didn't have to do anything, he just had to be there and she couldn't ignore him. Edwin? I looked across at my brother, who was crowded back against the steps that led down into the room. He looked bored but uncomfortable and I guessed the embarrassment stemmed from the way Galina and her father were behaving. She was far too big a girl to sit on his lap, or whisper in his ear, little secrets that they both laughed at. He kept stroking her hair and putting his forehead against hers, the way he had once done to me.

"I'll wait outside too," said Edwin.

Daisy May came back with her mother's hat, and I felt a surge of commonplace affection for dear, ordinary, plucky little Daisy May who didn't upset anyone except perhaps Brenda Jefford.

"We're all ready now, Mother," she said very kindly, and Mrs. Barshinskey fluttered and flapped and let Daisy put the hat on her head. They were alike, those two, but Dais had more guts.

I noticed, as we walked up to the Mission Hall, that Mrs. Barshinskey's illness was making her fatter. I wasn't supposed to know about things like that and, indeed, I was rather hazy about what actually happened. But I knew enough to realize that eventually that poor soul would be trying to rear a tiny baby in the Owl House, in winter, and that most of the worry and work would fall on Daisy May.

But tonight was one of Daisy's triumphs. She led her mother into the hall, and preened herself like a peacock when one or two of the other girls from Bible class nodded to her. She belonged.

Dad gave a special welcome to "our two new sisters" and although I think Mrs. Barshinskey was rather mortified, for Daisy May it was nearly as good as being presented with her first Text. She didn't play with her gloves, not once. She learned very quickly, did Daisy May, when she was given the chance.

It was a very long meeting that night. Several of the brothers were moved to prayer and Mr. King was moved five times, which I felt was not only hard on us (it was the third meeting we'd attended that day) but also very hard on God. I looked at the clock—half-past eight already, and there were still some brothers who hadn't had their chance to be moved. I thought enviously of those fortunate enough to be Church. They began earlier than we did, but they never went on for longer than an hour. I had pins and needles in my foot and the starched collar of my best summer frock had made a sore place on my neck. I eased a finger round the neckband, Mother glared, and Dad at last stood up for the final blessing. But still it wasn't over.

After meeting came the gossiping which was nearly as tedious as the meeting. This evening Mother was in superb and flashing form. Mrs. Barshinskey, shabby and apologetic, was a prize exhibit and was led from group to group. She was patted, spoken kindly to, and given many gracious and encouraging examples of what she should aspire to. I looked at her and suddenly realized that she didn't really care about being patronized, or even about belonging, the way Daisy May cared. Mrs. Barshinskey was a totally exhausted woman who had found another woman, strong and inexhaustible, on whom she could lean. Part of me pitied her, but I also felt shame and not a little contempt for her condition. It was *her* fault that the Barshinskeys were where they were. She should have fought back against her life. She should *mind* about wearing Mother's cast-off clothes and about being patronized by the good ladies of the Mission Hall. She was embarrassing to be with.

"Ma, can't we go home?" Mother didn't even appear to have

heard me. She had a scalp to wear on her belt that evening and no one was going to rob her of it.

"Don't you think we should go home, Ma?"

This time she heard me. "We'll go when I'm good and ready, Sophie," and then, seeing that a fidgety child hanging around her skirts was going to be an irritation she added, "There's nothing to stop you and Edwin going on if you want. Your father and I will be home when we've finished here."

Lillian of course stayed with Mother. Daisy May was torn— the dilemma of remaining with her newly respectable mother, or walking home in the company of Edwin. She looked from us to her mother, then pressed into Mrs. Barshinskey's side. Later I was glad that she had.

Edwin and I left the Mission Hall and began to wander down Cobham's passage toward the church.

Cobham's passage was haunted. There was a high brick wall on either side of you, and under your feet was a hollow echo that was supposed to come from the sanctuary tunnel that lay there. No one had any evidence that such a passage did exist, but it *sounded* as though it did. Some old earl of Cobham, hundreds of years ago, was so wicked that he lived in fear that one of his victims would somehow wreak a just revenge upon him. So he had a special secret passage built from his castle to the sanctuary of the church—so that he could get there and cry feignits before they could kill him. But one of the people who hated him found out about the passage and blocked it off, just under the yew tree where Daisy May and I had hidden our pinafores. His moldering bones were said to lie there still.

"Look at the bats," said Edwin.

I didn't want to look at the bats. I wanted to get through Cobham's passage before it got really dark. The echo from our two pairs of feet sounded very loud indeed.

"I could tell you something you don't know," said Edwin in the tone of voice which usually portended some unpleasant piece of information. "I bet you didn't know that tonight is the anniversary of wicked Lord Cobham's chase through the tunnel."

"I don't believe you. . . ."

"S'true! We learn things about history in the top class that you junior ones don't know." That was said with such a lofty air that I knew it must be true.

"Tonight's the night he was chased screaming along the passage by the three knights from Fosborough Castle—and when he thought he'd nearly got to sanctuary, there was a gray stone wall in front of him, absolutely impassable. When the Fosborough knights caught up with him he was a gibbering wreck—gibber, gibber, gibber!" He flapped his hands in my face and said "gibber" again.

"You stop it, Edwin Willoughby!"

"So do you know what they did?"

"I don't want to know." I put my hands over my ears and began to run along the passage.

"They cut off his legs and left him there. And then they sealed off the tunnel at the other end. Gibber, gibber, scream, gibber!"

And at that moment I reached the end of the tunnel, and as I got level with the yew tree something moved, something at low level, the level of a man standing on his stumps. I turned and raced back to Edwin.

"Behind the yew tree!" I whispered. "Something horrible . . . a man on his stumps . . . by the yew tree!"

"Don't be silly, Soph," said Edwin, but suddenly his voice wasn't quite so sure as it had been. When I moved close to him he didn't push me away.

"What sort of . . . thing was it?" he asked.

"Big, and breathing horribly. And I'm sure I saw blood flowing."

Edwin didn't answer, but he began to march purposefully along the passage.

"You're just frightening yourself with silly ghost stories, Soph," he said loudly. "You don't want to believe all the nonsense I tell you."

We reached the end of the passage and he paused, but only for a moment. Then he jumped onto the yew tree and hit it about with his hands. "Come on out! You come on out, whoever you are."

There was absolute silence, and with growing confidence he began to search in the branches.

"Nothing there," he scoffed. "It was a rabbit or a fox, that's all."

"No, it wasn't."

Just as Edwin turned to walk away there was a movement right on the other side of the churchyard, where the gate led out into the lane and station fields. "Over there," I whispered, and Edwin caught my hand and we began to tiptoe around the great bulk of the church, hiding in the shadows of the buttresses, darting in and out among the tombstones and the trees. Edwin reached the gate before me, and when I got there he suddenly pushed me back.

"It's all right, Sophie. Nothing to worry about. We'll go home now."

He was very, very still, and his voice had changed. It was grown up, cutting me off from whatever he had seen.

"What is it?"

"Nothing," he said quietly. "Nothing at all. We'll go home now."

He turned around, pushing me back with his body. I knew that whatever he had seen wasn't a ghost or anything like that, but whatever it was it had upset him.

"I want to see what it is."

"Do as you're told, Soph!" he snapped. "Why are you forever asking questions? Just leave things alone, do you understand? Leave things alone!" His voice rose and cracked a bit. Usually I felt sorry for him when that happened. It couldn't be much fun having a voice that you never knew what to do with, whether it was going to come out high or low, but now I was just indignant and underprivileged. Both Mother and Lillian talked down to me, and now Edwin thought he was going to start as well.

"I'll do as I please," I said indignantly, and I twisted under his arm and darted out into the lane.

I just caught a glimpse of them before they ran and vanished around the corner at the end of the lane. Two women, and one I was sure was Galina. I could tell by the huge knot of hair at the nape of her neck.

"It was only Galina and some other woman," I said scathingly to Edwin. "I don't know why you should make such a secret of that . . ."

Edwin didn't answer.

"Who was the other lady?" I asked. "She wasn't wearing a hat —did you notice?"

"Why don't you shut up, Sophie."

"Why were they running away from us? What do you think they'd been doing to run away when we came?"

"Shut up!"

"Who would it be not wearing a hat. . . . She had a black dress and . . ." An image flashed through my mind, Galina with her huge knot of hair at the top of her slender figure, and beside her a figure in a long black shapeless dress, no hat, and suddenly the image resolved itself into startling revelation.

"Why . . ." I breathed, "it wasn't another woman at all. It was Mr. Hope-Browne in his cassock. . . ."

Edwin stopped and turned to face me; his temper, or distress, or whatever it was had totally evaporated.

"Look here, Soph, I don't think you'd better talk about this to anyone. It's best if we pretend we didn't see anything."

I was silent, the enormity of what I had seen still absorbing into my consciousness.

"You're fond of Daisy May, aren't you, and of him, Mr. Barshinskey? Well, I think it's better we don't say anything about this to anyone."

"I suppose they were just walking back to the vicarage after church," I said slowly.

Edwin didn't answer me; he didn't need to.

Church had finished ages ago, about an hour and a half, and even then it was unlikely that Mr. Hope-Browne would have been seen walking alongside the vicarage housemaid. And why were they running? And there was that sinister movement behind the yew tree. It was odd . . . . odd and unpleasant.

Edwin turned me to face him. He looked much older in the dusky light.

"You're too little to understand, Soph," he said gently. "You don't know what it's all about. Neither do I really. But I know it would be better if we didn't mention it to anyone."

"All right."

He was wrong. I wasn't too little to understand. Oh, I didn't understand exactly what was happening, any more than I understood how Mrs. Barshinskey would eventually produce a baby. But I knew the *feeling* that hung over those two scurrying through the twilight. I knew the guilt and the excitement and the terror of being caught. Whatever it was, it was frightening, more frightening than the ghost of Lord Cobham gibbering on his stumps.

We walked home, a leaden lump hanging in the air over us, a sense of oppression because something unpleasant and unrecognizable had entered into our lives, something that I, at any rate, was not ready to cope with. And Edwin? I think Edwin was affected more than I, for it was after that day that our separation began. Nothing violent or unhappy, just that Edwin moved across the line that divided childhood from the adult world. He was always nice to me, but from then on there was always a gulf between us.

5 YEARS AFTERWARD DAISY MAY TOLD ME THAT THE PEAK of her life was Edward VII's coronation party. I felt rather amused when she told me, and then I began to remember. I remembered poppies everywhere, fields golden and red where they had showered themselves among the corn, and the banks along the ditches covered in flame and Mr. Barshinskey's hat smothered in them. I remembered a morning when I looked out of the bedroom window and saw the plum tree full of bullfinches; there must have been thirty or forty of them. I remembered the field opposite the church with the marquee set up, and long trestle tables all covered in white paper tablecloths and every woman in the village setting out crocks of lemonade. I recalled how happy I was that August morning— with a feeling of something wonderful about to happen, and the end of the day when something wonderful did happen, and I realized that possibly King Edward's coronation was the peak of my life too.

There were games and races before tea and Mr. Hope-Browne in a striped blazer and a straw hat rushed up and down and fired starting guns and generally didn't seem as nervous and shy as he usually was. The vicar and Mrs. Lovelace sat in the marquee having tea with the gentry so perhaps that was why he was more relaxed. There was a sack race, and a three-legged race, and an egg and spoon race, and that was when it began to be wonderful for Daisy May. She won the egg and spoon race.

There she was, neat and smiling at the finishing post, holding her egg (hardboiled and later to be used for the tea) and everyone clapped and cheered. They'd clapped and cheered all the winners of the other races, too, but Daisy May didn't even think about that. It was the first time in her life she had ever received public praise and she was far too innocent to dissemble. Pride, pleasure, gratification were written all over her. My dad, who was manning the winning post, handed her the prize which was a needle book shaped like a heart, and Edwin, who was helping at the winning post, said, "Oh, well done, Daisy!" and suddenly she couldn't stop smiling.

Mrs. Barshinskey was there looking respectable. She was helping Mother put out the teas and Daisy May kept glancing over as if to reassure herself that, yes, that was *her* mother, along with all the others and looking like all the others in a cotton frock and a big hat. She rushed over to show Mrs. Barshinskey the needle book and, for a moment she ceased to be earnest, serious, responsible Daisy May, and was just any eleven-year-old.

Then Mr. Hope-Browne announced the three-legged race, a boy and a girl to be tied together and I suddenly knew what would make Daisy May even happier.

"Go and ask Daisy May to be your partner," I said to Edwin.

"But I'm helping judge the winners!"

"Anyone can do that. Go on. Go and ask her."

"She's only a kid," he said, embarrassed.

"Please, Edwin. She's my friend."

He hesitated, and then shrugged and said, "Oh, all right then," and made his way over to Daisy May.

"Do you want to run this race with me?" he asked kindly. Daisy May's blush would have done credit to Mr. Hope-Browne. She just nodded, obviously too overwhelmed to speak and Edwin took her by the shoulder and marched her over to the starting post.

"You tie the legs together," he said, anxious not to embarrass her further by touching her ankle. He was staring about, very grandly, as Daisy groveled at his feet, when I saw his attention suddenly focus on something. There were occasions when I had a sixth sense about Edwin. He was two years older than me and I had watched and copied him since the time I was a tiny child. And when you do that to someone for all of your life you can often tell what they are feeling, just by looking at them. I watched Edwin and felt my own body go tense in sympathy with him. I felt the unsureness, the nervousness in his neck and the control he was exercising over his hands. I followed his gaze, and there was Galina Barshinskey, tied up with her father. They were laughing—that wonderful, warm, happy Barshinskey laugh—and jabbering away to each other in Russian. And she . . . she looked out of place and foreign and ridiculous in that English field full of ordinary Kentish people. Her dress looked good on her—it was a cast-off made over from Mrs. Lovelace's—and instead of wearing her braids around her head her hair was loose in a great dark cloud reaching well down below her waist. She had a bunch of poppies tucked into her sash. They matched the ones in his hat.

Was it my imagination or did the field succumb to a sudden and chilly stillness? I glanced at Mrs. Lovelace, who had come out of the marquee, and saw her face turn sour with disapproval. She had given Galina permission to have the afternoon off and come to the party, but she was obviously surprised and angry about the hair and the poppies. Mr. Hope-Browne stood with his starting gun held foolishly in the air and his acne flared into a myriad of colors as the blush, forgotten until now, ebbed and flowed several times over his face. Mother looked distressed, Mrs. Barshinskey weary and resigned, and those two, they laughed and kissed and chattered in their own language and I hated her.

Mr. Hope-Browne recovered himself and fired the gun. Daisy May and Edwin promptly fell over. I don't know whether it was because Daisy May was overcome by Edwin's proximity or because he was still staring at the Barshinskeys, but over they went and never properly recovered.

The Barshinskeys won, not because they ran in unison but because Mr. Barshinskey just put his huge arm around her, held her into his side like a sheaf of corn, and carried her. She hung limp in his arm and her great swirl of hair fell down until it was nearly brushing the grass. That was the only race of the afternoon where there wasn't cheering and shouting—just a few polite handclaps from people who suffered from a sense of social obligation. But it didn't matter because those two didn't notice. They fell on the ground at the winning post and rolled over together, laughing and shouting, and then he swung her onto his shoulder and marched all around the field singing some kind of crazy foreign song. Everyone tried not to notice them, but you couldn't not. There was so very much of them. The one person who didn't seem to notice was Daisy May. She was on her knees again, undoing the handkerchief that held her to Edwin, and her happiness at being his partner, even though they hadn't won, appeared to have obliterated everything else.

During the tea I saw Mrs. Lovelace talking to Galina, quietly but furiously. The girl looked sullen and it was made worse because Mr. Hope-Browne was standing right beside them. Once he tried to move away but Mrs. Lovelace put a hand on his arm and wouldn't let him move. He went red and white by turns and tried to intervene in a nervous and mild kind of way. But Mrs. Lovelace steamrollered him down and went on hissing at Galina. And finally Galina tossed her head and vanished behind the marquee, and when she returned her hair was bound up again and the poppies had gone from her sash. She sat down at one of the tables and, very sulkily, began to pick a rock cake to bits. Edwin, sitting beside me, was watching her. I could feel him watching her and finally I turned. His face was expressionless and he said very quietly, "I wish she'd go away. I don't mind the others, not even him, but I wish she'd go away."

At about six o'clock she did go away. She'd had her time off and now she had to return to the vicarage and help get the supper. Mr. Barshinskey had already left before tea. He and my dad had to do the milking, even though it was Edward VII's coronation.

We all milled about a bit. The babies and little children were taken home and people began to drift into the Parish Hall for the concert. For the first time, we, the Brethren, were going to hear Mr. Hope-Browne sing "Come Into the Garden, Maud."

I sat on one of the long benches that were set up the side of the hall, with Daisy May on one side and Edwin on the other. Edwin was very anxious that Mr. Watkins, the stationmaster, should have solid applause when he played his trumpet and he was doing his best to organize it.

"Now understand, Soph, you're to clap when he comes on. Don't wait for it to be over, give him encouragement before he starts. You, too, Daisy May."

"Oh yes, Edwin," breathed Daisy May. I looked at her critically. Edwin was a fairly nice sort of brother—on the whole—but there was no need to treat him as though he were God. I certainly didn't think of her brother in that way. Perhaps, if I could have, it would have helped Ivan to behave in a more reasonable fashion.

Ivan was the one member of the Barshinskey family (always excepting Mr. Barshinskey himself) who remained entirely unaffected by my mother's missionary zeal. And the harder Mother tried, the more difficult and prickly he became. It wasn't only the clothes that he sent back. He refused to come and draw water at our pump, even though it was fully permitted, and could be seen several times a day humping back the buckets from the top of the fields. And although I hadn't told Mother, Daisy May had reported that he refused to sleep on our camp bed. "He's made himself one," said Daisy May, "a wooden frame with several sacks nailed across it. I laid on it and it's very uncomfortable."

There had been a typical example of Ivan's stiff-necked awkwardness when we had gone to collect them on our way to the party. Mother had looked at Ivan's bare feet and torn trousers, and said very firmly, "The clothes are still on the copper in my scullery, Ivan. You'd better get over and make yourself ready if you're coming to the coronation party."

Ivan had looked terribly hurt, terribly vulnerable. I realized that he had been looking forward to the party just like the rest of us, even though he had been disparaging about "kids' games" and "running a lot of stupid races against soft village boys." But now Mother's ultimatum had been presented: only those decently washed and dressed could present themselves in honor of Edward VII.

"I'm not coming."

"Do come, dear," said Mrs. Barshinskey gently, but Ivan turned and ran out of the house. Mrs. Barshinskey sighed as though she understood but didn't know what to do about it. I'd wanted to go after him, but Mother was marshaling us into departure and when we got outside he had vanished.

He'd been there though. All through the afternoon he'd been hovering on the outskirts of the field, close enough to see what was going on but not close enough for it to be said he was actually there. After Daisy May had won the egg and spoon I'd crossed the field (and it was a long way in my best shoes) to talk to him.

"Daisy May won the egg and spoon."

"Good."

"I think you'd stand a jolly good chance in the sack race. You're pretty strong."

"No, thank you."

"Are you going to come over for the tea?"

"No."

"Would you like me to bring you something from the table?"

"No," and then his face had screwed into hatred and he spat, "You're so bossy and interfering, all of you. I'm sick of you Willoughbys. You think you can turn us into great fat tabby cats like yourselves, but you can't. Leave us alone."

At first, when he'd spoken to me like that, it had upset me, but I was used to it now and didn't take any notice. I was the only one he could be nasty to and I got everything that was meant for Mother, and Lillian, and even Edwin. He always came around and tried to put it right (like the first time when he told me I wasn't a stuck-up cow) and I knew the best thing to do was leave him alone.

" 'Bye, then."

He didn't answer but I could almost hear him scowling as I walked away.

And now, as I sat on the long bench in the Parish Hall, I saw him sidling in at the back. He went to the alcove at the side of the door, where the brooms and ladders were kept, and he leaned between the wall and a stepladder.

Mr. Hope-Browne sang "Come Into the Garden, Maud," and then "Speak to Me, Thora," and really Peter Hayward had been quite right. If you shut your eyes you forgot all about his spots and thought what a lovely romantic sound he made. Such a pity.

Mr. Hayward did a funny monologue wearing a false mustache and a monocle and really one wished he hadn't, and Lillian and the girls in the Bible class recited "Oh, daffodils we weep to see" in unison. She was right in the middle of the front row and waved her hands about more than anyone else. There were lots of piano solos, and then came Mr. Watkins's trumpet. He was last, not because he was the best but because he had to fit in with the 8:02 freight train passing through to Edenbridge. I stood up and slipped quietly down the hall to where Ivan was.

"Edwin wants us to clap for Mr. Watkins before he begins. I don't think he's very good on his trumpet and Edwin's worried he won't get enough applause."

"All right," said Ivan. That was the way it always was. We both had to pretend that those earlier words hadn't been spoken.

Mr. Watkins came on, and Ivan clapped loudly alongside me. When Mr. Watkins started to play we realized that Edwin's worst fears were confirmed. Mr. Watkins kept falling off his notes. He managed to get them all right, but as soon as he'd got there he wobbled, and then slid off onto another note, a wrong one. And what was worse was that he crossed his eyes while he was straining. Behind the trumpet you could see the swollen red balloon of Mr. Watkins's cheeks and over that his eyes in a permanent swivel. I began to laugh. I thought of sad things, terrible things, but I couldn't stop. I held my breath and looked at the ground, shaking, praying to God to make me stop because if I exploded Edwin would never forgive me.

Beside me I felt Ivan's body begin to quiver in agonized sympathy. I looked at him and it was too much. We were lost. We allowed ourselves one burst each, and then slid to the floor, stuffing arms against mouths in an effort to stop. When the applause came at the end of the first piece (there was another to follow) we stumbled out of the alcove and through the door, and in the cool of the evening we staggered across the field, screaming with mirth, leaning on each other, gasping, and finally crashing into a

109

quivering heap on the grass. Every time we began to quieten one or the other of us would erupt again and it went on and on (and so did the very distant sound of the trumpet) until finally, bit by bit, the sobs subsided into no more than an occasional hiccough and an indrawing of breath.

It was quiet and the distant sounds of the hall made our own little world seem even more silent.

"Listen to the crickets."

Tick tick, they went, all around us.

"There goes the first bat."

We lay on our backs, our eyes adjusting to the gloom, and saw the bats begin their night flights. They were quick, much quicker than birds, and you couldn't really see them properly, just little aerial dark creatures flitting from tree to tree.

And then, from out of the gloom, came another sound, a thin magical sound, out of place among the clicking of crickets and the swish of bats, but yet in its way so right for a warm soft summer evening when everything was slightly—and wonderfully—off balance.

"Listen, Ivan, it's your dad!" I whispered, and I felt him stiffen beside me.

Oh, the magic of a fiddle playing in the night, and not that gloomy Russian music but the country sounds of "Sir Roger de Coverley." As though it were a signal from the Pied Piper, the doors of the Parish Hall opened and people began to swarm out into the field. The concert was over, the coronation party was over, but no one wanted to go home, and here, suddenly, was beautiful music that they all knew well and had known since childhood, and it didn't really matter that an odd foreign sort of fellow was playing it.

He wandered forward across the ground until he stood near the entrance to the hall and when "Sir Roger de Coverley" came to an end there was a little murmur of approval. Mr. Barshinskey bowed.

"And now," he said, in his deep laughy voice, "now I shall play the music for you. But not the tunes of my country. For the new King I will try to play the tunes of this people."

"What about the 'Cumberland Reel,' " shouted someone, and Mr. Barshinskey shook his head.

"It is sad but I do not know the names of the tunes. I can play them because I have heard them, but I do not know how they are called."

"I'll sing it, Mr. Barshinskey," I cried, running up to his side. "I'll sing the tunes and then you'll be able to play them." I began to hum the "Cumberland Reel" and he, genius that he was, picked the tune up after a few bars, caught it on his fiddle, and played.

Someone brought a chair out for Mr. Barshinskey to sit upon, and then another for me, and then there were quite a few chairs and people were sitting down or doing little dance steps as the fancy took them. He played "Gathering Peascods," and "Circassian Circle," and "D'Ye Ken John Peel," and it went on and on, all the old tunes that people could sing, and "Sir Roger de Coverley" again, only this time Mr. Hayward bustled up and down trying to form a set, making the more sporty types dance up and down the rutted surface of the field.

And between each tune Mr. Barshinskey would clap me on the shoulder, or pull my head up to his and call me "clever *kroshka*" or "*lapushka*" or "little Sophie" and the overwhelming nearness, the hugeness, the warmth of him permeated right through my skin and into my heart. I didn't even think about Mother or Dad or Lillian, even though they were there, listening and watching like everyone else. But it must have been all right because I never did get scolded. They must have relaxed like everyone else into this wonderful day of a party and an evening of Mr. Barshinskey's music.

There was happiness, gaiety in the air. Mr. Hayward kept saying what a pity it was that we hadn't a bonfire and a barrel of cider. In his mad, impetuous way he even started to organize wood collecting but it didn't get very far. People were too busy enjoying themselves to worry about working over a bonfire. And we didn't need one, for from that large dark figure with crumpled fading poppies around his hat emerged the greatest glow of all.

He didn't sit all the time. Sometimes he stood up, especially when they were dancing, and he jigged up and down beside them going "Dom-dee-dom-dee-domedy" and once he had mastered the movements of the dance he got very excited and would point his bow at the next one whose turn it was to set to his partner, and shout, "Now you, little man, to the fat lady, so! Now, now! It is your turn!" and nobody seemed to mind being called a little man or a fat lady.

I would have liked to dance, except that I couldn't bear to leave Mr. Barshinskey, but suddenly he bent his head and said, "*Kroshka*, please to go and dance with little DaiZEEmay. She don't dance enough. This night I would like her to dance."

So Daisy May and I whirled up and down, and then Edwin and I, and then I saw Dad and Lillian having a go.

I don't know, or remember, how the night ended. People drifted away, I suppose, and it finished with Mr. Barshinskey beginning to play once more his melancholy Russian tunes. Mother and Dad must have called me and taken me home. The only thing I really recall is Mr. Barshinskey lifting my hand as though I were a lady and kissing it. And even though he was laughing and winking at me it was lovely because it was just for me.

Ivan must have gone home very early because I never saw him after his father arrived.

6 I WAS WORKING IN HAYWARD'S DAIRY ONE SATURDAY IN August when I heard the terrible sound of my dad screaming. It was coming from the bull pen.

Mrs. Hayward and I looked at each other, and then I dropped the pail and ran as fast as I could. My dad never screamed.

The bull pen was right on the other side of the yard and you could only see inside it by climbing up on the bins that stood against the wall. I was up on them before I realized how I did it and I'd pulled myself up onto the wall before Mrs. Hayward could drag me back.

My dad was lying in the water trough, all silent and still. The bull was standing over him with his hump up huge. He pawed the ground several times, and then started to pulverize the bucket my dad must have dropped.

"Dad! . . . Dad!"

I scrambled down and ran to the door of the pen, but Dad, like the good cowman he was, had put the latch on so that the bull couldn't sneak out before Dad had got him tethered.

"My dad's in there!" I screamed at Mr. Hayward. The yard was suddenly full of people. Mr. Hayward, Peter, Mr. Barshinskey, the boy, all of them with faces either very red or very white.

"Get my dad out! Get my dad out!"

"Come out of the way, Sophie," said Mrs. Hayward sharply, trying to drag me away from the door. "Leave it to the men. They'll get him."

"Have to break the door! Peter, get the ax. And throw some more feed over, quickly, at the other end, try to divert him."

It seemed as though a whole summer passed before Peter came back with the ax. I thought I was going to cry but I didn't. If my dad was conscious he would hear me and it would upset him to hear me cry. I didn't want to upset my dad, not for anything. I'd never upset my dad again if God and Mr. Hayward would only get him out of there.

Mr. Barshinskey snatched the ax from Peter's hand and smashed the catch of the door with one blow. Then he and Peter went in, Peter with a fork, and Mr. Barshinskey with the ax.

"Don't damage the bull!" cried Mr. Hayward. "Don't damage him more than you have to. Leave that ax aside!"

I'd have smashed that ax right through the bull's head, that's what I'd have done. I'd have killed him, and then I'd have killed Mr. Hayward.

The bull began to bellow. Mr. Barshinskey began to talk to him in Russian but it wasn't a soothing noise, more a swearing one. I heard him and Peter both shouting, then Mr. Hayward went in with another fork and the rope and there was a lot of crashing and the bucket being smashed again. I'd have gone in, yes I would, but Mrs. Hayward was holding my plaits in one hand and both of my wrists in the other. Vaguely in the background I could hear her saying, "Now stop it, Sophie! Stop it!"

Then I heard Mr. Hayward shout "Got 'im" and the bull gave a final bellow as they got the rope through his nose ring and tied him up.

Then I heard my dad groan, and though it was terrible it was also marvelous because he wasn't dead so now I could cry. Mr. Barshinskey came out and in his arms was my dad. His foot was all dangling and twisted and his face bloody. He'd gone still again.

"What'll we do?"

"We'd better get the barn door, put him on and carry him home. Peter, you go up and tell the doctor to get down to Willoughby's cottage as soon as he can. Sophie, you run on home and warn your ma."

"I'm not leaving my dad."

Mr. Hayward looked angry and then, at a warning shake from Mrs. Hayward, he turned away.

"I'll go," said Mrs. Hayward. "I'll help her get ready for the doctor."

They got the door, and my dad was lifted onto it. Mr. Barshinskey and Mr. Hayward lifted an end each and began to carry him out of the yard. I trotted alongside, touching my dad's hand every few moments but it still didn't move. The door was heavy and so was my dad, and finally the boy took one of the corners, at Mr. Hayward's end, and trudged along with us. They were all sweating, even without having to carry a great weight because it was a boiling, sultry day. That's probably what had made the bull turn vicious.

When we got home Mr. Barshinskey lifted my dad up in his arms again and carried him up the stairs. By this time my dad's foot was dangling right down low from his leg. It made me feel sick just to look at it. Mr. Barshinskey laid him on the bed.

"Best not touch him till the doctor comes," said Mrs. Hayward. It was a bit late for those instructions. My dad had been pulled and pushed all over the place.

The men went downstairs, and we three women waited by the bed. My mother was white, totally white like a starched pinafore. She stared at me coldly once, as though it were my fault, but then I realized she wasn't seeing me. When she did see me she told me to go downstairs.

"No."

"She saw him, Mrs. Willoughby," said Mrs. Hayward gently. "We were in the dairy and we heard him scream. Sophie was up over the wall before I could stop her. She saw him in the bull pen."

Mother came back from wherever she was and gave a little wintry smile. I felt she wanted to be kind but didn't really have time for me.

"All right. You can stay until the doctor comes."

I stood by the bed holding my dad's hand. Horrors opened before me and the greatest of these (so selfish are we when tragedy threatens to denude our lives) was loneliness. Mother and Lillian had each other. Edwin lived a life apart, but even he, as only son, had a place in the family and a place in Mother's affections. I had no such place. If anything happened to Dad I would be completely alone.

"Shall I go and make a cup of tea, Mrs. Willoughby?"

"That would be nice," said Mother politely, and Mrs. Hayward left us. Even then, sitting silently together beside the body of the man who was our mainstay, our pivot, our moral and material hold on life, we were still apart. I did not belong to my mother. She did not feel that I was her child. I began to shake but she did not notice. It was not delayed shock, it was the realization that I was unloved by someone who ought to love me. She was fond of me. She felt a sense of family responsibility for me, but she did not love me.

They'd got Lillian from Miss Clark's and I heard her hurrying up the stairs. When she came into the bedroom Mother's face suddenly collapsed and she began to cry. So did Lillian. They were both gentle about it, just a few tears running down their cheeks, and then Lillian put her arms around Mother and said, "I'll bring you a cup of tea, Mother. Mrs. Hayward's just made some," and Mother smiled feebly and answered, "Oh, Lillian! What are we going to do . . ." and then she suddenly braced herself and said, "We must get some water ready for the doctor, and some old sheets."

"Mrs. Hayward's getting the water hot now, Mother."

"If we cleaned up his face a little it wouldn't matter. That can't hurt him if we do that before the doctor comes."

She was herself again. Competent. In charge of things. She cleaned Dad's face and made me drink a cup of hot sweet tea. She sent Lillian around to Mrs. King to borrow another hot water bottle to pack around Dad and keep him warm. Even on this hot day Dad's body was icy.

When the doctor came we were sent downstairs, except for Mother. They were up there for a long time.

Mr. Barshinskey and Peter had gone back to the farm, and that left me, Lillian, and Mr. and Mrs. Hayward sitting staring at one another in an atmosphere that was both intense and embarrassing. Lillian suddenly remembered her manners as daughter of the house.

"Would you like to come and sit in the parlor?" she said.

"No, thank you, dear. We're not really dressed for parlor

sitting. Mr. Hayward's still in his farm clothes and I doubt your mother would thank us for sitting on her sofa in our dirt."

Lillian flushed.

"We're just going to wait and see what doctor says, then we'll be off. I've still to finish in the dairy."

Edwin came in, fetched by the boy from Mr. Watkins's station.

"How is he?"

"Doctor's still up there."

"You all right, Soph?"

"Yes."

There was another long silence and then Mr. Hayward said to Edwin, "You're to tell your ma that I don't want her worrying about doctor's bills. I'll give a hand with those."

"That's very good of you, Mr. Hayward."

It was good of him. I nearly forgave him for those instructions about not damaging the bull.

And finally they came down the stairs and went into the parlor. I heard the doctor's voice rumbling away and then the front door opened and shut and he was gone. Mother came into the kitchen. Her eyes looked very blue and bright.

"He's got concussion and a broken ankle and broken ribs," she said. "Doctor's coming back tomorrow to see how his head is."

That was serious. If the doctor was coming on a Sunday we knew it was serious.

"We're just to keep him very quiet now," she said.

Everyone was still. Then Mrs. Hayward said in a nice normal tone of voice, "Now is there anything we can do, Mrs. Willoughby?"

"Very kind of you, but we can manage." People would help us, but they would be our kind of people. The Haywards were our employers and one did not make too many demands on them in case they got impatient. One looked for help from one's equals.

"Well, we'll be getting along," said Mr. Hayward. "We'll look in tomorrow. And I've just told your boy here, I'll give a hand with the doctor's bills."

"Very good of you, Mr. Hayward," said Mother tonelessly, and they went.

It was Saturday, but we didn't have our baths, just wash-downs at the sink. We didn't have our hair washed, or sluice down the yard and the scullery floor. It was quiet and different and that made us realize how ill Dad was. In the evening I got out my text and realized that Dad wasn't there to hear me say it and that was when desolation and overpowering grief struck me, and this time it wasn't entirely selfish. I thought of all the things I could have done for my dad, and of all the things he had done for us, things like getting up at four every morning and lighting the stove so that it was warm when we came down, like never taking second helpings at mealtimes so that we children could have whatever remained. He never shouted at us, or hit us, he was just there, quiet, unassuming, kind. He never told us stories unless they were from the Bible, and he couldn't play the fiddle or draw people to him like the Pied Piper. But he was my dad and now that he was ill I knew I wouldn't have him any other way. A terrible sense of my disloyalty toward him swamped me, just for a moment, driving out the misery of worrying about whether or not he was going to die.

The room was quiet, just the gentle sound of the clock and an occasional creak from upstairs. Mother was with Dad, and Lillian was with Mother. Edwin was shutting up the hens, and as that was something Dad usually did no doubt Edwin, too, was having his own worrying reflections.

All these thoughts flitted through my head. I saw Edwin standing by the hen run wondering if Dad would ever shut them up again. I saw Mother and Lillian upstairs and Dad's face on the pillow, and suddenly a great scream welled up inside my head and I knew I would have to run outside if the scream wasn't to come out and disgrace me. We had all done so well, hardly crying and not saying anything at all to one another about what we dreaded.

The silent scream sent me out of the kitchen and across the yard. I ran and ran and ended up in Tyler's meadow, and there I was able to lie under a hedge and cry, safe in the knowledge that no one could see or hear me.

"Come now, *kroshka*. What is this?"

He sat on the ground beside me and pulled me over onto his lap. His arms were around me and his beard rested on the top of my head. He held me tight and began a kind of rocking movement, backward and forward, very gentle. I didn't want him to be my father anymore, but I clung to him because he offered warmth and human sympathy. To touch Mr. Barshinskey was to drive away the specter of death.

"You must not cry, little one. Your papa is ill, yes, but he is big, strong man and I do not think God will let him die this time."

I could not answer and wisely he said no more, just continued with his rocking and hugging and at the back of his throat was a very soft gentle humming. The insidious pull of Mr. Barshinskey began to stir in me again but this time it was weighted by the memory of my dad's body crumpled and silent in the bull pen.

"I love my dad better than you," I wept accusingly, and for a second his rocking was stilled.

"Of course you do, *kroshka*."

"I thought I didn't. But I do."

"Yes."

He gave a great gentle sigh, and then put me from him, back on the grass at his side, his arm across my shoulders.

"Sophie," he said sadly, "when you are older you will learn that it is possible to love many people in many ways. You do not have to say, this one I love, therefore the others I do not love."

"But I wanted you to be my papa," I sobbed, "and now God is punishing me."

"Poof!" he said disparagingly. "Who do you think God is to listen to a little girl like you? God, who has the whole world to run, is going to waste his time and go to all this trouble just to punish you? No!"

"But I was disloyal to my dad! I loved you more than him!"

"No, Sophie. You just loved the things I could do that your papa cannot do. I am . . . different from your papa . . . and this you loved. But I would be a very bad papa for you, *kroshka*." He paused and then said to himself, "I am not a good papa at all. . . ."

And that terrible confusion of mixed emotion and loyalties made me answer, "Oh, you are! You are!" and in the darkness I heard him chuckle.

"Well, perhaps I am, just a little. For Galina I am good, the papa she would have above all others . . . yes . . . now if Galina had *your* papa she would be, oh, so very unhappy!"

"No, she wouldn't!" Misery made me cry, and he chuckled again.

"You must stop thinking, *kroshka*. Remember only that, if God is good, your papa will grow well again, and then you can love him because he is your papa, and me because I am man who plays the fiddle. So now . . ." He patted my shoulder. "Go home, and remember that whenever you are sad or lonely, your friend Nikolai Igorovitch is here to help you."

He stood up and reached down a hand for me. The touch of it gave me, as always, the feeling of safety and warmth and security. I knew he couldn't make things come right, but suddenly I didn't feel quite so lonely.

We none of us slept much that night. Before I went to bed I asked if I could see my dad and both Edwin and I went in and stood by the bed. Father's head was bandaged up, and his face had a bluish tinge about it that was terrifying. All night long the picture of it kept appearing in my head. I could hear Edwin coughing in the other room and I wanted to go in and climb into bed with him but then, I thought, that would leave Lillian alone and she wasn't asleep either. Just as dawn was breaking she got out of bed and pulled her wrapper around her.

"Where you going, Lil?"

"To see how Mother is."

"Ask if I can come in and see Dad."

Lillian didn't answer. She crept through Edwin's room and then I heard whispers from the front bedroom. Mother had spent the night in an armchair by the bed. The whispers went on and on, and finally I couldn't stand it any more and I hurried—none too quietly—through Edwin's room and into Dad's.

Mother and Lillian were bending over the bed, and something about the way they stood filled me with apprehension.

"What's happened to Dad?"

They turned, but their faces weren't the way I'd thought they'd be. I pushed forward and there was my dad, and his eyes were open. One was a great red-blood bruise but the other was just as my dad's eyes always were.

"Dad!" He gave a tiny little smile.

"You all right, Dad?" He closed them again, but the smile remained on his face. And he was still breathing.

"Will he be all right now, Ma?"

"Go back to bed, dear," she said tiredly.

"Will he be all right?"

"We must let him sleep, and hope that he'll be all right."

I put my face down against his hand that lay outside the sheet and that, more than anything, filled me with hope. The terrors of the night receded a little. His hand was warm at last, and there was even a little pulse beating in it.

"His hand is nice and warm, Ma," I whispered. "That's good, isn't it?"

She didn't answer, but she absentmindedly patted me on the shoulder.

"Can I sit up with him, Ma? I'll be quiet, I won't move or make a noise."

"No, dear. Lillian will stay with me. I want you to go back to bed like a good girl and after the doctor's been, well, we'll see . . ."

I knew, from the tone of her voice, that I mustn't argue, so I went back to my own room, clinging to the memory of Dad's warm hand and the smile upon his face.

121

7 HOW SLENDER THE LINE THAT SEPARATES THE AFFLU-
ent poor from the truly poor. Until that time we had
been the Willoughbys, envied, admired, modest benefactors to the poor. But Dad's accident brought
about a change in our fortunes so that, although we were never
reduced to the near-destitute standards of the Barshinskeys, our
days of financial supremacy were over.

It didn't worry me too much. I didn't have the responsibility
of financial adjustment, and as far as I was concerned everything
faded into insignificance beside the fact that Dad didn't die.

He was ill, badly ill, for several days, sometimes conscious
but for much of the time buried in a deep immobile sleep. The
doctor came every day, which frightened us all, but by the end
of the week Dad appeared to be conscious more than unconscious.

It was the head injury that had done the damage. In time the
ankle mended and so did the ribs, but Mr. Hayward's villainous
bull had in some way damaged Dad's head so that his sight wasn't
quite perfect in his right eye. Even then he could have managed.
There's nothing wrong with a one-eyed cowman, but about three
months after the accident the first of his headaches began—bad
violent headaches that made him virtually drop where he stood,
unable to see at all, unable to stand without vomiting, unable to
walk without overbalancing. When the headaches came he was in
bed for anything up to three or four days and a cowman who was
likely to be absent, without notice, for as long as that wasn't much
use.

Mr. Hayward was kind. He did, as he had said, help with the
doctor's bills. He paid half. And while Dad was laid up in bed he
sent down the milk just the same and gave Mother various sums
of money from time to time. But his kindness didn't implement
the loss of Dad's regular wages.

There was a small weekly sum from Oddfellows that Dad had

122

paid into for years and the money came out from the Penny Savings Bank. The harmonium lessons were stopped (I wasn't altogether sorry about that). Edwin, as well as continuing with his holiday job at the railway station, had to take over Dad's heavy jobs around the yard—chopping the wood, superintending the livestock, coping with the garden.

As well as my two mornings in Hayward's dairy, another holiday job was found for me, and I heard my fate with a sinking heart. The woman who did the laundry at the vicarage was unable to go in for a while. Her daughter, over Edenbridge way, was ill. And Mrs. Lovelace's cook-general had said she'd manage the laundry herself if she could have an extra pair of hands in the kitchen. Those hands, young, inexperienced, and therefore cheap, were to be mine. Four mornings a week I was to "make myself useful" in the vicarage kitchen and scullery.

I'd sooner have done anything than that. I didn't like Mrs. Lovelace. I didn't like her cook-general, and above all I hated Galina Barshinskey, who would be in a position of supremacy over me. I was about to protest when I saw Mother's harassed face, and thought of Dad lying upstairs in bed, and I determined to try to accept my miserable fate with fortitude. Dad was alive. I was earning money for him. What did anything matter apart from that? And it was only for a few weeks.

The one thing that Mother was determined upon in our time of emergency was that nothing should interfere with Lillian's apprenticeship. She was paid very little—only three shillings a week—and she continued to live at home. If she'd gone into service it would have helped tremendously but Mother decided that nothing should wreck Lillian's chances and, of course, although I resented the decision, hated Lillian, was jealous of Mother's preference, practicality forced me to admit that it was sensible not to waste the premium money Mother had saved so thriftily.

So, on Mondays, Tuesdays, Thursdays, and Fridays I reported promptly at 7:30 in the morning to Mrs. Puddingoyle at the kitchen door of the vicarage. There I washed dishes and pans, cleaned and scraped vegetables, helped with the rough copper washing, and scrubbed kitchen and scullery floors. I was not allowed in the rest of the vicarage, only in the kitchen and scullery.

Mrs. Puddingoyle gave the impression of being a large, jolly, happy woman, but she was not. She had a noisy laugh, but even while she was laughing and calling you a "good lassie" her eyes were shifting meanly over every job you'd done and she was giving you a hard jab in the ribs for not doing it quicker.

"Come on now, there's a good lassie, not strung those beans yet?" she'd bellow, as though it were the funniest thing in the world, and while she said it she'd shake me quite hard by the shoulder.

When Mrs. Lovelace came into the kitchen for the daily instructions, Mrs. Puddingoyle changed from pretending to be a fat, jolly, noisy woman to becoming a fat, loyal, warmhearted woman.

"Now don't you worry about the vicar's supper, ma'am. I know he's a bit below par at the moment, and goodness knows we've all watched you working and worrying yourself to a shadow with looking after him, and the young curate, and the parish. There's a nice duck come up from Tyler's, and I'll dress it up with a jar of apricots and some fresh runners. It'll make you both feel better. . . ."

Mrs. Lovelace would sigh and raise a hand to her forehead, and carry wearily on with her directions for the day. It was as though they were both acting in a play. I felt they didn't even like each other very much but found it convenient to have someone who gave the right responses. Mrs. Lovelace liked being told she was a brave saintly woman who spent her life doing things for others. And Mrs. Puddingoyle liked to think she was the mainstay of the vicarage rather than just a cook-general. I once heard her telling some distant relative, who called in to share a pot of midmorning tea, that she was the vicarage housekeeper and with that kind of experience behind her could go up to London any time and get a better paying job.

She couldn't have done, not to my way of thinking. She was

slatternly and wasteful. I knew the way my mother ran a house and it was not Mrs. Puddingoyle's way. Carcasses of poultry were thrown out with meat still on them instead of being boiled for stock. Flour and sugar were left uncovered in damp places so that they mildewed and mice got at them. The first time I scrubbed the kitchen floor I found that under the sink and up the sides of the stove hadn't been cleaned for years. The stove was encrusted with congealed fat and general kitchen dirt. And suddenly I discovered I was more like my mother than I knew—distaste and a fury for someone who did her work so casually made me scrub it as though it were my kitchen. The two things Mrs. Puddingoyle was good at were cooking and ironing. To see her with the goffering iron was fascinating; in and out it twinkled and starched frills appeared as if by magic. And when she was ironing she ceased to shout and laugh and punch me. She became quite human and sometimes let me have a go with the iron. That was the only time I ever liked her.

It was extraordinary to watch the way she and Galina behaved. It was like the Mrs. Lovelace performance all over again, only this time Galina played the flattering role, while Mrs. Puddingoyle pretended to believe that Galina was a meek, pretty little thing who thought the world of her.

I remembered how Galina hadn't wanted to come to work at the vicarage, and how I had even felt sorry for her at having to do so. I remembered how unhappy she said she was and, I supposed, this nasty creepy way she had with Mrs. Puddingoyle was just her way of surviving.

Whenever Mrs. Puddingoyle made one of her terrible, unfunny jokes, Galina would give a squeaky girlish giggle, and she would clap her hands over her mouth, nervously, her head on one side, as though she really liked and admired Mrs. Puddingoyle but was too shy to say so. When she got her month's wages she went out to the village and came back with a bar of chocolate.

"That's for you, Mrs. Puddingoyle," she said. "For being so kind to me and helping me when I wasn't too sure of my job."

I was scouring out slimy porridge pans at the time and I felt furious that such hypocrisy should actually be believed. Mrs. Puddingoyle's face, which in spite of the fat was a very hard face, softened and looked genuinely surprised.

"Well, thank you, dear," she said.

Galina turned to me. "I'd like to have bought something for you, too, Sophie," she whispered sadly, "but—well—you know how things are at home. I just allow myself a few pennies for necessary things, and the rest has to go to my mother."

That was a lie. I knew from Daisy May how hard it was to get Galina to contribute regularly with any of her money. If you caught her the minute she'd been paid it was all right. She didn't seem to mind parting with her wages. But usually she was out of the house and up in the village shop while it was still in her hand, and by the time she'd bought ribbons and artificial flowers, and scarves and cheap scent and all the other bits of rubbish that took her fancy, there wasn't any left. But, true or not, it worked beautifully with Mrs. Puddingoyle.

"You save your money, child. The day'll come when you need it. And I'm sure that if Sophie wants chocolate bars she can buy them for herself."

And later that morning, when the goffering iron was out, "Galina dear, fetch your shirtwaist and I'll do those frills for you."

There was a great deal of bantering and teasing between them about Mr. Hope-Browne too, about his spots and his blushing, and about his underpants which were of very good quality, better than the vicar's in fact.

"That's because Mr. Hope-Browne's family are very rich," said Mrs. Puddingoyle with an air of insufferable and knowing importance. "He's the youngest son of a Sir Somebody or other, down in Hampshire. I've seen the letters come from his mother and they've got a crest on the envelope. And his shirts are mono-grammed, too, including a silk one up in his drawer that he only wears when the bishop comes."

I didn't think it very nice to talk about Mr. Hope-Browne's underpants. Mother would have considered it common, but Galina and Mrs. Puddingoyle went off into squeals of laughter and made all kinds of jokes. And they laughed, too, about the fact that Mr. Hope-Browne kept making excuses to come into the kitchen, and when he came he stared at Galina and sometimes flushed. I hated it. Galina somehow managed to behave in a dual role. She would smile boldly up at Mr. Hope-Browne, gazing into his eyes just a moment too long for respectability, and then she would give a little sideways grimace at Mrs. Puddingoyle, inviting her to share the joke. And in some clever way she managed never to let Mr. Hope-Browne see the grimace, or Mrs. Puddingoyle see the liquid gaze of her dark eyes.

Every time I thought of those two figures running away out of the churchyard I felt sick. When, at one o'clock, I left the vicarage kitchen I would run all the way home through the clean fresh air. Those two, Galina and Mr. Hope-Browne, made me feel choked and dirty.

There were times when I wanted so badly to tell someone at home about it. Even if I could have mentioned the dirty places under the vicarage sink it would have helped but I didn't want Mother to think I was complaining, and anyway I never had shared things with her, and now was not the time to begin. Dad began to get a little better and was allowed to get up in the afternoons. He would come down the stairs on his one good ankle with both hands holding the banister rails. Then he would sit, his eyes closed, looking rather white, and although I wanted to talk to him I couldn't. It was enough just to sit near him and touch his hand now and again. At that time we didn't know about the headaches and we all thought that when his ankle and ribs were mended, and he had grown used to his restricted sight, he would be able to go back as head stockman at Hayward's.

In September, just before the new school term began, the Pilgrim Teachers arrived and set up their tent on the field at the side of the Fox. They went there, partly because the vicar disapproved of evangelical crusades and therefore wouldn't let them near the Parish Hall, and partly because they liked to catch the drunks coming out of the Fox. They had captured quite a few souls for Jesus in the first throes of alcoholic remorse.

Everyone in the village enjoyed the Pilgrim Teachers. There were those who said they were little better than strolling players, but as they performed under a banner of evangelism even we, the Brethren, were allowed to go to hear them. I thought them exciting, and I went as many times as Mother would let me.

They had lovely rousing hymns accompanied by two concertinas and the teachers all wore black cloaks with red linings. This year there were five of them, three men and two women, and their leader was new, Pilgrim Teacher Jones.

Mrs. Puddingoyle, who went on the first night, told us all about him in the vicarage kitchen next morning.

"A wonderful man!" she enthused. "Full of the spirit of the Lord. He's tall, you know, and I do like a big man, with good strong shoulders and a voice that can be heard right at the back of the tent."

"Was anyone saved?" I asked.

"No, not the first night. He didn't really try hard at the saving, not on the first night. Plenty of good hymns and a couple of solos, and then mass praying for what was going to happen in the next two weeks. . . . 'Every beggar and sinner, every drunkard and harlot in this village will be here, on their knees, praying for forgiveness' and then"—Mrs. Puddingoyle's voice pulsed in remembered sympathy—"then he flung out his arms and all the red in the cloak flashed beautifully, 'And I tell you brothers, sisters, as you kneel, penitent, miserable sinners, I shall be with you, kneeling with you, supporting you with my strength, sharing your secrets and giving you comfort. . . .' Oh, it was lovely. But I shan't be able to go again until Wednesday," she finished sadly.

"I'd like to go," said Galina suddenly. She and Mrs. Puddingoyle stared contemplatively at each other for a moment.

"We'll have to be careful," said Mrs. Puddingoyle. "*They*"—she pointed a finger up to the ceiling—"*they* don't like anyone from the vicarage going. She says they're vulgar, and he says they're blasphemous, but if we're careful and go on alternate nights they won't know. We'll cover up for each other."

Galina gave her soft, little-girl smile. "I think I shall enjoy it," she whispered.

I went the next night with Mother and Lillian and Mr. and Mrs. King. We left Dad sitting quietly at home with Edwin. I don't think Dad altogether approved of the Pilgrim Teachers, but Mother loved them and had suddenly looked more like her old spirited self at the thought of an evening out.

Mrs. Puddingoyle was quite right. Pilgrim Teacher Jones was a fine-looking fellow and very different from the older leader of last year. He had silvery curls over a very strong face, and his voice was something like Mr. Hope-Browne's. He sang some hymns all on his own, sad ones at first, about those who turn their backs on the Lord, and then they got brisker and jollier—fighting tunes about getting in the souls somehow. The Sisters had scarlet hoods up over their hair, and about halfway through the evening they came around with collection bags. They were both very pretty.

Just after the collection was taken I saw Galina slip into the tent. She looked around, and then came and sat on the bench beside me. I can't think why as she never bothered with me in the ordinary way. I suppose she wanted someone to tell her what to do.

There was a little excited rustle, and then the concertinas made a kind of "here-we-go" noise. They dropped to a gentle background noise, and the Sisters began a gentle humming. Pilgrim Teacher Jones stepped up onto a wooden platform and lifted his arms high in the air.

"Good people!" he trembled. "For some of you are good, some of you tread the narrow path to Jesus, the hard path, the path strewn with bolders, blowing with bitter winds, the storms of Satan raging around your heads. Who"—he lowered his voice and dropped his arms—"who would willingly choose this path? Who would go naked when they could flaunt themselves in cloth of gold! Who would choose the humble table when the devil offers a feast of rich foods and crimson wines. Who would choose to walk quietly with Jesus when they could join the revelries of Satan!"

He raised his right arm and pointed to us. "Who? I ask. And the answer is, not many." His voice began to get louder and I noticed that little beads of sweat were beginning to gather on his forehead. We were sitting right near the front as Mother always liked to see who was going up to be saved.

"In this tent are sinners," he cried. "You may not *think* you are sinners, but search in your hearts. I look about me"—he did so—"and I see more sinners than righteous. I feel, in my heart" —he beat it—"all the sinners in here tonight. I *know* who you are! I could *name* you! I could walk among you and touch your hearts and you would know that your sin was detected! In this tent, brothers, sisters, are thieves and liars, drunkards and har- lots. There are hearts filled with all the wicked longings of Satan, and these longings will *destroy* you!"

He was shouting and the concertinas were going at full blast. The Sisters were swaying from side to side singing and chanting a heady and compelling melody. I was enjoying it, but not with quite the same uncritical appreciation of other years. For I couldn't help thinking that the music wasn't as good as Mr. Bar- shinskey's fiddle.

"Come forward, brothers, sisters! Come forward, here, to me! Let me put my arms about you and bring you to Jesus. Let me show you the way. Let me take your sinful hearts, your sinful thoughts in my own two hands and tell you that . . . JESUS LOVES YOU! COME!"

His arms were held toward us, the red shiny lining of the cloak glimmering in the naphtha flares. The music had reached a crescendo and the other two Brothers had come forward and were standing in line with the Sisters. There was a great surge of noise, a kind of guttural cry from the congregation, a sensed quivering of emotion spreading through the tent like wind through a corn- field. I heard a little gasp beside me and looked to see Galina swaying slightly in her seat. Her head was thrown back and her

130

lips were slightly parted. She looked the way she did when she was dancing.

"COME!" cried Pilgrim Teacher Jones in a great throbbing voice. "Come and be saved. Step forward to the platform and I shall help you!"

Mr. Kelly was the first to go. He always was. He drank and knocked his wife and children about, but he was always saved most beautifully. He made a public confession, wept, and then sank on his knees before the platform. One of the pretty Sisters came forward and knelt beside him.

"One sinner? Only one sinner? Be brave! Only a short step to Jesus! Stand and come forward! Just a few steps and his arms are around you!"

Mrs. Jetson went forward, although I wouldn't ever have described her as a sinner, and sank to her respectable, plump little knees. One of the Brothers passed his concertina to the other Sister and came forward to kneel beside her.

The music and Pilgrim Teacher Jones's sonorous voice dragged people forward. Some of them looked sheepish, some excited. Finally he left the platform and began to pace up and down the passageway, exhorting us to come forward, to leave our seats and kneel before him. I felt a movement beside me and turned to see Galina, trancelike, stand up. And suddenly I was frightened.

"Yes! Come forward, sister! Come to my arms, to the arms of Jesus! Step forward and confess your sins!"

He stopped pacing and stared at Galina. She was breathing very heavily and the top button of her shirtwaist had come undone. She reached out a hand toward him but couldn't touch him because we were all sitting between them.

"Come, sister!" He was suddenly still, and I saw his eyes narrow. "Come! Even a young girl, a girl who resembles a perfect ripe fruit can have a heart throbbing with sin and wickedness!"

"Sit down, Galina." I tugged hard on her dress. "Sit down! Don't tell everyone! Please don't tell everyone!"

What was it I didn't want her to tell? I don't know. But a

memory of the figures flitting through the churchyard, of her moving toward Mr. Hope-Browne with her hands raised to her hair, made me tremble. Galina was different from the rest of us, and her secrets were dangerous ones. She turned her head and looked at me as though I wasn't there. "Don't tell," I whispered. "You'll lose your place at the vicarage."

I held her hand so hard in mine that she couldn't have moved without a struggle, and then slowly her eyes seemed to focus and as she looked at me the color ebbed away from her cheeks.

"Sit down," I hissed, and then, to my terrified relief, she did so. The Pilgrim Teacher stared at her and I thought he was going to start again, exhort her to come forward, or even rebuke me for interfering, but after a long, long pause he passed on.

I didn't notice too much of the rest of the evening. Those who had been saved put something more in the collection bags, and as we filed out the Sisters stood at the tent entrance holding them yet again in case anyone was moved to contribute a little more. All I wanted to do was hurry home and tell Edwin, but somehow when I got home I couldn't mention it. I was too ashamed.

The next morning at the vicarage Mrs. Puddingoyle wanted to hear all about the evening before, but Galina didn't say very much. She smiled to herself a couple of times, and said she wanted to go again.

"Yes, well, but it's my turn tonight, Galina. We agreed to go on alternate nights."

"Yes, of course, Mrs. Puddingoyle." She smiled sweetly. "I'll just look forward to my turn tomorrow."

The Pilgrim Teachers were there for two weeks, and those weeks became ones of constant tension and worry for me. I was terrified of what Galina might do, and so I lied and coaxed and persuaded Mother to let me go every night that Galina was going. All the fun of the Pilgrim Teachers had gone. I had to maneuver myself into sitting beside her; sometimes it meant I had to get up after the service had started, push along a row, and squeeze down where there wasn't any room. Sometimes she was all right. The fervor and excitement didn't touch her. But at the beginning of the second week it nearly happened again. I felt her begin to rise beside me. I panicked and did the only thing I could think of, which was to kick her hard in the shin. She blinked at me and frowned, but again I had broken the spell.

I began to hate that tent with its close-packed benches and sweaty congregation. I hated the music, and the flickering lights from the flares that made everything seem as though Satan were indeed present. Above all I began to hate Pilgrim Teacher Jones. Every night he seemed to be talking directly to Galina. Drunkards, liars, and thieves featured less and less in his peroration and harlots and Jezebels featured more. He spoke about evil disguised by beauty, about youth that was corrupt. He gazed at her with his narrowed eyes and she stared back at him and as the week went on she seemed not so much mesmerized as fascinated. She was looking at him the way she looked at Mr. Hope-Browne. One night she came with her hair down. It was tied back off her face, but the great mane of black curls around her shoulders made Teacher Jones's eyes narrow even more.

The end of the week came, and there was only one more night. Just one more night and then we would be safe. I couldn't eat, and I felt sick all the time. If only I could have told someone.

At tea time I began my usual plea to Mother about letting me go to the crusade. And this time, for some reason, she was adamant in her refusal. The more I pleaded, made excuses, lied (I said that Ivan Barshinskey had agreed to go and surely he was one person who needed saving), and wept, the more implacable she became.

"I'm beginning to think your father's right about these evangelical crusades," she said tiredly. "You've become more and more difficult since they arrived. I've enough to do with your father ill. I'm not having you on my hands too."

"But I must go!"

"No, you must not, my girl. And we'll hear no more about it, otherwise it'll be bed for you straight after tea."

I thought I was going to burst into tears, but then Dad smiled at me and I knew I mustn't do anything to upset him when he was ill.

I could feel my stomach turning in a ferment of worry. The

last night of the crusade was always the worst, singing and shouting and everyone crying and falling on their knees. There was no one I could trust, no one I could tell, for in a curious way there was nothing to tell. How could I say that I didn't want Galina to be saved? How could I say I was sure something dreadful would happen if she was? I thought of Mr. Hope-Browne with his gentle manners and his spots, his good quality underwear and his lack of confidence. How young he was. When one compared him with Ivan, or even Edwin, Mr. Hope-Browne seemed a very feeble young man. But I didn't want anything dreadful to happen to him.

I finished the washing up and then went out into the yard.

"Where are you going, Sophie?"

"I'm going to tell Ivan I shan't be able to take him to the crusade."

"Don't be long."

Once outside I ran up the lane toward the church. I didn't have much time if Mother thought I was only popping next door to the Owl House. When I reached the vicarage I had to face the dilemma of whether to go to the kitchen door or knock at the front. If I went to the kitchen, which was my proper place, either Mrs. Puddingoyle or Galina would be there, and they'd want to know why I'd come. One or other of them would still answer the front door, but if I knocked there they would think I had come from my mother. I swallowed and banged the vicarage knocker. It was Mrs. Puddingoyle who answered.

"Saints alive! What are you doing here, Sophie?"

"I've got to see Mr. Hope-Browne."

"What about?"

"My dad says I've got to see him."

Mrs. Puddingoyle hesitated, then held the door open a little. "All right. Come in. But stand on the mat there. I don't want you walking about over this clean floor. You wait there now."

She went through one of the doors leading off from the hall and I heard her talking to someone. Then she came back with Mr. Hope-Browne.

"There you are, Sophie. Now you tell Mr. Hope-Browne what it is your dad wants."

She waited, and so did Mr. Hope-Browne.

"It's private," I finally blurted. Mrs. Puddingoyle's mouth hardened and I knew I was going to have a rough time in the kitchen on Monday.

"I'm sorry, Mr. Hope-Browne," she said. "Sophie's manners are no better than you'd expect. I'll send her away."

Mr. Hope-Browne blushed. "Can't you tell me what you want, Sophie?" he asked gently, and I shook my head, raging silently at him for being so unhelpful, so stupid when I was doing it all for his sake.

"We'll just step outside, Mrs. Puddingoyle," he said. "I'll walk her down to the gate."

Mrs. Puddingoyle made an angry snorting noise, but she could do nothing to me for the moment. All my anxieties, all the panic churning over and over in my stomach was for now, this evening in the Pilgrim Teachers' tent.

"What is it, Sophie? Is your father ill again?"

"No." Now that I was here I didn't know how to tell him. I wasn't nervous or in awe of him, the way I was of the vicar, but how was I to shatter an illusion, to break through the gentle, respectable façade that was the life of our village and tell him that soon Pilgrim Teacher Jones would know everything that had happened.

"It's Galina," I finally choked.

All the years I had known Mr. Hope-Browne he had lived in a constant state of embarrassment, changing from pink to white as his shyness manifested itself. But now, when I mentioned her name, his color didn't change at all. I wish it had. His face just seemed to—drop away, as though he wasn't there anymore. I wanted to look away but the terrible emptiness of his face held me.

"She's going to the Pilgrim Teachers' tonight," I gabbled. "She's been going for the last two weeks and twice she's nearly been saved. He wants her to confess—Pilgrim Teacher Jones.

135

He's been staring at her every night, *making* her come forward and tell him everything, only I stopped her. And she's going tonight. She likes him, I can tell that, they like each other. I can't go tonight . . . but somebody must go and stop her. Sometimes when people are saved they stand up and say dreadful things. It's terrible there, Mr. Hope-Browne, like a fever with everyone going mad."

The churning in my stomach got worse, and with it came an overwhelming desire to weep for dear Mr. Hope-Browne. Whatever he had done I didn't blame him. He was just a shy, gentle, lonely young man.

"I'll have to go now, Mr. Hope-Browne."

He stood there with his empty clown's face, looking at nothing.

"I have to go!"

He turned and began to walk back toward the vicarage.

"Mr. Hope-Browne! What are you going to do?"

He went in and shut the vicarage door, and after a few moments I began to trot back home again, more worried than I had been before.

When I got in Mother took one look at my face and asked what was wrong.

"I don't feel very well."

"Too much gadding about," she snapped. "And if you'd had your way you'd be up in that wretched tent again tonight. You get up to bed now. Kiss your dad goodnight and don't let me hear anymore from you."

I went across to Dad and kissed him. He still looked tired and ill and, oh, how I wished I could talk to him. Dad was the only one who would have known what to do. If Dad had been well it would never have got to this stage. Somehow he would have stopped Galina from going to the crusades, and would probably have stopped the secret thing concerning Mr. Hope-Browne too.

"I shan't be long behind you, lassie," he whispered. "I'm ready for my bed too."

It had been such a wonderful, wonderful summer, and then

Dad had been kicked by the bull and since then it had all gone wrong. I went to my room and tried to cry but couldn't. The memory of Mr. Hope-Browne wouldn't go away. What was he going to do? Was he going to do anything? Why hadn't he answered or shown he understood me? What was the point of warning him if he took no notice?

It was dusk, and finally I opened the bedroom window and climbed out on the windowsill. This was the ultimate sin and Mother would never forgive me, but her forgiveness, like Mrs. Puddingoyle's anger, seemed unimportant compared with other things.

The coal shed backed onto the cottage at the back and I slid down the roof, then took a deep breath and jumped. I heard Mother call, "What's that?" but I was up and racing the length of the garden, getting through the thicket and into Tyler's fields before she could see me. This was the long way to the village and when I got to the Pilgrims' tent the crusade had already begun. The concertinas were playing their pounding background music, and I could hear Pilgrim Teacher Jones alternately chanting and shouting.

I pushed through the crowds standing at the back of the tent. There was always a vast congregation on the last night. I raced up the gangway, looking for Galina, but somehow in the hysteria and flickering light I couldn't find her.

Pilgrim Teacher Jones was crooning now, in a rich soothing voice, and lots of those in the congregation were swaying backward and forward. He looked huge and runnels of sweat were pouring down his face. When he lifted his arms to us I could see great circular patches of damp staining the armpits of his dark suit.

"Sisters . . . brothers . . . do not feel shame at your thoughts. The devil puts lust in our hearts and bodies, and we must fight him."

I saw Galina. She was sitting right by the gangway, near to the front, where he could get at her. I hurried toward her and tried to push in on the bench beside her. And suddenly *he* was there, Pilgrim Teacher Jones, looking down at me as though he wanted to squash me.

"This young girl," he cried, putting his hand on Galina's head. "This tender young girl has been here many times, and I have watched her wrestling with her sin. This beautiful young creature, pulsing on the threshold of womanhood, in her heart is deceit and lust and lies."

"Come away, Galina. Do come away."

I tried to stand between them but he gave me a hard thrusting push, back up the gangway, and then he placed his body between me and Galina.

"So much beauty! To hide so much evil! But the Lord is good. The Lord knows and understands. Come to Him . . . to me! Place yourself on His bosom, share your thoughts, your sinful thoughts, with Him. Let Him take your lust!"

Galina rose and to my horror I saw him open his arms and sweep her into the crimson cloak. Surely someone would protest! Someone would say it was wrong! But nobody did. They were all chanting and swaying. The whole village had gone mad. Only when I looked again I saw that it wasn't the whole village. And I realized that, slowly, over the last two weeks, the saner, respectable members of the village had ceased to come. Pilgrim Teacher Jones had infused something different into the crusades—something unpleasant and dirty—and the right people, the ones who would have stopped it, weren't there. I looked and saw they were nearly all men—men from the Fox, men who weren't Church or Brethren or anything. And the women were, with a few exceptions, the odd ones, crazy Miss Durand who lived alone in a crumbling farmhouse and never washed, the laundry women who lived down by the railway line, several girls from the jam and pickle factory. And their faces were all greedy and hot.

The great cloaked figure moved up to the platform and then he moved away and Galina was standing there alone, her eyes black and shining, her head thrown back, swaying in time to the music.

"See, sisters, brothers, see this child. I am going to wrest her from the devil! I shall squeeze the sin from her body. I shall tear the lustful thoughts from her soul! I shall make her stand before you, her spirit bared, the lust driven from her, a pure, untouched vessel for the Lord!" He put his arms up toward her, then lowered them slowly just an inch away from her, then he climbed up onto the platform and stood behind her, close, touching her with his body, his hands splayed huge across her waist.

"Daughter of Eve, child of Jezebel, have you sinned?"

Smiling, Galina nodded.

"Will you share yourself with us! Confess your lewd thoughts and come to the Lord?"

She did what I had seen her do before. She raised her hands to her hair and thrust her body forward. Then she began to take the pins from her hair. There was a horrible guttural noise from all around me as it fell over her shoulders. He, that terrible man, pulled it all down, ran his hands through it and lifted it around her like a cloak.

"Pure," he cried hoarsely. "I shall make you pure . . ."

I tried to get out of the tent but a solid block of mesmerized bodies barred the way. I got down on the floor and tried to crawl through the legs, but they were all moving, treading up and down, feet squirming excitedly on the ground. Someone trod on my fingers.

"Let me through! Let me through!" I began to punch, and got pushed roughly to the front again.

"Shut up!"

I tried not to look at the platform, but I caught just one glimpse. Galina, smiling that horrible trancelike smile, had raised her hands to her neck and was slowly unbuttoning her shirtwaist. And when I thought my head was going to burst I heard, as an echo of my own fear, a terrible loud scream and there was a heaving movement in the crowd, and then Mr. Hope-Browne burst through and ran, screaming and screaming up to the platform.

"You whore!" he cried, and then he collapsed weeping on the ground, an agonized keening noise that smashed through all the music and the hysteria and reduced the tent to silence. The chanting stopped and there was no sound except for that nightmarish sobbing. Jones, his hugeness suddenly diminished so that he was just a sweating man in a shabby cloak, bent over Mr. Hope-Browne in a nervous, unsure manner.

"You're ill, brother . . ." he fumbled, and Mr. Hope-Browne reared up on his knees, sobbing, coughing, and when he saw Jones over him he began to punch him in the stomach. He wasn't a very strong man but he must have caught the preacher on some nerve because Jones doubled over and clapped his hands to his belly, grunting. Then Mr. Hope-Browne stood up, trying to speak, his face screwed into a mask of agony, and when he found he couldn't speak he just fell off the platform, then got to his feet again and staggered down the gangway, holding his hands over his eyes, still making that heartrending noise. The crowd at the back of the tent parted and let him through and then a nervous, evasive embarrassment swept over the crowd, and furtively, not looking at each other, they began to drift away.

The Pilgrim Teachers and Galina were clustered together in a frightened little heap behind the platform. It was uncanny, the sudden emptying of the tent, no voices at all, no calling out, no music, just the scuffling of hurrying feet and people vanished, anxious not to look into each other's eyes.

I tried to walk home, but outside in the lane I began to be sick. I lay down on the ground and a huge white weight pressed down on my head. I stood up and was sick again. The pain that had been in my stomach for the last two weeks began to throb so badly I didn't think I would be able to walk.

"It was a nightmare, that's all, just a nightmare. It didn't really happen," I whimpered to myself. And I managed to get on a little way, got the length of the lane and crawled under the stile where the pain and sickness was so bad I just lay on the ground and let it sweep over me.

After a long, long while I began to feel cold, but the pain had numbed to an ache and I tried to move on a bit farther. I'd reached the top of Tyler's when I had to lie down again, but I knew I wasn't far from home and soon, soon there would be Mother and bed and an escape from the horrible dreams.

There was a clanking and a rustling, and the sound of the pump going up and down.

"Ivan," I whispered. "Ivan, is that you?"

Out of the gloom, slightly nervous, he appeared, bucket in hand.

"Ivan, I'm ill. Will you help me back home?"

Oh, the blessed comfort of him, even the smell that Lillian complained of was good because it reminded me of simple things —of us fighting by the pump, and me walking to school with Daisy May, and the ordinary, everyday life that we passed together.

"I can't carry you, Soph. You're too heavy. D'you want me to get your ma?"

"Just help me walk a bit. Help me up off the ground."

He pulled me up, and together we staggered along. Every time I thought I was going to faint he'd say, very firmly, "Only a bit farther, Soph, not far now," and finally he pushed through the hedge and pulled me after him.

Edwin was in the garden. They were all looking for me, he said, but when he saw I was ill he held me on the other side and between them they got me indoors. Nobody scolded. The smooth, white shape pressed down onto my head again and nearly obliterated me, but I was home, in my own bed, and Lillian was there, hard and grumpy but safe to press up against. With Lillian there I could drive out the devils of the evening, push them away and pretend they hadn't happened.

I didn't get punished, and I didn't have to go to meeting next day, even though it was Sunday. I was allowed to stay in bed, and then Mother came up and told me—in a brusque way—that perhaps it had all been a lesson to me. Then she gave me some neatly folded old towels and explained all about monthly periods.

"You can stay in bed, just for today," she said. "But don't go making an invalid of yourself. We all have to get on and work even if we don't feel too good. Everyone's the same." She paused and looked down at my face. "I'll give you some aspirin, and then you can have a good sleep today, and you'll be ready to go to the vicarage tomorrow. With Dad poorly I can't afford to have two of you ill. So you pull yourself together as soon as you can."

"Oh, I will, Ma. I will!"

It was lovely in bed, with the covers pulled right up to my chin. I slept a lot, and reread all my *Elsie* books, and then Edwin came in and brought me a railway book to look at.

"Ivan came around," he said. "He says, are you all right?"

"Yes."

He dithered with the book and then, not looking at me, said, "What happened last night, Soph? Where did you go? What happened to you? Mum's very worried."

Outside there was a lovely late September sky, all blue and clean, and I could see the trees in the thicket just beginning to turn gold at the tops. The white thing began to press on my head again.

"I've got a stomachache," I said, and Edwin blushed and looked awkward and uncomfortable.

"Did you go to the crusade?" he asked.

"I don't like the Pilgrims. I'm not going anymore." The pain got bigger. It was a big white thing trying to swallow me. Every time I tried to climb away from it I slid on the smooth sides. The sky outside was nice but I began to cry again.

"Oh, I say, Soph. I'm sorry. Look, I'll bring you another book. I'll bring you the big one with colored pictures, but you must promise not to turn the corners of the pages down."

"I promise." The pain receded, and when Edwin brought his book in it had nearly gone.

In the afternoon I heard Mrs. King's voice downstairs. She was talking and talking in a loud voice, very excited, and from time to time I could hear Mother saying something. Then the back door opened and shut again, but although I knew someone else had joined them I couldn't hear who it was.

I got up for tea, and as it was Sunday, and as I'd been ill, I was specially privileged and allowed to wash in the bedroom. Lillian, looking a little resentful, brought me up a jug of hot water.

"D'you feel better?" she asked grudgingly.

"Yes, thanks." I felt a bit wobbly, and strangely lightheaded, but all the pain in my stomach had gone, and the white thing pressing on my head had totally vanished.

She paused, and then said in a curious voice, "Do you think you'll feel well enough to go to work at the vicarage tomorrow?"

"Oh, yes. Mum told me all about . . . you know . . . she said I wasn't to make a fuss of myself. Just get on and try to take no notice."

"Yes . . . well . . ." She went over to the window and fiddled with the curtain. "You'd better know, I suppose." She looked at me, a strange, sly look. "Mum said we wasn't to ask you what happened last night. Whatever it was, she said, you'd been punished. That's what monthly periods are all about, you know. It's woman's eternal punishment for the original sin."

"What original sin?"

"The original sin in the Garden of Eden. And what you did last night, disobeying Mum and going to the crusade was all part of it. . . . But anyway Mum—and Dad—said we wasn't to ask you about it." She waited, curious, but I just sloshed my face flannel around in the wash-hand basin and didn't answer.

"But if you're going to the vicarage tomorrow, you'd better know."

"Know what?"

"Mr. Hope-Browne's been taken very ill."

The white pressing pain didn't come back, but my legs suddenly felt weak and I sat down on the edge of the bed.

"What's the matter with him?"

"I don't know," said Lillian evasively. "Just that he's very, very ill. They had to get the doctor in last night. And a telegram has been sent to his parents down in Hampshire."

"Will they want me at the vicarage, then? If all that's going on they won't want me." I didn't want to go. It wasn't my fault that Mr. Hope-Browne was ill, but perhaps his mother and father would think it *was* my fault. "What made him ill?"

"I don't know," said Lillian, and I knew she was lying. "But of course they want you at the vicarage. They're extra busy with Mr. Hope-Browne ill. Mrs. Puddingoyle sent down a message special asking you to be there tomorrow."

"I see," and then, "Lillian, have the Pilgrim Teachers gone yet?"

"They were taking the tent down when I came back from Bible class."

"But they haven't gone yet?"

"No." She came across, stood by the bedhead and said waspishly, "But I'd think if you knew what was good for you you'd keep away from them. That's what caused all the trouble, wasn't it?"

"I'll keep away. I just want them to be gone, that's all."

I felt she was going to ask me all about it, but the door at the bottom of the stairs opened and Mum called us down to tea. When I went into the kitchen there was a very strange atmosphere. Mrs. King was there and everyone was being very careful to be normal and ordinary and not talk about my escapade or Mr. Hope-Browne's being ill. Once or twice during that strained meal I began to feel a great burden of guilt descending on me, and every time that happened the pain in my head and stomach came back. I didn't fully understand my guilt but I wished I'd never spoken to Mr. Hope-Browne about Galina going to the crusade. I tried to think through what would have happened if I'd done nothing. If I'd not gone to Mr. Hope-Browne or to the crusade.

"That child's going to faint, Mrs. Willoughby."

Mum pushed my head down between my knees and after a while all the vague flitting images in my head went away.

"Up to bed with you, Sophie." I was suddenly frightened of going up to bed. Something had happened the night before but now it was blurred in my mind, dim shadows of naphtha flares and Mr. Hope-Browne weeping and someone treading on my fingers. I didn't want to go upstairs and be alone.

"Let the child sit with me, Maud. When you've all gone to meeting, Sophie and I will sit quiet together. Couple of old invalids, eh, Sophie?"

I remember that evening as one of the coziest of my childhood. I think in fact it was the last evening of my childhood. Mother and Edwin pulled the sofa around so that it was right in front of the range, and Dad and I sat together on it. When it got dark we didn't light the lamp, but watched the room grow soft in the flickering glow of the coals. Dad, for the first time since his accident, seemed to be really better. There was more color in his face and, even though he had his leg stretched out along the sofa, the splints were off and I could tell from the way he moved that his ankle was stronger. He told me all the old stories I loved, not the Bible ones, but about Grandfather Willoughby who could lift a hundredweight sack of potatoes on his back when he was a young man, and how he and Grandmother Willoughby had had eleven children and none of them had died and one had gone to Australia and never been heard of again.

"Do you think he's made a fortune, Pa?"

"Shouldn't be surprised, lassie. And one day he'll turn up here, in a carriage and a silk top hat, and he'll carry us all off to Australia to be sheep farmers."

"When I'm grown up, Dad, I'm going to work hard and I'll be housekeeper to a rich old man, and then you can come and live with me and I'll look after you."

"I'll look forward to that," said Dad soberly. "What about the others?"

"Well . . . I expect Edwin will be a stationmaster by then, and we'll be able to have lovely trips on the railway—go to marvelous places like . . . like London and Wales all for nothing. And Lillian will have her own dressmaking shop, and of course Mum will want to stay with her. So we'll all be very happy."

"Yes, I suppose we shall," said Dad very seriously. "But we'll try and stay together a bit longer—all of us, eh?"

And there, alone with my dad, I didn't mind the others at all.

145

Mum wasn't so bad really, and if Lillian was her favorite, that was only fair because here I was with Dad, just the two of us. After a while I made the cocoa and we sat there in the firelight, sipping the hot fragrant liquid, listening to the owls outside and the distant barking of the fox. After an evening like that I was able to cope with anything.

WHEN I ARRIVED AT THE VICARAGE NEXT MORNING, AT 7:00 instead of 7:30, it was to find Mrs. Puddingoyle a mass of quivering, disorganized confusion. The scullery was full of dirty supper dishes from the night before and Mrs. Puddingoyle was trying to get the early-morning tea trays ready, even though they should already have been on their way upstairs.

"Ringing and ringing for their tea, they are. And Mrs. Gallagher, too—she's been up sitting with him all night—and she's run off! Run off, not washed up last night's things, not lit the fires this morning. Start on those dirty crocks—no—see if the kettles are boiling and put some water in these teapots. Late getting the stove going, and they'll be wanting their washing water too. I can't do everything!"

"Do you want me to take the jugs up, Mrs. Puddingoyle?"

"Yes . . . no . . . I'll have to get the tea trays first . . . Here, that's all right . . . the kettle's boiling, the small one. I'll take theirs . . . you take Mrs. Gallagher's . . . she's in his room, Mr. Hope-Browne's, you know where that is, don't you?"

"No."

To my horror Mrs. Puddingoyle burst into tears. It was like seeing a large blancmange smashed to pieces. "What am I going to do?" she sobbed angrily. "His parents are coming today, and there's the nursing, it's too much and I'll have to tell her so."

"Have a cup of tea, Mrs. Puddingoyle," I said feebly, because that was what one always said in an emergency, and it appeared to be the right thing because she sank into a chair by the kitchen table and poured herself a cup from Mr. and Mrs. Lovelace's morning tea tray.

"After yesterday, to say nothing of the night before—I saw it, you know. It was me that saved him. And yesterday we didn't stop for a moment—had to clear up after the doctor. You never

147

saw such a mess, and it was trays of tea all day, and I had to sit with him till they got Mrs. Gallagher in. And now she's run off. I came down this morning, no fires lit anywhere, supper things not washed, morning trays not done, nothing . . ."

"Who?" I asked, but I knew.

"That pesky girl. Should never have been taken on. Don't know what Mrs. Lovelace was doing. Trouble, that's what she's been. And she's mixed up in it somehow. I knew that when I saw her face yesterday. Frightened she was when she knew what he'd done. Wouldn't go and take a turn sitting with him either. Wouldn't even go into the room to take something for Mrs. Gallagher. And now she's gone—must 'ave gone last night—bed's not been slept in. Have you seen her at home?"

"No, Mrs. Puddingoyle. But I was ill all yesterday. I didn't go out."

"All happening together like this, it's too much. They still think he might die, you know. It's the fumes. I got to him, you see, just as he had the bottle in his mouth. 'My Gawd! What are you doing, Mr. Hope-Browne,' I shouted. Right here in my kitchen, and the Lysol bottle to his mouth. If I hadn't come down for my tablets he'd be dead on the kitchen floor."

A cold tingling began to spread up from my feet and the memory I had forgotten—Mr. Hope-Browne weeping—suddenly blazed into my vision.

"When was it, Mrs. Puddingoyle?" I whispered.

"Saturday night. She went to the Pilgrims, you see. And she wasn't home when she should have been. He kept coming down to see where she was, and finally I went to bed, and then I heard her running up the stairs and he was shouting. Then it all stopped, and I went down for my tablets and thank Gawd I did. Smashed it away from him before he properly swallowed it. They came down—heard me shouting—but he'd collapsed by then. On the floor unconscious. Doctor said he thought he hadn't swallowed any, but best to use the stomach tube in case. Worked on him nearly all night. Milk, lots of milk. But his poor face, all burned . . ."

She stopped suddenly, and stared at me, aware of what she was saying.

"Get a clean cup and saucer and I'll take these up."

I was so cold I could hardly move. I reached a cup and saucer down from the dresser and remembered how lovely it had been drinking cocoa with Dad the night before.

"You forget what I've said, Sophie. Don't you go telling people what I said. . . . Here, you sit down for a moment and have a cup of tea."

She hovered over me, and then she moved off with a tea tray. When she'd gone I threw mine down the sink and started the washing up.

I got jugs of hot water ready. Went into the breakfast room and laid the table. Set a tray to be taken to the sick room for Mrs. Gallagher. Dusted the drawing room and lit the fire there ready for Mr. Hope-Browne's parents. Then I washed up the breakfast things. Helped Mrs. Puddingoyle make the vicar's bed and dusted that room. I didn't think about anything. I tried very hard not to think about anything. But it was all my fault. If I hadn't said anything to Mr. Hope-Browne none of it would have happened. Please God, don't let him die. It will be my fault if he dies. I will have killed Mr. Hope-Browne.

I worked very hard because then I didn't have to think. Also I felt that if I worked hard God might take it as a very small count toward saving Mr. Hope-Browne's life. I achieved a pitch of desperation in my work: "If I have all the vegetables peeled by ten-thirty, Mr. Hope-Browne won't die. If the front step has dried in five minutes' time the burns on his face will go away." Every so often I would go back to Saturday—if Mother had let me go to the crusade none of it would have happened. I would have guarded Galina from being saved, just like all the other nights, and nothing would have happened. If I hadn't told Mr. Hope-Browne to go and stop her, he wouldn't have seen her on the platform unbuttoning her shirtwaist and then he wouldn't have come back home and taken Lysol. If . . . if . . . Cold waves of panic swept over me from time to time, and when that happened I would scrub or polish or sweep twice as hard, trying to drive the panic away with physical activity.

Mrs. Puddingoyle sent a note home to my mother by the garden boy, asking if I could stay through dinner to work on in the afternoon because Galina wasn't there. But at half-past twelve, Edwin stood at the back door and said he had come to take me home.

"But I explained to your ma," screeched Mrs. Puddingoyle. "I told her in my note what trouble we're in here. I need Sophie to stay on."

"Mum says she's to come home to dinner," Edwin repeated stolidly, "and then Mum'll decide if she can come back this afternoon."

"How am I supposed to manage if she don't?"

Edwin didn't answer. Just stood, a stubborn block of silence, not moving until I put my coat on and accompanied him home.

"She's run off with the Pilgrim Teachers," he said, expressionless.

"How do you know?"

"Peter Hayward saw them last night. They were pulling out on the Eastbourne road and she was sitting up on the cart."

"Oh." I tried to work out if it was my fault.

"And she's taken Mr. Barshinskey's fiddle with her."

A last remnant of childhood made a pang of pure disappointment sweep through me. Everything else was nightmarish, terrible guilt, more than I could understand. But, like a child, I nearly wept at the thought that I wouldn't hear Mr. Barshinskey play his fiddle anymore.

"He's gone off after her," said Edwin. "He's going to get her back. He just went off without saying a word to Mr. Hayward, and what with Dad laid off, too, Mr. Hayward said he doesn't know what he's going to do. Lady Audley's going to calve soon."

"It's funny, isn't it? They've only been in the village a few months, and now, because two of them have gone off, nobody can manage without them."

"Ivan's gone up there—to Hayward's—and offered to help.

He's quite good with milking, and he can muck out, I suppose. Mrs. Hayward's going to help with milking too. She's asked if you'd go up until Mr. Barshinskey comes back. Would you rather go there than the vicarage?"

Oh, would I not. To work with dear, nice, sane Mrs. Hayward, and Peter, who was ordinary but kind. To get away from the vicarage, where everyone was silent and careful, trying to hide what had happened, where the door of Mr. Hope-Browne's room hid an unconscious young man with a burned face. I never wanted to go back there again.

"I must go back to the vicarage. They need me more than Mrs. Hayward."

Edwin stared at me. "Is he very bad?"

"Very bad."

After I'd eaten my dinner, Mother asked me if I felt I could go back to the vicarage. She said she and Dad had discussed it, and decided the greater need was there. After all, Mr. Barshinskey might return to Hayward's at any moment, and it wasn't a case of sickness as it was at the vicarage.

So back I went in the afternoon, and the next day too. And my bargain with God paid off because Mr. Hope-Browne didn't die.

At the end of the week his parents took him home. Lady Hope-Browne was crying. She was a tall gray lady, not a bit like her son, but she held his hand as he was carried out to the carriage. Mr. Hope-Browne had a silk scarf tied over the lower half of his face and he was very, very thin. It seemed impossible that anyone could get as thin as that in a week.

I hoped that he would turn his head and look at me. I just wanted to see his eyes, to see if he blamed me for what I had done. But he didn't seem to know anyone was there. He didn't look at anyone, not even the vicar, and he didn't say goodbye.

Later I found out that he couldn't say goodbye. Mr. Hope-Browne would never be able to talk in anything but a whisper. The Lysol had damaged his vocal cords. He would never be able to sing "Come Into the Garden, Maud," ever again.

MR. BARSHINSKEY WAS GONE FOR EIGHT DAYS, AND HE came back without Galina and without his fiddle.

I'd been waiting for him every evening; every moment that I wasn't working I hung about at the top of the Eastbourne road, looking for a distant moving spot that would enlarge itself into a big man in a flower-covered hat. I wanted him desperately. I needed to talk to him about what I had done.

On the eighth day the miracle happened. A dark moving dot grew bigger and when I saw who it was I began to run.

"Mr. Barshinskey! Mr. Barshinskey! You're back!"

He strode on toward me, but there were no flowers around his hat and he didn't carry his fiddle. Galina wasn't there, but then I hadn't expected her to be.

"You didn't get your fiddle back, Mr. Barshinskey?"

He didn't answer me. He didn't even look at me. He didn't seem to know I was there. I ran along beside him, pulling at his hand.

"Mr. Barshinskey, are you all right? Did you find them?"

He was walking so fast it was hard to keep up with him. "No. I didn't find them. They are gone." He still didn't look at me, just stared straight ahead.

"Mr. Barshinskey . . . please! Don't walk so fast, I need to talk to you . . . I can't talk when you're walking so fast!"

He stopped and stared down at me. He had never looked at me in that way before. Always his eyes had been warm and twinkling and friendly. Now they were narrow, not seeing me, empty.

"Mr. Barshinskey . . . ?"

"I have lost my child," he said simply. "What can you say to me?"

"I . . ."

"Can you tell me where she is? Can you tell me why she has done this thing to me?"

"It's . . . yes . . . it's Mr. Hope-Browne, at the vicarage. He . . . he got ill and Galina was frightened and ran away. I . . . it was my fault . . . I . . ."

"Paa!" He shook his head angrily from side to side. "What do I care for them all—for him—for you. It is *her*. She has run away. She has left me, her papa. She did not say goodbye. She did not tell me she must move on—me—who knows what happens, that you must move on, that one place becomes bad for you and you feel you will choke if you do not move on. Why did she not tell me this? I, too, would have gone. We would all have gone."

"Mr. Barshinskey," I cried. "You must help me. You must tell me what I've done . . . I don't understand it . . . I only tried to stop something bad happening and now Mr. Hope-Browne will have a scarred face for the rest of his life . . . and he'll never be able to talk again. . . ."

When I'd cried before he had helped me, had sat beside me on the grass and put his arm around me and told me my dad would get better again. Now, as I stood before him, a heaving sodden heap, he just stared, and then said sadly, "I cannot help you, *kroshka*. I am too filled with misery to help you."

"Mr. Barshinskey! Wait . . . please wait . . ."

"Leave me." He thrust one hand into the air. "I can do nothing . . . nothing . . ."

If only I could have prayed. I suppose I did pray really, in a blind, not-expecting-to-be-listened-to kind of way. A yawning pit of panic opened before me. I was alone with my guilt, my confused guilt because I couldn't see what I had done wrong. Mr. Barshinskey, he whom I loved more than anyone except my own dad, had shown that I meant nothing to him.

I walked across the meadow and bathed my face in Sandy Bottom, then went home to tea.

That night, even though it was a Tuesday, there was shouting and crashing from the Owl House. This time I didn't pretend not to hear it. I went into Edwin's room and looked out across the two gardens. A light flickered in one of the windows of the Owl House, and there was more shouting, mostly his, but other softer voices too.

"He's very drunk this evening," I said tonelessly to Edwin.

"Wonder where he's got the money from. It's only Tuesday."

We both watched the flickering light. Then it went out, but the noise didn't stop.

"I hate him!"

"And I hate *her*," Edwin said softly. "I hated her when she first came."

We stood silently together, bound by nothing, our hatred for the Barshinskeys not enough to make us speak freely to each other.

Mr. Barshinskey went back to the farm. Mr. Hayward was very angry with him for walking off like that, but he couldn't get anyone else in a hurry and Mr. Barshinskey was better than no one. Every day he did his work in the sheds and every night he got drunk. Ivan had a black eye one morning, and Daisy May became taciturn and proud. When school began again, and I started to call for her every morning, she wouldn't let me come in, and she hardly spoke to me on the way. Because I could think about little else except my guilt, I assumed it must be because she knew it was my fault that Galina had run away.

"Daisy May . . . about Galina . . ."

"I don't wish to talk about it."

"But you see, I think it was all my fau—"

"I don't want to talk about it. I shan't walk with you if you're going to talk about it."

And so, in silence, we plodded along the lane, the sad smells of autumn all about us, both totally, and selfishly, absorbed in our individual miseries. It did not occur to me—because then I didn't realize just how great was Daisy May's craving for respectability—that the humiliation of Galina's behavior had shattered her precarious hold on self-respect. By this time it was common whispered knowledge that there had been "carryings on" between

Mr. Hope-Browne and Galina. And among the village people Mr. Hope-Browne was no longer blamed because he had been punished. But Galina, who ran off (taking not only her father's fiddle but also a silk petticoat and two of Mrs. Lovelace's best shirtwaists), had not been punished. She was a harlot and a thief and everyone in the village knew it, and her disgrace was also Daisy May's.

Too absorbed in my own problems, I never thought of how much courage it must have taken Daisy May to walk into school on that first day of term, to brave the Jefford set, the giggles and nudges of the rest of the class, the nervous embarrassment of Miss Thurston. She bore it all, including the playtime jeers of the Jefford, with stoical, stony silence. She ignored the rest of the class, and finally they came—if not to ignore her—to treat her with indifference. It becomes rather boring trying to bait someone who never answers or even looks at you and in time even Brenda Jefford ceased to shout, "Thief's sister! Thief's sister." (The other matter was too dreadful to be mentioned. Officially we children were not supposed to know about it and Brenda Jefford knew that if she even mentioned it she would be in shocked disgrace both at school and at home.)

Life friendship is formed in funny ways. We used to stump to school together, not speaking; at playtime we hovered together in a corner of the playground, not speaking, and at dinner time and at the end of school we walked home together, still in the same selfish silence. But the habit of friendship (that friendship which had blossomed so bravely and gaily all through the summer) persisted and later I realized that those silent walks contributed just as much to our lifelong bonds as had the happier periods we'd spent together.

The condition of the Barshinskeys grew worse at the same time as ours grew temporarily better. Dad returned to the farm. He couldn't take over his old job as his ankle wasn't strong enough yet to stand on for too long. He limped up to the farm with the help of a stick, and did as much milking as he could manage. Mr. Hayward paid him part of his old wages and, although it wasn't enough for us to live the way we used to live, at least it was regular. If you have a regular wage coming in, no matter how small, you can live to some kind of plan. There is regularity in your life, and that in turn brings peace.

The Barshinskeys had no such peace.

We discovered eventually where Mr. Barshinskey was getting the money from to start his drinking bouts at the beginning of the week instead of the end. The news threw Mother into the wildest temper I had ever seen on her. I was with her when we saw their kitchen table—which was really *our* kitchen table—together with the armchair that had been Grandmother Willoughby's, being carried out of the Owl House by Mr. Kelly.

Mother was too proud to ask Mr. Kelly where and why he was taking them. Mr. Kelly never really worked. He did a bit of digging sometimes, and a bit of ratting, and a bit of poaching. And he bought and sold things. His yard was full of old rain butts and wheelbarrows, rusty shovels, warped chests and cupboards, and you could pick up almost anything there for a few pence. Mother knew only too well where her things were going. She stormed across and into the Owl House. She knew, I knew, everyone knew, that those things had been lent "for as long as they were needed." She came back in a fury of rage, not at Mrs. Barshinskey, but at him.

I think she would have gone over that evening and faced him with his "stealing," but Dad wouldn't let her. Mr. Barshinskey had turned into a morose silent man by day, and a violent drunkard by night. He was quite as capable of hitting my mother as he was of hitting his own wife and children. He did his work at Hayward's efficiently; efficiently enough not to be sacked, but the rumors of his violent drunkenness were making Mr. Hayward mutter about "looking around for a new cowman." Mrs. Barshinskey had sunk to a frightened shadow, so cowed and terrified that Mother had not had the heart to remove all the rest of her things. The truckle beds came back but she left the duck-shaped boiler and the linen. In time they went to Kelly's yard too.

There came a night in October, when Peter Hayward banged

156

on our kitchen door. We were all in bed but the banging woke us, and both Edwin and I crept out onto the stairs after Mum had gone to see who it was.

We heard Peter Hayward's voice in the kitchen, and then Mum came upstairs again, saying, "Out of the way, you two," very crossly before going back into the bedroom.

"Mr. Hayward wants you," we heard her saying to Dad. "Lady Audley's calving and it's not going right. Peter's tried to rouse *him*"—she hated Mr. Barshinskey so much by now that she wouldn't even say his name—"but . . . well, you'll have to go and help as best you can."

"I knew there'd be trouble," we heard Dad say, and I thought he meant about Mr. Barshinskey. The bedsprings creaked as Dad got up. "I knew there'd be trouble when he put her with old Cowper's bull. I told him at the time—the Friesian's too big, I said. She's a good cow for breeding, but you can't do this. The calf'll be too big . . ."

He hobbled out of the bedroom (his ankle was always worse when he hadn't moved for a while) and said, "Back to bed at once, you two," and then sat on the top stair and shuffled his way down to the bottom. We heard the back door shut and as there wasn't anything else to see or hear we went back to bed.

That night in the cowsheds must have been one of the most horrifying any cowman had ever seen. When Dad finally told us what had happened I didn't know whether to be sick or cry. Maybe he shouldn't have told us, but when he returned in the morning, sickened, weary, he was too far gone to consider restraining himself before us. He loved cows, my dad, and the needless waste of that night nearly destroyed him.

Lady Audley was bellowing. She was frightened and in pain. An experienced mother, she had always dropped her calves effortlessly until now. But, as Dad had so rightly predicted, the Friesian bull had sired a calf too large. To be fair to Mr. Hayward, the mating hadn't been quite so foolhardy as it seemed. He had crossbred before, and it had worked. He always chose the cows to experiment with with great care. Lady Audley was large

for a shorthorn and had a history of effortless calving. The Friesian bull was smaller than most, and if it had worked he would
have produced some excellent milk and meat cattle. But it hadn't
worked and now he was frantic with worry. It needs skill to get
a large calf out of a small cow and he couldn't do it. Dad could
do it, providing he could move about properly on his ankle and
use his arms above the just healed ribs. You need to be strong to
help a cow with a difficult calving.

They struggled with Lady Audley most of the night, Mr.
Hayward holding her head and trying to soothe her, and Dad
trying to ease the calf from her while avoiding her frightened
kicks and sudden spasmodic upheavals. Time after time he managed to get his arm around the curled body of the calf, tried to
gentle it into place, and then heave. It went on all night—the
shed lit with oil lamps making it hot and fetid, my dad growing
more and more tired. Finally, when he really began to feel he
didn't have the strength to continue any longer, he managed again
to get the head in position and, with a last superhuman heave,
pull it into the open. And just at that moment, the door of the
cowshed burst open and Mr. Barshinskey—fired by some dim
recollection of duty, answering Peter Hayward's midnight call in
a kind of drunken delayed memory—burst into the stall with a
mighty roar.

"I can do! I can do! Out of way!"

He pushed Dad aside, which wasn't difficult to do after the
night my dad had had, and when Mr. Hayward and Peter went
to pull him away from the cow he reared up like a great bear and
thrust them hard, one to each side, so that they crashed against
the sides of the stall.

"My task! You think I, Nikolai Igorovitch Barshinskey, cannot do this! I am best cowman in Russia—in the world! You
think because my daughter is run off I cannot make calf come!"
And then he took hold of the calf's head and staggered back, and
that would still have been all right if only Dad or Mr. Hayward
had been able to leap forward and hold the calf and knock Mr.
Barshinskey out of the way. Dad was nearest and he reached
up but was kicked, this time by Mr. Barshinskey. The calf,

wrenched from Lady Audley, lay still on the floor. Lady Audley gave a final bellow of pain and then was quiet, blood pouring from her where the calf had been too savagely extracted. Mr. Hayward gave a great anguished shout and Mr. Barshinskey turned and stared uncomprehendingly at him; the front of his black suit was covered in blood.

"You think I cannot do this," he mumbled, and then turned and shuffled out of the shed, or at least he would have if Peter, in a fury of rage and misery, hadn't hit him hard over the head with a bucket. He fell over and they left him there.

They tried to save Lady Audley. My dad did everything he could but there comes a point where a cowman's greatest skills are no use. Lady Audley lay very quiet, not bellowing or making any sound, and after about an hour she died. The calf never breathed at all. Its neck was broken.

They had all loved that cow. She was the star of the herd, the capricious one, the temperamental one, the one who could be most endearing and most exasperating.

When dawn came they were all silent and Dad was nearly unconscious with tiredness and pain. Young Peter Hayward, who even though he was a farmer's son, was only sixteen and had never seen such a bloodbath before, was shaking and covered in sweat. It was he, though, who took some kind of control.

"What shall I do with Lad—with them, Dad?" he whispered, and Mr. Hayward turned savagely toward the recumbent figure of Mr. Barshinskey.

"Just leave them!" he shouted. "Leave them, and leave him to see what he's done when he wakes up. Let him see what he's done for one night's work."

"You can't leave them, Mr. Hayward," said Dad wearily. "If it's left this place will smell like a charnel house. And . . . and he won't remember. He'll wake up and wonder how it all happened and he'll go home. Best to clear up. And see him later. Get rid of him then."

He left them to clear up, and he hobbled home as the morning sun showed above the trees. When he came in he looked as though he was going to cry. For a cowman to lose a cow and a calf in one night is the most depressing thing in the world. And to lose them in such a way . . . In after years it was strange to hear Dad talking about the things that had happened on the Hayward farm. He hardly mentioned the cups he had taken at the county shows. He dismissed the accident with the bull in a few passing words, even though it had permanently damaged him and reduced our standard of living. But when he spoke of Lady Audley's death it was obviously the thing he remembered most clearly. It was the most disastrous thing that had ever happened to him.

That was one morning I was especially glad that Daisy May and I didn't talk much when we went to school. It wasn't her fault. She was, most certainly, more sinned against than sinner. But such is the human condition I felt I hated all the Barshinskeys who had cruelly and brutally murdered a cow and its newborn calf.

Everything happened so swiftly after that I didn't really have time to think about how or why it happened. Only at the end did the old guilt return. Was it all my fault? If I hadn't told Mr. Hope-Browne then he wouldn't have tried to kill himself. If he hadn't tried to kill himself then Galina wouldn't have run away, and Mr. Barshinskey wouldn't have got drunk so often, and he wouldn't have killed Lady Audley and Mr. Hayward wouldn't have sacked him and . . .

When Daisy May and I came home from school at dinner time there was no longer any need to pretend that nothing had happened. Halfway down the lane we could hear Mr. Barshinskey shouting and Mrs. Barshinskey screaming. And this time it was a different screaming. Daisy May and I looked at each other, her face blanching with fear, and then we began to run toward the Owl House.

The cart—that pathetic cart with which they had arrived—was standing outside the door and he was throwing things on at random. Throwing them anyhow, china, chairs, pots, so that things were smashing and falling on the ground. Mrs. Barshinskey was screaming at him, begging and pleading, her capacity for apathetic endurance finally snapped by this precipitant departure.

"He said we needn't go until we've found somewhere!" she screamed. "It was for me he said that. Not for you, not for you!"

Mr. Barshinskey elbowed her out of the way and went back into the house. He looked dangerous. I don't think he had sobered up yet.

Mother's face suddenly looked over the hedge and then she quickly broke through the gap. Mrs. Barshinskey turned to her. She was even more ragged and disheveled than usual. Her hair hung down in wisps and her face was distorted with fear. Not fear of him, she'd learned to live with that, but fear of being out on the road, this time with not even the pretense of a new job or a new beginning before her. Homeless, pregnant, and the winter coming on, and in the charge of a mad drunkard.

"Speak to him," she cried. "There's no need to go at once. Mr. Hayward said we could stay here until after the baby's come. He said I could stay as long as he doesn't set foot on the farm. We don't have to go now!"

Mr. Barshinskey came out of the house and threw the wooden chest on top of the cart. A basin smashed.

"We go!" he roared. "No man speaks to Nikolai Igorovitch Barshinskey as he speaks to me. I do not take his charity. I spit upon it. We go, now. We leave this filthy village that has stolen my child and broken my life. We go!"

Mrs. Barshinskey didn't cry, not crying with tears. What she did was even worse. She put her hands on each side of her head and began to scream again, that same screaming we heard in the lane, a wild, mad noise that had no reason, no grief in it, just terror and a total snapping of control. Beside me I felt Daisy May tighten, withdraw right into herself.

"Mr. Barshinskey," said Mother breathlessly, trying to be heard through the screaming, "I think you should consider your wife. With the weather growing cold, and nowhere to go . . ."

161

"You, shut up, you!" he shouted, but whether to Mother or his wife it wasn't clear. Certainly Mrs. Barshinskey took no notice, and finally the hysterical screaming broke through his drunken anger and he turned and hit her, hard, right across the head.

Daisy May plummeted across the ground and began to punch ineffectually at his legs. And I suddenly realized this was an old scene many times reenacted. To us it was terrible. Mother, myself, Edwin who had now joined us, were shocked into temporary immobility. But some small detached part of me recognized that this was nothing new. This was how Mrs. Barshinskey and Ivan and Daisy May got their bruised faces and black eyes.

He plucked Daisy May from his legs as though she were an ant, and threw her to one side. Mrs. Barshinskey hadn't stopped screaming, and Mother suddenly regained her common sense and walked forward to try to lead her away.

"Come into my kitchen, Mrs. Barshinskey," she said. "Come with me now."

But that poor, ineffectual, driven soul had gone too far. Too many years of shame, and poverty and bullying and insecurity had driven her to the point where she was no longer afraid of him.

"I don't leave! I don't leave!" she screamed. "I stay here!"

He hit her again, hard, and she spun around and tumbled to the ground. We all hurried forward, our own fear of him submerged in the shocking prospect of a man knocking his wife to the ground. He disappeared back into the Owl House again, and this time, thank God, he didn't come out.

"Come into my kitchen, Mrs. Barshinskey," said Mother again. We helped her up. She was groaning a little but that last blow had at least broken her hysteria. We led her back through the hedge, Daisy May and Edwin following, and when we got inside Mother locked the scullery door.

"You make some tea, Sophie. And fetch two aspirin from my bag. And then you dish up the dinner. It's stew and all ready, just the potatoes to mash. I'll take Mrs. Barshinskey up to my room for a bit. I'll write you a note if you're going to be late for school. And listen for your dad at the back door. You'll have to unlock it and let him in."

She led Mrs. Barshinskey away, and Edwin, Daisy May, and I were left looking at one another.

It was strange. I wanted to help Daisy May, wanted to show her how sorry I was for her, to say just the right words, but I couldn't even look at her, I was so embarrassed. The terrible scene had left us all white and shocked, but my immediate reaction was one of humiliation—for her. I thought how I would have felt if it had been my father and my mother behaving like that in front of strangers and I knew I would die from shame. And so I failed her. Instead of showing her that I loved her, I made a lot of noise draining and mashing the potatoes. I kept on talking; the noise of my voice was shrill and irritating but I couldn't stop—asking Edwin to get the plates from the dresser, wondering why Dad was late (which he wasn't), making a fuss because as well as dishing up the dinner I had to make a cup of tea. I hated myself, but I'd been hating myself for quite a while —ever since the Pilgrim Teachers had come and I'd turned into a woman.

It was then that Edwin did one of those curious un-Edwin-like things that seemed so out of character. Like giving Daisy May one of his precious railway books. And there was the time he'd tried to stop me from seeing Galina and Mr. Hope-Browne in the churchyard. He went across to the sofa and sat down beside Daisy May. Then he smiled at her, and took one of her small grubby paws in his. He didn't say anything—and heaven knows I was saying enough for all of us—but he sat beside her holding her hand, just smiling.

It doesn't sound like much, but it was an awful lot for our family, and especially for Edwin. We didn't kiss or touch each other much. We didn't talk about feelings or love; that I suppose explained why I couldn't help Daisy May the way I wanted to. But Edwin—from somewhere—knew what to do with that poor humiliated child. And what he did was right, just as my incessant talking was wrong. Daisy May fixed her eyes on his face. She didn't look grateful, she looked fierce, as though by staring hard at Edwin's smiling face she was keeping herself sane and silent.

I took the tray of tea upstairs and into Mother's bedroom. Mrs. Barshinskey was lying on the bed, on top of the coverlet, with her shoes off and the pillow from Dad's side propped up extra behind her shoulders.

"Will you be coming down to dinner, Ma?"

"Not for a bit. You serve it, Sophie. Mind how you dish it up now."

I knew what that meant. If we had to make it go around to Daisy May and Mrs. Barshinskey, the portions would have to be measured very carefully.

Dad rattled at the scullery door and I let him in and gave him a quick, whispered explanation of why things were as they were in our house. He looked dreadful from his long sleepless night and the shock of losing Lady Audley, but he was still Dad, and he sat Daisy May at the table and said the grace as though it was just a normal day.

I needn't have worried too much about the stew going around. No one had much of an appetite. We all sat pushing the good food around and around on our plates, and then we heard Mum coming down the stairs, and we all looked expectantly toward the door. Mother came in looking tired and resigned.

"Sophie, I'd like you to get up to Mrs. Pritchard and ask her to come down."

"Yes, Ma." Mrs. Pritchard came for lying-ins and laying-outs.

"And, George, I don't know what you'd better do about that benighted heathen next door. I suppose someone ought to tell him, but I don't want him coming anywhere near me or near this house. I'd feel safer if he was locked in the shot tower until this is all over."

Daisy May put her fork down and stared at Mother with a lumpy, ugly face. Mother suddenly recollected herself.

"I think you should go back to school, Daisy May. In fact you can go with Sophie now to Mrs. Pritchard's, and then straight on to school."

164

"Is my mother ill?"

"No, dear. Just a little tired. She'll be much better later on. You and Sophie go to school."

And so we went, and on the way I explained to Daisy May what little I knew about Mrs. Pritchard and about babies. Daisy May went quiet again, just stumped along and into school without saying a word. Once, at playtime, she opened her mouth and said almost to herself, "I wonder where we can go with a new baby," and then she was silent again for the rest of the day. We walked home together and when we reached the Owl House she suddenly veered off.

"Where are you going, Daisy May?"

"To find Ivan. He usually comes home around about now. He'll be worried when Ma's not there. And my father . . ."

And her father might still not be sober, might still be locked in that place waiting to lash out at anyone who came in for whatever reason. Ivan lived a strange half-life. He went out in the morning, having got the water from the pump, and was seen only spasmodically and irregularly throughout the day. Sometimes I met him in the woods hacking away at an old tree stump with his ax and filling sacks with kindling. Sometimes you could see him in the village, going from house to house trying to sell that kindling. Once I stumbled over him skinning a rabbit that he'd caught. I didn't ask how he'd caught it—I hated animals being trapped and I didn't want to know. I couldn't really blame him whatever he did. The only time the Barshinskeys ate meat was when Ivan caught a rabbit or a hare.

He was a funny boy, proud and silly like Daisy May, but wild, too, like his father. But I liked him, and even though he was prickly and stubborn I think he liked me.

Bravely I turned into the Owl House garden with Daisy. She went up to one of the windows and peered in. I did the same. There was nothing to see and the quietness over the place suggested no one was there.

"He'll be waiting outside the Fox," said Daisy May woodenly. "We'll go up to the hedge and see if Ivan's getting the water."

He was, and when he looked down the field and saw us standing at the gap in the hedge he dropped the bucket and began to run toward us.

"Where's Mother?"

"She's in next door . . . with them. . . ." Daisy May jerked her head in my direction. We were *them*, and it suddenly made me realize that they must often talk about us, the way we talked about them.

"Why?"

Daisy May paused, then said with studied carefulness, "Father's funny . . . you know . . . and Mrs. Willoughby took Mother in there because she wasn't feeling too good and . . ."

She didn't have a chance to finish. Ivan was through the hedge in a flash and vanished down the garden. We followed more slowly.

There was no one in our scullery or kitchen. I could hear voices upstairs, Mum and Mrs. Pritchard I suppose, but Dad was at milking, Edwin was doing his outside jobs, and Lillian hadn't returned from Miss Clark's yet. Ivan stood in the middle of our scullery, glaring around as though we had spirited his mother away.

"Where is she?"

"Upstairs . . . but you can't go up there . . ."

I might have saved myself the trouble. He pushed past, into the kitchen, and through the door, and the next thing was an outraged Ma marching him back in by one ear.

"You keep out of the way, my lad," she said, very angry. "You don't go walking into people's houses, much less their bedrooms, without so much as a by-your-leave."

"What's wrong with my mother?" He wriggled against her hand like a young savage. "What's wrong with my mother? What have you done to her?"

Mother looked at him, then at Daisy May, and some pitying instinct must have been aroused by the two grubby, undernourished figures.

"You can stay to tea," she said kindly. "Sophie, you get on and lay it, and when Lillian comes home send her up to me."

"What's wrong with my mother?" he shouted, but she had gone back upstairs.

"Nothing's wrong," I said. "You're going to have a baby." Ivan glared at me.

"What you talk about?" he said angrily, suddenly sounding like his father.

I lowered my voice. "We're not supposed to know about what happens," I said. "But your mother hasn't been very well, and she's been getting fat. And Mrs. Pritchard's been sent for and whenever that happens there's always a baby around."

"No," he said stubbornly, and then a slow burning flush crept up his face. "No! It's not true!"

He glared at me again, and then ran to the scullery door.

"Don't you want your tea?"

"I want nothing from you. Nothing . . ."

I was wrong. Mrs. Pritchard's presence didn't always mean a baby.

Daisy May slept in with Lillian and me that night, and Dad was bunked up in Edwin's room, and at some time in the middle of the night I heard the door open and felt Mum's hand on my shoulder.

"Sophie, are you awake? Is Daisy May awake?" She sounded very gentle, and that soft gentle voice in the darkness, so unlike Ma's voice, suddenly caused a faint stir of disquiet.

"I'm awake, Mrs. Willoughby," whispered Daisy May.

"I want you to get up, dear, very quietly. There's no need to wake the others."

Daisy May got out of bed, her breathing began to quicken. "Shall I get dressed, Mrs. Willoughby?"

"No, dear. Just a minute and I'll light the candle." We heard the match striking, and then Mother's face appeared, worn and tired, palely circled in a nimbus of light.

"You come, too, Sophie," breathed Mother, very softly. "You come with Daisy May."

That was such an unusual thing to say that I knew then that something awful was going to happen. Very quietly she led us

167

through Edwin's room and across the little platform at the top of the stairs into her bedroom.

It smelled in there. It smelled like it must have done in the cowshed the night before, and suddenly I understood what my dad had suffered, only this was worse, far worse, because by my side Daisy May was beginning to tremble.

"Hold Daisy's hand, Sophie," said Mother. "She's your best friend. Hold her hand."

I couldn't do that because she had them clasped in front of her chest, but I put my arm around her and we went to stand up near the head of the bed.

Mrs. Barshinskey was all pale and washed out. She'd never looked much, but now she seemed like a dead leaf on the pillow. Her eyes were closed and her hands, misshapen and grimed from work, lay outside the blanket.

"Mum?" Daisy May's small body was shaking and I felt a huge terrible lump come up in my throat. Only a little while before I'd stood in the same place praying my dad wouldn't die. I could tell there was no point in praying for Mrs. Barshinskey, so I prayed for poor Daisy instead. It just wasn't fair that so much could happen to Daisy.

"Mum?"

The pale lids lifted and, when she saw Daisy May, she smiled a little and moved one of her hands. Daisy covered it with her own.

"You've been a good girl, Daisy," she whispered. "I don't know what I'd have done without you."

"Mum . . ." Sobs racked the shoulders under my arm, and all I could do was hold her tighter. Daisy May had always been so brave.

"Daisy . . ." Her voice was very quiet. She wasn't in pain I think, just very tired. "Daisy, I want you to do what Mrs. Willoughby says from now on. D'you understand?"

"Yes, Ma," she sobbed.

"It won't be easy, love, but you're the best . . . you're the best of my children. It'll be harder for you, but do what she says . . ."

"I will, Ma."

"It doesn't matter about the others," she said quietly, talking to herself. "It's too late for Galina . . . she's like him. She'll always be all right. And Ivan's a boy, he'll manage . . ."

Mother bent over the bed on the other side. "Don't worry, dear," she whispered. "We'll do the best we can for all of them . . ."

"No!" The sick woman tried to pull herself up in the bed and then slumped back on the pillow. "No—the others don't matter. The others . . . they're Russian, like him. But this one . . ." She looked at Daisy May and she managed a slight smile that showed where her front teeth were broken and discolored. "Daisy May's like I was," she said sadly. "I knew it when she was born . . . that's why I called her Daisy May. He had another Russian name, but this one was mine . . . it was the only time he gave in to me."

She sighed softly and turned her face to my mother. "I don't want her left just to grow up like the rest of them. I don't want her father to keep her. He'll make her like he is . . . I don't want that . . ."

She tried to raise her head from the pillow again.

"Promise me, Mrs. Willoughby . . . promise me. I know you can't have her . . . you've troubles of your own, but I want her brought up respectable. I don't care how hard it is. I want her to be decent."

"Don't you have any family, Mrs. Barshinskey? No sisters or cousins she could go to?"

Mrs. Barshinskey shook her head. "She's to go to the Union . . ."

"Oh no, dear! Surely there's someone . . ."

"There's no one. I tell you there's no one. Only him, and I don't want him raising her . . . turning her into a gypsy . . . living rough so that decent folk won't have anything to do with her. She's to go into the Union, or the parish, anything. So long as she's respectable. You promise me . . ." She began to breathe heavily, the exertion of talking too much for her. "She's to go into the Union . . . they'll see she's raised respectable . . ."

"Mum!"

"You're a good girl, Daisy . . ." she breathed. "Such a good girl . . ."

"Mum!"

I'd never seen anyone die before and I didn't really want to stay there, but Mother had known what she was doing. Sometimes she had great insight, for in later years Daisy always remembered that I had been with her when her mother died.

We stood by the bed for what seemed a long time. Mrs. Barshinskey didn't open her eyes again and her breathing seemed slighter and slighter. And then she gave a deep sigh and a single tear ran down one side of her face.

"She's gone, dear."

Daisy's face screwed up into a silent cry, and then I led her out of the room and took her downstairs. The kitchen range was still alight and I lifted the lid and stirred up the coals a bit.

"Would you like some cocoa, Dais?"

"Yes, please."

She sat by the fire, staring into the coals, and when I'd heated the milk and poured it on the cocoa she took the cup, very graciously, and sipped it in a ladylike fashion. I felt very in awe of her. It was terrible to see your mother die and I didn't know how to treat her.

"Are you all right, Daisy?"

"Yes . . ." She paused and thought for a moment. Her small tear-stained face, all grubby and plain, looked important for a moment and she said, "They'll have to be nice to me now. Brenda Jefford and all of them. They'll have to be nice to me because I'm an orphan." And as she said the words realization swept over her and she began to sob and cry. She put the cocoa down on the table first, and then she laid her head over the side of the chair and cried and cried, and I didn't know what to do except hold her hand and cry too.

My dad came in then, wrapped in his coat over his nightshirt, and he picked her up in his arms and hugged her tight, just the way Mr. Barshinskey had done to me when Dad was ill.

170

He sat on the sofa with her in his arms, gazing out over her head, and I heard him say, "What kind of monster is he to let a child cry alone when her mother dies?"

I went outside. It wasn't right, what she had said about Ivan. He wasn't like Galina. He loved her too. Yes, he was strange and dirty and couldn't be made respectable, but he loved her, too, and someone should have tried to find him.

He was huddled by the woodshed. He'd got hold of Tibby, who was nearly full-grown now, and she was purring and rubbing her face up against his. I sensed him grow still as I got near.

"She's dead, isn't she?"

I didn't have to answer him. I just went and stood as close as I could.

"I knew she was dead. There's been lights in the bedroom all night, and I looked through the window and saw Dais crying. I knew she was dead . . ."

"Come in, Ivan. Come in and have some cocoa. It'll be nice for Dais if you come in."

He put the kitten down, very gently, and then he stood upright and pulled himself even taller and wider. I couldn't see his face properly but I knew he'd gone into one of his strange moods.

"He killed her," he sighed, not angrily, but it sounded menacing. "He killed her. He hit her, didn't he?"

"He didn't kill her, Ivan."

"He killed her. He hit her. You don't have to pretend. I know that's what happened."

"She wasn't well anyway, Ivan."

"He killed," he said again, and then he slid away from me in the darkness.

I called him, but he'd vanished, and I waited for an instant, knowing that something else was going to happen.

Just as I was turning indoors I heard a terrible roar, a deep roar, and then another shout from the Owl House, and I flung the back door open and shouted, "Dad, Dad! Come quickly. Something's happened!"

As we broke through the hedge I saw a shape flit past me and I called "Ivan," but the shape vanished into the darkness and I knew we'd never find him. We broke into the Owl House but then realized we couldn't see. But we could hear and, thank God, it was a noise that meant Mr. Barshinskey was still alive. He was roaring and swearing in Russian, and as we groped our way through that labyrinth of rooms and stairs we saw a figure ahead of us, leaning against a wall, shouting and lurching along toward the door at the back.

"Go back, Sophie," said Dad. "Get a lamp, and send Edwin over with it. And don't come back."

As I ran away I felt something against my foot. Afterward I realized what it was. The ax that Ivan used to cut his wood.

They had to get the doctor to Mr. Barshinskey and he wasn't best pleased. He knew he wouldn't get paid but then he couldn't let a man bleed to death. Ivan had slashed his father in the leg and they had to put a tourniquet on and then the doctor stitched him up.

He lay in the Owl House for four days and only Dad would go over. He took food and water and changed the bandages. Mrs. Barshinskey was buried on the parish and of her family only Daisy May was there. The rest of the village turned out in full strength. Not because they cared about her but because nothing like this had ever happened before in our village, and, please God, would never happen again.

I nearly went to see Mr. Barshinskey once, but I was too afraid. I had loved him but now he was a killer and a madman.

The night after Mrs. Barshinskey was buried I heard an owl hooting outside in the garden—an owl that was no owl.

Lillian and Daisy May were both asleep, and I went down and opened the back door. He was there—I could smell him before I saw him, and it was worse because he'd really been living wild for the last few days. He hadn't been near a pump for a long time.

"Are you all right, Ivan?"

" 'Course I'm all right. How's . . . he . . ."

"He's all right. He's got a bad leg. But the doctor says it'll be all right."

"Are they looking for me?"

"A bit."

"I don't care if they are. They won't do anything to me!" His voice shook, cracked a bit, and stumbled on a half-sob at the end. "I put flowers on my ma's grave. I stole some from the gardens. I wanted nice flowers for her. She liked nice flowers."

"I'll see she has nice flowers, Ivan. I can't promise all the year-round, but I'll do my best."

We stood quietly together. It was cold and the damp chilly mist of October seeped through my coat and nightclothes. The garden looked different at night. The apple tree was sinister and all the little rustlings in the hedge seemed extra loud, as though very large animals were there instead of shrews and field mice.

"Are you going away?"

"Yes." He paused, and then said in a voice that was curiously young and defenseless, "I'll have to, won't I?"

"I . . . I suppose you *could* stay here . . ."

"No." He choked on the words a bit. "They'd have to take me in and punish me, wouldn't they? They might even lock me up. I couldn't stand that."

"Where will you go?"

He braced his shoulders back and said loudly—too loudly—"I'm going to go to sea, or perhaps I'll join the army."

"Ssh . . . they'll hear you."

"I don't care." And then I felt him shudder beside me, a deep harrowing shudder and I was suddenly sorrier for him than I was for anyone else. I'd been sorry for Mr. Barshinskey, and his poor wife, and there was Mr. Hope-Browne with his face all scarred, and above all there was Daisy May. But Ivan was sadder, more pitiful than any of these. Mr. Barshinskey had his drink and his moods and his adoration of Galina who had betrayed him, but whom he still loved. Mrs. Barshinskey was dead, and Mr. Hope-Browne had gone back to his nice home and parents to be cared for. And Daisy May didn't have too much, but she had me and she had the memory of being "the best of the lot" in her mother's eyes.

Ivan had nothing and no one. He was pitiful, but must not ever be pitied.

"I'll miss you, Ivan," I said, very carefully in case he thought I was patronizing him. "After Daisy May you've been my best friend."

"I don't have girls as friends."

"No. I know."

"But if I did . . . well . . . you're not so bad."

"Will you stay here a moment, Ivan? If you're going away I'd like to give you some things—at least some food to take with you."

"I don't want anything . . ." and then he broke again, his voice broke and the shudder ran through him.

"Wait here." I dashed indoors, not taking too much care to keep quiet, and I took half a pie and a loaf and a great slab of cheese from the larder, and I wrapped it all up in a pillowcase that I took from Mum's pile of washing waiting to be ironed. I reached up to the mantelpiece and took down my money box. Dad had the key so I couldn't open it, but I'm sure Ivan (so handy with an ax) wouldn't have any difficulty about that.

"Here you are. Take these."

"I don't want nothing. . . ." But he took it, and as I met his hands in the darkness I felt them trembling.

"You'll look after Dais for me, won't you?"

" 'Course I will."

"I'll come back one day. Tell her I'll come back, just to see how she is. Tell her to stay here, so's I know where to find her."

"I'll tell her. And if you want to write you can write here." Too late I realized that was a stupid thing to say. I wasn't really sure whether he could write or not.

" 'Bye, then."

" 'Bye, Ivan." And because he just stood there, and because it was dark, and because I'd been driven to a trembling crisis of emotion over the last few days, I suddenly reached up and put

174

my arms around him and kissed him where I could reach him, on the chin.

"Soppy," he said, and he didn't move. He stood there, letting me keep my arms around him, the smell of him wrinkling up into my nostrils, the grimy feel of him unpleasant against my face and hands, the shaking of his thin body growing quieter. There was a moment when he leaned his face down on my hair, leaned and sagged a little, and then, "All right then, I'm off," he said, and he was gone, flitting through the rows of dead dahlias and away out into the lane.

" 'Bye, Ivan!" I called, not caring a hoot for who could hear me. " 'Bye, Ivan. God Bless!"

When I crept back upstairs Lillian was awake. We had the bed to ourselves again, for Ma had put up one of the tiny truckles in a corner for Daisy May. The room was so crowded that the beds touched, but still it was nice not to have to sleep three.

"You've been seeing that boy, haven't you?" hissed Lillian. "Don't pretend you haven't. I can smell him."

"I hate you, Lillian!"

She was silent, and I wondered if I'd gone too far, but I didn't care. She'd been absent all this summer, not absent from the house, but absent in spirit, not helping with any of the awful things that had happened, not helping to make things easier for Daisy May, detaching herself all the time from Mrs. Barshinskey's death, from everything.

"Where's he going?" she asked into the silence.

"He's run away to sea."

"Did he . . . did he say anything . . . about any of us . . ."

"No. Just a message for Daisy May. And he asked me to put flowers on his mother's grave."

She flung herself over in the bed. "I never knew what you could see in him. What did you use to talk about?"

What did we use to talk about? We used to argue and fight. But once we had laughed together, when Mr. Watkins had played his trumpet, and once he had been kind to me, on the night I had been so ill at the crusades. We'd been quiet together, just walked, or sat, not talking.

"Oh . . . nothing really . . . I just liked him, that was all. . . ."

I was just falling off to sleep when she said, "Did you give him anything? Any food or something for the journey?"

"Hmm-hmm."

"Any money? Did you take anything out of your money box?"

"I gave it to him."

And just as I was falling off to sleep again, she said, "Well, I don't suppose we'll be seeing any more of him. And good riddance too. I always knew he was a bad lot, the first time I set eyes on him."

I didn't answer, because I didn't want to talk to Lillian about Ivan Barshinskey. He had been my friend, and she was already trying to intrude in my memories of that friendship.

I saw Mr. Barshinskey when he left. It was a few days later, and he had sobered up because no one would sell him any liquor and in any case he didn't have any money to buy any. Not even Mr. Kelly would take the few bits and pieces that remained in the Owl House.

He just walked out of the Owl House one morning, limping badly, and with not a single flower around his hat.

He stood at the top of the lane and stared back, shouted something in Russian, and then stumped off. He'd told Dad he was going to go on searching for Galina. I hoped, for the sake of Pilgrim Teacher Jones, that he never found her.

Daisy May didn't have to go into the Union, but Mother kept her promise to Mrs. Barshinskey. Mum and Dad, with the best will in the world, couldn't afford to keep Daisy May. Dad never got his old job back. He remained at Hayward's as a general dairyman and handyman, on a reduced wage of course, and he didn't get paid when he had his attacks. So Mother went to the parish who said that Daisy May would have to go into an orphanage. And that upset Mum so much that finally she went to Mrs. Fawcett at the White House, because Mrs. Fawcett, although Church, was a good Christian woman. And there it was agreed that Daisy May would be taken into the White House to live and help out after her school hours were done. And in return for a good home she would promise to go into service proper when she left school. It was unofficially acknowledged that school, in Daisy May's case, would be attended only irregularly and probably not at all after she was twelve. And a further concession was that Daisy would be allowed out on alternate Sundays to spend her half-days with us. Mrs. Fawcett agreed that as her mother had been a Quaker, and as Daisy May had already been going to the meeting with us, she should continue in the same form of worship.

A month after her mother died she went up to Fawcett's.

The Owl House was empty again. The few pitiful things remaining were stored in our shed for such a time as Daisy May could have use of them. Mrs. Barshinskey, whose face I could hardly remember after a few weeks, lay in a parish grave, with flowers that were put there sometimes by me and sometimes by Daisy.

I thought of them often—him with buttercups around his hat, and Daisy May winning the egg and spoon race on the happiest day of her life—and Ivan plugging my bleeding nose with a rag wrapped around his fingers.

And I thought of Galina, wreaking her trail of havoc through the village, of Mr. Hope-Browne with a face now scarred instead of pimpled, a ruined voice, a ruined reputation. I thought of Lady Audley and her calf, and of a woman beaten once too often who had given up and died too.

I thought of the train of tragedy I had begun when I told Mr. Hope-Browne to stop Galina from going to the crusades. It was many years before I understood that the guilt was not mine, other than in my own mind. All those things that happened were bound to happen when a family like the Barshinskeys came to our village.

I thought of how much I had loved him, and what he had done to me. He had opened a world, had given me a dream.

That was the summer of the Barshinskeys.

Part Two

———◆◆◆———

Edwin
and
Daisy May

10 HE WAS AT THE NEW CROSS EMPIRE, SEATED IN THE fourpenny gallery, when he saw Galina again. He was so shocked, so disbelieving, that he thought for one moment he was suffering a delusion brought about by too long a period of relief link duties at the power depot. He looked at the side of the stage—Item Nine—and then down at his program. There she was, Olga, the Cossack Princess, and on the stage, dressed in a white-and-gold dress with swirling skirts that came to her knees and a pair of red high-heeled boots, was the Galina of his childhood. The orchestra gave a screech of gypsy music, and Olga, the Cossack Princess, stamped her way to the middle of the stage, threw off a small white-and-gold cape, and began to dance. And suddenly he was transported back twelve years. He was thirteen again, standing at his bedroom window watching a fire in the garden of the Owl House and a black-haired girl dancing around the flames. He felt his stomach give a disbelieving lurch and for a moment a sense of panic, of terrified claustrophobia, made him want to rush from the gallery as quickly as he could. He looked around to see if anyone had noticed his sweaty fear. No, of course, they were not looking at him but at the stage, at the Cossack Princess and, reluctantly, forcing himself to remain calm, he turned his eyes once more to the stage.

He was at once fascinated, and relieved. Fascinated, because she was still beautiful. Relieved, because now that the initial shock was over he believed he was old enough not to be disturbed by that beauty, that alien quality of taunting, pulsing life that had upset him so when he was a boy.

She finished dancing, and someone in the wings stepped onto the stage and handed her a violin and bow. She took them with a theatrical, rather foolish gesture, flourished the bow in the air, stamped one small high-heeled boot, and began to play.

The melodies were well chosen. Those poignant, Slavic tunes that her father used to play would not have done for Saturday night's second house at the New Cross Empire. These were good, easily understood songs that the audience, made benevolent by bottled stout and port and lemons, could hum and wax sentimental over, songs from *The Merry Widow*, "Black Eyes," and to round off, a couple of nice Strauss waltzes. The audience was happy. Not quite good enough, or vulgar enough, to top the bill, but quite good enough for the end of the first half. And then, when everyone was nicely mellowed by the lush, popular old tunes, she set down her fiddle, raised her arms over her head and waited. The lights were lowered so that she stood in a shining white glow. The audience, experienced, knew what was expected of them and obediently hushed, and through the silence came the first drums of the Cossack horsemen and the first movements of Olga—the Galina of his youth.

It was all a cheap trick, the lighting, the soft drumming, but it worked, and as the music grew louder, more strident, faster, so did Galina's whirling and twirling, her body swaying so much it seemed as though it would snap at the slender waist. The white-and-gold skirts flew out revealing more white-and-gold petticoats, and beneath them the long brown legs that appeared, shockingly, to be bare above the boots. The dark hair swung around her face and suddenly she was what she had been all those years ago. Profoundly and elementally disturbing.

A small pulse beat in the side of Edwin's temple, not so much because of what she was doing now, but because it rekindled that summer twelve years ago, the summer when his body had tormented him, when he had seen brutal unthinking violence for the first time, when he had been unable, even while hating her, to think of anything else but her body and her smell and her glowing, mocking eyes.

It had taken him a long time to get over that summer. Perhaps, in a less well-ordered, less disciplined family he would have recovered sooner, but the Willoughbys, with their dread of showing emotion, with their reluctance to talk about happiness, or misery, or anything that wasn't humdrum and respectable, were no help to a boy suffering the confusion and turmoil of adolescence. There had been no one he could talk to, for who would have understood that he hated and was in love with a tinker's raffish child? Until that summer he had been able to talk to Sophie, but after Galina he was separated from Sophie by a wide sexual gulf. And he had, in any case, always detected in Sophie a tendency to give way to feelings, an erraticism which wouldn't have helped him at that time. Sophie had also been too deeply mixed in with the Barshinskeys to be of any help to him. That summer she had been nearly as wild and emotional as they were.

After that wonderful, dreadful summer, he had had, slowly, to rebuild his sanity, his equilibrium, his silence and stoicism. It had taken him over a year—a year before he realized, quite suddenly one day, that he was no longer absorbed with his own misery, that life once more held the promise of enjoyment. He had spent that year of misery incongruously, ridiculously, in Mr. Watkins's railway station, finding, in its very ordinariness, a soothing calm that he could find nowhere else. He looked back now, from the maturity of his twenty-five years, and was amused at the specter of a boy recovering from a broken heart by cleaning the brasses and sweeping the platforms of a village railway station, but in the well-ordered familiarity of the station, in the execution of humble and routine tasks, he had discovered once more his sanity.

There had been a period when he had wanted to run away, as Ivan Barshinskey had done, when he believed that nothing would ever be normal again, when every night his twisting, tortuous mind thought of Galina and Mr. Hope-Browne, Galina and her father, Galina and the Pilgrim Teacher. On those nights he had begun to understand Mr. Barshinskey's violence. Violence seemed to be the only way that such tormenting anguish could be relieved.

But eventually stability and peace had been restored to him, and once restored he had felt he never wanted anything violent or emotional to occur in his life again.

Strangely, his crisis had produced material results. For his escape, his frantic work at the station, his constant studying under the benevolent eye of Mr. Watkins, had made everyone realize positively that Edwin *must*—somehow—join the railway, and not just the railway but the elite locomotive section. Mr. Watkins himself had found the three necessary references and had coached him for the test. He had found him lodgings with a railway widow near the depot at Three Bridges and Edwin, armed with a brand-new pair of overalls, boots with steel caps and heel studs, and a letter to the shed foreman, had begun his career as a locomotive cleaner at ten shillings and sixpence a week. Edwin, the second of the Willoughbys to bring glory to the family, was on his way to becoming an engine driver.

His dedication had never wavered, his year of misery was behind him and, indeed, in the well-ordered discipline of the power sheds, he sometimes wondered if that year had been real, if the violence of the Barshinskeys had really happened. He knew he was a very ordinary young man, and ordinary young men did not spend a whole year of their lives longing for the exotic. If, at the back of his mind, that restlessness was still there, he ruthlessly subdued it. He looked forward to a life of variety and excitement made possible by his work. He was young and at the beginning of a career that contained everything he could ever want.

He had done well. Of course a Willoughby would do well. At twenty-one he had asked for a transfer to a London depot, partly because he had heard that promotion was quicker there, and partly because the restlessness refused to be subdued. Since that summer of the Barshinskeys he had known how narrow, how restricted the life of his parents was. When he thought of living all his life in one place as they had done he felt a sense of suffocation rising in him. He had to get out, see things, new things, experience a life that his parents wouldn't begin to understand. Now, after four years in London, he was—when he went home —vested with the glamour of a big city. He wore shoes instead of boots, smart off-duty suits, and had grown a mustache. He had money and was generous with it, never forgetting his family or Daisy May whom, in some strange way, he didn't associate with that year of the Barshinskeys. To him, Daisy May was the small girl he had saved from the Jefford set when they were both young. He had friends, mostly young men with whom he worked, and he had a life in London that he enjoyed, and that his family didn't know too much about. He thought that probably, one day many years in the future, he might marry, but it would be a tranquil, well-ordered affair, the kind of relationship that his mother and father had.

And now he watched Galina, and suddenly he remembered it all, the misery, the violence, the distortion of his own private childhood world.

The music grew faster, louder, and Galina spun around on one leg, revolving like a white-and-gold top about the stage. She was a very good dancer, much better than she had been as a girl. It was energetic and clever as well as being provocative. With a final clash of drums, a blast from the trumpets, she stopped, one hand swung up above her head, a wide smile on her face.

He didn't applaud. He couldn't. He watched her standing there, smiling, bowing, fluffing out her skirts, and he thought, how strange to see her on a stage, she who had caused so much misery, who had become, with the passing of time, no more than a remembered phantom, so that sometimes he wondered if she had really existed at all outside his own fevered imagination. But he hadn't imagined her, and there she stood, beautiful and admired, the way—he supposed—she had always wanted to be.

"I'm going to get a stout. You want one?"

"Eh?" He stared at the face beside him, good-natured, sweaty, and realized after a moment that it was the face of Bassy, his particular friend at the depot and his companion on several evening sprees.

"She was all right, weren't she? Do you think she had stockings on or was her legs bare?" He guffawed and nudged Edwin in the ribs. He felt a sudden swift revulsion for Bassy. For a moment he wanted to rush away and think his own thoughts, but the moment passed. It would be much better not to go away and think about her. It would be better to watch the rest of the show and forget about her.

"I used to know her," he heard himself saying to Bassy. "When we were kids I used to know her."

"Go on!" Bassy—short for Sebastian—was impressed, then cynicism crumpled his face. "Some Cossack princess then, ain't she? Comes from Kent I s'pose, like you . . ."

"Her father was a Russian. A real Russian. He taught her to play the fiddle." And she stole the fiddle and broke his heart.

"Fancy you knowin' a real actress! 'Ere, Ed . . ." His face lit up and again he nudged Edwin in the ribs. Edwin moved away a trifle. "If you know 'er, let's go round to the stage door and say 'ow-d'ye-do. I haven't never been in through a stage door before."

"No. I don't think so."

"Aw . . . come on! Just for a laugh. See what she says. I'd like to find out if she 'ad them flesh-colored stockings on 'er legs."

Two railway lads in their Saturday night suits, hanging around the stage door, waiting to see Galina Barshinskey. . . .

"No. I don't want to see her." He sounded shorter, more brusque than he intended and Bassy, who was not as insensitive as his looks suggested, was hurt.

"No need to be like that," he said with wounded dignity, and gazed distantly over several heads to the safety curtain which advertised Hudson's soap powder. There was a strained silence, and Edwin mused how strange it was that as soon as Galina entered his life again, however remotely, there was discord. *But I mustn't let there be discord. Galina isn't important anymore. She never was.* "I'll get the stout, Bassy," he said. Bassy didn't answer so he pushed his way past the knees and handbags and feather boas out onto the stairs. He bought Bassy a stout and, as a peace offering, a baked potato as well, balancing the potatoes on the top of the glasses as he made his way back to the seat.

Bassy, who was unable to hold a grudge for very long, allowed himself to be mollified and they drank their stout and ate the potatoes in fairly amiable silence. Marie Kendal ended the second half and by the time Bassy was joining in "Just Like the Ivy" he was completely restored to good humor and didn't notice that Edwin wasn't singing with the rest of the audience. They ambled their way home, eating a fish and chip supper out of the paper as they walked, and then Bassy turned into his lodgings just off the Tower Bridge Road with a cheerful, "G'night, Ed. See you Monday. Early turn."

He was alone, able to stop being jolly and matey, but strangely he found he missed Bassy's presence. He was unsettled, disturbed, and he knew he wouldn't be able to sleep. Partly it was because of seeing Galina again, but that was only a part of it. He felt restless with himself, with his life, his future. Suddenly there seemed nothing to look forward to; nothing strange or exciting would ever be likely to happen to him. He shook himself and began to walk. What did he expect, or want, to happen? Wasn't it enough that he had a good job, better than his father, that his life would, with luck, be comfortable and rewarding? He was a man now. No need to be baying at the moon for things he couldn't have—even if he knew what those things were.

He walked and walked, right up to Tower Bridge, where he stood looking down at the water, a thin trickling mist dampening his hair and clothes. When he finally turned and began to go back home he felt better. Galina was in proportion again, just a music hall act he had happened to know several years ago.

He was off duty the next day and, as was his custom on free Sundays, he went home, mostly from a sense of duty, for he was at that stage of his life where backward ties and old disciplines were increasingly irritating.

"Oh, good, you're in time for the morning meeting" was the greeting of his mother, and he wondered why he had been so keen to get the early train down from London. But then later, watching his father behind the reading desk in the Mission Hall and seeing how old he had become, he was suddenly filled with a sense of love for them both, for their loyalty and their total commitment to the standards they had set themselves.

Now, away from home, removed from them in both distance and emotional pressures, he recognized them as good people— simple, good people who had morality and generosity.

"Are they all right?" he whispered to Lillian suddenly, but she only frowned at him to be quiet and crossed her hands gracefully over her Bible. Lillian, as they had all expected, had turned into a beauty, tall and slim with a thick mass of creamy-colored hair. She was partner to the village dressmaker now, taking more and more work from Miss Clark, who suffered from eyestrain. Edwin, curious, wondered if Lillian had ever had a suitor. Other girls, whom he had grown up with, less attractive than Lillian, had married and were already absorbed with small incomes and large families. As he looked around the Mission Hall he could see them—tired young women with untidy hair and harassed eyes. When he glanced from them to Lillian they seemed to be of a different species. And then, unbidden, into his mind came the image of Galina Barshinskey.

They had cold lamb, baked potatoes, and beetroot for dinner —exactly the same Sunday dinner they had had for the last twenty-six years and, in his strange mood, he ate as though it were a last meal, a ceremony of things as they had been but would never be again. He felt once more that uneasy sense of concern for his parents, worrying that they were all right on their own even though, with Lillian still living at home, they weren't exactly on their own. When Lillian and his mother went into the kitchen to wash up and fetch the tea, he suddenly broke the rule of a lifetime and tried to talk intimately with his father.

"Dad . . . are you all right? You and Ma . . . are you all right?"

His father looked at him, surprised. "Why yes, son. Why shouldn't we be?"

"Well . . . your headaches. Do you still get them?"

"A bit, lad. A bit. But Mr. Hayward's been good to me. There's a job for me on the farm however long I have to lay up. Always something for me to do."

"But what about money, Dad? You don't get paid when

you're ill, and you don't get the money you used to when you were headman there."

His father's face cleared. Concern over practical matters of money was something he could understand. "Don't you worry yourself, lad. Your mother and I are all right. Sophie and Lillian are good to us—and so are you, son. We're all right, your ma and I. No need to worry about us."

How could he explain? What was he worried about? In some curious way his parents had become like children to him, innocent and too trusting of the world. They didn't understand about . . . things . . . about shattering emotions and the disturbances of life.

"Your mother and I are all right, Edwin," his father said quietly. "We had our worries when we were young, but we've seen you children settled all right. You and Lillian have done better than any in the village. We don't have anything to worry about now." He moved his hand slightly on the table and for a moment Edwin thought his father was going to reach out and touch his hand. But he changed the movement to a gentle tapping of his fingers on the table.

"I expect your mother and I will have a rest now. Why don't you go up and meet the girls when they come off duty?"

He gave up. Years of restraint, of disciplined emotion, could not be thrown aside just because he had seen Galina Barshinskey again.

The afternoon took on the quiet somnolence of a Sunday in January after a week of hard work. As he strolled along the lane he had the same curious sense of distance, of seeing things for the last time, the way they always had been but would never be again.

It was a clean day, with an intermittent sun dusting branches that stood black against the sky. He was wearing his best Sunday shoes but the day and the mood he was in made him climb over the stile at the top of the lane and walk through the woods to the White House. Under the trees were patches of white frost, kept hidden from the day's warmth, and when he ventured off the track a little he saw a clump of wild snowdrops clustering around the bole of a tree. They must always have been there. Why had he never noticed them before? Every so often a fine spray of moisture would fall on his head and shoulders from the thick tangle of branches. He didn't hurry. The girls usually didn't get off until about half-past three, after they had cleared and washed up the luncheon things and prepared and set the tea trays for the afternoon. They always came out together, even though Daisy May had more tasks to do than Sophie.

He opened the gate that led to the road from the side entrance of the White House. Callers were not allowed to the servants of the Fawcett menage but even Mrs. Fawcett found she was unable to issue an edict forbidding the brother of her parlor maid to wait for his sister.

The kitchen door of the White House was as quiet as the rest of the village, for the boiler boy and cook were both allowed to leave the minute the lunch was on the table. He tapped lightly on the door and it was opened by Daisy May, still wearing her morning dress of pink-and-white-striped twill.

"Edwin! Oh, Edwin!"

He thought of them, as did the rest of the family, as The Girls, and the reactions of The Girls to his homecomings were always the nicest part of his Sundays off duty.

"Did you forget it was my Sunday home?" He grinned. Daisy, flustered and flushed, wiped her hands on the kitchen towel.

"I get mixed up with your on and off turns. Oh, but look! I'm not even changed yet. But the washing up's done and the tea is ready to be taken in to the drawing room."

"Hurry, then."

She smiled and untied her apron which somehow, even after a morning's dirty work and the washing up of a big roast lunch, was still immaculately clean.

"I'd better not ask you in. Mrs. Fawcett's in a bit of a mood today."

"It's all right. I can wait here."

She vanished, leaving the kitchen door open, and he leaned against the door frame with his hands in his pockets. The Fawcett kitchen was huge, with a big double-sided kitchen range along one side, and a dresser that was hung with gleaming copper pots. The kitchen staff consisted of cook and Daisy May, so he knew whose task it was to keep the pots so clean. A fat ginger cat stretched itself on a rag rug in front of the range, and then as a draft from the door touched its fur it turned and glared at him.

" 'Lo, Edwin." Sophie was in her Sunday clothes—a dark green coat and a felt hat pulled well down over her coiled braids. Since Lillian had taken over the renovating of the family wardrobe Sophie looked a lot smarter.

"The hem of your coat's coming down, Soph."

"Oh, never mind about that." She came across and gripped his arm. "That old bag's been foul to Daisy May today. She's always rotten to her on Sundays—doesn't like her coming back with us and going to the Mission Hall. She always finds an excuse to make her work late when it's her Sunday off."

"I've brought her a tin of toffees," he said, and Sophie's angry face immediately cleared. "Oh, Edwin," she said, "how kind of you! Daisy May will love that!"

Walking back down the road between them, he thought what *nice* girls they were. Of the four of them, he and Lillian had achieved the most, had moved up a step in the hierarchy of class structure and had brought most honor to the family. But, if truth be told, Sophie and Daisy May were the nicest, the most willing, the ones most given to pleasing and spontaneous enthusiasm. He thought of them as sisters, partly because they looked so alike (except that Sophie was always so appallingly untidy) but also because of their fierce loyalty to each other. He guessed that Daisy May's life at the White House wasn't too easy. She had need of a good friend like Sophie.

Later, around the tea table, he realized how the girls brought life into the house. Sophie's chatter, Daisy's bright, smiling little face brought the quiet house to life again. Tea was cheerful where dinner had been moribund. Even the evening meeting was gayer with them present. Sophie turned to him and winked when prayers went on too long, and she sat and picked a hole in the finger of her glove during the reading. Daisy, neat and quiet, just looked happy and, with a repetition of the gloomy forebodings that had dogged him all day, he suddenly felt terribly sad for her. She had so little.

He prepared to walk the girls back to the White House after the evening meeting and was disconcerted to find he was not alone. Two young sprigs strolled alongside and, by just being there, established themselves as having a right to walk among the party. He found himself, at one point, maneuvered on a narrow path so that he was walking alone at the back of them. But it was only for one brief moment, for Daisy looked around, then dropped back to join him.

"Thank you *so* much for the Sharp's Kreemies, Edwin. The toffees are nice, but then, when they've all gone, there's still the nice tin."

He felt a spasm of unexpected annoyance with her. Why did she have to be so pathetic, so grateful for even the most trivial things? Why didn't she put up more of a fight, reach out and grab things for herself as others did? Her humility, her expectance of nothing made him suddenly want to jolt her.

"I saw your sister last night. Galina. She was on the stage of the New Cross Empire. It's a music hall. Calls herself the Cossack Princess."

Beside him Daisy faltered. He turned to look at her but could not see her face properly in the darkness. Already he was ashamed of himself, appalled at his streak of cruelty.

"Sorry, Dais," he said gruffly. "Shouldn't have told you like that. Shouldn't have told you at all probably."

Daisy May didn't answer. They scuffled along in silence.

"I don't know whether you ever think about her . . ."

"Yes," said Daisy tonelessly. "Yes, I do think about her. And about the others. My mother, father, Ivan."

"It was quite a nice act she had," he said placatingly. "She danced, and she played the fiddle. She was very good really."

"I expect it was my pa's fiddle. She stole it, you know."

"Yes. I know."

Ahead of them he could hear Sophie chattering away to her two young men. He suddenly longed for Sophie to come back and walk with them. Sophie would know how to handle this awkward situation that was entirely his own fault.

"Did she say anything? Did she ask after me?" said a small voice at his side.

"I didn't speak to her. Just saw her on the stage."

"I never really liked her, you know. It's wicked to say that, isn't it? But I never did like her. She was on my father's side, you see, and I . . ."

"You were always your mother's girl."

"But still, she's my sister. I don't want her coming back here, no, never! But she's still my sister, she's all I've got. I wish you'd spoken to her."

"I . . . it was difficult, Daisy. I was with a friend, and anyway, it's been so many years that . . . well, I just thought it wouldn't look right somehow."

"No. I suppose it wouldn't." He heard her sigh, a gentle sibilant noise that seemed part of the evening breeze. "But I still wish you'd spoken to her. Could you go and see her again? Tell her I'm all right and . . . and that she could write to me if she wanted. She could just about write, you know. And I expect she's got a bit better if she's on the stage. She'd have to read for the stage, wouldn't she? She'd have to read letters and songs and things, wouldn't she?"

"I don't know if I could find her now, Daisy. The program changes on Mondays and she won't be at the New Cross Empire next week." There was a small breathless pit of excitement in his stomach—like there had been the first time a driver let him take an engine around the shunting depot.

"But you could find her if you asked, Edwin, couldn't you?" She turned to face him. He couldn't see her face in any detail. It was just a white blur. "And anyway, you might see her again, at another music hall. You go a lot, don't you?"

"Well, yes, but . . ."

"Oh, it's all right. I won't tell your folks. It would only upset them." She sounded unlike Daisy May, rather knowing and superior. It was a new role both for her and for him and he wasn't sure he liked it.

"If you find her, tell her I've heard from Ivan."

"Have you?" Edwin asked, astonished.

"Yes. He wrote to Sophie about three years ago. He wasn't sure where I was, you see."

"Sophie never told me." He was deeply affronted. He had been God to these two girls. They didn't do a thing without asking him, and here they were, keeping secrets from him for three years.

"No. I made her promise not to. It was so badly written. I was—no—not ashamed of it, but I was ashamed for Ivan. He never really had time to learn to write properly and I didn't want anyone else to see it. If I'd told anyone he'd written they'd have asked to see the letter."

Yes, of course they would. For so long Daisy May had been the runt of the family, the poor relation, the one who did as she was told and had no privacy of the soul. Oh yes, they had all been kind to her, very kind, and had made her one of them. But the price she had paid was to be totally *theirs*, no privacy allowed, no independence.

"What did he say . . . I mean, if you want to tell me," he said stiffly. He could tell from Daisy May's voice that she was smiling.

"Just that he was all right. He joined the army, joined as a boy soldier. He was out in India. He said he'd come to see me if I was still here when he came home. It was such a pretty stamp on the envelope. I wrote back to him. So did Sophie. He changed his name of course. He didn't want anyone knowing about . . . about what happened here . . ."

"No, of course."

"It was lovely, knowing that he was all right and had remembered me. I felt I had a family again."

"Yes."

"And although I don't feel like that about Galina . . . oh, well, she's still my sister. I'd just like to know where she is . . . and if she ever thinks about us."

"Yes, well. I'll see what I can do. I may be able to find out where she is next week. I'll see what I can do."

He left in a slight state of shock. Going back in the train that evening he kept examining what Daisy May had told him. He couldn't believe that there was anything about her he didn't know. When she surprised him, as she had done this evening, he felt uneasy. But even while he felt uneasy, at the back of his mind was a small joyous core of excitement. He wondered how he would go about tracking down Galina Barshinskey.

He met with an instant rebuff at the stage door of the New Cross Empire, for the man there gave him an old-fashioned look and said, "Oh yes? Wanting to chase up one of the lady artistes, was yer? Well, I'm afraid I don't know where she's performing this week, and if I did I don't know as I'd be telling everyone as hangs around this door."

Edwin had flushed, not with embarrassment but with anger. An explanation that he was searching for the Cossack Princess on behalf of her sister brought a knowing leer to the man's face and Edwin left before he smashed his fist into the leer.

He tried at the ticket window that night, and again from the man who stood in the foyer. It was no good. The matron with dyed hair who sat behind the ticket desk didn't know, and the house manager all but threw him out. He bought as many of the local London newspapers as he could and scoured them all for news of local entertainment. Galina was not there, though that didn't necessarily mean she wasn't on at any of the advertised places. He was on early turn that week, and every evening he caught a tram or omnibus and went to a different music hall, checking the bills outside the theaters and asking the doormen whether Olga, the Cossack Princess, was on that week. By Friday he was desperate, knowing that the greater the length of time that elapsed since her week at New Cross, the harder it would be to track her down. She might have gone anywhere, might be touring the provinces for all he knew. The need to find her was now an obsession, a personal obsession that had nothing to do with Daisy May's request.

On Saturday morning, as he was firing on the run to Charing Cross, the answer suddenly came to him—the public house close to the New Cross Empire. The variety performers were sure to go there, both before and after the show. The publican or the barmaid might remember Galina, or at least know some of the other artistes who were on last week. If he could only find one of them he should be able to get some news of her.

As soon as it was time for the first house at the Empire, he settled himself in the saloon bar, ordered a half-pint of stout, and began to question the barmaid. Olga, the Cossack Princess, meant nothing, but she did vouchsafe that several of the artistes came in to wet their whistles between the houses. Edwin settled down to wait.

It was easy for him to make casual acquaintance with people, to exchange comments with passersby or people he met only briefly for he was, although he was unaware of it, a personable young man, good to look at, with a pleasant and inviting face. Tall, big-boned, he was nearly always lightly tanned and his thick brown hair was always clean and shiny looking. The most striking thing about him was his eyes. They were gray and had an almost translucent quality about them. When he laughed the eyes shone and sparkled and women particularly found him attractive. He had a natural warm and friendly manner and it didn't bother him that he was going to have to speak to total strangers when the first house at the Empire ended.

First two came in, then a group of three, two men and a woman. They were all talking to one another and he didn't like to interrupt even though the woman glanced over to where he was sitting. Then the door opened and a man came in on his own. Edwin recognized him from one of his stage performances. It was Leonardo, the sketch artist. Edwin stared at him until the man looked back, then he smiled and nodded. Leonardo gave a slight nod in return and Edwin, unabashed, picked up his glass and moved toward him.

"Leonardo, the sketch artist, yes?"

"That's right."

"Saw you last summer at the Brixton Empress. Jolly good."

"Thanks," Leonardo grunted, and buried his head in his mug.

"Can I buy you another?"

Leonardo's head emerged from the mug, his expression considerably warmer. "Thanks. Stout."

The courtesies were exchanged. Edwin expressed admiration and Leonardo, after another stout had been purchased, mellowed and expanded about himself. Edwin, remembering the rebuff from the stage door man and the house manager, worded his request with care.

"I wish," he said, "there was some way of finding out where your favorite acts were going to be. Take you now, I've had to wait all this time to see you drawing on the stage again. And last week—here at the Empire—there was two acts, really good, I'd like to see again. But who knows where they are now?"

"Oh yes? And what was they?"

"Datas, the Memory Man, and Olga, the Cossack Princess."

"Well, I don't know for certain about the Cossack act, but Datas is probably on the circuit. When we're in London we do a regular circuit, see? Unless you're right at the top of the bill it's easier to arrange that way. Mostly from here we go to the Holborn Empire, and after that the Crouch End Hippodrome. Then there's the Oxford, and the Met at Edgware Road. You'll likely find Datas at one of those this week."

"Thanks very much, Mr. Leonardo." He tried to hide his elation. "Can I get you another stout?"

Mr. Leonardo wiped his hand over his mustache. "No thanks, son. Three's my limit before a show. Any more than that and my eye slips. Very important to an artist, a steady eye. Without it you're lost."

"I'll say goodbye, then."

"Eh?"

"I have to go. It's been very nice meeting you."

He left his drink half finished and rushed out of the pub. If he hurried he could catch most of the second house at the Holborn Empire. He raced to the tram stop and managed to leap on a tram as it was grinding off. All the way to the Elephant and Castle, where he had to change trams, he was fighting a sense of surging excitement. He hadn't even thought what would happen if he did find her. The chase had almost become sufficient in itself.

He'd missed nearly all the first half when he got to the Holborn Empire, but as he charged up the stairs to the gallery he heard a sound that made him halt, his hand tensing on the rail. It was the sound of Galina's Cossack dance. He closed his eyes for a moment, and swallowed hard. Then he turned and walked slowly down the stairs again because he had to catch her now, before she left the theater. Ignoring the curious stare of the man in the ticket desk, he walked out and found his way to the stage door. When he opened it he found a fat man eating pease pudding and faggots out of a paper, seated behind the doorman's window.

"Yus?"

"I want to see Gali—Olga, the Cossack Princess."

"All right," the man said, to his astonishment. "Who is it?"

"I'm . . . tell her, Edwin Willoughby, with a message from her brother, Ivan."

"All right . . . *Bertie* . . ." A small boy appeared from down a flight of steps.

"Bertie, tell the Cossack act there's a bloke wiv a message from 'er brother. Says 'is name is Willoughby."

"Edwin Willoughby. And her brother's name is Ivan."

"Like I said, Bertie. Get along now."

Edwin waited, and the man chewed, slowly turning the pages of the *London Illustrated News* with his free hand.

"All right. You can come up."

Suddenly it was all too easy. Only now did he stop to think what he would say. How would she look? Would she recognize him? Through his head passed a blur of memories: Galina at the coronation party with her hair hanging down and poppies tucked into her belt. Galina dancing around the fire. Galina in her house-maid's uniform, looking clean and demure and infinitely seductive.

The boy, Bertie, tapped on the door.

"Come in." The voice was soft, gentle, a little voice. He opened the door and went in.

It was a dirty, scruffy room, but he didn't notice. It seemed all glamour and light to him. Her white-and-gold costume was flung over a screen and gas lights blazed at each side of a mirror. And Galina stood up and reached her hands out toward him and smiled, that warm, glowing, wonderful Barshinskey smile that he hadn't seen for so many years.

"Edwin!"

He couldn't speak. He felt like an oaf, as he had done all those years ago. Oh yes, he'd tried to feel superior to her because she was a tinker's child and he was respectable. But all he had ever felt was an oaf, a thirteen-year-old hayseed. She didn't look like a tinker's child now. Her eyes were brilliant, and her great thick mane of curling hair swept over her shoulders to her waist.

"Edwin," she said, staring at him across the room. "But I would never have recognized you! You have changed so much . . . so big! Who would have thought you would have grown so big . . ."

"Yes . . ." he said foolishly, and laughed at himself to cover his discomfiture. She came across the room, took his hands, reached up on her toes and softly kissed his cheek. Something exploded softly within him. Her nearness, her smallness, the very smell of her, flowers and powder and sweat, nearly made him lose control. He gripped hard on her hands. They were tiny, delicate in his.

"I remember you as tall, Galina. Yes, tall. But you are tiny. You can't have grown at all since you left."

"But now I am better dressed, yes?"

"How did you . . . I mean, what happened? After you ran away, what happened between then and now . . . all this . . ."

He waved his hand around the dressing room and Galina shrugged and sat down in front of her mirror.

"I don't like to talk about the past. For us Barshinskey children it was not good. Now is better, much better."

Edwin, embarrassed, remained silent.

"He was no good, that man, Jones. At first I liked him, and then I was afraid, you know, all that terrible night, with the poor young man with the pimples on his face." She shuddered and smeared grease over her face. Edwin stared, fascinated. He had two sisters but he had never seen anything so careless, so intimate before. She didn't even seem to care that he was watching her.

"I do not like ugly things, death, and illness . . . horrible . . ."

"If you'd rather not talk about it . . ."

"There is little to tell, Edwin dear. Jones, he became so serious. Always talking of my soul, and praying for me. It was worse than the vicarage, so I left."

"And what happened?"

She shrugged again. "I did a little of this, a little of that. I was housekeeper for a while. . . ." She looked at him sideways, from beneath her lashes, and then said naughtily, "He was a very *old* man. . . ."

"And then?" He wanted to know. He realized what she was telling him, of the life she had led but, strangely, he felt no jealousy. He just wanted to know.

"So then I met someone who taught me how to dance—properly, you understand. He was my manager for a little time but now I do not need him."

She had wiped all the greasepaint from her face and she looked younger and somehow more vulnerable, like a child scrubbed for bed. Slowly she began to reapply cosmetics, cream, rouge, eye kohl, and powder.

"And now you must tell me everything from your home. Ivan! You have a message from Ivan?"

"Well, not really a message. Daisy May heard from him some years ago. He joined the army and now he's in India."

"Daisy? You still see Daisy?"

"She's still in the village. Working at Fawcett's."

"Poor little Daisy. You are to tell her that Galina sends her fondest love! Remember now, her fondest love!"

There was a knock at the door and she tilted her face up to the mirror for a final inspection. She had high cheekbones and a small pointed chin that gave her a fragile elfinlike quality.

"Come in!" she cried, and turned, smiling, to the door. "Heikki! Dear Heikki!"

He was a shortish, roundish little man with a bald head and a small pointed beard. He wore a dark suit that was almost an evening suit, but not quite. He bounded across to Galina like a small black India-rubber ball and kissed her on both cheeks.

"Heikki darling, see here is an old, old friend who has known me since I was a child. He comes from my brother. He has known me—oh—since the time when I had no shoes and was ugly and dirty." She laughed, a delicious, gurgling laugh that somehow indicated that life was wonderful because she was no longer poor and dirty.

"Oh . . . no, Galina," Edwin began to stammer. "You were never like that. You were always . . . different . . . exciting, even when you had no shoes."

The little India-rubber man beamed at Edwin. He didn't seem to mind finding him in Galina's dressing room.

"So," he said, surprised. "And why does this young man call you, who are Olga, Galina?"

Galina turned to Edwin and laughed again. "You must know, Edwin, that Heikki saw me when I appeared at the Tivoli . . . yes . . . your shabby little Galina has appeared at the Tivoli, no less. And Heikki only knows me as Olga, not Galina." She shrugged. "I do not mind. Galina . . . Olga . . . it is all the same."

The little man bounced over to Edwin and held out his hand. "I am happy to see you," he said cheerily, and then he peered hard up into Edwin's face. "A very *English* young man," he said approvingly. "Yes, very English."

"Heikki is from Finland, Russian Finland," said Galina, turning back to the mirror and her face. "And, oh, Edwin! Just think. He has a house in Moscow and an apartment in St. Petersburg, and a dacha in Finland, and one day, one day, he is going to take me to St. Petersburg on one of his ships!"

"I am merchant," said the little man jovially. "Timber and flax." He gave a polite bow and said, "Heikki Rautenberg."

His English was good and, funny and fat though he was, to Edwin he was already vested with an air of glamour—that same glamour that the Barshinskeys had had in the old days. He was Russian, and he spoke with an accent and he was obviously the possessor of Galina. Edwin waited for the old familiar agony of jealousy to smite him, but nothing happened. She was exciting and beautiful and as far above him as any other will-o'-the-wisp fairy creature. Obviously she would belong to someone who was different, who came from a foreign world, who was rich and odd and colorful.

"Edwin Willoughby," he said shyly, and Mr. Rautenberg pumped his hand up and down again in a frenzy of good will.

"And now," he said, clasping his hands together in front of his chest, "now, Olga, your friend must come to supper with us. No . . . I insist. Old friends do not appear from the past every night of the life, and we must celebrate. A party, yes?"

"That's very kind of you," Edwin stammered. "But really, I . . ."

"Good. We shall go then. Olga, you are ready?" He went to a peg on the wall and took down a sealskin coat which he wrapped around Galina. She had put her hair up—it took his sisters hours to get their hair up. He had never seen anyone do it as quickly as Galina—and now, in the smooth, gleaming silver coat she seemed elegant and very distant.

"I'm not really dressed for going out to supper," he faltered weakly. He wanted to go with them, desperately he wanted to go. They were so exciting, so different.

"No matter," said Mr. Rautenberg peremptorily, waving his hand in the air. "Young man, you go and find a cab, and in two moments we shall join you."

He rushed down the stairs to the stage door. At the back of his mind he was thinking that Bassy and his mates at the depot would never believe what was happening to him, and then he realized at once that he would never tell any of his workmates of his entree into bright cosmopolitan life. They wouldn't understand and anyway he didn't want to share it with anyone. He could tell Sophie. Sophie would understand what it meant to him —meeting people on the other side of life!

They went to a restaurant in Long Acre. It was all red plush and there were drawings on the walls. Mr. Rautenberg went in first and had a whispered word with a waiter. Edwin saw that money was exchanged and then they were led to a table in a little side alcove—"Because we are not dressed, you understand"— and as Edwin looked about him he saw that indeed everyone was wearing evening clothes. He suddenly began to worry about money. Should he offer to pay, and did he have enough? Anxiety beset him, made worse when he heard Mr. Rautenberg order something that sounded suspiciously like "shampanyer."

"I should . . . er . . . like to contribute something toward the evening," he blurted, feeling gauche and awkward.

"Tonight is my party," said Mr. Rautenberg airily "Tonight you are my guest. It is good for Olga—but no, it seems she is Galina—to have a young friend from her past. Always she is with me, an old, old man, and sometimes I think she must become tired of such an old, old man." It was said with such confidence, such ebullience, that it was obvious not for one moment did he believe it. Galina gave him a warm melting look and said, "Ah, no, Heikki!" resting her small slim hand on his, and still Edwin felt no pang of envy. They were different, these exotic creatures, and he was grateful to them for taking him into their lives.

Several times that evening he had to stop, in his mind, and say, look, hold it, for nothing like this will ever happen to you again. I am here, Edwin Willoughby, drinking champagne, sitting with elegant ladies and gentlemen as though I were one of them.

He was sensible enough, old enough, to know that champagne, caviar (which Mr. Rautenberg ordered when he learned that Edwin had never tasted it), and deferential waiters were, in fact, only a more expensive version of an evening at the Variety followed by a sit-down steak and Guinness supper at the City Tavern. An evening out was an evening out and the people in this red plush restaurant just had more money, that was all. But nonetheless he was part of it, part of a world he had never seen before, and with two people he would never have met at the City Tavern.

He kept thinking of Sophie, how Sophie would have enjoyed it, especially she would have enjoyed Mr. Rautenberg who was Russian—Finnish—and whose conversation was liberally sprinkled with words like St. Petersburg, Moscow, Riga. . . . The champagne and the wine that followed made his shyness vanish. He listened, fascinated, to the stories of Mr. Rautenberg's journeys, and Galina's theatrical career. He asked questions, forgetting to be ashamed of showing his lack of sophistication. He ate, and drank, relishing the new flavors, the new sensations, as much as he relished the presence of Galina and Mr. Rautenberg. He listened and he noticed. He observed that Galina's voice had changed from the old days, not the pitch and tone, but the accent. As a child she had spoken with a curious mixture of Kent and her father, but now every word was clearly and carefully enunciated. Sometimes indeed she appeared to be speaking like a foreigner who is determined not to show her accent. And her eyes—when they were young he had likened her eyes to those of a cat. They were still slanting, but now the slant carried something mysterious, something inviting and beguiling. Several times he caught her looking at him, staring in a wondering, musing kind of way. When she looked at Mr. Rautenberg it was different. Then she laughed and her eyes crinkled up into two sparkling crescents.

"I can't believe it," he said to her warmly. "I can't believe that I am here with you, Galina Barshinskey. You're so different, and yet so much the same. And you're rich, and beautiful, and successful . . . I can't believe it."

She laughed and inclined her head in a gracious movement of

acknowledgment. "And I cannot believe you, Edwin," she said. "You were always so stern and disapproving, staring at me all the time and never smiling. You were always so . . . so righteous, you Willoughbys. You always thought that the way you lived was the right way. You never understood about my papa and me."

"Oh, we did, we did! Sophie and I, we thought you were all wonderful, but you upset us, disturbed us. All the things we had been taught were so important, you treated as nothing. I think you made us afraid. You were so . . . Russian, I suppose . . ."

Mr. Rautenberg suddenly broke in, pouring more champagne, patting Edwin's shoulder, Galina's hand. Just for a moment they had forgotten he was there.

"I, too," he said vehemently. "The first time I see her, so beautiful, on the stage of the Tivoli Theater, I knew she was Russian! Not because she was called Cossack Princess—so silly to call her this—but because of the way she played and danced and looked. At once I say to myself, Heikki, that is Russian girl, and you will go to see her and discover what Russian girl does on stage of the Tivoli Theater in England. That was . . . how long . . . since two years. And since that time every visit I am in London—I am in London many times, you understand—I come to see my Russian girl with the English voice. Once she comes to Edinburgh with me, to see my ships. And one day, perhaps, I will take her to St. Petersburg, for a little holiday, to see the land of her papa. . . ."

"I always wanted to go to Russia, Edwin," Galina said dreamily. "All those years my father used to speak of it, always promising to take me there. He used to say that in Russia I should be a grand lady and ride on a sleigh and wear furs and jewels."

"And this is true, my Galina, for already the furs and jewels are yours. You do not have to go to St. Petersburg to possess the furs and the jewels."

For the first time Mr. Rautenberg's voice ceased to be benevolent. There was a note, not of admonishment, but of a statement of fact, as though she needed to be reminded of something. Galina responded immediately.

"Ah, Heikki darling. You are so generous to me. You see, Edwin"—putting her hands to her throat and hair—"these pins, and the necklace, they are from the Baltic Sea—amber, Russian amber, so beautiful."

"Indeed," said Edwin, suddenly uncomfortable, and then Galina said something in Russian—or so Edwin supposed—and both she and Mr. Rautenberg laughed.

He was at once aware that he was an outsider. He looked around at the restaurant and realized he was in the wrong place, with the wrong people. He had no right to be there. He was badly dressed. In the ordinary way it was his about-town suit but, compared with those about him, it didn't fit properly and was the wrong color. He didn't look right, or speak right, and he had no place being there.

"And now, Edwin Willoughby, you are to tell us what you do. Where you come from, we know, the same place as my Galina-Olga, but how do you pass your days?"

"I work on the railway. I'm a fireman. That's someone who travels with the driver, firing the box, making the engine run. In time I'll be a driver. An engine driver . . ."

"But this is wonderful!" said Mr. Rautenberg, beaming happily at Edwin, all his brusqueness gone. "This is romantic, to drive a great engine is the same thing as to drive a great ship, my ships, they, too, have drivers and fire boxes and all these things. They run on steam, so, like your engine. It is romantic, is it not romantic, Galina?"

She gave a little giggle but this time it didn't make Edwin feel uncomfortable. He wanted to giggle, too, but felt it would be rude to Mr. Rautenberg, who was really so very nice. And, beneath all his reserve and dislike of extravagant emotion, he felt that what Mr. Rautenberg had said was true. Engines were romantic, driving them was romantic. Anyone who had stood on the footplate of a great engine, and felt the pistons begin to move, knew that it was romantic. Two men pulling thousands of tons of steel and iron and goods behind them was romantic, especially when he was one of the men.

"We shall do all this again," said Mr. Rautenberg approvingly. "It has been fun to have a party and now we shall plan to do it again. Next week, you will sit with me—I have a box, it is more comfortable, is it not?—and after, we shall have another little supper."

Edwin was once more conscious of embarrassment. "That's very kind of you, Mr. Rautenberg, but I don't think . . . you see . . ." How to explain that if he couldn't afford to entertain in the same manner as Mr. Rautenberg he could not accept his hospitality. "You see, we're not really . . . the same kind of people. If you lived here you would understand. You would have your friends and I would have mine."

"This is nonsense! For we are both friends of Galina, and Galina and you, you were children together."

"It's different for Galina," he answered stubbornly. Gently she placed her fingers on his lips.

"Please, Edwin," she said softly, and when he looked at her face he was startled to see an urgent plea there, an entreating look. Her eyes were open wide, very serious. "Do not be like this, Edwin. So stuffy and disapproving. I thought you were not like this anymore. You must come. Heikki and I want you to come, don't we, Heikki?"

"I have a different idea. Next week, Galina, we shall return to your rooms after the performance, and we shall both bring something for a party."

She clapped her hands together like a child. "Oh, what a lovely idea! A surprise party. And I will ask Mrs. Keith to cook supper for us, and perhaps we shall ask someone else, someone from the theater."

"Good. It is arranged then," said Mr. Rautenberg, summoning a waiter for the bill.

At once a horde of questions flew through Edwin's mind. What should he bring? How much could he afford? Should he take food or wine or both? Or "shampanyer"? Should he refuse? But how could he when Mr. Rautenberg was being so gracious and understanding and Galina's eyes were full of unshed tears?

"That will be wonderful," he gulped. "Where are you playing next week, Galina?"

"Next week, the Metropolitan. But, oh, how I wish you had seen me at the Tivoli. I shall go again. They told me I should be there again." Her eyes shone, and although they always gave the impression of being black, Edwin realized that in fact they were a deep golden brown, like the amber round her neck and in her hair. The pupils were always so large that they seemed darker than they were.

"A cab, fetch a cab," said Mr. Rautenberg jovially, and Edwin hurried away once more to do Mr. Rautenberg's bidding.

When the cab came he couldn't bear to leave them, and they insisted that he travel with them. Mr. Rautenberg talked and laughed all the way to Bayswater where Galina had her rooms. Once more the evening took on a magic, fairy-tale quality. The clopping of the horse in the empty streets, the crisp January night, the laughter, and above all the shining brilliance of Galina Barshinskey shed a glow over the journey. When they arrived at Galina's rooms, Galina kissed him on the cheek and so, to his astonishment, did Mr. Rautenberg. They told him to take the cab home but when he got around the corner he paid the disgruntled cabby off and prepared to walk back to the New Kent Road. It was a long way but he was young and strong and in love with Galina and Heikki Rautenberg and with London and his whole life. The city, so quiet in the January night, belonged to him.

Just as he was dropping off to sleep in a euphoria of champagne and exotic recollections, he was jarred by an unpleasant thought. Why had she never asked what had happened to her mother? Why had she never even asked after him, her papa, whom she appeared to love so much?

Of course he should have told her, should have told her the whole of that dreadful time after she had run away. But how could he when she was so happy? And anyway, perhaps she already knew. Yes, that was it. That was why she hadn't asked. She already knew.

11 IT WAS QUITE SOME TIME BEFORE MRS. FAWCETT CAME
to realize that in fact she didn't like Daisy May Barshinskey.

There was a long period when she felt quite genially disposed toward the child. There she was, orphaned, the
child of disgraced parents with no one to give her a character
(other than Mrs. Willoughby, who really had known her no
longer than anyone else in the village) and she, Mrs. Fawcett, had
acted as a good Christian should. She had provided the child with
a home and a future.

There was a year or two when she saw very little of Daisy
May. On arrival at the White House, Daisy had been given a
room at the top of the house (a whole room to herself) and passed
over to Mrs. Bramble, the White House cook. Daisy May had
been told to keep her room tidy, her clothes and person clean,
and to help Mrs. Bramble in the kitchen when she returned from
school. Mrs. Fawcett had supplied her with a good serge frock
for winter, and a poplin one for summer. There were two pinafores from the Church Mission box, stockings, undergarments,
and a stout pair of boots. She already had a Sunday frock that
Mrs. Willoughby had given her so that was one expense saved.
Daisy May had proven quiet and docile. Mrs. Bramble had no
complaints. She was a good little worker, she said, and on the
whole Mrs. Fawcett rarely saw the child, who shifted between
the attic and the kitchen with mouselike timidity. Mrs. Fawcett
had experienced that sense of well-being that comes with a good
deed done at no personal inconvenience.

At some point of time, Mrs. Fawcett wasn't quite sure exactly
when, Daisy May stopped going to school altogether and was
seen a little more often around the house. Mrs. Fawcett was
aware of her in the kitchen every morning when she went in to
have her morning consultation with cook.

209

The first time the child really impinged on Mrs. Fawcett's consciousness was when cook had let a casserole boil over in the stove, and Daisy May was kneeling on the floor, her sleeves rolled up, scouring out the inside of the range. Mrs. Fawcett, talking to cook about what should be done with the remains of the saddle of mutton, vaguely noticed how clean and fresh the child looked, in spite of her dirty job. Her hair gleamed. Her fresh pink-and-white complexion was further enhanced by the composure of her features, unusual in one so young. Her dress and apron were spotless, although considering the dirtiness of her task, a few spots of dirty water and grease could have been excused. When Mrs. Fawcett had first come into the kitchen, Daisy May had stood up, given a respectful little bob, and then continued with her work. Mrs. Fawcett couldn't complain, but something about the neatness, the orderliness of Daisy May, irritated her, not strongly, but enough to make her say as she was leaving the kitchen, "I hope you're not taking too long over your tasks, Daisy May. You're here to help cook, remember."

Daisy May had bobbed again, said, "Yes, 'um," and continued scrubbing out the oven. Mrs. Fawcett had left the kitchen somehow aware that her own hair wasn't quite as tidy as usual.

She saw Daisy May again, a few weeks later, going off after Sunday luncheon to spend her afternoon and evening with the Willoughbys. Once more the girl was immaculately fresh. Her hair shone as though it had just been washed. Her face was demure and glowing over a lace collar fixed to her Sunday dress. She wore a dark blue straw hat and carried a Bible. Usually the staff left by the kitchen entrance and went through the vegetable garden to the lane, and so were never seen by the inmates of the house. But Mrs. Fawcett had taken a notion to look at her own strawberry beds and intercepted Daisy on her way out.

"Daisy May!"

"Yes, 'um." She turned and came down the path to the strawberry beds. Now that she had called her, Mrs. Fawcett couldn't think what to say.

"Have you finished all your tasks?"

"Yes, 'um."

"Have you washed up the luncheon dishes and set the trays for afternoon tea?"

"Yes, 'um."

Mrs. Fawcett caught a sudden whiff of something but she wasn't sure if it was the scent from the strawberry beds.

"Come here, child." Daisy May shuffled closer.

"Are you wearing scent?"

"Hungary water, ma'am. It was a Christmas present from Mr. and Mrs. Willoughby." A faint pink tinge crawled up her neck. "I only wear it on Sunday, ma'am."

Irrationally Mrs. Fawcett was pleased by the flush on Daisy's face. She had discomforted her.

"I don't approve of servants wearing scent, Daisy May."

"No, 'um."

"But I suppose as your friends gave it to you I can say nothing. Make sure you wash it all off before you go to bed tonight."

The flush deepened. "Yes, 'um."

"You may go now."

She watched her walk between the rows of peas and runner beans, a small girl; she hadn't really grown all that much in the last few years, but with good straight shoulders and a trim walk. Mrs. Fawcett knew a spasm of irritation that she had allowed Daisy May to remain with the Brethren. She should have insisted when she took her in that she turned to Church like the other servants. Those Sunday afternoons and evenings with the Willoughbys gave Daisy May a measure of independence that Mrs. Fawcett acutely resented.

It was a trivial matter, but she found it continually nagging at her, intruding on her consciousness at odd times with a sudden and uncomfortable clarity. It became so disproportionate that the sight of Daisy May leaving for the Willoughbys on alternate Sundays would upset Mrs. Fawcett for the rest of the day. Sometimes she wondered why she didn't just issue an edict that Daisy was to attend evensong with the other servants, but Mrs. Fawcett prided herself on being a good Christian woman who kept her word. And she had given Mrs. Willoughby to understand, at the time of taking Daisy May in her house, that on alternate Sundays, Daisy May belonged to the Willoughbys and to the Brethren.

She had a chance to raise the matter when Mrs. Willoughby asked to see her with a view to taking Sophie into service.

Mrs. Willoughby came into her private sitting room accompanied by a scrubbed fourteen-year-old whose braids had been twisted into a huge and untidy bun at the back of her neck. Mrs. Fawcett asked Mrs. Willoughby to sit. Sophie stood fidgeting slightly, balancing herself on one leg.

"So this is your youngest, Maud," Mrs. Fawcett said graciously. "How many years is it now since you left me?"

"Nineteen years, ma'am."

"Your family are well?"

"Oh yes, ma'am. Mr. Willoughby's as well as he can be—after his accident you know—and my son is into the railways—over at Three Bridges. Lillian, my eldest, she's nearly finished her training with Miss Clark."

"And now you would like . . . Sophie? . . . to begin her training?"

"If you had an opening, Mrs. Fawcett, ma'am. I heard that Meg Jenkins was leaving, and thought that perhaps you'd have a place for Sophie in the house." She paused and then added, "I'd prefer her to go in the house and not the kitchen."

"Yes . . . well . . . I see. I could make a space for her, I suppose. She's young of course and will need training."

"She's good about the house, ma'am. I've seen to that. She knows the right way to do things."

"I see." Mrs. Fawcett bit her thin lips together and stared hard at Sophie. The child had quite a bright, intelligent little face, not pretty, but intelligent. She was clean, but a little untidy. One stocking was slightly wrinkled and the thick mane of hair needed attention.

"Does she have her uniform?"

"Oh yes, Mrs. Fawcett. Her sister's made all that for her. My eldest girl you know, Lillian, she's apprenticed to . . ."

"Yes, quite. So you said. Well, I think we could take her on for a six months' trial period. Living in, of course."

"Of course."

"I'll start her at fifteen pounds a year, and we'll see how she shapes."

"Thank you, ma'am." She turned to Sophie and "ticked ticked" at her. Sophie, a trifle sullenly, Mrs. Fawcett thought, bobbed slightly and said, "Thank you, ma'am." Mrs. Fawcett gave the child a gracious smile. Sophie was just the kind of house-maid she liked, strong, clean, from an excellent background, and yet needing several edges knocked off. Mrs. Fawcett was very good at knocking edges off.

"While you're here, Mrs. Willoughby, I would like to raise the matter of the Barshinskey child."

Mrs. Willoughby looked faintly puzzled. "She's giving satis-faction, isn't she, Mrs. Fawcett? She's such a good, quiet little thing, and so tidy and well turned out I can't imagine her being any trouble."

"No trouble, Mrs. Willoughby, except perhaps in her manner sometimes. She is not quite as . . . respectful as I would like. I cannot help feeling that, in spite of my undertaking to you about her Sundays off, she would be better going to church with the other servants."

Mrs. Willoughby said nothing.

"For one thing there is my Sunday afternoon girls' Bible class. On her Sundays in, Daisy May naturally attends my class. It seems a pity that every other Sunday she misses them."

"But she goes to the Bible class at the Mission."

"Yes . . . well . . . but that is exactly what I am talking about. It would be far more sensible if she just worshiped in one place."

Over Mrs. Willoughby's face came an expression of stubborn politeness. Mrs. Fawcett recognized the look. She had seen it before on the face of the village nonconformists.

"I shall have to ask my husband about that," she said tone-lessly. They all said that, these Mission women who were as tough and self-opinionated as any man, but when it came to asking them for a decision they always pretended they were timid creatures bowing to the authority of the male. Mrs. Fawcett knew a spasm of really quite justifiable anger.

"I don't actually see that it has a great deal to do with Mr. Willoughby," she said firmly. "Daisy May's home is here in this house and she was placed in my charge with the full permission of the vicar and the Parish Council. Mr. Fawcett and I are responsible for both her moral and physical well-being."

Mrs. Willoughby sat very straight on her chair. "That's very true, ma'am. But you see, when Daisy May's mother died she trusted her to me, to see that she was brought up rightly. We couldn't keep her ourselves, but we would always want to do the right thing by her. I don't think changing horses in midstream, as it were—begging your pardon, ma'am—would be at all the right thing."

Mrs. Fawcett's nostrils flared slightly. "Of course, I should never have made the concession at the beginning. I should have insisted on church attendance the first day she came here."

"And of course," said Mrs. Willoughby, steamrolling on as though Mrs. Fawcett hadn't spoken, "Daisy May's mother was a Quaker. I think our form of worship is more in keeping with her mother's faith than the church."

There was a stony silence in the room as the two ladies reached an impasse. Mrs. Fawcett wasn't prepared to use her position and status to override Mrs. Willoughby, and Mrs. Willoughby wasn't prepared to be overridden, even in view of the fact that her daughter had just been taken into Mrs. Fawcett's employment. Sophie's eyes darted from one to the other, her interest thoroughly roused. She backed her ma to win.

"Myself," said Mrs. Willoughby coolly, "I think the present arrangement is very fair. One week she attends your Bible class, the other week she comes to the Mission with us. When she is old enough she can choose for herself where she wants to go."

Another silence, while Mrs. Fawcett waited in vain for Mrs. Willoughby to back down. But she knew she wasn't going to and

Mrs. Fawcett suddenly realized how very foolish she would look if she continued to battle over the soul of an unimportant servant girl. She had given her word to Mrs. Willoughby three years ago, and if she broke it now she would lose face.

"As you wish, Mrs. Willoughby," she said icily, and rose, signifying that the interview was over.

"Oh! We didn't agree to Sophie's time off," said Mrs. Willoughby on the way to the door.

"Alternate Sundays, and one evening on alternate weeks. I shall expect her in by nine o'clock on her afternoons off." She had been thinking of giving the girl an evening off every week, but Mrs. Willoughby deserved to be punished.

"That will be all right. When would you like her to begin?"

"You can send her box up on Saturday evening."

She had the satisfaction of seeing Sophie's face fall and settle into lines of despondency. She felt quite genially disposed toward her. It was her mother who had caused the annoyance after all. . . .

Yet strangely, after a few days, she felt no animosity at all toward the Willoughbys. All her resentment over the matter was directed toward Daisy May Barshinskey. Somehow it was all her fault.

Another truckle bed was put into Daisy May's attic room, and on Saturday evening, Sophie arrived, her father accompanying her and carrying her box. He came into the kitchen and then took it up the four flights of stairs. When he came back, he nodded to Mrs. Bramble, winked at Sophie, and was gone. Sophie stood looking depressed. Her career in service had begun, three years after Daisy May.

If she felt despondent about her new position, she quickly came to realize that, compared with Daisy May, she had nothing to complain about. Daisy May was senior to her in service, and that seniority should have manifested itself in small but distinctive ways. Being served first at kitchen meals, being allowed to pop out of the house for a few minutes when it wasn't her day off. But it became apparent that Daisy May was still the tweeny, still the charity child at the beck and call of anyone who couldn't get through their work quickly enough. Sophie, at first astonished, quickly became furious on Daisy May's behalf, and her wrath blew into open indignation when she discovered that Daisy May received no salary for her services.

"But how can she!" she squealed indignantly. "How can she employ you when she doesn't pay you any wages? I shall tell Ma, and I shall tell my pa and he'll do something about it. How *dare* she! When I'm getting fifteen pounds a year and I haven't even trained yet!"

"I'd rather you didn't tell anyone, Sophie," said Daisy May firmly. "I've worked it out in my own mind. She kept me for two years while I went to school, so I'll work for her for nothing for another two years. Then I'll ask for wages."

"But that's not fair," cried Sophie. "Even while you were at school you were working, and all she gave you was a bit of old food and some aprons. I mean, how do you live? Where do you get your collection money and your stockings and things like that?"

"Mrs. Bramble tells Mrs. Fawcett when I need new stockings or my shoes mending or anything like that. And Mrs. Fawcett gives me stockings and aprons for my Christmas box. And then I do all Mrs. Bramble's mending and laundry for her and she pays me a bit each week—enough for the collection and to save up for little odds and ends."

"Well, I'm going to tell my ma! She'll get you out of here and find you another position. It's just not right. Not right at all!"

"Please don't tell anyone, Sophie," said Daisy, with rather a hard, authoritative note in her voice. "I've thought out for myself what I'm going to do. I don't want to leave here—it's the best place in the village to be trained. Your ma knows that. That's why she got you in here. And the food's good—just look at the way the servants eat at Borer's or the vicarage."

"You could get just as good a place somewhere else, Dais! Oh, not in this village perhaps, but over Edenbridge way. There's lots of big houses there."

"But I don't want to leave the village." There was desperation in Daisy's voice. She knew, from past experience, that Sophie's loyalty and determination, once given its head, was almost impossible to control. "I like this village and I don't ever want to leave."

Sophie looked at her, amazed. "Stay here for the rest of your life? Never go anywhere or do anything exciting! Oh, I just wish I had the chance! If only I were a boy then I could go on the railway like Edwin. Just think of all the places he goes to!"

"I've done enough of that," said Daisy May tersely. "All I want for the rest of my life is to stay in one place, and have a nice cottage with a garden and friends, and the meeting on Sundays, and a cat and a dog and nice china, and everyone knowing who I am when I go to the village shop. And when I die I want to be buried in this churchyard right alongside my ma." She smiled at Sophie, who was looking puzzled and a little cross. "You've never really understood, Soph. But only because you've got all the things that I want. You've always had them so they don't mean anything to you. But that's why I want to stay here, at Fawcett's, even though I know she doesn't like me. If I stay here I'm making a place for myself in the village and one day they'll forget about my pa and about"—she swallowed—"about Galina. I'll be Daisy May Barshinskey from Fawcett's."

She was implacable and nothing that Sophie said would move her. Most of the time Daisy did what Sophie told her to, but when her mind was made up nothing would budge her.

She worked her extra year out, just as she said she would, and then she asked to speak to Mrs. Fawcett one morning just before she left the kitchen.

"Yes, well, what is it, Daisy May? I'm sure whatever it is you can say it in front of Mrs. Bramble."

"It's a private matter, ma'am."

"Nonsense! What could you possibly have to say that would be private? Whatever is it you want? I don't have all the morning to spend chatting in the kitchen."

"Please, ma'am, I'm fifteen now."

"I'm well aware of that, Daisy May."

"You very kindly gave me my keep for two years while I finished my schooling, up till I was thirteen, and I've worked for another two years full time now, and I was wondering, ma'am, if you could see your way to paying me a wage."

A slow flush began to suffuse Mrs. Fawcett's face. She glared at Mrs. Bramble who, interested but not impervious to the glare, hurriedly vanished into the scullery.

"I'm not sure I quite understand you, Daisy May. I had thought this was your home."

"Oh, no, ma'am," said Daisy May politely. "You was very good and took me in when I had nowhere to go, but it isn't my home. Home is where you live with your relations, isn't it?"

"I was not aware you had any relations with whom to live," said Mrs. Fawcett coldly, and she had the satisfaction of seeing Daisy May falter.

"That's true, ma'am, but all the same I was wondering if you could see your way to paying me a wage, like the other girls."

"I shall give the matter some thought," said Mrs. Fawcett, rising majestically and making her way toward the kitchen door. As she was leaving she heard Daisy May saying respectfully, "Thank you, ma'am." She would have been infinitely gratified if she could have seen Daisy May, after she had left the room, leaning against the table to steady her shaking knees. She didn't like the girl, but to be fair the matter of the wages was an oversight. She'd given the girl a home while she was at school and had then really ceased to think about her. She was a mean-spirited woman but she wasn't miserly and she resented the fact that Daisy had had to point out her shortcomings as an employer. She couldn't bear to tell Daisy herself that she would pay her a wage. Instead she sent for Mrs. Bramble.

"Do you find Daisy satisfactory, Cook?"

"Yes, indeed, ma'am. She's an able and willing little body, and she's the makings of a good cook. I'm training her nicely, ma'am. It's a pleasure to teach someone who wants to learn as much as she does."

"Yes . . . well . . . you may tell her that I shall pay her a wage of thirteen pounds a year, but of course from now on she will have to pay for all her own clothes and boot repairs."

"I'll tell her, ma'am. I don't think you'll find it'll be money wasted."

Mrs. Fawcett had her slight revenge the following Sunday when Daisy May attended her Bible class. In the prayers, Mrs. Fawcett made a special plea to the Lord that one especial child present should be blessed with the gift of gratitude, should be humbly aware of the great advantages heaped upon her by unselfish benefactors. A glance at Daisy's face after the Amen did much to restore Mrs. Fawcett's good humor.

Daisy never, in the years that followed, caught up with Sophie's salary. But it never bothered her and in some curious way she always had more money than Sophie. Sophie was given to whims and extravagances, like putting a down payment on a set of encyclopedias and then never having the money for the payments. She spent her money on a wide variety of what her mother called "fripperies"—a secondhand silk shawl that looked as though it had come from China, an Indian brass elephant bell, an ivory crocodile said to be carved from the tusk of an elephant. Sophie could never resist the exotic and their attic bedroom sometimes resembled an Eastern bazaar (hastily cleared into the box before Mrs. Fawcett made her weekly inspection). Sophie could never understand how Daisy, who received less, always seemed to have more.

"Don't you ever want to buy things, Dais? Books and frocks and things? Don't you get tired of mending all your old things and making do with passed-down clothes?"

"I'm going to spend it all one day. I'm saving it now, but one day, you'll see, I'm going out and I'm going to spend the lot!"

"But when, Dais?"

"I'm not sure. But I'll know when the time comes. Perhaps Ivan will come home one day and we'll have a cottage together. I'll have monogrammed sheets and Royal Derby china and cut-glass dishes. Everything will be new and beautiful."

"Oh, Dais," said Sophie dreamily. "Don't you just wish you

were like Edwin and Ivan? They lead such exciting lives, not like us. Nothing exciting ever happens to us."

"I think life's exciting," said Daisy. "I think it's very exciting."

Sophie stared at her in horror. "You can't think that, Daisy! How can you possibly think that? What exciting things ever happen to you?"

It was their Sunday off and they were changing into their off-duty clothes ready to go home. Daisy put down her hairbrush and stared out the dormer window.

"Today I made a soufflé, and Mrs. Fawcett told Mrs. Bramble how good it was. She thought Mrs. Bramble had made it. And spring is coming—it's always exciting when spring comes. And"—she gave Sophie a guarded look—"and it's Edwin's off-duty Sunday, so we'll be seeing him."

"That's true," said Sophie gloomily. "I suppose Edwin is something to look forward to."

Their tall handsome brother was invested with the kind of glamour that could only come from living in London. To his family he epitomized cosmopolitan life, sophistication, and when their parents weren't around he always had some enlivening anecdote about city life—the theaters, the grand hotels, the public houses, everything that was at once wicked and infinitely desirable.

"Yes, there's Edwin," Sophie repeated, cheering a little. "That's something to look forward to."

Often he was waiting for them outside the kitchen and both their faces took on a crestfallen look when he wasn't there.

"Expect he's still talking to Dad at home," said Sophie, and they hurried along, taking the short cut through the fields and lanes to get home, both of them suddenly restless, possibly because of the bright winter sunshine or perhaps because they had talked themselves into a state where Edwin was more exciting than usual. When they got home, Lillian was just getting ready for Bible class and was putting her hat on in the parlor. The house seemed empty.

"Where's everyone?" asked Sophie peremptorily.

"Don't tread all the mud on your shoes through the house! Why are you so muddy anyway?"

"We came through the lanes. Where's everyone?"

"Mum and Dad are having a rest upstairs."

"Where's Edwin?"

"Not coming. He sent a note. He's had to do extra shifts."

It took them awhile to recover. It was silly really. Edwin wasn't there every weekend, and time off was time off, to be enjoyed as much as possible. It was just that they'd been expecting him and now, Sunday with just Mum, Dad, and Lillian seemed a bit flat. Still, there was always the next time. . . .

But the following month, when whatever shifts he was on he should have had one off, Edwin still didn't come.

It started slowly at first. He saw Galina and Mr. Rautenberg once a week and that once a week stood out like a beacon of light, beckoning the days forward, drawing the hours until they took him once more into their magic circle. All the week he would think about her, the way her profile looked when she turned her head, her eyes, sometimes gold, sometimes black, that gazed at him so that he was lost, unable to look away first. She had a way of touching him, carelessly intimate, laughing at some statement of his, saying "Dear Edwin" and placing her smooth brown hand alongside his neck in a way that sent the blood coursing through his veins. Everything about her was beautiful, exciting, warm. Sometimes she had the naïveté of a child and a walk by the river eating hot chestnuts would charm her just as much as dinner at the Café Royal. Not that Edwin ever went there with them, but when she told him she was going she would clap her hands together and laugh in just the same way.

He tried to pay his share of their amusements, dipping into his savings for bottles of champagne he could not afford, for cab fares, and on one occasion for good seats at the theater. He bought a secondhand evening suit from a stall in Petticoat Lane and had it altered to fit him. He could see it wasn't the same as

221

the suits worn by the people around him but he had to buy it. It made him feel less of an outsider, made him part of a wonderful illusory world that he knew would last for only a short time. He paid for what he could, trying to hold onto his pride and self-respect, but even so he knew that their gay convivial evenings were mostly financed by Mr. Rautenberg. Twice they went to parties given by Galina's theatrical friends where nobody paid. That was fine. There he felt on equal terms with them. But nearly always it was Mr. Rautenberg who paid for the boxes at the theater, the suppers, the excursions, the long rides in the hackney cabs.

That Saturday in Galina's rooms had set the pattern for the rest of their evenings. Edwin had arrived there with a bottle of champagne that had cost him five shillings—a huge hunk of his weekly wage—and a posy of spring flowers. Mr. Rautenberg had arrived with caviar, smoked salmon, a ham, grapes, marrons glacés, and more champagne. He had made much of Edwin's bottle, insisting that it be opened first, saying it was of excellent vintage (Edwin had had to trust the man in the Soho wine shop), that toasts drunk in Edwin's champagne were the ones that counted, but nothing could disguise the fact that they were really still eating Mr. Rautenberg's supper. Galina had invited another artiste from the theater, a blond girl who sang comic verses. Edwin could not even remember her name.

In February came their last supper. It was six weeks since they had met, six weeks of incredible, unreal, glamorous life, a life that Edwin knew would come to an end when Mr. Rautenberg went back to Russia. For how could he afford to finance the parties and outings that made their every meeting so memorable?

For their last evening Mr. Rautenberg said he had a surprise, and the surprise came when the cab (summoned as usual by Edwin) drove not to the restaurant in Long Acre, or Pagani's, but into the labyrinth of small streets behind Leicester Square. Edwin was not altogether a stranger to Soho—the place fascinated him with its cosmopolitan population and foreign food stores. Frequently he spent part of his Saturday evenings wandering through the late night market, looking at the strange dark faces lit in the naphtha flares on the stalls. He bought the "shampanyer" there, and humbler foods that he tried out for himself. But he had never entered any of the cafés or restaurants there, deterred somewhat by the feeling that he would be an outsider intruding into a private house.

But now Mr. Rautenberg led them to a quiet and unobtrusive green door from which strange smells issued. They were shown into a smallish room, no more than twelve tables, the walls papered dark red and bordered with mosaics. A crimson plush curtain hung down from the ceiling halfway across the room, and behind it was a piano and an open space.

"Good," said Mr. Rautenberg. "First we shall eat a real Russian dinner—this is the *only* place in London to eat Russian food, and then we shall dance."

Edwin felt a glow of desperate happiness engulf him. It was their last evening and already he knew that it was going to be their best. He couldn't dance but that didn't matter. He was here in this world of light and shade and color with two people who had, for some inexplicable reason, decided to include him in their lives.

Mr. Rautenberg ordered the meal in Russian, and Galina laughed and clapped her hands together and said, "I know everything he says. It is like when my papa and I would speak together. I understand everything!" She tilted her face toward Mr. Rautenberg and said, "When you take me to St. Petersburg, Heikki, I shall understand everything! I shall be able to talk to everyone!"

They drank champagne and vodka and ate a meal which Edwin hardly noticed. As the evening advanced he tried to comfort himself with the thought that perhaps this would not be the end of their meetings. For he could go to see Galina on the stage, and afterward he could see her for just a few moments in her dressing room and, perhaps, when Mr. Rautenberg returned . . . but no, reason and pride prevailed. He could not continue taking, being a permanent guest, the one to call the cab, to say thank you, to admire, feeling always that he was in the presence of lustrous beings.

"You are silent, my young friend. It is the food. Russian food is perhaps a little heavy to English stomachs."

"Oh no, Mr. Rautenberg. The food was good, very good. Wonderful."

"So. What is wrong?"

"It is the last evening."

"For now, yes! But you will still see my little Galina, no? And when I come again, then we shall have more parties, more excursions."

Edwin smiled but said nothing. He didn't know how to begin explaining his confusion over money and pride.

A thin, white-faced man in black sat down and began to play the piano and immediately Galina wanted to dance. She and Mr. Rautenberg revolved gently around the floor, a strangely incongruous couple, Mr. Rautenberg bobbing with energetic clumsiness, beads of perspiration breaking out on his forehead, Galina gliding and whirling with fragile ease. When they returned Galina looked expectantly at Edwin.

"I can't dance," he muttered. "You must dance with Heikki again."

"Please try!"

"I can't."

"You must! I will teach you. Now!" She pulled at his arm and suddenly the touch of her made him angry. She was so spoiled and so beautiful. If she wasn't so spoiled he could go on seeing her. If it wasn't for Mr. Rautenberg buying everything for them, being so generous, so kind, he could ask her to share simpler pleasures. If Mr. Rautenberg wasn't so nice he could betray him, try to steal this wanton elusive woman from him. He realized he wanted to cry, he was so confused, so troubled and unclear about why he couldn't do it. Their last evening was suddenly painful and unhappy—unhappy because he knew that once more he was condemned to the misery of his boyhood.

"Come now, Edwin! You must dance with me!"

"Leave me alone!" He jerked his arm roughly away from her and her eyes grew round with petulant anger then, to his amazement, filled with tears.

"I'm sorry . . . I didn't mean . . . I just . . . I can't dance and I don't want to. You must understand that . . . but I didn't mean . . . I'm sorry, Galina, so sorry."

"And see," said Mr. Rautenberg quietly, staring at each of them in turn. "See, here is someone who wishes to dance with you. And no, sir, I have no objection to my young friend dancing with you." A thin middle-aged man from another table had come over and bowed, first to Galina, and then to Mr. Rautenberg. Galina smiled, blinked, and stared again at Edwin.

"Go on," he muttered. "Have a good time and dance."

She went away with the stranger and silently they watched her. Mr. Rautenberg took out his cigar case and began to cut the end of a cigar.

"You must look after Galina until I return again," he said.

Edwin closed his eyes for a second. "I can't."

"Why? Because you do not have money for all this?"

"That's part of it."

"I do not want to know the rest. You are mad if you think I do not know it already." He finished cutting the cigar and took a long time lighting it. Then he stared at the glowing end.

"I do not know how you can arrange your life without money, but even so you must look after Galina until I return again. If it were possible I would leave money for you, but this would be wrong, very wrong, you agree?"

Struggling in misunderstanding, and with a sense of growing oppression in his heart, Edwin nodded. Mr. Rautenberg flicked his cigar ash onto the floor at his side.

"Good. That is understood." He sighed a little. "It will not be easy for you. It is never easy without money. I hope your nice honest simple life on your railway engine will not be destroyed."

"I . . ."

"I will probably be back in about six weeks. I shall try to make it less. It is difficult for me too. I have a wife and child in

225

Moscow. But I think you know you must look after Galina while I am gone. I think, even if I did not say this thing to you, you would still see her. I think this is so, is it not?"

"Yes. I suppose it is."

"Sometimes one has no choice. There is only one way to go."

"Yes."

Mr. Rautenberg stared down at the table, at his fattish hand covered in small black hairs. "You and I, between us, we have everything she wants," he murmured.

Edwin felt his heart pounding. He was afraid and even while he was afraid he knew it was too late to do anything about it. Whatever Mr. Rautenberg was saying—and he only half understood—it was too late to do anything about it and it had been from the moment he had seen her on the stage of the New Cross Empire.

"You don't understand," he said, suddenly desperate. "This, all this, is so wrong for me. My family, where I come from, everyone I know, they would think I was mad."

"We are both mad."

"What will happen?"

"What will happen?" He stood up and Edwin, puzzled, realized that Galina had returned to them. Her face was glowing and all resentment at Edwin's refusal had been forgotten.

"What will happen," said Mr. Rautenberg jovially, "is that after this wonderful evening you will both enjoy yourselves just a little—only a little because you will miss me—until your Uncle Heikki returns to you."

"Oh yes, Heikki dear! We shall want you to return—every minute we shall want you to return!"

"You would like to dance some more?"

"I think we should go," said Edwin suddenly. He felt he could take no more. "I will get a cab."

If Galina protested he did not hear, for he was out in the Soho street and down into Shaftesbury Avenue to find a cab. The fresh air soothed a little but his overwhelming feeling was one of unhappiness, not only for himself but also for Mr. Rautenberg.

When the cab came he didn't get in with them as he usually did. He wandered around the Soho streets, ignoring taunts and invitations, wondering what he should do, feeling trapped and desperate but yet not knowing quite what had trapped him. When he arrived home it was three in the morning and, as he was on early turn, it hardly seemed worthwhile going to bed. But he lay down and slept for an hour, then changed his clothes and went to work. And in the sanity of the locomotive sheds he felt his uneasiness evaporate a little.

He didn't go near her for three days, and during that time he came to an acceptance of certain things and a methodical planning of others. He accepted that whatever Mr. Rautenberg had been saying, he had to see her again and see her frequently, for now he could not imagine his life without her. Sometimes, in his wildest moments, he envisaged a life where he was married to her, living in a neat little house in Southwark, taking her home to the village to meet his family once more, this time as a respected and respectable wife. And when bitter reality broke the dream he would laugh sourly at himself and then make up his mind not to look ahead but just accept that life without her was unthinkable.

But because he was a Willoughby, and had his share of that family's common sense, he knew that his immediate life must be mapped out with some degree of order. He could not afford to look after Galina the way Mr. Rautenberg did. But he could manage the lesser attractions—tea at Slater's instead of dinner at the Café Royal, the pleasure steamer to Southend instead of the private cab all the way to Richmond. He went back to Soho and painstakingly studied the foreign menus outside the cafés. It was possible to have a late supper there for as little as eightpence. He could manage that. With what he earned, and with his savings, he could manage until Mr. Rautenberg returned, or until something else happened. . . . And when, after three days, he had arrived at the decision that he could temporarily cope with a life that included Galina, he went straight from his early shift to her rooms in Baywater. Mrs. Keith gave him a curious glance when she let him in.

"I suppose you'll want to go up and see 'er?"

"Yes, if that's all right, Mrs. Keith."

"Well, you know your way, I suppose. You were 'ere enough with 'im. She's in."

He was aware of her watching him up the stairs, curious and yet not critical. He knocked on the door of Galina's sitting room and when there was no answer he turned the handle and called to her. There was no answer but from the bedroom he heard what sounded like a stifled sob.

"Galina!"

He opened the bedroom door. She was lying in a crumpled heap on the bed. She wore a white silk robe that was dirty and her hair looked dull and knotted. When she turned her face toward him he could see she had been crying.

"Why, Galina! What's the matter?"

She slumped her head down on the pillow and muttered, "Nothing."

He had imagined many things when he saw her again, but this sad, sulky, woebegone creature was none of them. He crossed to the bed and gently touched her wrist.

"What's the matter, Galina? Are you ill?"

Tears began to run down her swollen face. She turned her head into the pillow and began to sob.

"Galina, what is it? You must tell me."

He put his hands on her shoulders and pulled her in to his chest. She felt small and fragile held against him, like a tiny, shaking bird. "What's the matter? Please tell me!"

"I felt so alone!" she sobbed. "Heikki went away, and suddenly you weren't there either. And nobody came near me, not for days and days. And I haven't a booking for two weeks, and there was nowhere to go, and no one to see." She caught her breath and sobbed afresh. "I was so alone," she cried.

"But it was only three days, Galina. Only three days."

"It was three days! All on my own!"

"I can't always see you, Galina. I have my work, my shifts. I can't always be with you."

"But if I know you're coming, it's all right! Only I didn't know if you'd ever come again. And I don't know how to find you . . . I don't know where you live or where you work. I couldn't find you . . . oh, Edwin . . ."

He closed his eyes, trying to subdue the surging sense of elation rising within him. She was small, shaking, soft. She was clinging to him and her cries were those of a frightened, abandoned creature. He stroked her tangled hair and rocked her gently to and fro in his arms.

"Why didn't you go out with your friends?" he asked quietly. "What was her name, Rose, the girl who was here that night. And your other friends, all your friends from the theater, why didn't you see them?"

"I don't have any friends," she sobbed. "I only have you and Heikki . . ."

He smiled over the top of her head. "That's silly, Galina. You have lots of friends."

She lifted her head and stared up at him, tears still welling over onto her cheeks. But when she spoke it was quietly and in puzzled surprise.

"But no, Edwin," she said. "I don't have any friends. I never did. You know that. I never had friends. Only men."

In the silence that followed he felt her grow still in his arms. There was a part of him that wanted to crush her, squeeze the breath out of her until she hurt the way he hurt. He didn't want to think about her men. There were too many and he felt savage with her for reminding him of them. And there was another part of him, the adult part, that felt a terrible pity for her. She was so beautiful, so enchanting and charming and winsome. Why did she have no friends?

"Edwin?"

The voice was no longer tearful. There was a heady excitement about the way she said it. He was aware, again, of the smallness and softness of her against his body. When she raised her face again he could not believe it could have changed so quickly. The flush of tears had changed to a feverish glow that made her eyes bright.

"Edwin . . ."

She put her arms up around his neck and raised her face to his cheek. He felt again that surge of excitement that always happened when she touched him. She began to kiss his face, small, soft kisses, pressing up against him, murmuring, "Edwin, I love you. Oh, Edwin, I love you," and suddenly he could stand no more and the blood coursing through his veins, beating in his heart so loudly he could hardly hear her, exploded into a total loss of control. He forgot his doubts, his planning, his caution. He forgot Heikki, and all the others that had been before Heikki. As he felt her mouth against the side of his throat he groaned and pushed her back onto the pillow, rejoicing in the feel of her body beneath the thin white silk.

12 EVERY MOMENT THAT HE WASN'T WITH HER SEEMED empty and wasted. He could think of no one, nothing except her. He found himself wanting to talk about her, to Bassy, anyone, just because talking about her when she wasn't there brought her closer. But then, just about to tell Bassy of his dream, his love, a sense of distaste would make him draw quickly away. To speak of her to anyone who was ordinary was to defile and put the stamp of common human beings upon her. She was too rare to be spoken of by ordinary mortals.

Every moment he wasn't on duty he rushed to be with her, depriving himself of sleep and the company of any but her. He watched her from an infinite variety of galleries until they all blurred into one another, and he could not remember whether he had been there before or not. Often, during the other acts, he would find he had dozed off into an uncomfortable slumber, only to wake with a sense of pounding excitement as he heard the first few bars of her music.

Afterward there was the cab ride to a Soho eating house, then back to her rooms and while she was still sleeping he would rise and let himself quietly out of the house and begin the long walk home to his lodgings, where he changed and went straight to work.

At first he was afraid that she would miss all the places Heikki Rautenberg had taken her to—Gatti's, the Trocadero, the Café Royal. But she didn't seem to mind where she went or what she did so long as it was new and gay, with bright lights and music. She liked doing almost anything providing she hadn't done it before. Once he took her to the Zoological Gardens and, to his amazement, she went up on the back of an elephant with exactly the same cry of delight as when Mr. Rautenberg had taken them all the way to Kew Gardens in a motor taxi cab.

On another day off, he took her to Brighton, but the wind blew roughly from the sea, and she became bored and uncomfortable. Sometimes, in one of his rare, sane moments, he would reflect on how she could make him behave in a way, and do things, that no one else ever could. She never demanded anything, was never bad-tempered or angry, but her small frown, her shrug of boredom or irritation made him quickly want to put things right, to see the slow, wonderful smile spread over her features, feel her hand slip softly into his arm with, "Oh, Edwin, I do love you! I do love you!"

He bought her things—things that were nothing compared with the largesse showered upon her by Heikki, but things, even so, that he could ill afford as his savings steadily diminished—a pair of gloves that she admired in a shop window one day, a string of glass beads that were worth nothing compared with the amber and pearls that Heikki had given her. But they were pretty and her eyes lit up when he said he would buy them for her and she behaved as though they were just as valuable as the finer jewels.

Occasionally, not very often, a fine sweat would break out on his brow and with a sinking of the stomach he would think, how will it end? What will happen to us? But he would thrust such thoughts quickly away, and lose himself in the memory of the smell of her, the feel of her, and the recollection of her eyes looking up into his, submissive and adoring, loving him. He did not doubt that she loved him. What she felt for Heikki, for the others, he did not know. But he knew without doubt that in her amoral, guileless way she loved him, and he gave himself up entirely to the dream he was living in, determined not to spoil it now by thinking of what must come.

The dream broke at the end of March. He arrived at Galina's rooms and had to pass Mrs. Keith on the stairs. She gave him what was almost a malicious smile. He didn't like her but was honest enough to admit that it was probably his own conscience that made him feel so. She never remarked on the hours he spent in Galina's rooms—it wasn't the kind of house where anyone worried about that kind of thing—but he hated the way the woman looked at him, knowing and derisive.

"She's got some news for you today," she said, grinning. "Oh, full of 'erself she is today—just wait till you sees 'er."

He tried to walk slowly, calmly up the stairs, knowing Mrs. Keith's eyes were on him, and when he arrived at the top he knocked quietly on Galina's door.

"Galina?"

"Edwin! Oh, come in, come in!"

When he opened the door she flung herself at him, her arms around his neck, eyes shining with excitement.

"Edwin! Oh, Edwin! Such wonderful news . . . Heikki is coming, and Edwin! This time when he returns to St. Petersburg he is going to take me with him. I cannot believe it! After all these years, all the promises that my papa made to me, I am really going back to Russia. I never thought it would happen. . . . Oh, Heikki promised that one day . . . but then my papa used to say one day, too, and it never happened. But now it is going to happen. See"—she waved a sheet of paper in the air— "I have a letter from him, a little letter, and he says it is all arranged. I am to stay in his apartment in St. Petersburg, stay there for as long as I wish. Oh, Edwin! Can you believe that at last I am really going to Russia!"

So this was how it was going to end. There was a leaden weight in his stomach, a cruel sense of hurt that she could not even think how it would be for him.

"Isn't it wonderful, Edwin?"

He couldn't answer. Despair choked his words and he could say nothing. He looked at her, light and ephemeral as she darted about the room, and tried to absorb the fact that soon she wouldn't be there anymore. She would vanish. The purpose would be gone from his life.

"We must celebrate, Edwin! Let us go somewhere exciting for luncheon. Let us have champagne. I am so excited I must do something to celebrate."

"No!"

She stared at him, eyes widening as she saw his face.

"I can't bear it, Galina! I can't bear it . . ."

"Why, Edwin . . ." she faltered.

"You say you love me. Hundreds of times you have said you loved me. And I believed you. I could not believe we would have been so happy if you had not loved me. And now . . . here you say you are going . . . going right away and you want to drink champagne? Galina! Don't you know . . . don't you know . . ." He put his hands up to his face, unable to look at her, unable to cope with the misery inside him.

"But, Edwin," she said slowly, "I do love you. And I will miss you, but only for a little while. I expect I shall come back and then I will see you again."

"No." Suddenly he hated her, hated her shallowness, her wantonness, her childlike inability to hold anything in her head or heart for very long. Anger flared in his heart. He took two quick strides across the room toward her and caught her shoulders roughly in his hands. Violently he shook her.

"How could you? How could you?" he cried.

"Edwin!"

The pretty, soft, frightened voice fueled his anger even more. He put his hand inside the neck of her shirtwaist and wrenched it open. Buttons tore off and she gave a tiny breathless scream. He placed one hand around her throat. It was so small that his hand totally encompassed it, and he pushed her, pulled her back toward the bed.

"You bitch!" he cried despairingly. "You selfish bitch!" Then he threw her onto the bed and hit her when she tried to struggle. Always when they had loved before he had been gentle, carried away on a tide of sensual indolence that was slow and deep and moving. But now he just wanted to hurt her and he relinquished any last control and used her body to express his bitterness, his hatred. Every time she cried or tried to beat his chest with her soft hands he struck her until finally she was pinned helplessly beneath him, a few last butterfly movements indicating her fear.

Afterward, drained of hatred, when she lay weeping in his

arms, he felt the tears running down his own face, and the despair was even worse than it had been before.

"Oh, Galina, Galina, forgive me! I've hurt you! I shouldn't have hurt you . . . I didn't want to hurt you . . ."

Her arms were suddenly raised around his neck and she began to kiss him. "I do love you, Edwin. You must believe me that I do love you. You . . . you see, you are different, Edwin . . . different from all the others . . ."

"Stop! Isn't it bad enough that you're going away! Do you have to speak of the others?"

"But I just wanted you to know, Edwin. I never . . . I never felt *young* with any of the others. They were always old, or if they were young they were sad and ugly, like that poor young man in the village. And then you came along . . . and you were so tall. . . ." Her voice faded away on a little choking sob.

"You'll meet other tall men," he said bitterly, and then as she began to kiss his face, his neck, despair flooded over him again, despair and love and the desire to possess her again, not cruelly this time, but in misery and anguish.

Afterward they dressed in silence and went out to eat in a small restaurant in the Bayswater Road. Galina was subdued, her eyes red and swollen, and her hand shook as she raised her fork to her mouth.

"How long before Mr. Rautenberg comes?"

"Three weeks." A long pause and then, "I shall miss you, Edwin. I really shall. . . ."

"Then why go?" he burst out, ignoring the curious looks of the other diners. "Why don't you stay here? You have a good life . . . you have plenty of theater bookings. You like playing and dancing on the stage. Why go?"

"Because I must," she answered in her little-girl voice. "We cannot go on as we are now, can we? We would get tired of each other, tired of doing the same things, of never having anything different to look forward to . . ."

"I wouldn't," he said wearily. "I wouldn't because I love you, Galina. I really love you."

"You don't understand, Edwin," she sighed. "I shall miss you . . . of course I shall miss you, and one day I shall return here and then it will be wonderful again . . . for a little while . . ."

"Would you marry me?" he asked roughly, and for a moment his heart stopped as he saw a look of wondering consideration come over her face. "Would you marry me, Galina? I have a good job. We wouldn't be poor and you could go on with the stage if that was what you wanted. I wouldn't mind . . ." he stopped as he saw her frown, then shudder slightly.

"Perhaps . . . one day we might marry. Not now."

"Why not now?"

"No. When I am richer perhaps then I might marry. But not now. . . ." She shuddered again. "Do you remember my mama? To live like that . . . terrible. And your mama, not much better . . . just work and drab clothes and no fun and no . . ."

"No. Of course not." It was ridiculous of him even to have thought of it. And slowly, as the knowledge of her coming departure became more settled in his mind, a fatalistic acceptance of despair began to envelop him. He had known that somehow it must end, and now that time had come. But he still had three weeks . . . three weeks when she belonged to him . . . three weeks, every moment of which must be savored and enjoyed to the full.

Strangely, in the next three weeks, their roles became reversed for he, with a frenetic desperation, threw himself into an interval of fun and enjoyment, determined to use every second with her as intensely as he could, while she, realizing at last that she would probably not see him again, became subject to moods of sudden sadness, of "this is the last time we shall do this together." He determined, to himself, that once Mr. Rautenberg arrived he would not see her again, even though she would not be departing immediately for St. Petersburg. He could not see Heikki Rautenberg now. There had been that curious conversation between them, when it seemed as though Mr. Rautenberg had known what was going to happen. But now that it had happened, Edwin did not want to see the fat little man again. He liked him and, curiously, he was not jealous of him, but he did not want to meet him, face to face. Sharing Galina as they did, it was impossible for them to meet.

And so the last night came, the night he had been dreading, and strangely it was all right because it was also unreal. He kept trying to tell himself that this was the last time he would be able to touch her, see her, love her, but he could not believe it, and it was with a sense of calm that he lay beside her in the darkness, listening to her gentle breathing. He had written a note already to leave by her bed. Galina thought they would meet again before she left, even though Mr. Rautenberg would be there. In her foolish, shallow way, she had spoken of them having their dinners and excursions together as they had done before. And Edwin, even now anxious to spare her the pain of a farewell, had let her go on believing this, even while he wrote the note, even while he passed his last evening with her.

He rose quietly and dressed, then placed the note on the table by her bed and left. As he walked through the silent streets he knew a mood of fatalistic acceptance. Later the misery would come—weeks and months of it most probably—but for now he felt calm and unreal, as though he were walking through an imaginary world, as though he did not really exist, as though, he realized with a sudden shock, his life had come to an end.

13 THERE SEEMED TO BE A LEADEN WEIGHT IN HIS HEART. He had read that phrase somewhere once, probably in one of Sophie's dreadful romances that she was given to reading. At the time he had thought how foolish it was, but now, in a detached, interested way, he realized that that was exactly how he felt. On the left side of his chest was a heavy lump, a weight of misery that never left him, not even when he slept. Sometimes it was just dull, hopeless despair. At other times it was a sharp anguish that made him want to burst out sobbing.

Pride made him hate her sometimes. She was wanton, a whore, and she had made him as bad as she was. He had never met anyone as selfish, as fickle-brained, as cruel as she was. But when he said these things to himself he found his despair grew worse. Everything that he thought about her was true. But it didn't matter. It didn't make any difference to the way he loved her.

The gods and Bassy somehow ensured that he got through his work without too many mistakes, although he knew he was working badly and several times his driver had to reprimand him, once —when Edwin had fired so incompetently they hardly got into Sevenoaks—angrily and severely. Edwin, shaken, did his best after that to concentrate during his hours of work. Strangely, all those weeks he had spent with Galina when he had had little or no sleep, he had never felt tired. Now he was constantly weary, longing for his shift to be over and then hating it when he had finished and had nothing to stop him thinking of her.

He couldn't go out with Bassy. It was too much of a strain and he knew he was miserable company. After a while Bassy stopped suggesting outings together. He couldn't go home. He was too ashamed. No one, except possibly Sophie, would understand, and why should he burden Sophie with a problem that

238

had been caused by his weakness, his own stupid infatuation, his own madness.

There were ten such days of misery, and expectation of many more. He came out of the sheds' entrance at the end of one of his shifts and began to walk up the Old Kent Road, vaguely aware of a hackney cab moving along beside him. It passed him, and then a small gloved hand fluttered urgently out of the window and he heard her voice.

"Edwin. Edwin! We want to speak to you. Heikki and I want to speak to you."

He was so confused, so bewildered, and so unable to cope with whatever was about to happen that he took no notice of the hand or the voice, but just began to run along the road. The cab moved faster.

"Edwin! Please wait, we must speak to you."

He stopped, aware suddenly of the ridiculous spectacle he was making of himself. Several of the men from the depot who had left at the same time as he were staring. He moved slowly toward the now stationary cab.

"Edwin. We must talk to you. Heikki has some wonderful news."

Slowly he raised his eyes to her face. She seemed thinner, her eyes even huger and blacker, and there was a nervous diffidence about her that he did not remember being there before. Just to look at her was agony.

"I think, my young friend, it would be well if you came with us into the carriage."

With the blood draining from his face, he opened the door and pulled himself up. He sat down, and then looked straight into Mr. Rautenberg's eyes. There was a moment of shared misery between them, then the moment passed and Mr. Rautenberg smiled.

"So. We have missed you, my young friend. It has not been easy to track you down. Our little girl here has never troubled to discover your address. All she knew was that you worked here, at the Bricklayer's Arms."

"But I was able to remember the times of your shifts, Edwin. Wasn't that clever of me?"

She was nervous, a little unsure of herself. Her hand, clutching a parasol, trembled a little.

"Heikki has a wonderful suggestion," she said breathlessly. "I told him . . . what a wonderful friend you had become . . . how you looked after me when he wasn't here . . . how you were . . . such an old friend, from my childhood. I don't have anybody else like that . . . not anyone who has known me for so many years . . . who knew me before . . ."

He just stared at her, listening to the bizarre words, unable to believe what she was saying, unable to believe that Heikki Rautenberg was sitting there with a smile on his face while she talked.

"And Heikki has said . . . I asked and he agreed . . . oh, Edwin! Why don't you come to Russia too? Not like me of course. Not properly . . . but you could work on one of Heikki's boats! And every ten days or so you would come to St. Petersburg and you could see me and . . . oh, Edwin . . ."

For he had begun to laugh, a laugh compounded of misery and shame and a sense of the ridiculousness of the whole scene. He laughed until tears ran down his face and he began to choke. Mr. Rautenberg sat there the whole time, saying nothing, the smile on his face unblinking, immovable.

"Edwin," she faltered, "why are you laughing?"

He just shook his head at her and let his sobs die away, then he stared out of the window at the passing streets. He wondered if now he was truly going mad. He hadn't slept properly for several nights. He knew he was off balance, holding onto his self-control with difficulty. Perhaps he had not understood Galina's words because he really was beginning to go mad.

"Do you think it is a good idea, Edwin?" she whispered, her eyes huge.

"What?"

"To come to St. Petersburg on one of Heikki's ships . . ."

He giggled again, didn't answer, and stared again out of the window. The cab had continued up into St. George's Road, going toward Westminster Bridge. Pigeons whirled and hung over Parliament and the trees were at their best, bursting with young green leaves.

"You could work on a ship just as easily as an engine, Edwin, couldn't you? And you'd like to see other countries, wouldn't you? You always said you wanted to see other places. And now, here is Heikki, dear, dear Heikki"—she turned suddenly and placed her hand over Mr. Rautenberg's, smiling at him with the same tremulous delight that she had used on him—"my dearest, dearest Heikki . . . he saw I was unhappy and so he said he would do this for you, Edwin . . . so that we can all see one another again . . . and soon, in St. Petersburg."

"No!" said Mr. Rautenberg suddenly. "Not all see each other. We shall not all see each other."

A motor taxi cab overtook them and the horse bridled slightly. Edwin could hear the cabby talking to the beast, and then they clopped on, over the bridge, up Whitehall and into Trafalgar Square. He stopped thinking he was mad and began to wonder if Mr. Rautenberg was mad instead. He stared into his face and said, "Why are you doing this, Heikki? You cannot be as miserable, as desperate as I am, so why are you doing this?"

The smile didn't fade from the little man's face but it took on a set look so that it seemed he was grimacing. Galina turned her head from one to the other. She was breathing heavily and her eyes looked the way they did just before she was going to cry.

"I don't understand!" she said. "It's all so simple. We can still all go on being good friends, seeing each other, having fun together. It is all so simple. Why are you behaving like this, Edwin?"

"I think, my dear little girl, that we shall take you back to your rooms, and then we shall speak together, your young friend and I. And from now on we shall travel in silence." He leaned out of the window and gave the cabby Galina's address. The smile faded from his face and he rested his two hands on the handle of his umbrella and looked out of the window. Galina

241

frowned, then smiled and nestled up close to Mr. Rautenberg. She was dressed from head to toe in a shade that reminded Edwin of primroses. Around her gloved wrist he noticed a bracelet of sparkling stones. She'd not had it before and he supposed they were diamonds, or something akin to diamonds, and a present from Mr. Rautenberg.

How was it possible to love her, knowing what he did of her past? How was it possible to love her, and not hate Heikki Rautenberg? He thought of all the people she had ruined, Mr. Hope-Browne, her father, her mother, her sister and brother. The Pilgrim Teacher, whatever his name was, how had she left him? Crushed and ruined like everyone else? And there were the others she had mentioned. The old man she had been house-keeper to, the man who had taught her to dance. What havoc and tragedy had she left in her wake? And now it was his turn. And whatever she did to him, however much he suffered he knew it would be worth it. For she was something special and rare and while she was there he had to love her and give her whatever she wanted.

"So. Here we are, my dear. Now you shall go in and rest a little. Later I shall return and take you to the theater in time for your performance."

"Goodbye, Edwin," she whispered nervously. "I will see you again, won't I?"

"Go in now, my dear."

She stood on the pavement, watching them as the cabby turned and went back toward the park. Edwin leaned out of the window and looked back at her. She was small and somehow pathetic in spite of her new spring clothes and her diamond brace-let.

"Do you wish to eat?"

"No. No, thank you."

"Neither am I hungry. I think we shall walk in the park."

The cabby put them down at the Bayswater entrance to Hyde Park and silently they walked through the gate. With a curious sense of detachment Edwin noticed the flowers and how brilliant they were against the season's new growth of grass.

"The tulips are pretty," he said, but Mr. Rautenberg didn't answer. They came at last to a seat overlooking the water and Mr. Rautenberg sat down, leaning his hands once more on his umbrella. Edwin sat beside him.

"These ten days, since I returned to London, have not been happy for me. I must think that for you, too, they have not been good."

"No."

"She has wept, and begged, and been so happy when I told her I would do what I could. I do not know how she has been able to do this thing to me. I am a mature man—a middle-aged man—and my life has known many women. I am thought to be clever in my business—certainly I have made much money. I tell myself that she is worthless. It is no use."

"No."

Mr. Rautenberg breathed softly to himself and closed his eyes for a moment. "So. This is what I will do. I will give you a letter that you will take to William Thomson and Company in Leith. This letter will mean, I think, that you will be taken on as a fireman in one of their ships." He turned his head and stared owlishly at Edwin. "I do not think it will be too different for you, being a fireman on a railway engine and a fireman on a ship."

"Your ship?"

"No. I have no ships. I am merchant. But to William Thomson and Company I am important. I think this letter will mean you will work on a ship going to St. Petersburg."

"I see."

"I will also give you a paper on which will be the address of my apartment in St. Petersburg. This address I will write in both English and Russian. You will not be able to read the Russian, and I do not know how you will manage in St. Petersburg. Everything is very different in St. Petersburg. You will not understand anyone. You will not be able to read the names of the places where you are. You will not know how to travel to the address of my apartment. All these things you must manage for yourself."

He didn't answer. The old feeling that he was going mad had

243

come back. Mr. Rautenberg was taking it seriously—the fact that he, Edwin Willoughby, fireman and sometime driver on a London freight service, was going to sign on as a stoker in a ship going to Russia. And to sign on, moreover, with the help of a man who should hate him.

"When you are in St. Petersburg I shall know. I shall acquaint myself with the information of what ship you are on, and when you are in St. Petersburg I shall not be there. I shall be with my family in Moscow, or traveling on my business, or at my dacha in Finland. I shall not want to see you again. Please do not try to see me. I think it best this way. Do you agree?"

"I agree."

Mr. Rautenberg stared out over the water. He looked tired and old, and Edwin tried to stop himself from thinking of Mr. Rautenberg and Galina together. A sudden wave of nausea hit him as he stared at the older man's thick neck covered in coarse dark hair. He turned quickly away, and then said, "Why are you doing all this?"

"Why? Yes, indeed, why . . ." He sighed. "You are a good young man . . . the best of what, in Finland, and Russia, we think of when we speak of an Englishman. I do not like you, but you are honest and kind and when you have given your word you will try to keep it. You will not betray me."

"I have betrayed you already," Edwin said bitterly. "Once, all those things were true of me, but no longer."

"You will not betray me, and you are what Galina wants. Between us we have everything she wants. . . . If I do not give you to her, she will wander somewhere else . . . she will go on looking for the things she wants. I would rather it was you whom I know, and who are poor and can give her only little glass beads and cheap gloves than someone who might take her from me. This is why I am arranging for you to come to St. Petersburg. You agree to come to St. Petersburg?"

"No, of course not," said Edwin wearily. "How can I? I am ordinary and English and I come from ordinary people who do nothing extraordinary with their lives. How can I give up my life, my work, my family, and roam like a madman over the face of Europe?" He became angry suddenly for the way Mr. Rautenberg had so carelessly thrown this disruptive idea into his life. "You must see how ridiculous all this is. It is ridiculous that you and I are sitting together here discussing how we are to rearrange our lives, how we are to share her. . . . How can I go to Russia? What will become of me! What will happen to the life I planned for myself . . . everything I planned and . . ." He dropped his face into his hands and could say no more. He heard the crackle of paper and looked up to see Mr. Rautenberg putting two envelopes on the seat beside him.

"All these things are yours to worry. I do not know the answers. You must decide what you will do. I have done everything I promised to Galina. There are the papers. Now I shall go. I do not want to see you again, not here, nor in St. Petersburg."

He stood up, nodded his head, and walked quickly away from the bench, a short, funny little man who had just managed to smash Edwin's thin façade of normality into total confusion. Edwin watched him disappear into the distance. Then he picked up the two envelopes from the seat, placed them in his coat pocket, and left the park.

14 SOPHIE ALWAYS DATED DAISY MAY'S CHANGE OF CHAR-
acter as occurring from the time of the arrival of
Edwin's letter. That was how she thought of it, as
Daisy's change of character. For most of their lives
together—and they had been firm friends since they were eleven
—Daisy had been quiet, contented, grateful, and apart from a
few instances of atypical stubbornness, docile and tractable. But
when Edwin's letter arrived all that changed.

It had been a shock to all of them, that letter. Obviously there
had been something wrong. He hadn't been home for months and
all they had received from him had been postcards from London
saying he was well but busy. And then the letter had come, the
letter, and the five-pound postal order. And it was the postal
order more than anything else that had shocked them, made them
realize how serious was Edwin's decision to alter his life.

The letter spoke of a new and wonderful opportunity on a
merchant shipping line that ran from Edinburgh to St. Petersburg. That word, St. Petersburg, looked alien and dangerous on
the lined white notepaper and Pa had faltered over it when he
read it aloud. The letter spoke of good wages and a chance to see
the world, of having to make a quick decision and being unable
to come home and see them before he set off for Edinburgh. But
the wages were good, so good that he wanted to send them the
enclosed to help out with any emergencies in case he couldn't get
to see them again for a while.

The letter had come during the week, but when they had
arrived home the following Sunday, Pa had read it to them. The
postal order was still intact, tucked into the envelope so that they
could see it for themselves.

"A splendid opportunity," Pa had read tonelessly. "A position
as fireman with William Thomson & Co. on the Ben Line Steamers. . . ." His voice had faltered away, then he'd stared at the
postal order.

"He's a good boy . . . to send us all this. It must have taken him a long time to save all this money."

"But I don't understand," Sophie cried. "He's always wanted to work on the railway, ever since he was a little boy. And he never wanted to be a sailor. Don't you remember? Even on the Mission outing to Brighton he was sick when we went out in a rowing boat. . . ."

"A splendid opportunity with William Thomson . . ." Pa had repeated, as though trying to understand, and then Sophie had caught sight of Daisy's face and had decided to say no more.

Daisy was white, all the color drained away, and she was staring at Pa as though she and no one else understood. All through the ensuing conversation, the worried discussion of why he had done it and what would happen to him, Daisy had remained silent, staring ahead of her at nothing and sometimes flushing an angry red as though some secret thought had struck her.

Walking back to Fawcett's, Daisy's answers to Sophie's constant questions had been monosyllabic and, later that night, in the attic bedroom, Sophie had listened to Daisy turning restlessly in her bed, sighing and punching her pillow.

"Is anything wrong, Dais?"

"No."

"Are you upset . . . because Edwin's gone to be a sailor?"

"Oh, don't be so stupid, Sophie! I don't spend all my life thinking about the Willoughby family, you know."

Sophie felt as though she had been hit. Never, in all their years of friendship, going to school together, working together, had Daisy attacked her so savagely . . . so unfairly. . . .

"I never thought you did. I . . . ."

"Do be quiet and let me go to sleep, Sophie. I have to get up earlier than you, remember. I'm only a kitchen maid, not a house-maid."

In silence they had lain there, each perturbed and smoldering. Sophie was hurt and angry, but beneath the anger was a dim understanding. Daisy had always worshiped Edwin, much more than either of his own sisters had. In some curious way, because

247

Daisy was not his sister, his desertion had hurt her more. Her idol had proved to be unreliable.

In the days that followed Daisy May had banged around the kitchen with grim-faced efficiency. She was bad-tempered and uncommunicative. She snapped several times at Sophie about the untidiness of their shared room. Before, she had tidied it up for both of them without complaint.

On Daisy's next weekly half-day off she vanished without a word in the direction of the station and returned a few hours later with several packages. By this time Sophie knew better than to ask to see her purchases but they were there for all to see on their next Sunday off. As they got ready to go home Daisy undid a large hatbox and lifted out a purple velvet toque. It was a glorious hat, more expensive than either of them had ever owned. There was a wide satin swath around the crown, and a large copper-headed pin for decoration. Defiantly, Daisy lifted it onto her head. It was quite huge and beneath it her face looked small and overshadowed.

"Oh, Dais . . ." breathed Sophie. "What a splendid hat."

Daisy, mollified, rummaged in the bottom of the box and produced a purple boa. She hung it around her neck with a jaunty flourish. The effect of the toque and the boa was overpowering.

"Are you going to meeting in those?" faltered Sophie.

"Why shouldn't I?"

"No reason, Dais, no reason at all. . . . It's just that you, well, you usually dress so quietly and . . ."

"And look so dull and uninteresting that nobody ever notices me, or cares about me or anything!" There was a rising note of hysteria in Daisy May's voice.

"I didn't mean that, Dais! You know I didn't."

With hands that trembled, Daisy took out a box of face powder and began to dab it on her nose with a piece of handkerchief. Sophie stared, appalled and fascinated.

"Whatever would Mrs. Fawcett say if she saw you? Whatever will Mother say . . ." Daisy didn't answer, just went on dabbing.

"Could I try some, Dais?" Silently Daisy handed over the box and the cloth, then she began to pull on a pair of cream elbow-length gloves, also new.

"Gosh, Dais. You've been having a real spend. Did you get anything else?"

"A pair of silk stockings."

"I thought you were saving your money for when Ivan came home?"

"Well, I'm not."

"All right, Dais."

And then the days of accumulated misery suddenly broke and Daisy sat down on her bed and began to cry. Sophie took a step toward her and then stopped when she realized the tears were more of anger than sorrow. "Is it because of Edwin . . ." she began, and Daisy May suddenly banged her fist down in fury.

"It's *everything*, everything," she cried. "I've spent years, *years* being helpful and good and quiet, hoping everyone would forget about my family. All I wanted to be was ordinary, like the rest of you, but it's no good. Everything's spoiled. It's no good trying to make life the way you want it to be. You might just as well smash things, and take what you want, and say what you think . . . and stop trying!"

"But, Daisy, I don't understand . . . people do like you . . . you are ordinary, if that's what you want to be. You're part of the village, part of us. Everyone thinks of you as a Willoughby now."

"Well, I'm not a Willoughby. I'm a Barshinskey. One of those wretched miserable Barshinskeys who spoil everything and ruin everything and . . ." Her angry sobs, the tears falling down her cheeks, stopped her from continuing. In fury she scrubbed at her cheeks with the new kid gloves.

"You haven't spoiled anything, Dais . . ." Sophie faltered.

"Yaa!" Daisy screamed derisively. "What do you know about it? It's *her* that's spoiled it, but me, I asked him to go and speak to her. If I hadn't done that he might have forgotten about her, might still be working on the railway, coming home to see us once a month. . . ." She choked into silence.

"Daisy, what are you talking about?" breathed Sophie.

"Galina! That's what I'm talking about. He saw her in London. He told me about it the last time he came home. And like a fool I asked him to go and see her. And since then he hasn't been home. And now suddenly he's left his job and is signing on for a seaman to Russia. And if you don't think that's something to do with her . . . that scheming, evil, hateful *cow*, then you're as stupid as I've been all these years!"

"Oh, Daisy . . ." Sophie sat suddenly on her bed.

"For years I've thought, if I make myself like one of his family, if I become respectable like your ma and sister and you, then I thought I'd be good enough for him! He liked me all right, but still I wasn't quite like the rest of you . . . I was a Barshinskey and had to live that down. And I tried and tried, and now it's all come to nothing . . . nothing. And it's because of her. I'm sure it's her. . . ."

The blood had run out of Sophie's face. She stared at Daisy but instead of Daisy she saw Galina. Memories she thought she had forgotten flooded back. "It can't be her," she said weakly. "Surely just meeting Galina couldn't mean that he'd give up his job and sign on in a ship . . ."

"Of course it could! You remember the things she did. And she's grown up now. She'll be worse, much worse!"

"Oh, Dais, what are we going to do?"

"What are we going to do? Well, I'm going to stop trying! I'm going to spend my money and be different and forget Edwin Willoughby."

"There must be something we can do to stop him. Remember how dangerous she was? Remember what she did to Mr. Hope-Browne?"

"There's nothing you can do," Daisy said savagely. "Whatever has happened, he doesn't want you to know. He's been very careful to make out he's doing it because it's a better job. What can we do? Go all the way to Edinburgh and get on the next ship?"

"I could write . . . yes, that's what I'll do. I'll write to him care of the shipping line. He'll be sure to get it at some point. When he comes back to Edinburgh he'll be sure to get it. Don't you think that would be a good idea, Dais? To write?"

"You can try. But it won't do any good. It's too late for that."

They sat in silence on their beds, staring at each other. Their intimacy was restored but the balance of their friendship had changed. Sophie had always been the strong one, the dominant one. But now Daisy suddenly seemed older than Sophie, older and tireder and disillusioned.

"Whatever we do we mustn't let Mum and Dad know," said Sophie slowly. "It's bad enough him going for a sailor; if they thought Galina had anything to do with it, it would kill them."

"No. We'll make sure they don't know."

"And I'll write to him."

"If you want."

"I suppose we'd better go now."

"Yes."

Daisy suddenly lifted the hat from her head and put it back in the box. "I can't manage it today," she choked. "I can't live up to that hat, not today. I'll wear it next time. Next time I'll show everyone that I'm different."

"All right, Dais."

Daisy put her old navy blue boater on and, silently, they descended the stairs and began their afternoon off.

The shared secret helped them to be friends again, but it was not easy living with Daisy May for quite a time. There was an aggressiveness about her, a defiance that sometimes took the form of an attack. She began to flirt with some of the village boys and that didn't seem right either. It was almost as though she was trying to behave like Galina, and it didn't suit her. She flaunted her purple hat and boa at the meeting on Sundays and she began to talk about looking for another position.

"But I thought you said you never wanted to leave Fawcett's, or the village?"

"So now I do. I don't want to spend the rest of my life

scrubbing old Mother Fawcett's kitchen. You're always saying how you want to go off and do things, so why shouldn't I?"

"Because . . . because you're more contented than I am. And you enjoy being in the same place. You like living with people who know you."

"Not anymore. Now I want to be different."

She went for an interview as assistant cook over at a big house at Edenbridge, but as she wore the purple hat and boa she was not accepted. The rejection made her more angry, more bitter with her life. She grew thin. She caught a summer cold that would not go. And one morning, at the beginning of July, Sophie woke up to realize that Daisy was still in bed when she should have been up lighting the kitchen range and getting staff breakfast, and that she was muttering to herself.

"Daisy?"

She was turning her head from side to side on the pillow, and when Sophie put her hand on her forehead it was soaking wet.

"Oh dear, Dais. Are you ill?"

She scrambled into her clothes and went to knock on Mrs. Bramble's door. When cook had huffed up to the attic, Daisy was trying to climb out of bed. "Got to get Mum's breakfast," she muttered. "Mum's ill, got to get the breakfast."

"Back to bed, lovey," said Mrs. Bramble. "Sophie, was she like this last night?"

"Her cold was bad, and she said she felt hot and her chest hurt."

"I think the doctor should see her. We'll have to tell Mrs. Fawcett when she gets up. Now, Sophie, you get down to the kitchen and get the range going. I'll look after staff breakfast. And after you've done the drawing room you come up here and sit with Daisy until I've seen Mrs. Fawcett."

"Oh dear . . . poor old Daisy. . . ." She looked at her friend's feverish face and wondered how much more Daisy was going to have to take. A sudden pang of fear made her wonder if perhaps Daisy was going to die, but then common sense asserted itself. She was too young and healthy to die.

"She's too thin, that's the trouble," said Mrs. Bramble. "Picking and pecking at her food. She's got no resistance."

A succession of people climbed the stairs that morning: Mrs. Fawcett to confirm that Daisy May wasn't malingering, then the doctor who announced that Daisy had pneumonia and needed careful nursing. Mrs. Fawcett was extremely cross.

"I suppose, Sophie, it had better be you who looks after her, but it is *most* inconvenient. We have house guests this weekend and I cannot spare a single girl, let alone two of you. She should have looked after herself. All you girls should look after your health. It is your duty to remain healthy, both to your parents and your employers."

"Yes, Mrs. Fawcett." She was furious with Mrs. Fawcett. She knew very well that had it been she who was ill, a message would have been sent home and Sophie would have been moved down into the room next to cook's. She was so angry that she wrote a note to her mother and bullied the boiler boy into running home with it.

When, at dinner time, she saw her mother and father standing at the kitchen door, come to collect Daisy May, she felt a sudden surge of love and pride for them. She had known all along that that's what they'd do.

Mrs. Fawcett was happy to have the dogcart brought around and her unwanted invalid shunted off. Daisy, wrapped in a blanket, was carried down from the attic and taken back home to be properly cared for, and Sophie, feeling both defiant and contemptuous of Mrs. Fawcett, went home every evening to see how she was, without asking permission.

Looking infinitely small and pathetic as she lay in Edwin's big bed, Daisy looked as though she might indeed die. And Sophie, through her fear and anxiety, felt also a spurt of anger with Edwin who had disrupted everyone's life by wandering off to Russia, just to please himself. "If she dies, I'll write and tell him it was all his fault," she said childishly to herself. It helped to blame Edwin. It covered some of the fear that Daisy might die.

She didn't die, and when she recovered it was as though all

the aggression had been burned out of her with the fever of her illness. But still she was different, withdrawn, uncommunicative. And on her return to Fawcett's at the end of July she dropped her next bombshell. It was done gently, quietly, and Daisy May was obviously sorry if she was causing any hurt. But behind the gentleness was the stubborn determination of a Daisy who would not change her mind.

"I've told your parents, Sophie, and now I'm telling you. It isn't that I'm ungrateful. I certainly don't want to seem so and I hope that just because I'm not coming to meeting anymore, or to tea on Sundays, you won't stop being my friend."

Sophie swallowed, wondering what form this new revolt was going to take.

"I've been very happy spending Sundays with your family, Soph, and going to the meetings and knowing everyone there. But you do understand, don't you, that I can't go on my whole life like this. I've got to find more than that. I've got to find out about me."

"What do you mean . . . find out about you?"

"I've got to find something to help me get through the rest of my life. I don't seem to belong to anything, or anybody. There's nothing that is just mine . . . nobody to whom I'm the one important person in the whole world. There doesn't seem to be a place for me, not anywhere." It was said without self-pity. It wasn't a complaint, or a plea for consolation and reassurance. It was a plain statement of fact and Daisy had obviously considered it long and hard.

"So what are you going to do on Sundays, Dais?" Sophie asked. She was a little afraid of this new Daisy May, this cold, matter-of-fact, self-contained Daisy.

"I'm going to join the Quakers, in Reigate. Only they don't like to be called Quakers. They're called Friends."

"I see."

"I thought about it, Sophie, and I tried to go back to where everything went wrong, and the further back I went, the more I realized that if my ma had never left the Friends, everything might have been different."

"But if your ma hadn't left the Friends, if she hadn't married your dad, well, you'd never be here, Daisy May."

"No . . . and maybe that would have been better too," said Daisy quietly. "I don't think any of us, except Galina, have ever enjoyed our lives much. Ma didn't, and Ivan and I didn't. Perhaps if Ma had never left the Friends some other, nicer, happier children would have been born."

And that was that. Sophie knew there was no point in trying to dissuade her. Why should she? Daisy had as much right to do what she wanted with her life as anyone else. And, as though emphasizing the change in Daisy's condition, fate took a hand. Mrs. Bramble, after years of service as White House cook, gave in her notice. Her sister had been left a legacy and a house in Clapham and they were going to run it together as a boarding-house. Mrs. Bramble pointed out that Daisy May was more than capable of taking over as cook. Prejudice fought with common sense and expediency in Mrs. Fawcett's breast. It would cost far less just to give Daisy a raise than it would to employ a new cook. And she knew, in moments of honesty, that Daisy *was* a good cook and a good organizer. With a great deal of grudging and cautionary remarks—"A trial period only"—"Until I can get a proper cook from London"—"Just as an emergency measure"— Daisy May, at twenty-three, was elevated to the rank of cook. It seemed to Sophie that now Daisy was doubly removed from her, at work, and during their leisure. And it felt strange on Sundays, going home by herself, no Edwin, no Daisy. The family was shrinking and the day was dull and restrained with just Ma, Pa, and Lillian. No fun, no laughter, her parents still puzzled by Edwin's behavior, and hurt by Daisy's, not understanding either of them. Everyone, even Lillian, seemed to be disoriented, thrown off balance by the curious behavior and family defection of first Edwin, then Daisy May.

When, a few days later, they heard that war had broken out, it seemed no more than just an additional strangeness, an added confusion that had somehow been precipitated by Edwin's letter.

15

"I DO NOT THINK IT WILL BE TOO DIFFERENT FOR YOU, being a fireman on a railway engine and a fireman on a ship."

He remembered those words, many times, with a sickening sense of fear and failure and shame. For the first few days he could remember nothing. He could only try to cope with the horror, the enormity of what he had done, the life he had condemned himself to. But afterward, when he learned how to bear and work in the hell of the stokehold, he remembered the words and wondered, for an instance, if Heikki Rautenberg had deliberately offered him this chance in order to kill him. For, he thought, no man could survive this kind of life for long, this terrifying, grueling, mindless life of fire and scorched flesh, and dirt and sweat, and the unintelligible men—animals—who worked with him.

Why had he, too, thought that a fireman on a ship would hold the same honored, respected place as a railway fireman? On the railway a fireman was a skilled, knowledgeable engineman, only one step removed from the elite aristocracy of the drivers. It took years of examinations, experience, study, to become a fireman of an engine. In this nightmare of a ship the firemen were the dregs of the Scottish docks, distinguished by only one thing, their enormous brute strength that enabled them to withstand the turn-about four-hour shifts of raging inferno in the bowels of a steel ship.

At the end of each shift, when he fell burning, sweat-soaked, and nearly delirious into his bunk, he tried to remember why he had done this thing. Galina. The memory of her was isolated, distant. It had nothing whatsoever to do with his present life. He looked back on that soft, spoiled young man, who had worn good clothes and been clean for much of the time, and he wondered at how that young man had turned into the prisoner that he now was.

There were three on each shift, two firemen and a trimmer in the stokehold, and in the adjacent engine room an engineer and greaser. He quickly realized that he had more in common with the engineer and greaser than with his fellow stokers. Apart from anything else he could understand the engineer and greaser. They had Scots accents but they were not so broad as to be unintelligible. But his fellow stokers, both on and off his shift, spoke a language he had never heard before, thick and guttural and, he guessed, filled with curses and profanities. One among them was different. He didn't speak at all and when off shift he lay in his bunk reading a Bible. Edwin tried to speak to him once but a pair of mad blue eyes staring from a blackened face didn't acknowledge Edwin at all. He might have been invisible.

He had been used to the noise of an engine. Why then did the noise of the furnaces and the ash hoist thunder in his ears until he felt his head would crack? There was no air, no contact with the outside world. On the footplate of an engine the air was there, all about you. You could see the world, trees, fields, passing you by. Here there was nothing but a great flame-lit steel cavern, insufferably hot, filled with sweating, heaving men.

The round trip, Leith to St. Petersburg and back, took about three weeks and on their first docking he was hardly aware that they had, in fact, arrived in St. Petersburg. He did not go ashore. Some minor infringement of regulations with the port authorities resulted in shore leave being banned but, in truth, he could not have gone ashore anyway. He was too confused, too humiliated and bewildered by what he had done to face the hurdle of making his way through a foreign city to see Galina. When the passengers disembarked and the dockers began to come aboard for the cargo, he went up on deck and stood gratefully breathing in some good, crisp air blowing in across the Gulf of Finland. There was little to see that he had not already seen in Leith and Revel—sheds, cranes, and warehouses. It was cold, colder than England would be at the beginning of May, but a pale sun shone and the late afternoon was reflectively light. The water, even in the gray dock area, was dappled with ice blue and the strong breeze slapped tiny waves against the hulls of merchantmen and icebreakers.

Idly he stood watching the dockers and the customs officials moving up and down the gangways. Odd sounds of an unintelligible tongue drifted up to him and then, suddenly, a word arrested his attention and he was cast back many years, to a summer of magic and misery when the future beckoned with promises of unknown excitements. The word—it sounded like *"nitchevo"*— brought a sudden image of Mr. Barshinskey to his mind, huge, black-bearded, and so unlike the smallish, sturdy fair men whom he could see from the deck. And with the memory of Mr. Barshinskey came also the memory of the undefinable longing of that summer, the longing for space and adventure and new horizons. And, washing through the waves of tiredness, of exhaustion, came the realization that that was why he was here, searching, not just for Galina, but for that restless boy's dream that had never been satisfied. He looked at the dreary gray and brown dock, and at the customs officials in their braid-trimmed uniforms, and a small tingling glow of that old excitement began to course through him. He was here, in St. Petersburg, many, many miles away from home, from the village and the old small, confining life. He had done it. No matter what the cost he had done it, and this was only the beginning. If he could come so far, then he could go farther, accomplish more, assuage that dream of which Galina was an ineffable, an integral part.

He would survive the stokehold—of course he would survive. He was young and strong and if he pulled himself together and stopped wallowing in self-pity he could achieve whatever he wanted. It was hard work, hideous work, yes, and he was condemned to loneliness because he was "different" from his fellow stokers. But did that matter? Wasn't it much better that he should be apart from them, free to follow his own pursuits, to see Galina whenever he could? And in his mood of rising hope and determination he knew that he would do whatever he had to, follow whatever path was necessary to continue seeing Galina. One day she would tire of Heikki Rautenberg and men like Heikki Rautenberg. One day she would tire of the life she had been leading since she was fourteen. Already she was changing, although she did not realize it. He remembered the way she had been with him, her tears when she thought he had gone, her insistence that he should throw up his life and follow her. He felt a surge of triumph as he remembered these things, as he realized that he was becoming as necessary to her as she was to him. Always before in her life she had moved on, fecklessly, irresponsibly leaving behind a man she no longer had use for. But this time she had been unable to leave him behind. In a while, he thought with rising optimism, her latest diversion—of a visit to her father's country—would pale. Heikki Rautenberg would grow a little older and providing he, Edwin, could earn enough money to take care of her, he would be able to persuade her back to England and normality and a life of permanence.

While they were in port the duties of the stokehold were reduced to a minimum, that is until they began to build steam for their departure. Refreshed, revitalized, he lay on his bunk and, for the first time, studied the map of St. Petersburg he had purchased in London. It was not going to be easy The city was vast and he wasn't even sure where they were docked. There were, apparently, two dock areas for heavy shipping One of them was the Kommercheski and the other the Gutuevskaya, but there was no way to tell which dock he was in.

When he was next in the stokehold he put his head through into the engine room and asked the greaser, "Where are we? What port is this?"

The greaser stared blankly at him. "What're ye talking about, mon. It's St. Petersburg."

"But which dock? There's two of them."

The greaser waved an oily rag at him. "What the hell does it matter? One dock's the same as any other in this bloody country."

Behind the greaser a figure leaned across. "We're in the Kommercheski Dock."

"Thank you, sir."

"Usually we berth at the Gutuevskaya. But for some reason we've been told to come in here for the next few weeks." The deputy engineer stared curiously at him for a moment and continued, "Does it make any difference?"

"I just wanted to see where we were on the map, sir."

"There's no going ashore this time."

"I know, sir."

The engineer looked at him a moment longer, then disappeared.

Back in his bunk he studied the map again. He was right on the other side of the city from Galina. He had to travel the length of this island where they were docked, cross the river, and then travel farther down what appeared to be the mainland. He began to look at the guidebook. Mostly it was useless, being intended for rich and language-fluent tourists, but it did give the routes of the new electric tramways. Painstakingly he followed route after route on his map—*Lafonskaya Square, via Suvorovsky Prospekt to Smolenskoye Cemetery*—the print on the map was small, and many of the names seemed the same until you looked hard at them and realized that just a few of the strange little letters were different. At the end of his off-duty time he had discovered that a number 5 electric tram—always providing he could find where it started —would take him to where he could walk to Mr. Rautenberg's apartment.

On the return journey he had little time for studying the book. He was still too exhausted and when he came off watch he found, in spite of fighting his tiredness, that he fell at once into a deep sleep. But once they were back in Leith he took a small room near the railway station and settled down to fill the short time ashore with a concentrated study of his guidebook.

There were letters from home waiting for him at the shipping office and when he wasn't reading his book and trying to learn the curious Russian alphabet, he wrote what he hoped were positive and reassuring letters. On his last day ashore he took a train into Edinburgh and bought, for one and sixpence, a manual of the Russian language, then he wandered about the city in the bright May light, feeling that by acquainting himself with one strange town, it would prepare him for the next.

Back on the *Moscow II* the stokehold hit him afresh, but resolutely, not allowing his mood of optimism to evaporate, he struggled against heat, coal dirt, and frustration. Determinedly he thought, not of what he had given up, but of what he was going to do. He must not whine, not even to himself.

This time when they docked there was a sense of comforting familiarity about it. This bit he had done before. With a sense of elation he waited until he was told he could go ashore, then queued outside the master's cabin for an advance on his pay in rubles and kopecks. He knew the worth of the ruble, he had read it in his book and he asked for a largish sum. He remembered Galina's expensive tastes.

Captain Patterson paused, his hand over the metal cashbox. He glanced up at Edwin and repeated, "Seven rubles?"

"Yes, sir."

"Have you been ashore before?"

"No, sir. But I have a friend living in St. Petersburg and I am not sure how much I shall need on this journey."

The captain, as the engineer had done previously, eyed him curiously, then he counted out a mixture of rubles and kopecks.

"Be careful with your papers, and with the authorities," he said tonelessly. "Things are different here. Sometimes offense is taken at the most minor of infringements."

"I'll be careful, sir."

He listened to the men in the hold and, because he could now begin to understand them, realized they were making plans for their jaunt ashore. He was not asked to join them and again he was thankful for the isolation that had been thrust upon him in the stokehold. He was not one of them yet, although no doubt in time it would change. When that time came he would have to think of excuses that would not offend.

As they filed past the dock gate and were given their passes, the spurt of excitement rose again, strong and exultant inside him. He had done it. He was standing on the soil of Russia and, not too far away, was Galina. . . .

It took him an hour to find the street where Galina lived, and he walked all the way. He could find nothing that looked like an electric tram stop, and he was too impatient to search. Outside the dock area a wide boulevard stretched before him, strangely empty, depressingly scuffed and dirty. A few carriages and carts rumbled over the cobblestones, and once a motorcar passed him. The buildings, tall and cavernous on either side, were grubby and the pastel-colored stucco and brickwork was badly cracked. St. Petersburg seemed noticeably unexotic.

He turned right, carefully following his map, and then as he came out onto the river embankment he stopped, a smile spreading across his face. All his optimism was suddenly renewed and justified. Excitement and confidence rose within him. This was Galina's city.

Across the river of sparkling marine blue, ruffled up by the wind, lay a vista of colonnades and spires and arches rising up in splendor against a pale blue sky. It was St. Petersburg, a city he had been hearing about since he was thirteen years old, since the Barshinskeys had come into his life. Foolishly, happily grinning, he stared across at the great buildings and gilded domes that stretched up into the air and he knew that because of Galina and the Barshinskeys, and because of this city, his life would never be the same again. He thought back to the village, to the tiny circumscribed life he had led there, the life his parents still led because they didn't know anything about this bigger, mightier, more splendid world, and he knew that whatever happened to him in the future, the one thing he would never know again was contentment.

He crossed a bridge—the Nicholas Bridge, his map said—and plunged into the labyrinth of streets, canals, and palaces that would lead him to Borovaya Street. Close up, St. Petersburg was still scruffy, curiously uncrowded, and covered in the hiero-glyphic writing that he was only just able to decipher. Street vendors stood with their backs to the high buildings, their baskets filled with huge red and brown mushrooms. Once he smelled coffee, strong and aromatic, wafting out from a café set a little below pavement level. The air was cool and clean, and there was a constant slight breeze that sometimes, as he rounded a corner and turned into another boulevard, became a wind. He discovered, in later months, that St. Petersburg was never without the small, fresh river winds that blew across the islands.

When he came to Borovaya Street his heart was pounding. It had been nearly two months since he had seen her and he was suddenly afraid in case something had changed. He couldn't find her apartment building and he began to panic. The street was a long one and the high buildings appeared to be unnumbered. He showed his envelope bearing Mr. Rautenberg's writing to one or two passersby but they were unfriendly. One just brushed his hand away and hurried on, and it was several moments before a man in a black suit finally read the address and pointed to the other side of the road. He found the apartment at last, the number high up on the inside of the dark entrance. There was a courtyard at the back with a flight of steps rising from it, and before he had time to worry about whether he should enter the courtyard or climb the steps he heard her feet running down the stairs and her voice calling to him from above.

"Edwin! Oh, Edwin . . . I thought you would never come!"

And then she was in his arms, the familiar magic of her working on him yet again, dissolving sanity and reason. Everything he wanted was here. Nothing else mattered. A day and a night with Galina once a month more than compensated for everything else.

"Edwin! Edwin! My dearest, dearest Edwin!" She was kissing him in full view of the old man in a short fur jacket who had emerged from a cellar near the entrance. She was kissing him as though she had missed him as much as he had missed her. He felt his senses swirling as her arms pulled his head down to hers, felt a soundless cry burst from his chest as the familiar feel of her, scent of her, pervaded and swamped every part of his body.

"Why didn't you come sooner? The last time . . . your ship should have been here last month. Heikki went away and I waited for you. . . . Why didn't you come? I couldn't believe you wouldn't come . . ."

He tried to explain but could think of nothing but her in his arms. All he could finally blurt out was, "I'm here, Galina. I'm here."

"Oh yes . . . yes . . . you're here. It's wonderful! Everything is wonderful now that you're here, Edwin!"

Laughing, chattering, she began to pull him up the steps.

"I knew your ship was in again. . . . Heikki goes away, you see, like he said he would . . . and I've been waiting and waiting, looking out of the window hoping to see you!"

They came to a dark gloomy landing where a huge door stood slightly ajar.

"Here we are . . . let me look at you, Edwin. And you must look at me. Do you think I have changed? Do you think I am more beautiful? See, I have all new clothes, and the apartment is wonderful, is it not? So much more exciting, so rich and wonderful and . . . Russian."

She darted about the apartment, touching pictures, vases, chairs with her hands as though to reassure herself. Then, like a butterfly, she danced back into his arms. "Oh, Edwin! I love you so much!"

He could do nothing but close his eyes and swallow. He was trapped. This elusive, fragile creature had trapped him for the rest of his days. Suddenly she pulled him toward a sofa and they sat together, listening to the street sounds that came in through the window. She was holding his hand and then she lifted it tenderly and held it against her cheek. He was astonished to see tears in her eyes.

"Promise me you'll never leave me, Edwin," she said quietly, and as he began to remonstrate with her she interrupted hastily, "Oh, I don't mean that you shouldn't return to your ship, or anything like that. That's not what I mean. You'll have to go away sometimes, I know that." She gave a frightened little laugh. "Promise me you'll never stop seeing me, never leave me altogether. You're the only one I have, you see. You're the only one who . . . knows about me."

With a strange burst of tenderness in his heart he stroked her hair back from her face.

"You won't believe things that people might say about me, will you, Edwin? You'll always love me and stay with me, won't you?"

"Yes."

And again, that swift change of mood, a sudden bursting smile, a throwing wide of her arms. "Oh, Edwin! How long can you stay?"

"I have to be back on board at seven tomorrow morning."

She gave a little moue of disgust, then leaned toward him, fluttering her mouth across his, softly teasing until at last, as it always did, the urge to dominate her overtook him.

"Enough," he said hoarsely, and as he crushed her arms behind her back and forced his mouth down on hers, he felt her give a little sigh and relax against him.

She had become, if anything, more beautiful, more Russian. Her hair was braided into a great crown on her head, and around the collar of her high-necked dress she wore a deep band of pearls, a new present from Heikki, he thought, but for the moment without bitterness. For he knew, somehow he knew, that with Heikki she was not like this, joyful and trusting and insecure, uncertain of him.

She sent out for lunch that first day. She had a servant—a woman who came in every day to clean and shop—and he heard Galina rush out into the hall and there was excited giggling, squeals of laughter, and the sound of money clinking. When he went to follow her she spun him around, back into the bedroom.

"No. No. No!" she cried, the corners of her eyes crinkling up with laughter. "You must keep away and wait for my surprise."

She shut the bedroom door and he smiled to himself, listening to furniture being pushed about and her voice shouting instructions that she constantly contradicted. The bedroom was magnificent, with huge inlaid and gilt furniture and a bedhead embossed in gold. There were crimson curtains over the top of the bed and at the windows. Everything was . . . opulent, exotic. It made him think of all the evenings the three of them had spent together.

"Now!" she said, laughing as she opened the door. "Now you can come and eat."

A table covered in a white cloth, a silver tureen, glasses, a huge crystal centerpiece filled with apple blossom—how had she found apple blossom in the middle of St. Petersburg?—and a bottle of "shampanyer" in a silver bucket.

"Yelena has gone. Now we can have our party! But first, a little present for you, to welcome you to St. Petersburg." Her eyes were glowing, black, full of delight and fun and happiness. Everything else was forgotten, the stokehold, the guilt, everything. She was enchanting.

"What is it?"

"Open! Open! It is a special present for you, for me. You must promise that only you and I will ever drink from it."

It was a small leather case shaped like a cylinder. He unclasped it and inside were two silver cups that fitted so tightly into one another they appeared to be one.

"But Galina . . . I can't . . ." Swiftly she placed her fingers over his mouth.

"Pouf, pouf, pouf!" she said, shaking her head from side to side. "Don't be so *righteous*, Edwin Willoughby. I buy you this with my own money. I know what you will say—so proud!—if I use Heikki's money, so I carefully spend the money I have brought from England. You must say thank you, my dearest heart, my own precious Galina, and then you must open the champagne and we shall drink our first toast together!"

"Thank you, my dearest heart." He reached across the table and encircled her tiny wrist with his hand. Then he leaped up and clasped her around the waist, throwing her up into the air. "You are my own precious Galina, and I have never met a woman like you and I never shall!"

"Oh, Edwin, how lovely . . . at last you are learning to say lovely things to me."

She gazed down at him, her hands resting on his shoulders. They were so close, so close in every way, that he could feel her heart beating, sense her thoughts. He saw her eyes fill with tears, but knew that she was happy, happy as he was happy. They were still, silent together, knowing such a bond of love it was almost pain, almost too much to bear.

"The champagne," she said breathlessly.

As they raised the silver cups to each other, her face was framed across the table by an arch of apple blossom. She looked like a bride.

In the evening they went out. She put on a different dress, a red one with a little jacket trimmed in sable. They walked and walked. She wanted, she said, to show him "her city." She took him to the Astoria, the Summer Garden, the canals, the palaces of Prince this and Princess that. Once, just as they were about to turn into the Nevsky, a party of young officers stepped to one side and bowed slightly to her. Edwin heard, among the gabble of words, the unmistakable sound of "Barshinskaya." Galina flushed and smiled and slightly inclined her head, and resolutely he shut out any thoughts that might mar this wonderful day.

They must eat their dinner, she said, in one of the intimate restaurants off the Liteiny, and then they would walk up the quays to watch the way the light night shone over the water. They finally found a place close to the Nicholas Station, a small, dark restaurant that was dingy and depressing and yet didn't depress either of them. Edwin, content to let her order, found at the end of the evening it took all his shipboard allowance to pay for the meal and he realized that next time he would have to draw a bigger advance on his pay. And after supper it was suddenly too far to walk up to the quays to see the light, long night, and they hurried back to the apartment, now aware that they had only a few more hours together.

Throughout the night, holding each other, they whispered of how it would not be long, only a little over three weeks before he would be with her again. She clung to him when he left and he was reminded of all the times he had left her in her Bayswater rooms, times when she hadn't even wakened at his departure and he had left without her knowing or caring.

He left at five, because although he knew now where to wait for the tram he had no money left. It didn't matter. In a curiously euphoric state he set out amid a different kind of St. Petersburg, one he recognized, a hurrying population of workmen in caps and shabby coats, making their way to factories and mills in the bright white light of a northern dawn. He made it back to the ship just in time.

When the ship was in dock there was a minimum crew in the stokehold, usually no more than one senior man and a stoker, just to keep the boiler alight and the engine room ready. Leith was the port where everyone wanted to go ashore, to see families or visit familiar haunts, and on the return trip, Edwin volunteered to do the maintenance duty every time they were in Leith. He had no desire now to spend time on shore in Scotland, wasting money on lodgings when he needed every penny for Galina in St. Petersburg. He was happy to stay on board with his Russian grammar and his guidebook, dreaming of Galina. And, in the silent watches of the docked ship, a gentle deferential camaraderie grew up between him and the engineer, an awareness of each other that helped to decrease Edwin's sense of isolation. As the engineer greased and carried out his routine maintenance Edwin's knowledge, considerably more than that of the average stoker, became apparent and the engineer, curious, asked how he came to have such detailed knowledge of a steam-driven engine.

"I was a locomotive man, sir, before I joined Thomson's."

The engineer looked startled. "A locomotive man? You mean a driver . . . a railway driver?"

"I hadn't quite got to that, sir. I was a fireman, at a London depot."

"I see . . ." He suddenly ceased to ask questions and Edwin was relieved. He didn't regret what he had done, but to explain his demotion, his loss of status and skills was embarrassing. No one would ever understand.

When the rest of the crew came aboard, when they began to get a head of steam up, when the heat and the noise and the work started again, he was glad. No longer did he view it with eyes of horror, for all this activity meant that in ten days' time he would see Galina again. He felt that now he was an experienced traveler, able to find his way about on trams and read the odd word. When he arrived in St. Petersburg for the second time he was able to notice things he had not noticed before: the uniforms, everyone appeared to be wearing a uniform, even the old women in their black headscarves and dark coats were all dressed to a pattern; the changing vistas seen through the dirty windows of the tram; some of the city was ugly, huge dark buildings separated by bad roads, but then there would be a glimpse of a canal lined with trees and wrought-iron balustrades, or a huge porticoed palace with a carriage turning through an arch into an open courtyard.

That second visit they didn't go out of the apartment until ten o'clock at night. It was light, and they walked, holding hands, right up to the English Quay. It didn't grow dark but the light slowly changed and became a golden, unreal, fairylike color. Little light wisps of mist floated above the Neva and sometimes seeped up onto the stone quay and they were both silent, feeling that because they loved each other, the city had changed into this elusive lover's dream. After a while they sat on the steps and watched the colors change as the sun rose behind them. When they got back to the apartment it was already time for him to leave and they clung to each other whispering, next time . . . next time . . .

He became two people. There was the organized, industrious, silent stoker who worked and saved his money and studied his Russian grammar. That Edwin, the Edwin who got through the weeks as best he could, was a calm, rational being who became, after a while, tolerated by his shipmates. He always remained on board at Leith, cleaning the fires and stoking. He would exchange rational but unintimate conversation with the donkeyman or the second engineer. They would exchange tales of boilers that had blown back, of cracked fireboxes, but never of what he did in St. Petersburg with his large advances of pay and his solitary expeditions.

That Edwin, the cool, rational Edwin, was waiting only for the one day and night when he could live again in his dream world.

At the beginning of August he said goodbye to her for the fourth time. The atmosphere in the city had pervaded even his absorbed introspection. There had been vast crowds standing outside the Nicholas Station and the streets were full of young men, not just the usual officers in a variety of colorful uniforms, but ordinary young men in deep crowned caps, dark shabby jackets, and boots. Everywhere there were religious banners and pictures of the Tsar in shop windows and cafés and carried along on poles by little groups of men.

"It's the mobilization," she had explained carelessly, "and the war. Germany is supposed to have declared war on us. But Heikki and some of the officers we are friendly with say it's all right, it will all go away in a few days."

"Are you sure?" he asked, feeling a momentary stir of unease.

"Oh yes, it happened before, a couple of years ago, or something like it happened, Heikki says."

"If there is to be trouble, shouldn't you ask Heikki about going home?"

She stared dreamily out the window of the apartment. Through the heavy white lace curtains narrow passages of sunlight streaked the air.

"Home?" she said distantly. "Where is home? I like it here, I think." Her eyes narrowed. She was distanced from him again, suddenly Russian, alien, not the same creature who smiled in his arms or clung to him absorbed in her own passion. Then she turned, smiling, "I like it when you are here."

It was growing harder to say goodbye. The division of his life, the short ecstatic periods with her made their affair more intensified, more acute and agonizing. He found himself wanting to speak to her of Heikki. Was she growing tired of him, that sad, fat little man who could give her only some of the things she wanted? He noticed, how could he not notice, that every time he was there she had more presents, more clothes, more jewelry, and he guessed that Mr. Rautenberg was trying, even as he was trying, to win her with the only things he had at his disposal. Several times he dreamed agonizingly of wealth—how could he acquire wealth? If only he were rich enough he could keep her, at least he *thought* he could keep her. A few hours out from St. Petersburg he shoveled and sweated and dreamed. He became aware, only distantly, that something was amiss in the engine room. The chief engineer had come down and the greaser and second engineer were talking in low anxious voices. The news seeped through to the hold—the ship must put back to St. Petersburg. His heart thudded with excitement. Back to Galina—but if something was wrong with the engine there would be no shore leave. But to go back was to be near her, to have the chance of seeing her for just an hour.

When they docked there was a strange atmosphere running through the ship. He was off watch, seated in the mess room preparing to eat his off-watch meal of stew and plum duff, when the greaser came in looking stunned.

"We're to gae on deck. The cap'n has to tell us bad news. There's a war breakin' out. We're fightin' the Kaiser. . . ."

He couldn't grasp it at first. He'd lived with his own tiny problems for so long he couldn't absorb this greater calamity. On deck passengers and crew were gathering in silence. They had two lady passengers aboard and they had come up without their hats. The wind blew tendrils of hair about their faces. Captain Patterson came to the rail of the bridge.

"I expect most of you have heard the somber news. It won't come as a surprise to any of us. Yesterday German troops invaded Belgium and His Majesty's government sent an ultimatum to Berlin. The ultimatum expired a few hours ago and we are now at war with Germany."

A little rustle moved along the crowd, a noise that was half a sigh and half a murmur of approval.

"Aye. I think most of us knew what was to happen over the last few days. I'm only sorry, ladies"—he gave a small bow to the two lady passengers—"I'm only sorry that I was unable to get you home before the war broke out."

"Is there no way the ship can get through?"

Captain Patterson rested his hands on the rail of the bridge.

"Orders from the British government are for all shipping to remain in St. Petersburg for the time being. There's no way we can get through the Baltic Sea. Libau has already been bombarded by the German fleet and is in flames. All British ships in Baltic waters have been told to put back."

"Can we get out overland? It's important that I get back to England as soon as possible."

A babble of noise broke out among the passengers as the news and its implications began to permeate. Into Edwin's mind came the image of a map of Europe. St. Petersburg on one side, Leith and home on the other, and between the two the Gulf of Finland, safe for the moment, leading into the Baltic Sea, which wound around the German coast.

"I suggest that as soon as we have cleared with the port authorities—and that may take a wee while—you all report to the consulate. As far as I know there is no danger as yet on the overland route, although there's still the North Sea to be crossed."

"Can we stay on board until we've made arrangements?"

Captain Patterson hesitated. "I think it would be best if as many of you as possible disembarked. The ship will have to remain here for some time. There's no chance at all we shall sail for home."

The passengers made no attempt to move, and neither did the crew until the first mate began to disperse them. Slowly they returned below decks. The isolation that Edwin had lived in for the last three months was broken down. Every man was hoping that someone else would have the answers.

"It's all right for the passengers—but how are we to get hame?"

"Overland. Ye haird the cap'n. He said the overland route's fine."

"Fine for the passengers. We canna just leave the ship, mon."

"They'll be wanting us for the navy," said Edwin slowly. "They won't just leave us here."

272

"Aye, weel, the Russkies have a navy too. If we canna get hame, they'll maybe put us into that!"

The war had suddenly made comrades of them. Cigarettes were shared and when the men on watch had left the mess room, the remaining crew raised enamel mugs of sweet tea to each other.

"Death to the Kaiser!"

"Aye, let's drink to that."

Death to the Kaiser? He hardly knew anything about the Kaiser. He knew nothing about Germany, or why this war had broken out. He hadn't read a paper or heard any news for three months. He had been living in a world of furnaces and Russian grammar and Galina. He had known a moment's panic when he had realized that the small group of them were isolated from the safety of home. Just one moment when he had suddenly felt homesick, known a longing to see his mother and father and Sophie again. But the homesickness passed, leaving in its place a profound relief and exultation that he was stranded here, where Galina was.

16 THE WAR, WHICH HADN'T IMPINGED ON HIS CONSCIOUS-
ness at all until then, suddenly became a pressing and
dominating factor. Old newspapers were produced
from lockers and bags and the events of the past
month, since the assassination of the Archduke Franz Ferdinand,
were pieced together. They were confined to the ship for the first
few days; nobody knew quite what would happen, what should
be done with them, this aimless piece of British flotsam cast
ashore on the wrong side of Europe.

On the evening of the captain's announcement they heard
cheering from the dockside and, hurrying on deck, they saw
bands of workers and Russian merchantmen marching along the
dockside waving flags and caps in the air. As they approached the
Moscow II they stopped for a moment and cheered and waved
afresh. A Union Jack appeared, then the French Tricolor, then
several standards and religious banners that were, presumably, of
great Russian significance.

"They're shouting, 'Long live England,' " said Edwin suddenly. He didn't know quite how he knew that except that he
recognized "Anglia" and in some strange way the other words
seemed to link up with odd things in his Russian grammar. And
there was also a brief whiff of the past—of Mr. Barshinskey
making sounds like this. The language was foreign but it no
longer sounded alien to him.

The second engineer, staring at the departing band, said
softly, "Aye, well, they're relieved that we've come in at last."

"What will happen to us, sir?"

"I can't say . . . not yet . . . we may be taken over by the
Russian government. We can maybe get some of the men home
through Sweden and Norway, and keep a master crew here—
just a few key men to work wi' a Russian crew if they decide to
try and use us for the war."

"If some are to stay here, sir, I'd like to be one of them. I'd prefer to remain with the ship. . . ." He said it without thinking, without weighing or considering what would be the right, the most sensible course of action. He was just filled with panic that they might suddenly all be shipped overland, away from Galina. The second engineer turned and looked at him. "Do you speak Russian, Willoughby?"

"I'm trying to learn, sir."

Again, that cool, hard, dispassionate stare. "It may not be too comfortable, remaining here. Everyone says it will be over in a few months, but if it isna', then we could find ourselves stranded and in a nasty spot, aye, very nasty."

They went below, although there was little or nothing to do below and after a week it was decided to let the fire go out and just maintain the donkey boiler. With no shore leave, and little to do in the stokehold, lethargy settled over the ship. There was an air of stolen time where nothing counted. Most of the men played cards or dice. The few books on board were circulated. Letters were written. Nobody wanted Edwin's Russian grammar, and he sat on his bunk, making hieroglyphics in an exercise book and learning all the tram routes around St. Petersburg.

At the end of ten days a few of them were allowed to go ashore for a few hours each. With some trepidation he made his way to Borovaya Street. This was an unscheduled visit and he remembered Heikki Rautenberg's words: "I do not want to see you again, not here, nor in St. Petersburg."

But surely the war made a difference. If he was going to be based here all the time, how could he avoid Mr. Rautenberg?

When he got to the building in Borovaya Street, the old man in the basement room popped out of his subterranean door, the way he always did.

"*Gde Barshinskaya?*" Edwin said, not really expecting to be understood but handing two kopecks to the old man in order to allay suspicion.

"*Dojidat,*" said the old man to Edwin's amazement. He pocketed the kopecks and laboriously began to drag himself up the stairs. What did *dojidat* mean? Should he follow the old man or wait—better to wait in case Mr. Rautenberg was there.

And then the hurrying feet, the enraptured little cry, and Galina in his arms again.

"Oh, Edwin! I knew you'd come back . . . I knew you would. And now you'll have to stay here with me, won't you? You can't go home . . . everyone says it is too dangerous to go home. All the English people will have to stay here!"

"Where's Heikki?"

"In Moscow. He is very worried about his business. He must see if the government want his timber and flax for the war because he cannot send it to Scotland anymore. Are you going to stay in St. Petersburg, Edwin?"

"I don't know."

"Oh, you must stay! You must!"

She was pulling him up the stairs, then they had to flatten themselves against the wall to let the old man come down. He passed them impassively, not seeming to be interested in them at all.

"I have only a little time, Galina," he said, when they were in the apartment. "First we must work out a way that I know I can come here—when Heikki is away."

"The porter will tell you." She shrugged carelessly. "He'll say if you can come up or not."

"But, Galina." He felt a sudden shaft of impatience with her childishness. "I cannot speak Russian well enough to ask all that. And what will he think . . . what does he think anyway when I arrive every few weeks, and Heikki is paying for the apartment?"

"Poof! What does it matter what he thinks. He is only a peasant . . . he will do anything for a few kopecks."

Added to the impatience was a new emotion—resentment, not at Galina, but at what she had said . . . only a peasant. That's what they both were. Galina and he were both the children of peasants. She sensed his withdrawal and was afraid even though she did not know what she had done to upset him.

"Don't be cross with me, Edwin," she cried. "I can't bear it if you are cross with me. I only have you, no one else. Heikki doesn't care." She grew more impassioned. "Heikki doesn't care about me at all. He is too worried with his business and his family to think about me on my own here and . . ."

"That's not true, Galina! Heikki has done more for you than any man alive."

She drew back as though he had slapped her. Her eyes were suddenly very dark and black as the pupils dilated.

"What do you mean?"

"All the things he has given you, looked after you in London, brought you here just because you had set your heart on coming to Russia, and . . . and arranging for me to come here just because you want me too. Can't you imagine what that must have meant to him, how it must have hurt him? Can you think of anyone else who would do such a thing for a woman?"

"I am not just a woman," she cried. "I am Galina Barshinskaya! I am entitled to everything I can get from men!"

"Galina!" They stared at each other, white-faced. Was that how she thought of him, too, just a man to be used for her purposes? Then, swiftly, she crumpled, cast herself sobbing into his arms. "I didn't mean it! I didn't mean it! Please don't leave me, don't hate me. You must love me . . . you do, don't you? You really love me, don't you? Whatever I am, whatever I do, you will love me, please!"

"Oh, Galina! Galina . . . surely you must know it by now. Don't you know what I have done because I love you?"

"Yes . . . yes. But I'm so afraid you won't stay . . . that you'll grow tired of me."

"Has anyone . . . any of those others . . . all the men before me . . . did they grow tired of you?"

"No . . ."

"Then why should I?"

"Because you know me. You know what I'm really like." She smiled, a child's heartrending smile that made him pull her roughly close to him, murmuring, comforting, reassuring. Now,

277

was now the time? Perhaps now she was ready to stay with him for always, to commit herself to him and to his way of life, safe in the knowledge that he would always love her, always look after her.

"Galina," he said into her hair, "what if Heikki could get you home again? Many of the English people are leaving and it isn't too difficult. The consulate is helping—recommending that all those who don't have to stay here should go home. Heikki could arrange for you to go overland. Most of us on the ship will probably be sent home too. And then, when we got home we could get married. I'd look after you. If you were married to me you would feel safe . . . you would know I'd never leave you."

She sighed a little and turned her face into his arm. "No."

"Why not?"

"I like it here. It's better than it was in London. More . . . elegant. Don't you think this apartment is far finer than my rooms in Bayswater?"

He wanted to shake her but knew it would do no good.

"And anyway, the war will be over by Christmas. Everyone says so. And then I can go back to England on one of Heikki's ships, whenever I like."

He closed his eyes for a moment, drawing on strength he knew he must find if he wanted to keep her. "How will I know if Heikki is here when I come?" he asked wearily.

"I shall tell the porter. I shall tell him not to let you up when Heikki is here. You know enough Russian if he says no."

He kissed her, then said goodbye, and hurried back to the ship.

17 MANY OF THE LETTERS THAT CAME FROM EDWIN WERE
censored, large lumps of them blacked out in heavy
Indian ink, but one came through which had somehow missed the censor. The letter said that their ship
was working as a carrier up and down the Gulf of Finland and as
far into the Baltic as they dared go. They had Russians working
with them on the ship, taking the places of the men who had been
sent home over the land route, and he was learning Russian so
that he could talk to them.

Left unanswered was the question in all their hearts—why
had some been sent home and not Edwin?

Once Lillian suggested that they should write to the head
office of William Thomson in Edinburgh and find out when the
rest of the crew of the *Moscow II* were coming home. Everyone
had looked at Sophie because she was the official letter writer in
the family.

"No," she said carefully. "We don't want them to think we
are asking for special favors. If, because of the war, they feel they
need Edwin on the ship, then it's right that he should stay there."

"That's right," said her father. "He's got to help where he's
needed most. If they want him there he must stay."

Sophie didn't believe it. She didn't know why Edwin was
still in Russia and she was afraid to find out. Sometimes she
thought of Mr. Hope-Browne, his face all scarred with Lysol,
and she became terribly afraid for Edwin. Suppose Daisy May
was right and it was something to do with Galina? What
chance had her gentle, kindhearted brother against a woman like
Galina?

Later, as it became apparent that the war would not be over
by Christmas, as 1914 led into 1915, and as the casualty lists from
the Marne and Ypres started to come in she began to realize that
there was no place in the world her brother, or any other young

man, could be safe. The boys from the village were all leaving. Peter Hayward had gone in a blast of glory to join the cavalry. The Tyler boys went, and so did the Jenkinses. They nearly all came back once, at the end of their training period, showing off in their khaki uniforms, looking huge and brimming with enthusiasm before they vanished into the maw of France.

"No men, and no horses," Sophie muttered to herself as she stumped back to Fawcett's after her evening off. At the end of the lane a platoon of R.A.S.C. troopers was lining up the horses requisitioned from Hayward's and from Fawcett's. Mr. Fawcett's streamlined hunters looked incongruous and out of place beside the working horses from the farm. "Nothing left in the village except women and cows."

She felt tired and dispirited. She missed Edwin, and she missed Daisy, who was still there, still working at Fawcett's, but was a quieter, withdrawn, and rather isolated Daisy May.

She turned off the lane and into the drive, and suddenly her stomach gave a swift, excited lurch. In the dim April evening she saw a figure she knew walking ahead of her. She knew the shape and size and walk of him; the way he strode was as familiar to her now as it had been all those years ago. She observed, blindly without understanding why, that he was in khaki but that was the only thing that was different, just the clothes. Everything else was exactly the same.

"Mr. Barshinskey! Mr. Barshinskey!"

She was back in that wonderful summer. She forgot all the bad things, the death of Lady Audley and Mrs. Barshinskey, the drunkenness, the cruelty. She just remembered him . . . *kroshka* . . . the violin . . . the smile.

"Mr. Barshinskey!"

She began to run, trying to catch up with him, with his long bold stride. Panting, her heart pounding with excitement, she chased after him.

"Mr. Barshinskey!"

The figure turned. "Hello, Sophie."

Clean-shaven, young, younger than Mr. Barshinskey had ever been. A big young man with brown eyes in a corporal's uniform.

A young man who was not Mr. Barshinskey but who smiled at her in such a way she wanted to burst into tears.

"Ivan . . . is it you, Ivan?"

"That's right." His voice was deep, a big slow basso voice like his father's had been. Everything about him was like his father, but he was not Mr. Barshinskey.

"Ivan . . . I can't believe . . . It just seems impossible that it could be you! Why are you here? Have you come to see Daisy May?"

"Daisy May, and you."

"Oh, Ivan!" She wanted to cry again, but this time it was because he had said something as nice as that. She stood beside him and looked up. He was enormously tall, or was it that she was so short?

"You're so huge, Ivan. When did you grow so big? I wouldn't ever have recognized you if it wasn't that you're so like your . . ."

"I'm like my father," he said blankly. "I'm like him to look at, that's all. I don't play the fiddle and I don't drink."

"Oh no. Of course not . . ." Sophie faltered, embarrassed.

"I'd know you anywhere, Sophie. You haven't changed one bit."

"Oh." She felt curiously deflated. Surely there should have been some improvement in thirteen years.

"I like your letters. They meant a lot to me. With you, and Daisy, I felt I had a family waiting for me back here."

"You didn't write back much," Sophie said tartly.

"No . . . well . . . you could see I wasn't much of a one for writing. I've improved a bit though. One of the sergeants has been giving me some help. I've been promoted, see? And if I'm going on in the army, I'll need to write better. I'm not bad now."

"Splendid. You'll be able to write me lots of letters from France."

He laughed, the same, big, heart-lurching laugh that she remembered so well.

"Sophie . . . Sophie . . . you're just the same. The first time we met you reminded me of a little terrier, full of bristle and spunk in spite of your size."

"Thanks."

"Any minute now you're going to charge me in the stomach with your head."

"I presume you are on leave preparatory to embarking for France," she said with sudden dignity, and his eyes crinkled up at her, the way his father's had done.

"Shipped back from India to reinforce the front. There's too many new recruits and not enough regulars. Has Edwin joined up?"

"He's in Russia," she said bleakly, and had the dubious satisfaction of seeing she had surprised him for the first time. "Daisy May will tell you all about it," she said quickly. She didn't want to talk to him about Edwin and Russia.

"You go on in, on your own," she said. "Daisy'll be in the kitchen. Go and see her, and I'll come in soon."

He lifted his big Mr. Barshinskey hand and touched her cheek gently with one finger. "Thank you, Sophie. For everything."

She stood outside, smelling the spring evening, looking up at the clouds scudding across the moon. She could feel the mark of his finger on her cheek. All her earlier depression had vanished. She felt alive and filled with hope. Edwin would come back. India was much farther away than Russia, and Ivan had returned. She heard the murmur of voices from inside, but she was in no hurry to go in. This moment in the cool night was one to be savored, enjoyed, a moment of pure happiness and hope, a moment of looking forward, anticipating. She tried to remember Ivan as he had been, dirty, with a running nose and no handkerchief and trousers that were always torn. She grinned suddenly as she realized how now he had tried to patronize her. He was daring her to remember that sad, miserable little rag of humanity who had allowed himself to be comforted by her and then ran away into the night.

He had twenty-four hours' leave, and it was agreed that Sophie should return home with him and see if her ma and pa would give him a bed for the night. She pushed to the back of her mind the memory of her mother's old disparagement of him. He was a gallant soldier now, a corporal in the infantry. He was entitled to all possible honor—one of the brave boys going to fight the Hun.

Daisy May, suddenly the old Daisy, flushed, excited, fiercely hugging her huge brother before he left, announced that she was going to demand the whole of the next day off to spend with him. Mrs. Fawcett, like Mrs. Willoughby, would have to bow to the honors of the war.

They set off back through the night, Sophie hurrying to keep up with his long strides.

"Do you have any luggage? A kitbag or anything?"

"I left it at the railway station."

"I expect Ma will be able to fix you up with some of Edwin's things."

"Ah, yes . . . Daisy told me about Edwin . . ."

They both fell silent. The presence of Galina hovered in the air between them.

"It's funny how things look when you come back," he said after a while. "When I was in India, I used to remember you all, all you Willoughbys, and you were much bigger than I was. And you all spoke well, and dressed very grandly and seemed separate . . . more special than anyone else, certainly more special than we were."

"Not me. I didn't seem special and separate, did I?"

She felt him lift his hand and tousle her head, and for some reason the movement irritated her.

"No. You were all right when you were on your own. But when you were with the rest of them, with your ma and Lillian, and your brother, there was that same kind of . . . untouchableness about you. And now I've come back, and the village is smaller and the houses aren't as grand as I remembered and you . . . you're just a nice little girl like Daisy. Not aloof or stand-offish at all."

They drew level with the old Owl House and he turned his head and stared at it.

"No one's lived there since you . . . the roof's fallen in over the scullery. It will probably fall right down one day."

He didn't answer and they turned into the path leading up

the side of the Willoughby house. As they came around into the yard, Ivan stopped. Her ma hadn't drawn the curtain in the kitchen and Lillian was sitting sewing in the window. The lamp was on the old writing desk in front of her and it threw an aureole of soft light around her face and hair. The material she was working on was blue, and as she bent her head over the cloth she looked like an illustration in a book, all soft blues and golds. Ivan didn't move.

"Is that Lillian?"

"Of course it is."

"She's very beautiful."

"Well yes, she always was," Sophie said sharply. "You used to hate her because she was so beautiful, and so patronizing."

He didn't answer and he still didn't move, just stood there staring at Lillian, and Sophie finally lifted the latch of the back door and pushed him roughly inside.

"Look who's here," she said brightly, trying to ignore Lillian. "It's Ivan Barshinskey, home from India and going out to France tomorrow."

"Ivan! My dear boy," said her father, getting up from his chair and coming around the table to reach for Ivan's huge hand.

"I'm Brown now," said Ivan. "I changed my name when I went into the army. Ivan Brown."

He filled the room with huge masculinity. Her father looked tiny and frail beside him and her mother seemed even thinner, more brittle.

"Ivan hasn't anywhere to stay for tonight. I thought he could sleep in Edwin's room."

"Of course he can," said her pa, and then to her relief her mother came forward, not smiling but quite gracious, and held out her hand.

"How nice to see you, Ivan, and a corporal too. Of course you must stay with us."

"I don't want to be any trouble . . ."

"No trouble. It's the least we can do for our boys going off to fight the Huns for us. Sophie, get some of that cold meat out of the larder and see what kind of meal you can find."

"I have to go back now, Ma. I'm late already."

Lillian carefully folded up the blue cloth and laid it on the desk. She smoothed it once with her long white fingers. "I'll get it," she said softly, and then she turned her face toward Ivan and smiled at him. It was only her polite smile, the one she used when she wished to impress people with her ladylike ways, but Ivan just stared at her.

"Lillian . . ." he said, and she inclined her head.

"How nice to see you, Ivan, and looking so well." She edged past through the tiny space he had left at the side of the table. There was one moment when it seemed to Sophie that she was standing right up close to him, and he had his head curved down over hers.

"I'll have to go now," she said.

"All right, dear. Will Daisy be down to see him tomorrow?"

"I expect so. Goodbye, Ivan. I have to go now."

"What? Oh yes, goodbye then, Sophie. Thanks for walking down with me. Thanks for everything." He turned to her and gave her briefly that wonderful Barshinskey smile.

She paused. "Goodnight, Pa."

"Goodnight, lass."

There was no point in staying on. Everyone was surrounding Ivan, eager to hear about soldiering, the war, about his life. She went to the door, through the scullery and out into the yard. She hadn't hated Lillian so much since she was eleven years old.

18 WHEN THE FIRST SNOWS CAME HIS LIFE, AND THE LIFE of those left on the *Moscow II*, began imperceptibly to change. For the last few weeks of the summer and in the rainy season that followed—that brief season which passed for autumn in northern Russia—a token Russian crew came on board. The ship was to act as a carrier up and down the Baltic coast. They ferried coal, sometimes machinery, and on one occasion crates of antiquated rifles which had been discovered in an old military depot and which had been eagerly seized to supplement the disastrous shortage of arms at the front. For, despite all the propaganda, the cheering and flag-waving in the streets, elements of bad news filtered through from the British Embassy to the consulate and down to Captain Patterson. The Russians had begun the war by suffering a big defeat and, rumor had it, their vast armies were unskilled and unarmed. The Russians who came on board the *Moscow II* were older than the British crew; sad, big, gentle men with deep-set eyes and low voices. They did not look at all like his memory of Mr. Barshinskey, and yet about them was a quality that reminded him of that long-ago village eccentric. He recognized words they used, he could sometimes make himself understood to them, and then their passive cold faces would warm into a flashing smile, a smile of such love and intimacy that he found himself confused, mixing their smiles with his childhood dreams and his love for Galina.

When the snow came they left the ship and so, in small groups of three and four, did many of his shipmates. There was nothing for them to do in the long Russian winter and they began the long journey home through Finland and Sweden. Volunteers to remain in Russia were asked to speak to Captain Patterson and Edwin was now one of a minimum crew. When the greaser and the second engineer were sent home he took over the maintenance of the engine room and kept the donkey boiler going. They shut

286

down the main boilers and drained them, a precaution against the savage Russian winter. When the snows came he went on deck every morning to help the hands shovel snow off the deck onto the frozen Neva below. He relieved the cook in the galley and organized the melting down of snow for water supplies. He ran messages from the ship to and fro across the city. His weeks of studying the guidebook, his summer city-strolls with Galina, made him confident of finding his way about, to the consulate, to the Russian police and civil offices, the commercial attaché, the embassy. There was much to do in that first winter. The crew, even those going home, had to be issued with special winter clothing. They were given food vouchers, but they had to go into the streets and markets of St. Petersburg or Petrograd, as it had been renamed, and purchase their own provisions. There were forms and papers and temporary passports to be arranged. A stranded alien crew, even if they were allies, were in some ways an embarrassment to the unwieldy bureaucratic machinery of the Tsar's state.

And then, as the winter advanced and the days became darker and shorter, as more and more of the crew went home and as the first flurry of wartime activity settled into a routine, he found he had both time and freedom on his hands. Those who remained ceased to be master and crew but became instead a small band of exiles experiencing for the first time the alienness of a Russian winter.

He found, that first winter, that he was filled with a kind of inward joy, a happiness that was only partly due to the presence of Galina. That winter the city took hold of his imagination. He had never known such cold before, cold that burned the inside of the nostrils and throat, that cut right through the body in spite of the special issue of clothing. He had known bad winters in his Kentish village, but they were cozy, Dickensian affairs compared with this giant descent of snow, wind, and ice that enveloped the city.

When the thin gray light of a late dawn would finally glimmer from the east, he would go on deck and stare about at the ships trapped in ice, at the occasional lumbering movement of an ice-breaker, at the sheds and cranes and quays all blanked out with white. Like ants, the black figures of men and carts could be seen making their way through the snow. A few sweepers, great bundles of dark clothing, tried to make inroads on the night's fresh fall. He liked it best early in the morning before the snow was cleared from the streets. As he traveled about the city on leisurely ship's errands he came to exult in the violent gusts of wind that showered him with fresh snow every time he turned a corner. After dark it grew even colder, so cold that the lanterns along the quays seemed to shine with a tinsel, brittle quality as though one more degree of frost and they would explode into shards of ice.

He was amazed at the endurance of the traders of Petrograd. They stood on the wet pavements between the piles of swept-back snow, still hawking their wares, rye bread, old clothes, milk, pieces of pickled herring sold on squares of old newspaper.

There was no part of the city, that first winter, that did not enchant him; even the depressing Viborg side, with its factories and tenement buildings, took on a mysterious quality when the poverty was distanced by flurries of snow.

Inevitably he saw Galina many times, but because there was an unwritten rule on the ship that they should stick together, and that no one should be absent for very long, his meetings with her were reduced to periods of no more than two or three hours. Heikki came only four times that winter. His business concerns, which had always been based in Moscow, had taken a new upward thrust as a result of the war. Old markets had closed, but the government was buying anything it could and was paying a good price. He couldn't afford to leave his affairs. Even the war seemed to be on the side of the lovers.

Sometimes, on his forays around the city, he would see her, catch glimpses of her leading her separate life. Once he saw her going into a café on Mikhailovskaya with another woman. They were stepping from a one-horse cab, laughing, their wind-flushed faces looking young and lovely against their fur collars and hats.

Another time, with the same woman, in the Gostiny Dvor, he stopped in one of the arcades and waited for them to see him. She laughed delightedly and introduced him to "Lizka" who was, she said, a singer at the Arcade Theater. She seemed to have formed a little circle of friends—acquaintances—very similar to the one she had in London, bit players from some of less grand theaters, a middle-aged woman and her daughter who ran a teashop at the unfashionable end of the Nevsky, a piano teacher, a little crippled hunchbacked man, who had an apartment on Vasilievsky Island.

He was taken—slightly—into her world of the demimonde. There was a little evening party once at Lizka's apartment, and coffee one morning in the piano teacher's room. They were all gay, gossipy people who didn't seem to notice the war very much, in spite of the shortages. They passed their time shopping and sitting in the teashops discussing the love affairs of their friends. He supposed he ought to disapprove of them all, such useless butterflies . . . but like butterflies they were charming and harmless and he could not help but like them. In the winter, when the theater season opened again, Lizka introduced Galina to the director of the Arcade and from then on she was intermittently taken on as an operetta dancer. Her life fell into almost the same pattern as when she lived in London.

Often, when he called at her apartment in Borovaya Street, she was not there, but the uncertainty of their relationship somehow lent excitement to it now that they knew they were both in the same city and would never have to wait for more than a few days before they saw one another again.

He felt, that winter, that he had indeed become a citizen of Petrograd. He had a place in the city, he knew people, not well, but enough to cease feeling that he was a stranger. He felt proud that he was not at all disconcerted by the size and strangeness of this great city. All that winter he felt a mood of rising gladness, an awareness that all this was going to culminate in an explosion of happiness. It was a familiar feeling. He had had it years ago, standing by his bedroom window watching Galina dancing by a fire. He felt the same now, but it was more intense, more sure . . . sure that fulfillment of a dream utter and complete, was not far away.

The moment came, but he did not recognize it as the climax of his winter until after it had passed. He was crossing the Nicholas Bridge on a morning at the end of April, when something different in the breeze, in the color of the sky, made him stop and look over down at the ice. As he looked there came a faint crack, like a pistol shot, and the ice began to tremble. Fissures opened and the miracle of a moving, heaving river of ice began to swell around the bulwarks of the bridge. The sun, out of a thin blue sky, caught the ice and the river was alight with sequins and spangles. And as he looked he heard two young girls speaking behind him and he discovered that he could understand what they were saying, not in detail, but the music and the sound; the melodic rising and falling which had mostly baffled him until now was suddenly familiar. They were talking about the spring. Spring is here, said one, although he couldn't have analyzed the grammar or even formed the sentence himself. He turned and stared at them, and because he was so unbelievably happy he smiled and they smiled back. "It's good," they said. "At last it is spring. Next week all the ice will have gone, and soon the war will be over. . . ."

"Yes," he said. "Spring," and the girls waved mittened hands and hurried away, their boots clearly visible beneath the hems of their gray coats.

"It is spring," he said to himself in Russian, echoing exactly the words they had just spoken. "It is spring, and I am happier than I have ever been in my whole life."

As the trees began to bud and the troikas vanished from the streets, the atmosphere in Petrograd began to change. It should have improved. The long dark winter was over and Petrograders could come out into the streets and promenade in the gardens, but there was a sullen mood hanging over the city. Even though he knew no real citizens (for he could not count Galina and her rather raffish circle as typical Russians) he could sense the gloom and resentment that had taken the place of religious and patriotic fervor. The black of mourning was everywhere, worn by women in all walks of life, and one morning as he crossed the Fontanka Canal he saw a soldier on crutches, his trouser leg pinned up over an amputation. After that he saw more and more wounded soldiers on the streets. He learned, from one of the clerks at the consulate, that all the Russian achievements at the front during the winter had been reversed and that the German and Austrian armies were rolling back over Galicia. He found he had to wait longer in the food queues and on some days there was no bread. He was drawn more and more over to the Viborg side. He could sense the mood of the city there just by walking along the streets; watching the faces of the workmen he could feel the apathetic unease of the city.

He was now the only member of the stokehold still on board. He and two of the deckhands were responsible for mounting a round-the-clock watch and maintaining the ship. It became apparent as the summer advanced that the captain and the chief engineer, who both spoke fluent Russian, were engaged in something vaguely secretive. There were occasions when Edwin was told to hire one of the few taximeter cabs and the three of them would drive to the Russian and English Bank in the Nevsky, and then back to the ship with a strongbox on the seat between them. He became aware, over several weeks, that the two senior seamen were busy hiding British securities and assets at various caches throughout and outside the city. Whether they were being smuggled out of the country, or hidden for the duration of the war, he did not know, but when he realized what they were doing he reflected, rather sadly for he had begun to love the city, that obviously the British government had little or no faith in any chances of Russian success.

There came a night in July, a glorious misty white night, when the light from the sun never really vanished, when he and the chief engineer delivered what the chief jokingly referred to as "one of our little packets" to a building in Zadovskaya.

"We'll walk back, Willoughby," the chief said when they

stood outside on the pavement and, in a mood of casual relaxation, they sauntered back toward the Nicholas Bridge. As they drew near the Old Donon restaurant a large party of young officers from the Imperial Staff College burst onto the pavement. They were noisy, drunk, and milled to and fro in a disorganized throng. Edwin and the chief engineer stood back and waited for them to disperse. Two women, laughing and shouting as noisily as the men, emerged from the restaurant and were swept into the arms of two officers. It happened so swiftly, so briefly, that Edwin wasn't even aware when his idle interest turned to shock. One moment he was looking at the woman in the scarlet jacket with the sable collar who was being kissed, and was kissing, a fair-haired officer, and the next moment he was consumed with incredulous disbelief when he saw the woman was Galina. He surged forward, unable to see anything but her face lifted up toward a blond mustache.

"Steady, lad. We don't want to draw attention to ourselves, do we?" His arm was fixed by an iron hand. Furiously he threw it off. A blaze of hatred, searing jealousy, and betrayal sent him forward into the throng, elbowing the drunken young men aside with vicious strength.

"Willoughby! Stop now!"

He heard, but didn't hear. He caught the young officer by the shoulder and spun him around, then threw his fist at the blond mustache.

"Edwin!" he heard her scream, then was hit in turn and went down under a weight of bodies, surfaced to the top, and found himself held, his arm screwed up high behind his back. The chief engineer began to speak in fast and eloquent Russian. Galina was staring at him; her face was white and she had one dainty gloved hand raised to her mouth.

"You whore!" he spat. "You dirty whore!"

"Edwin!" She began to cry and the other woman—he saw it was Lizka—put her arm around Galina and led her away weeping. There seemed to be a blaze of red before his eyes and only when Galina vanished around the corner did the red begin to disperse. He could hear, from a long distance away, the chief engineer apologizing, explaining, making excuses. The officers were very drunk and very arrogant.

"You must apologize, Willoughby. At once," said Mr. Bathgate urgently.

"No."

"You have no choice. I am ordering you to apologize. I am here as a representative of our government, and to a lesser degree so are you. Your personal affairs have no place here. You are behaving in a dangerous and undignified fashion."

The bile turned in his stomach. He took a deep breath and fought for control.

"I apologize," he said tonelessly in his bad Russian. "It was a mistake."

Mr. Bathgate began his long and profuse explanations once more. Edwin divined that he was saying something vaguely amusing about young men who were inexperienced with women, and he felt his fury returning, this time against the chief engineer. Then suddenly the mood of the angry young officers changed. One of them laughed. The blond mustache wiped the blood from his mouth and bowed stiffly, not to Edwin but to Mr. Bathgate. Edwin felt his arm gripped in an iron grasp once more, and he was hustled on up Blagovyeshtchenskaya toward the river. In silence they marched through the streets back to the dock. As his anger abated he began to feel sick—sick and tormented. He couldn't understand. Had it all been lies? Had everything she said been lies? Had she been laughing at him? But why had she bothered? Why had she asked him to come here? Why? Why? And another wave of hatred and anger engulfed him. He wanted to kill her.

"For the time being, Willoughby, you can consider yourself confined to the ship" came the cold voice beside him. "I shall naturally have to discuss this whole affair with the captain. I don't know whether it is possible, right at this moment, to have you shipped back to England. We kept you because you volunteered and because you seemed to be of above average intelligence and skills. We seem to have made a mistake."

"I'm sorry, Mr. Bathgate."

"I suggest you go at once to the messroom and see to your face. You have blood running into your eye."

He'd thought the red haze was entirely in his mind, but now he realized it was from a more mundane source.

"I can only say I'm sorry, sir."

"Who was that woman?"

He swallowed. "She was . . . she was the girl I was hoping to marry, sir."

"A Russian?"

"No . . . at least, only by blood. She was born in England. I have known her since she was a child. She lived in my village." *A whore, a dirty whore! But didn't you know she was a whore? Remember Hope-Browne. Remember the Pilgrim Teacher. Why did you pretend she was any different? Oh God! Why did you let yourself love her? Why did you let her creep under your guard? She's a whore.*

"I see. You're to remain on board until I have discussed this matter with the captain."

Dimly he was aware that he was probably in practical trouble, but for the moment he could think of nothing else but the misery in his heart and the confusion in his brain.

He was confined to the ship for several weeks but he did not mind. He cooked and polished and scrubbed decks, and greased every part of the engine that could be greased and did everything he could to stop himself from going mad. He had an interview with the captain, who was angry.

"You know very well, Willoughby, what Mr. Bathgate and I have been doing over the last few months. It isn't illegal, but it is something we do not want to be generally known. If the Russian authorities realized the British government had so little faith in their prospects of winning the war it could prove very embarrassing. We used you to help us because you seemed reliable and discreet and because you understand Russian. You didn't mix with the other crew members and you appeared to be self-reliant. We were obviously wrong. I cannot send you home at this moment. We are already down to a minimum crew and cannot spare anyone else. I shall have to contact Edinburgh and see what provision they can suggest. You have let us down, Willoughby."

"I'm sorry, sir. It won't happen again. There were . . . unusual circumstances."

"So I believe. I presume that is why you joined this shipping line. Because of the young woman."

"Yes, sir."

"If I had known, I would have refused to have you on my ship."

"Yes, sir."

The interview ended. He felt humiliated. He tried to turn her out of his heart, his consciousness, but at night he lay on his bunk staring into the darkness tormented with "why's" and "if only's."

Eventually they had to use him again for moving around the city. The other two crew members could speak only pidgin Russian and it was impossible for the captain and chief engineer to act as government couriers as well as queue for food and wait in the innumerable state and police offices for permits and food vouchers. He had to go out again into the streets of Petrograd, and all the time he was afraid that he would see her, terrified that every turn around a corner would bring her face to face with him. And when he didn't see her he felt a sense of loss, of emptiness that it was over and done with and he would never, as long as he lived, understand why she had done this to him.

As though reflecting his own personal life, the conditions in the city suddenly grew worse. Food, all kinds of food, was scarce. He had, during the winter, taken the precaution of buying some sacks of dried beans and these, with preserved sausage, gave them a staple diet of sorts. Once, when they had had no bread for several days, he was told to go to the kitchen quarters of the embassy and a bag of flour and a pail of butter were passed to him. The porter at the embassy was an ex-master sergeant of Hussars with whom Edwin had struck up an amiable acquaintance. He told Edwin that the Russian army was in a serious plight, and that the Germans were outside Warsaw. If their advance continued at the same rate, soon Petrograd itself would be in danger. Depressed, Edwin returned to the ship to find that MacKenzie, one of the deckhands, had gone down with summer cholera. Captain Patterson was both concerned and angry, and his anger with the prostrate MacKenzie served to restore Edwin, very slightly, to his favor.

"I've given strict instructions that no water is to be drunk without being boiled first. He couldn't have drunk tainted water on board, therefore he's disobeyed instructions and drunk it ashore. You'll have to report it at the consulate, Willoughby, and then take whatever papers they give you to the Alexander Hospital and arrange for him to be taken in. The doctor has seen him. It's definitely cholera."

As he left the dock and began his trudge back over the river, he saw a woman coming toward him, a Russian, whom vaguely he recognized. She wore the black coat, skirt, and headscarf ubiquitous to the poor, but she was neat and her black boots were made of leather. When she saw him she stopped.

"*Gospodin.*" She reached into the pocket of her coat and handed him an envelope. And as he looked at the large childish handwriting, *Mr. Wilerby, S.S. Moscow*, he remembered who the woman was and what she was called.

"Yelena?" he asked.

"*Da, Gospodin.*" She was the woman who came into Galina's apartment, cleaned, and did her shopping. Heart thumping, he stared down at the envelope, wishing he had the courage, the dignity, to tear it up in front of this servant so that she would go back and tell Galina. But she suddenly turned and hurried back down the wide boulevard. He made no attempt to call her back. The letter was illiterate and blotched.

Dear Edwin

I no I have been wrong and I am sory. I am very ill. You said you woud love me whatever I did. Do you remember? Plese come, plese come. I am very ill and I have no one. Heikki has come but I am afrade to tell

him I am ill. If you do not come I do not no what to do.
I do love you Edwin

Galina Barshinskaya

There was never an instant of doubt that he would go to her.
He knew nothing about what he felt for her any longer, but the
instant, blazing thought was that he must go at once. If he hurried
he could get to the consulate and the hospital and then down to
Galina's before Captain Patterson realized how long he had been
gone. At the tramway stand there was a long queue and no tram
in sight and, recklessly, he called down a passing horse cab and
jumped in. He wanted to go to her at once, but knew he must
not. All through the interminable filling up of forms at the consulate, and the even longer wait at the hospital, he wondered
what was wrong with her. Had she got the summer cholera? Was
she dying? Had he forgiven her? He didn't know. Every time he
recalled the memory of her standing on her toes to kiss the
drunken officer he knew he would never forgive her, but he had
to go to her.

When at last he had finished at the hospital and had seen an
ambulance go to collect MacKenzie, he jumped once more into a
passing cab and headed for Borovaya Street. All the way there
his thoughts, his heart, were in turmoil. And beneath the turmoil
was a heavy, saddening depression. Was he never to be free of
her enchantment?

The woman Yelena opened the door of the apartment and he
pushed past her and hurried into the bedroom.

"Edwin? Oh, Edwin!" She began to cry. There was a yellow
look to her skin and her hair, braided over one shoulder, was limp
and flat. He wanted to pull her into his arms and cry with her,
but suddenly the memory of the young officer intervened and he
couldn't touch her.

"What's the matter with you?"

"Oh, Edwin, don't be so cross with me! I'm sorry, I'm sorry!
But I'm ill and I'm alone and I'm so frightened! Oh, Edwin,
supposing I die? I don't want to die here on my own!"

297

Her eyes were huge and she looked plain and very frail. She had lost weight since he'd last seen her and when he moved close to the bed there was an unpleasant sour smell about her.

"Edwin, please . . ." she sobbed, and she raised her fists to her eyes and knuckled them like a small child. "I'm going to die," she gasped. "I know I'm going to die!" She reached out and clung to his hand. She was small, and ill, and infinitely pathetic. Somehow he had expected her to entice him, lure him into forgiveness, but this abject creature was beyond that. With a sigh he sat on the edge of the bed.

"What's the matter with you?" he said again, more gently.

"Edwin!" she sobbed. "Please say you forgive me! Please say you forgive me. I never meant to go out with them . . . but there was nothing to do here in the apartment all day. Heikki didn't come, and you were only ever free for a little while. . . ." She tried to catch her breath. "I was lonely, and Lizka said what fun it was going out with them after the theater. . . . I didn't mean it, Edwin! I didn't mean it!"

"Had you been with . . . with them before?" he asked, torturing himself.

"No . . . no, I swear I hadn't."

"MacKenzie on the ship said he had seen you with Russian officers before," he lied, hating himself for trying to trap her, but unable to curb the canker growing in his heart.

"Only a few times! Just when I was lonely and afraid . . ." She broke away and collapsed into the pillow, screaming and sobbing. "It's you I love! I only want you, Edwin. If only you could be with me all the time!"

A mood of sad, growing despair settled over him. She was lying . . . oh, not about loving him. In her own amoral way she did love him, but not as he loved her, not with an all-consuming, burning obsession. He would never want to kiss another woman, or even spend an evening with a woman while he loved Galina Barshinskey.

"Oh, Galina," he whispered, "do you know what you have done to me? Do you know what havoc you have created in my life? Do you ever think of what you do to the men you use and discard so thoughtlessly? Do you ever think of Hope-Browne? You were only young then and perhaps you didn't know what you were doing. But do you ever think of him and how you destroyed him?"

She seemed to shrink and grow smaller in the bed.

"What happened with the others? The preacher, and the others after him? Who taught you how to dance on the stage? What happened to him? Do you know what you do, Galina? Do you ever think of the lives you ruin?"

She gazed up at him with huge dark eyes, tears slowly running down her cheeks.

"I never mean to," she whispered. "I never meant to hurt Mr. Hope-Browne, nor you, nor Heikki. Heikki came to see me. Someone has told his wife about me and now she has taken his son away from him. He has had to promise he will never see me again if he wants his son back. He has left me some money and the use of the apartment for as long as I want. He was crying when he left. He said he wished he could leave his wife and marry me, but he cannot because his father-in-law owns much of his business. When his wife found out about me she tried to kill herself. He says she is unstable. . . ."

He just stared at her, unable to understand how someone so small, so defenseless, so *feckless*, could create so much destruction. He thought of that funny, sad, fat little man who had been so generous. Heikki was finished now, but he felt not the exultancy of the victor. Just pity for the little Finnish merchant who somehow had to put the pieces of his life together again.

"Didn't he suggest that you should go home?" he asked.

"I can't go home. I'm too ill."

"What's wrong with you?"

"I was going to have a baby. But it's gone now, and I can't stop bleeding. Every time I stand up I start to bleed."

He felt as though he had been kicked in the stomach. He felt shocked at the uninhibited way she spoke as much as anything. In his experience women never spoke of such things at all, let alone with such blatant coarseness. Childbirth, miscarriages, were dealt with discreetly behind closed bedroom doors while men were banished to dig in the garden. Galina's statement at first made no sense other than to shock him. Then, beneath the shock the old canker of jealousy began to gnaw again.

"Was it my child?" As she started to speak he suddenly grasped her roughly by the wrist. "You're to tell the truth . . . you understand, Galina? No more lies! If you want me to help you, to stay with you, you must never lie to me again. Now think very carefully before you answer, was the child mine?"

"I don't know," she whimpered.

"Oh, God!" He put his hands up over his face.

"You see," she began to gabble, "I couldn't tell Heikki what was wrong. He would know it wasn't his. He hasn't been here all the spring and summer. And I was afraid what he would do to me if he found out what was wrong. I wanted the money, you see, and the apartment . . ."

He didn't answer. He felt sick and ashamed. Men were dying all over the world, fighting for their countries, and he was wasting his life trying to save this selfish, thoughtless, totally useless piece of humanity. And yet, when he looked down at her, so small, so white and pathetic, he knew he could do nothing else because he loved her.

"How long have you been like this?"

"Several weeks . . . I don't remember properly."

"Have you seen a doctor?"

"No . . ." Her eyes evaded his.

"Are you crazy! You're afraid that you're going to die, and you still don't see a doctor!"

"I can't." She began to cry again. "Lizka made me promise I wouldn't send for a doctor in case she got into trouble. She took me to a doctor on the Viborg side, only I don't think he was really a doctor, and when I told Lizka I was ill and would she ask him to come and see me she said he wouldn't be there anymore. And then she went away and she hasn't been to see me again." She raised her eyes to his and said, in a sad and tired voice, "You see . . . I told you once, I don't have any friends. Only men, and girls I go around with."

Suddenly he felt he had to get out of the apartment or he would choke. The smell of her, the thought of what she had done, what she was, made him feel he was stifling to death.

"I must go now. I'll come back tomorrow."

Her face crumpled and she stretched out her arms. "Don't leave me! Please don't leave me! I'm so frightened!"

And because she was reaching toward him in anguish, because she was so totally helpless, suddenly she was in his arms, the small bird feel of her against his chest, the fear of her communicating itself to him, the fear, the utter dependence . . .

"Oh, Galina!"

"Don't leave me!"

"I must. But I'll come tomorrow and I'll bring a doctor. Somehow I'll find a doctor. What about Yelena? Will she stay the night with you? If I give her some money, will she stay the night and look after you until I can make some arrangements?"

"Yes . . . yes, I expect she will if I ask her."

"I'll tell her on my way out. I'll give her some money and ask her to stay with you until I come tomorrow with a doctor. You'll be all right until tomorrow. Just don't get up out of bed."

"Edwin . . . you won't leave me, will you? Promise you won't leave me!"

He kissed her gently on the cheek and laid her back on the pillow.

"I'll come tomorrow," he said quietly. As he walked across the room to the door he was conscious of her eyes—pleading—but he could not say the words she wanted to hear. Not just yet. He spoke to the woman and gave her what little money he had with him, then stepped outside the apartment and walked down the steps to the street. He took several deep gulps of fresh air, trying to rid his head of the stuffiness of the apartment, and his heart of despair. He wondered how he was going to sort out the trouble she was in, but he knew that he would. Whatever the cost, he knew he would.

19 WHEN SOPHIE PASSED THE TICKET COLLECTOR AND HUR-
ried onto the platform of the Newcastle train, she
couldn't, at first, see Daisy May. A huge number of
sailors were loading their kit into the luggage van and
she had to push through them. It was too early and too chilly for
the sailors to be in high spirits and in any case they were obviously returning to active service in the North Sea after their
leave. For sailors they were subdued and just opened a gangway
to let her through.

She hurried up the platform, quite a way up the platform,
growing depressed when she couldn't see Daisy. She had risen
very early that morning and caught the milk train to Victoria,
then crossed London in a cab to King's Cross, especially to see
Daisy off. It had become almost obsessively important to her that
she should see her friend off.

Near the engine a group of men and women milled, saying
goodbyes, loading luggage into the train, talking loudly above the
hissing of the steam. And standing to one side, with them but yet
not part of them, she saw, at last, Daisy May.

"Daisy!"

Daisy spun around, and over her tight pale face blossomed an
enormous smile, a smile of such surprised delight that all the
effort it had taken to get here so early was more than worthwhile.

"Sophie," she breathed. "Sophie, how on earth did you manage to get here? I never thought to see you!"

"I just told Mrs. Fawcett I was coming and she took it. Never
said a word. She can't afford to say anything now with everyone
leaving. Caught the milk train. I had to see you off, Dais, I
couldn't let you go without . . ." A choke suddenly stopped her
but she swallowed it. She hadn't come all this way, at this time
in the morning, just to send Daisy on her way with a flood of
tears and heavy emotion.

"It should be you going really, Sophie. You were always the one who wanted to travel. I never really wanted to do anything but stay at home. You'd enjoy it much more than I shall."

Sophie swallowed once more. "Yes . . . well . . . you're the one that's going. You've done it all on your own, managed it somehow. And once you get there you'll find it exciting and . . . and . . ."

It was the sight of Daisy May, the look of her that upset Sophie so much. Standing there in a dark suit and white shirt, with a round felt hat with the Quaker's badge pinned on the ribbon at the front, she looked . . . unloved . . . lonely. That was why Sophie had come to see her off. She couldn't bear the thought of Daisy, who had no one of her own, setting off without someone to stand on the platform and wave her goodbye.

"Have you got everything you need for the journey, for the ship and the train journey on the other side?"

"Oh yes."

Sophie looked at the nearby group. All the women wore the Quaker badge on their hats. The men had a kind of uniform, too, plain, and the eight-pointed stars were pinned on their jackets.

"Do you know any of them, Daisy?"

"Only a little . . . from the preliminary meetings we've had. I expect I'll get to know them on the journey." She smiled, a tense, determined little smile. Sophie put her hand out to touch her arm, then thought better of it.

She could hear the voices of the nearby group and she knew, as she had known all along, that Daisy May was going to be odd one out. They did seem nice, but they all spoke posh, like Mrs. Fawcett and Mr. Hope-Browne. Not affected or silly posh, but nice posh. She couldn't hear a single "country" accent, like Daisy's and her own. They were all educated, clever people— nice but clever. Daisy was going to be lonely.

"I know what you're thinking, Sophie," Daisy said suddenly, as the voices grew louder. "But I'm sure it's going to be all right. I know they talk like Mrs. Fawcett, but they're very nice to me really. And besides, there's a party already out there, and more are coming after us. There's bound to be some of them more like . . . well, more like me."

"Of course there is," said Sophie heartily. She still hadn't assimilated properly the enormity of what Daisy May was doing. It had been no more than five weeks ago that Daisy had dropped her bombshell. She had explained, in an aggressive and defensive manner, that she was leaving Fawcett's. She had applied to go to Russia, to Samara, with the Quaker War Victims Relief Unit. She had been accepted. She would be leaving England at the end of July 1916. Sophie, for once, was bereft of words.

"I'm going to work among the war refugees. All the Russians and Poles and Lithuanians who have lost their homes to the Germans. They've been sent to Samara. That's in the south of Russia, quite close to the Ural Mountains. We are going to a place called Buzuluk. You can see it in the atlas." There was a rather determined lecturing tone in her voice, as though she was convincing herself as well as Sophie. Suddenly Sophie was able to find her voice.

"You . . . go to Russia! Don't be so ridiculous, Daisy! However would you manage on your own in Russia? You don't understand Russian!"

Daisy stared at her, and then unexpectedly grinned. "Don't be silly, Sophie. Of course I understand Russian."

With a sense of shock Sophie suddenly remembered who Daisy was. They had all grown so used to her over the years—little, quiet Daisy with her soft Kentish accent and her prim, timid ways—that they had all forgotten that she was the daughter of that extraordinary man who had lived in their village for one brief summer. Of course, Daisy May *was* a Barshinskey, and she had spent the first eleven years of her life listening to her father and Galina gabbling away in their own tongue. She realized, yet again, as she had done at various times throughout their lives, that Daisy wasn't quite what one expected her to be. For ages, years, Daisy went on in her self-effacing, biddable way, bending over backward to please everyone and be grateful, sometimes so grateful it was irritating, and then without any warning she would do something utterly out of character, remind you that she wasn't quite the same as other people.

"I can't *speak* Russian. Ivan and I always refused to speak it, but we could both understand it. Even Ma understood a little in the end because Father never spoke anything else to Galina. I explained that I couldn't speak it when I applied to go to Samara, but they seemed to think that just understanding it was enough to qualify me for a place. I suppose there aren't many English Quakers who understand Russian."

"But how . . . why . . . ?"

"I didn't expect to be taken," Daisy said humbly. "All the other people who are going are nurses or doctors, or people who have been well educated. The only reason they want me is because of the language."

Sophie stared, unable to absorb the incongruity of it. If it wasn't so terrible, it would be laughable—mousy, frightened little Daisy going off to Russia.

"You're going because of Edwin, aren't you?" she asked, suddenly finding her tongue. "It was that last letter, wasn't it? I knew I shouldn't have showed it to you. I knew it was a mistake."

She had come almost to dread Edwin's letters. Even the ordinary ones, just talking about the Russian weather and the ship and Petrograd upset her parents, emphasizing as they did that their son was marooned on the other side of the world, doing something strange—they didn't quite understand what—in an alien city, when everyone else's son was being killed in Flanders. But in the spring had come a letter—which he had sent to Fawcett's so that their parents should not see it—which had been the most disturbing of all because of its honesty.

He had explained to Sophie why he had gone to Russia in the first place, no details, just that Galina Barshinskey had come back into his life, and he had followed her to St. Petersburg. And now she was ill. She had been ill for several months, had been in hospital and had had a serious operation. He had said he could not leave her, that he was committed to looking after her, that he did not know what was going to happen to them but for the time being he had to stay there. He asked her to tell Daisy May that he was looking after Galina, and hoped, eventually, that he would be able to bring her back to England. He asked her to look after their parents. He was ashamed, he said, because he had left everything that should have been his responsibility to her and Lillian. And then he wrote, "And although I say you and Lillian, I really mean you, Soph, for you're the best of all of us. You're the one who's holding it all together now that Dad is so sick. You never thought you were important, but you were because you were so normal, so ordinary, so good and practical in the things that really matter, like Dad. You were the one who really helped the Barshinskeys all those years ago. You reminded Ma that she ought to try and be human and kind to them, and you were a real friend, not like Lillian and me. You always did do the right thing, without even knowing you were doing it, and now I've got to ask you to go on doing the right thing, stay there keeping an eye on Mum and Dad, be a good friend to Daisy, a post office for me and Ivan, and a good stout stick for Lillian when she needs taking down a peg or two. I can't even help with money, Soph. I don't know if there's some way of allocating part of my wages at home, but even if there was I can't afford it. I'm saving every penny I can so that I can get Galina back home at the first opportunity. I'll try and make it up to you one day, Soph. I'm not very proud of myself, but I know I'd be less proud if I ran out on her now. She's sick, and weak, and frightened. I have no choice, but I know everything at home will be all right if you are there. God bless you. Love, Edwin."

As a family they never spoke, or wrote, emotionally to each other. Feelings were kept well buttoned up under stiff upper lips, and so the letter had disturbed her badly with its talk of caring for people and who was good and who was not. The letter touched her, and made her nervous, and a mite bitter too. He'd got Lillian all wrong, talking about her as though she was a dried-up old spinster. The letters from Ivan still came to her, but they came more frequently to Lillian. She'd seen them on Lillian's dressing table. Ivan had either learned to write letters of which he was not ashamed, or something had made him not care what they were like, so long as he had communication with Lillian. She longed to know if Lillian answered but the festering hurt in her heart wouldn't allow her to ask. Every time he wrote to Sophie she examined each letter minutely for some indication of intimacy, but they were the letters of a young man, proud but frightened, who considered Sophie a safe and familiar friend. Once he had written, "My mate was killed today, Soph. We've been mates since I joined the regiment as a boy soldier. I don't think I can stand much more . . ." and even through her fear for him she had felt proud that he could write to her like that. But her letters weren't anything like the ones he wrote to Lillian. She knew, because she had looked at one, had taken the paper out of the envelope and read it quickly when Lillian was downstairs, and she didn't feel a bit ashamed, just terribly depressed because all Ivan wrote about was how beautiful Lillian had looked that night sitting by the lamp in the window, and how much he thought about her. He'd said he was going to send her some of the special embroidered postcards from France and, one by one, they had come, exquisite pieces of gauze and muslin, finely embroidered in the daintiest of silks, and put into a card like a picture in a frame. Lillian had about ten now. Sophie longed for Ivan to send her one, but all she had was descriptions of the trenches. And finally, when she had considered Edwin's letter for a long time, she had decided that the only part of it that was true was that she was normal and ordinary.

She'd hesitated a long time before showing the letter to Daisy May, and then she did because, after all, Galina was Daisy's sister and anyway Daisy said she had always known that Edwin's going to Russia was something to do with Galina.

And, as a result, Daisy was standing on the platform of King's Cross in a Quaker uniform with a tin trunk at her feet.

"You've written to Edwin, I expect," said Sophie, not looking at Daisy's face, but when Daisy answered she was quite composed.

"Yes, and I've told him that the journey to Petrograd is expected to take about nine days. Apparently the train from Finland comes in about the same time every day. It's quite an event, so he's going to arrange to be there, at the station every day about that time. His ship will be in dock then. It's all worked out very well. We have several hours' wait in Petrograd before we cross the city and catch the Moscow train."

It was ridiculous, scrubby little Daisy, bandying words about like Petrograd and Moscow, as though they were Reigate and Tunbridge Wells. Then Daisy said, "I know it must seem silly . . . pathetic even, me going all this way just to see Edwin, but it isn't quite like that. I told you when I joined the Friends I wanted to do something with my life, belong somewhere. And now I'm going to do something, and I shall belong to the Relief Unit. That's something special for me. And, yes"—suddenly the words came in a rush—"I do care about Edwin, and at least if I'm in Russia I'm on the same side of the world as he is. Maybe there's something I can do to help him, even though I'll be miles away."

From the end of the platform came the guard's whistle and a great deal of shouting. One of the men in uniform came over and picked up Daisy's trunk.

"Off now, Miss Barshinskey," he said pleasantly. "I'll put this in with the others. Perhaps you'd like to get into the carriage with Miss D'Ete and Miss Stubbs."

The two girls stared at each other, suddenly appalled at the thought that they might be saying goodbye forever. Then Daisy leaned forward and kissed Sophie's cheek.

"Thanks, Soph . . . for everything."

"Miss Barshinskey!"

She stepped up into the carriage, holding her skirt up rather gracefully. The guard slammed the door and the engine began to crank and hiss steam. Daisy's black glove rested against the window and, as the train began to move, she waved. And Sophie, in spite of her anxiety, knew a moment's envy at the journey across seas and mountains and forests that Daisy was about to make. However it all ended, whatever happened, Daisy May was going to see the world.

They crossed the North Sea at night, with all lights out so the German U boats were not attracted to them. It never once crossed Daisy's mind that they were in danger. In spite of all the strangeness, the new experiences (of a long train journey up the length of England and the confusion of embarking onto a ship), she knew that whatever was going to happen to her, it wouldn't end here, in the North Sea. She was very afraid, but of her own inadequacies, not of the journey. She was a cook who knew how to organize a kitchen and the meals for a large household. But that, and her knowledge of Russian, was all she had, and she was worried that her party would find her a useless encumbrance. In spite of her brave words to Sophie she was still not sure that her small knowledge of Russian would be enough. Ever since she had known she was going to Russia she had developed the habit at night of shutting her eyes and trying to recall her father and Galina talking together. Once the thought came to her, Supposing when I get there I do not understand Russian after all, supposing I let them all down when they need me? But then, unbidden, an image had come into her mind of Galina sitting on her father's lap, and suddenly she could recall the way they had sounded, the words they spoke. She couldn't say them herself, but she could remember them. She was very careful on the journey not to join in the conversation too much. She had decided she must try to be as little trouble as possible and not show how ignorant she was. One of the other two ladies was badly sick on the crossing and she found that Miss Stubbs, who was a nurse, was quite grateful for her help in holding basins and emptying slops. And when, toward the end of the crossing, even Miss Stubbs had to lie down, she began to feel almost indispensable. She offered up a silent prayer of thanks that she was proving to be a good sailor. How terrible it would have been if they had had to minister to her.

When they finally got themselves and their luggage ashore they had no time for breakfast before boarding the train that would take them to Oslo and she went with Mr. Foulgar, who held the money for the party, to buy bread and butter and milk from a kiosk on the station. As they sat on the train she automatically (because she thought of herself as a domestic servant) shared out the food. An air of cheerfulness, of optimism prevailed. They were launched on their way and had survived the first hurdle. As small parties of travelers, isolated in strange surroundings always do, they cohesed quickly into a self-contained unit, each taking on, almost without realizing it, a role in the group.

They were all young (Mr. Foulgar was the eldest at thirty-six and the other four were all under thirty) and, with the exception of Daisy, middle class. Miss Stubbs, the trained nurse, was possibly the most useful of the group, and Miss D'Ete had helped raise money for charities in the Midlands. Mr. Goode, who was only one year older than Daisy, was training to be an engineer. He was full of energy and unbounded optimism, making them play word games on the long train journeys and bringing a sense of gaiety and excitement into everything they did. By the time they arrived at Stockholm, ready to begin the long ride up through the pine forests of Sweden, Miss Stubbs and Miss D'Ete were calling each other, and Daisy, by their Christian names. Daisy felt it would be presumptuous of her to do so and contrived to avoid calling them anything at all.

It took three days, rattling over the mountains and rivers of Sweden, to reach the frontier station at Haparanda. Sometimes Mr. Foulgar read to them, from the Bible and from *Barchester Towers*, which Daisy enjoyed very much. She'd never had time or opportunity to read books after she left school. Every time the train halted long enough they got out and walked up and down, trying to quell the jolting sensation that now seemed embedded in their stomachs and had become a permanent feature of their lives. Already the newness, the strangeness of travel had worn off. Daisy felt quite calm, quite unruffled. She felt she had left home several months before. It was difficult to remember that only a few days ago she had been cooking in the Fawcett kitchen.

When they crossed the river at Haparanda the Russians were waiting for them and with a small rush of fear Daisy knew her moment of trial had come. All through Norway and Sweden they had had train attendants who knew traveler's English, just enough to tell them how long the train was stopping and when they would arrive and how long they had in the station restaurants. She found herself praying that the Russian customs officers would also have the rudiments of English. Supposing, now that she was here, she couldn't understand a word! What would they do with her . . . send her back?

They waited by the customs sheds in the cool morning air, the scent of pines all about them and a high pale blue sky above them. And then a uniformed Russian came out and, without effort, she heard and understood him.

"He says we must open all our trunks and suitcases," she translated. It was a curious sensation. She didn't know how she understood, but she did, and when the officer asked her if these five people were all her party she found herself answering in Russian . . . "Yes. Five." She could remember just those two simple words.

The others all turned to her in relief, asking her hurried questions which she could not answer, but some newfound confidence made her say, "Just open the luggage and I'm sure everything will be all right. They most particularly want to see what books we have brought in."

She could say no more than Yes and No, and "I cannot speak, only understand," but necessity made her competent and what she couldn't explain she indicated, waving passports and travel permits and the documents from the Russian government which (she hoped) explained why they had come.

When they were once more entrained, young Mr. Goode said, "Oh, well done, Miss Barshinskey! We shall look to you to be our leader from now on." She smiled deprecatingly, but she could sense the change in the mood of the party. Her role had changed. She had blended into the group. And because she was Daisy May she began to worry again and to explain.

"I don't know if I will always understand. My father came from Novgorod which I think is in northern Russia. They speak the same kind of Russian that is spoken here. But they said—in

London—that what they speak in the south might be different, a dialect. I can't promise I shall understand."

"Don't worry," said Mr. Foulgar kindly. "We have been warned that we may have to hire local interpreters, but among the refugees you should be quite happy. They are all from northern Russia, remember, and in any case, it is most important that at least one of us should have the rudiments of the language. I think, from now on, we must pass the train journeys learning a few simple words from you."

On the last day, steaming along through the sunlit forests, Daisy mentioned, as casually as she could, that in all probability her friend's brother might be waiting for them at the Finland Station.

"He is the brother of my friend who saw me off at King's Cross," she said earnestly, as though a full and justifiable explanation of Edwin's presence was going to be necessary. "We grew up together. I've known him since I was eleven." Four pairs of friendly but curious eyes were fixed on her face. "He's a merchant sailor and he's had to stay in Petrograd with his ship. He said that if his duties permit he will meet us and help us in any way he can." She made no mention of Galina. She had not told any of them that she had a sister in Petrograd. When Edwin had written to her, a short, impersonal letter that sounded as though a stranger had written it, he had said that Galina would not come to the Finland Station to meet Daisy. She was not well. Her health would not permit it. And Daisy had been glad. She didn't want her Quaker friends to know she had a sister like Galina.

"How very kind," said Miss Stubbs. "It will be so nice to see an English face again."

"You can always look at me, Miss Stubbs, if you need an English face," said Mr. Goode, and they all laughed, more than the feeble joke warranted because they were tired and dirty and the length of the journey, still not completed, had begun to make them realize the size, not only of Russia, but of the work that lay before them. Beneath their cheerful, middle-class English confidence lurked a small, steadily growing pocket of fear.

As the train pulled into the Finland Station her stomach began to churn. Would it be all right? Would he be the old Edwin? Would he still be fond of her, kind, the way he had always been or had Galina totally changed him? The churning turned to a hot scalding sensation and she was suddenly terrified that she might have to rush to the lavatory. How awful it would be, to see Edwin for the first time in two and a half years, and have to rush past him to find the lavatory.

And then she saw him. He was pushing slowly through the crowds, staring up into the windows, and she forgot all about the lavatory and just felt a joyous relief because although he was thinner and perhaps a little strained, he was basically still the same Edwin, tall and broad and brown, a strong-looking young man who stood out in a crowd, who looked reliable and tough, as though he would always care for people who were weaker than himself.

She gazed at him, not knowing that a smile had broken out over her face, oblivious of the fact that Mr. Goode was watching her.

Mr. Goode was the first down the steps in order to assist the ladies. She hardly saw him, was only distantly aware of his helping hand, because Edwin was walking toward them, and when he saw her he smiled. It was a ghost of a smile, but a smile nonetheless, and then to her surprise he bent down and kissed her on the cheek. It was an avuncular kind of kiss, but she flushed. He'd never done anything like that before.

"Have you been waiting long?" she asked foolishly. If she hadn't said something as mundane and ordinary as that she might have burst into tears.

"Couple of hours. No more." He smiled again. "How are you, Daisy? You look just the same."

"So do you." It was a lie. Now that she was close to him she could see how much weight he had lost, and also there was a faint air of . . . foreignness about him, as though living in Russia all this time had set a mark of its own on him. She could feel the others gathering around her, slightly nervous, embarrassed.

313

"This is Miss Stubbs and Miss D'Ete, Mr. Foulgar, Mr. Goode."

"It is extremely kind of you to come and meet us," said Mr. Foulgar. "I believe we have a few hours before catching our Moscow train. We shall probably be met in Moscow by one of our advance party, but it's extremely nice to have someone help us here too." The others all murmured thank-yous and gratitude. Everyone had suddenly become very English, shaking hands, making inconsequential remarks about the journey and Edwin's great kindness. Daisy, torn between her joy at seeing Edwin again, and her pride in her new friends, was speechless.

"I'd suggest," said Edwin, "that you eat here in the station restaurant. It isn't like home. The station restaurants here are as good—or bad—as any in the city, and this station will be less crowded than the Nicholas Station. A troop consignment is passing through there and you will find it uncomfortable. I will arrange for a porter to look after your luggage, and I am sure the ladies would like to wash before they eat. Daisy"—with great tact and courtesy he drew her slightly to one side—"the *Damskaya* is over there, through the main hall. Do you think you will be able to find your way?" There was a slightly hectoring note in his voice, schoolmasterish. She should have been happy that he cared so much about their comfort, but she was, surprisingly, faintly nettled. Had he, too, like Sophie, forgotten that she was half-Russian and could understand?

"Thank you, Edwin. I've learned to read the word since we crossed the frontier. We've had quite a few stops in the last four days."

"I will reserve two tables in the restaurant while you are gone."

As she picked her way over the filthy station hall to the ladies' room, she tried to put her churning emotions into order. She had wanted him to be the same and he was, or very nearly. But she was aware of a faint tremor of disappointment. She was here to begin a new life. She was wearing the red-and-black star of the Friends, and she was accepted as—nearly—an equal of the clever and educated people who were with her. Edwin hadn't appeared to see any of this. As she pushed through the crowd, past an old peasant woman in a striped skirt and a black kerchief, she said "Excuse me" in Russian with exaggerated courtesy, as though she were proving to Edwin how capable she was rather than excusing herself to the old woman.

The restaurant was full. There were several youngish officers in field uniforms eating with small parties of civilians, mostly women, mothers and wives, Daisy supposed, seeing them off. Over everything hung the smell of soup. A samovar hissed gently, sending a thin spiral of steam into the air. Tactfully the other four seated themselves at one of the tables and left her and Edwin together. Suddenly, alone with him, Daisy found she had nothing to say.

"How's everyone at home?"

"Not too bad . . . well, your father isn't terribly well, but he still manages to go to Hayward's every day. He has to now, with all the men gone to the war."

"And Ivan?"

"In France, with his regiment. He's a sergeant now."

Edwin's face colored. He looked almost sheepish, and then the waiter came up and, with relief, he took a menu and leaned across to the other table, advising and helping on the ordering of food. Daisy, during the journey down, unable to read Russian, had had to rely on fumbling conversations with waiters trying to explain what food was available. Now she was impressed to see that Edwin took the menu and read it with a practiced eye.

"You can read Russian?"

"Better than I can speak it. . . . There isn't a lot of choice, I'm afraid, cabbage soup and roast mutton. Food is very short and meat is particularly scarce. Some weeks there's no bread either." He paused, then said, again in that slightly hectorish tone, "You shouldn't have come here, Daisy. Russia isn't safe for people like you. I think it very likely they may lose the war—it's open knowledge that the casualty lists are enormous and that there have been heavy desertions at the front. And the English

315

aren't very popular at the moment. They don't think we're pulling our weight."

"That's why we're here," said Daisy defensively. "To try and help . . . to pull some weight."

He looked irritated. And suddenly she realized it was a familiar expression. She had seen it many times when they were growing up and she had not obeyed his kindly instructions.

"Daisy, you really don't know what you're doing. You're like children, walking into a lion's den. This isn't like England . . . it's different . . . dangerous. Captain Patterson . . ." He paused a second, as though considering how much it was safe to say. "Captain Patterson and the people at the embassy think it very likely civil unrest will break out, riots and troubles of that kind. If that does happen, the first people to be attacked will be foreigners. Most of the English people have already gone home. It was very foolish of you to come."

"Then why are you still here?" She felt humiliated, hurt, and it was making her angry. She had wanted so much from this meeting, wanted the old relationship—for she knew she couldn't hope for more—but wanted also that he should see that now she was an independent young woman who had made some plans for her own life. Instead he was speaking to her as though she were a scrubby child, one of the Barshinskey tinkers. "Why have you stayed when most of your crew have been sent home!" she asked angrily.

A hunted expression passed across Edwin's features. He opened his mouth to speak and then the waiter arrived with a pot of soup and they both waited until he had ladled it out and gone.

"I expect Sophie has told you about Galina," he said stiffly.

"Yes."

"And in any case, there's no question of me leaving the ship now. The British government are determined that all British ships in Russian ports shall maintain some crew members. If anything does . . . go wrong . . . we have to protect British property."

"But you could have gone . . . earlier?"

"I don't know . . . perhaps."

316

"You stayed because of Galina?"

"Yes," he said angrily. "You know that. Why are you asking all these questions?"

"I think you have little right to tell me I don't know what I'm doing. I'm here officially, with the full approval of the Russian government. I am here with the Friends who have a long and honorable history of relief work in Russia. You don't know anything about the Friends or why they are here, Edwin. You don't know anything about us! I haven't drifted here by chance . . . nor come on an idle whim!" She was white and her voice, which she was trying hard to control, was shaking and high-pitched. She was aware the Elizabeth Stubbs and Flora D'Ete were staring at her from the next table and with a trembling hand she picked up her soup spoon.

"You think I came here on an idle whim?" he asked, tight-lipped, and a voice in his heart said, "What else? What else was it that made you drop everything and chase after Galina Barshinskey?"

Daisy's anger evaporated into sudden fear. Never before in her whole life had she defied Edwin. She had always deferred to him, hung on his words. For years she had watched herself in his presence, guarded her tongue and behavior so that he could never find anything in her to dislike. And now, when she had only a short precious time with him, she was risking it all by losing her temper. But why, oh why, can't he see that I'm different, her heart cried. Why can't he see that I'm grown up.

"I don't know why you came here, Edwin," she said sadly. "Except that I remember my sister, and I suppose I shouldn't be surprised at anything that happened . . . how is she?"

"Frail," he said stiffly. "She contracted septicemia after her operation, and then pneumonia. She still isn't very strong and she's depressed. She cries a lot."

Jealousy stabbed through her heart, making her forget her caution. "She always did when she wanted to get her own way," she said nastily, but Edwin ignored her. "What sort of operation did she have?" she asked, thinking, I wish she'd died. Why didn't she die?

317

Edwin hesitated. His eyes refused to meet hers. "Some kind of abdominal operation. I don't know exactly what it was."

"Cancer?"

"No. Not cancer."

"Well, that's all right then. As long as it wasn't cancer."

"Do you want me to give her a message?"

"Did she have any message for me?" She was filled with a bitter resentment. She was trying to control her tongue but she was tired, the journey had been long, and she was emotionally exhausted.

"She sent her love."

"Don't give her my love. That would be a lie, wouldn't it?" She knew she was destroying years of gentle affection but all the same there was a wonderful feeling of freedom, of saying acid things that were truly in her heart. She felt an urge to let go . . . to say terrible things about Galina, to tell him of all the awful things, hideous selfish things she had done when they were children. "You can just say that I hope she is better soon."

She became aware, through her trembling anger and disappointment, that Edwin was smiling at her in an amused, indulgent way, and she realized that he was thinking how childish she was.

"Don't be silly, Daisy," he said kindly. "Of course I'll give her your love."

She had to do something, anything, to make him think of her as a grownup, as an equal. She fumbled in her handbag and finally she found a piece of paper which she handed to him.

"There you are." She tried to speak in the tone of voice that Mrs. Fawcett used when she was patronizing the kitchen. "That's the address of the Friends' Unit in Buzuluk. You never know when you, or Galina, might need it. We might be able to help you if you get into trouble."

"Thank you, Daisy," he said solemnly, his eyes twinkling.

The waiter came, removed the soup bowls, and put down plates containing a tiny portion of stringy mutton and some pickled cucumbers.

"And you know how to contact me," he said. "Through the consulate. And I'll give you the address of Galina's apartment."

That hurt, too, although she didn't know why it should. Obviously he knew where she lived, obviously he went there. It was just the . . . the familiarity with which he spoke that disconcerted her. It opened up whole areas of speculation in her mind that she didn't want to think about. Dimly she realized that they must, *must* stop talking about Galina. It was destroying everything.

"Did you know that Sophie is now in charge at the Fawcett's?"

His face lightened.

"The other housemaid left, and the under-gardener and the boiler boy were called up, and then I gave in my notice. Mrs. Fawcett suddenly went doddery, didn't seem to be able to cope with all the changes, and Sophie took over. She's more like a housekeeper than a parlor maid now. One of the Kelly girls is in the kitchen, and a couple of dailies come in and Sophie manages the lot. I think your mother's quite proud of her, although of course she never says."

"And Lillian?"

"Oh, Lillian is very grand these days. General Harding's wife, over at Dormansland, saw a dress that Lillian had made, and said it was exceptional. Exceptional, that's what she said. And she recommended Lillian to some dressmaker up in London, in Bond Street I think. And now Lillian goes up to London two days a week to help out in what your mother calls a 'salon.' Apparently they were short of people because of the war. Lillian has put a card in Miss Clark's window. It says, 'Dressmaker and Couturier Clothes.' "

Edwin burst out laughing and there was suddenly a moment of the old intimacy, the old friendship between them. And then he killed it by saying, "And what will you do, Daisy? When you've finished your relief work, or whatever it is, will you go home, back to Fawcett's?"

Couldn't he see that she wasn't the same scrubbed kitchen

maid, content to remain respectable in Fawcett's kitchen? Couldn't he see that she was different? And then, in a moment of panic, she wondered if she *was* different. She had never thought beyond going to Russia, beyond making a place for herself somewhere, and seeing Edwin. What *would* she do when the war was over? Where would she go? She was suddenly lost, totally alone in the world without ties or a home or anyone who cared about her. And then, like an actual physical touch she felt the others standing behind her. Elizabeth Stubbs with her nurse's calm, and Flora, Mr. Foulgar, and cheerful young Mr. Goode. She was beginning to be one of them, bonded to them, not only because of the journey and being together in an alien land, but because they had accepted her as committed to the same things as they were. They depend on me, she thought. They depend on me. She clung to the thought. She didn't know what the future would be, but for the moment she would hold to her new friends.

"I wonder if we ought to see about getting to the other station?" said Mr. Foulgar anxiously. He looked deferentially from her to Edwin, and Edwin rose from the table.

"I'll get two carriages. And I'll arrange for the porter to bring your luggage through." They followed him out of the restaurant into the hall of the station. She noticed many things she hadn't noticed before; the signs of war, a queue of soldiers in gray uniforms, their rolled blankets strapped over their shoulders and tin cooking pots tied on behind. The floor of the hall was littered with sunflower seeds. Every soldier she saw seemed to be chewing and spitting and over everything hung the smell of *makhorka* tobacco. The entire concourse was a strange mixture of luxury and filth. Well-dressed officers and elegant women with parasols picked their way between huge bearded beggars, their feet bound round with rags. A vendor of *piroshki* pushed a small charcoal-heated cart through the crowd and just inside the main entrance a creature—it was impossible to tell if it was a man or a woman —was stretched out on the floor, face to the wall.

The Nicholas Station was worse. They could hardly push their way through the mass of soldiers and officers filling the concourse. Weeping women, crying children, silent men thronged together. She could vaguely understand some of the phrases she overheard—"The bread is good. It will last for many days." "Wear your holy" . . . something . . . "and the good God will protect you."

Edwin led them on to the train, spoke to the attendant, fought for seats, and helped them pack their trunks and suitcases away.

The second bell rang and Daisy, seated by the window, suddenly realized she was going away, hundreds of miles away, and she might never see him again. They had had a few short hours together and had spent most of the time quarreling. She had expected, wanted so much from this meeting, in spite of everything, in spite of Galina, but in fact nothing had really happened. As the third bell rang and the train began to move she realized that probably nothing ever would happen. She was still poor little Daisy May. That was how they thought of her. They loved her but felt sorry for her. She was poor and impersonable, a tinker's child.

A gust of smoke drifted past the window and when it cleared she peered back and caught a last glimpse of Edwin's smiling face, the old tender smile, kind, and at the same time so essentially male, the smile that attracted women so much, especially the Barshinskey women. As the train pulled out into the yards she felt the old familiar gnawing in her heart that was partly a sense of her own inferiority, and partly her love for Edwin.

It is difficult to have a sense of self-esteem when you have grown up without home or possessions, ignored by your father, and knowing that even though your mother loves you she is a weak, downtrodden, poor sort of creature. It is hard to believe in your own worth when you are poorly educated, poorly dressed, and the constant recipient of charity and kindly condescension. She had never met anyone who was more lowly than she but she realized that in some way it was her own fault. Because she had so little esteem for herself, no one else had either.

And yet from somewhere—certainly not from that poor spiritless woman who was her mother—she had inherited a core of stubbornness, stubbornness that had sent her, on that first Sunday, into the Quaker Meeting House at Reigate, with an air of almost defiant determination. There, she had discovered in the silent communal meditation a peace that came from somewhere outside herself. She realized, on the second Sunday when the same soothing calm took hold of her, that in the village she was never alone. She shared a room with Sophie, she passed her days in the noisy Fawcett kitchen, and she passed her leisure in the Willoughby's kitchen.

She believed in God. First her mother, then the well-meaning Willoughbys, had endorsed her belief in God but she had always thought of Him as a rather busy all-seeing person who ran a huge number of committees which guarded his many interests. And now she began to wonder if perhaps God was a quiet person, someone rather elusive, like the smell of the sea that sometimes drifted inland when the wind was in the right direction.

It was four weeks before anyone asked her name, and she liked that too. It was refreshing to be anonymous, to be left to find one's own level instead of being hustled into gossipy kindnesses. The sense of peace prevailed, grew stronger every time she went. It wasn't what she had gone to find, but the strength that she absorbed from the tranquil silences seemed to carry her home, soothed and detached from herself. And then, at one meeting, a woman whose distress was obvious, asked for help and prayer in her present deep trouble. She did not say what the trouble was but Daisy, with a sense of faint surprise, realized that it was not enough just to sit and absorb the peace. She must contribute to it as well. Naïvely she had squeezed her eyes tightly shut and willed comfort to the woman, not knowing if it would work but beginning to understand that what the Friends were doing was sharing with each other. And with that realization had come a sense of her own worth, just a frail awareness that the good intent of even so lowly a person as herself could contribute toward the common good.

The knowledge, the awareness of her worth, came and went,

sometimes she lost it altogether, but what she didn't lose was the sense of belonging to these people, of being part of them. As she sat in the crowded train, staring out the window at the flat everlasting landscape of trees and marsh, she wondered if she had been wrong to come to Russia. Had she come because she was needed, or because of Edwin? She wasn't sure, perhaps she would never be sure, but in her heart was a growing contentment with her new life. Nothing would ever stop her loving Edwin but until he needed her she was determined to find a place for herself, here, with these good and purposeful people.

The sense of shock hit them all, sensible, practical people though they were and bad though they had known conditions were going to be. They tried to seek strength from their faith and from their common sense, but for a while they remained stunned . . . overwhelmingly threatened by disease, poverty, filth, and above all the hopeless misery of two hundred thousand refugees.

"Most of them have lost everything except the clothes they stand up in," said Robert Tatlock on their first night in Buzuluk. They sat around a wooden table and through the window came the stench of a town without drains in summer. The train had arrived at eleven at night and they had only a confused impression of low shabby buildings, unmade roads, and clouds of flies.

"They have been driven before the advancing Germans and were finally shipped to Turkestan last winter. About a third of them died there, some from disease but most from cold and hunger. Those who survived the winter have been brought back here and billeted on the local peasants who don't like them very much." He paused and looked at the tired young faces around the table. "When I talk of peasants you can forget the country people at home. It's nothing like that here. The peasants here don't live much better than refugees themselves. They have one meal a day, they live in one room, scabies is practically endemic, there's no doctor or hospital in an area of a thousand square miles. In the summer there's typhoid, smallpox, and anthrax, in the winter they seal themselves into their huts with the stove burning, no fresh air and far too many people, and consumption breeds. That's just normal life here. The refugees have all that plus they have lost their homes, they have clothing totally un-suited to the climate here—another third will die this coming winter unless we can get warm clothes from home—all the men-folk are either dead or at the front, most of them don't even know where their men are. They've all seen their children and parents dying along the road. There's not a single family still intact; in many cases there's only one left and that one a child who can't remember his name or village. They're not only undernourished, badly clothed and ill, they're also totally demoralized, without hope. A lot of them will die because they want to."

He was a nice looking, kind young man with a thin face and a dark mustache. He looked typically British and you'd have expected to see him working in a bank or as a schoolteacher. His face was strained, but from him came an air of authority. It was the only thing that gave them any hope.

"What can we do?" asked Andrew Goode. Even his cheerful ebullience was subdued.

"We can do very little. There aren't enough of us and we don't have enough of anything—not enough clothing, nor food, nor medical supplies. We just do what we can . . . scratch the surface of the misery and try to learn Russian as quickly as we can. We have interpreters, but it makes everything take a long time and constantly there are misunderstandings. Miss Barshin-skey, at the moment you will be the most useful person we have and I am sending you to Mogotovo in the north." He pulled a map from a pile of papers to one side of him and placed it in the middle of the table. "It's forty miles north from here, but again don't think of it as forty English miles. The track is unmade and it takes eight or nine hours, sometimes longer, by *tarantas*. I believe it will be easier in the winter when one can travel by sleigh.

"At Mogotovo there is a large house which has been put at our disposal by the authorities and there we will house as many stray children as we can and also try to set up a small medical unit for the surrounding countryside, refugees and local peasants alike. Dr. Manning and Nurse Morgan are already there but have no interpreter. A consignment of clothing and boots has been sent there and they will have to be distributed to all the villages in the area. It's not so much a case of distributing it as sharing it so that every family gets a little of something, one pair of boots a family, one warm coat that can be shared among the children, and so on. That's why we need someone who can understand—everything must be shared very carefully over as large an area as possible."

Daisy just nodded. She was too tired to feel anything, anything at all.

"Miss Stubbs, you'll go to Lubimovka where we are trying to reopen the hospital." He pointed again to the map, to a spot as far to the south as Mogotovo was to the north. Daisy felt a stab of disappointment. Elizabeth Stubbs was a quiet, competent young woman and Daisy had grown to rely on her during the journey. Now she was going to be eighty miles away.

"Miss D'Ete, you will go to Mogotovo with Miss Barshinskey to try and set up the orphanage, as will Mr. Foulgar. Mr. Goode to Lubimovka for the time being. . . . Later I may ask you to open a new center in the south. Now then, a few precautions . . . you must wash every night in carbolic and if you have had to sleep in one of the peasant's houses—which you will do when you are distributing clothes—you must soak your clothes in carbolic, too, as soon as you return. For the remainder of this summer you must continue taking quinine, especially those working at the southern centers. There are frequent outbreaks of malaria. You must report any signs of illness immediately. All water must be boiled—it won't be for long. As soon as the winter comes snow can be melted for both washing and drinking purposes. You are to eat regularly, however much you are sickened or upset because those you are helping do not have enough. The food situation is easing and it will not help if you become ill. Sanitary arrangements are primitive—again, make sure you use carbolic wherever you have to dig a latrine. I suggest you don't use the same ones as the peasants."

Daisy was aware that Flora D'Ete was blushing and she suddenly realized how difficult it was going to be for some of the women who had never known poverty to use primitive lavatories or holes in the ground, to sleep in one-roomed huts with peasants, to keep fleas and lice at bay.

"I'm afraid that letters from home take a long time to get here. I don't quite know why when it has only taken you two weeks to get here. We try to have meetings and prayer when we can. Some of us at the smaller centers are very lonely—only two people at Bogdanovka—they need our prayers. It is sometimes"—his voice faltered a little—"it is sometimes difficult to remember that God is helping us when we are all so far apart. . . ."

In the light from the oil lamp their faces were white and small. Underneath the table Daisy felt her hand grasped by Flora.

"Shall we pray silently together?" Robert Tatlock asked hesitantly, looking about him. They huddled in, closer together. Flora lifted her other hand to the table. It was shaking and then Daisy saw Andrew Goode put his own hand over Flora's. One by one, around the table, they linked hands, small and afraid, praying for strength and resolution in the vast Russian night.

They set off the following morning in two carts that were little more than boxes on wheels with straw to soften the jolting over the uneven dirt roads. Daisy and Flora were in one, sitting atop their trunks, and Mr. Foulgar was in the other with several sacks of beans and rice. Almost immediately huge swarms of flies surrounded them, smothering their faces, crawling into their noses and mouths. Daisy gave a small, hysterical yelp and beat frantically in the air with her hands, a movement that threw the flies into fresh paroxysms of energy. She looked at Flora and saw that several of them were crawling in her hair and around her eyes.

"Quickly, Flora! Tie your handkerchief over your face."

"I hate flies," Flora said tremulously. "Hate them! Such dirty things!"

As the cart gathered speed out over the steppe the flies thinned a little and after about half an hour the driver, a big brown peasant in a cotton tunic, lit a cigarette and blew the smoke back in their faces. The smoke was mingled with the smell of onions and decaying teeth, but Daisy felt nothing but gratitude and said thank you with fervent warmth.

They had gone only a few miles over the flat, dry landscape when Flora was sick. Daisy wanted to stop the cart but Flora refused to let her. "I'm a bad traveler . . . as soon as we start moving I shall only be sick again and when we stop there's the flies. . . ." Daisy tried to wipe the dust and sweat from her pallid face. After a while she rested her head on Daisy's shoulder and began to breathe very quickly.

"*Stoi! Stoi!*" Daisy shouted to the driver, and after several yards, hauling and lurching, the cart stopped. Mr. Foulgar drew up alongside.

"What's wrong?"

"I think Flora's ill."

"Only travel sickness," she murmured, her eyes closed. "I'm always like this—remember how sick I was on the crossing."

"Perhaps if we rested a little while . . ."

The sun blazed down on them. The flies swarmed, and Daisy began to feel a little sick herself. "Perhaps if we could get to some shade, a village perhaps . . . I'll try . . ." She groped in her subconscious for words and finally remembered the words for house, and woman, and ill. The driver spoke in a thick dialect and it took her a long time to understand him.

"He says he will drive slowly to the next village and Flora can rest there."

The slow driving was only slightly better. There was still jolting and moments when it seemed as though the cart was going to turn on its side. After an hour Daisy saw, through the clouds of dust, the golden gleam of a church dome. The village, when they arrived, was a single wide track bordered by wooden houses with a draw well in the center. Towering over the dirt and dun-colored landscape was the church, all gold and blue and white. The driver took the cart up to a house near the church and said something to Daisy, who again wrestled with understanding.

"It's the house of the village headman," she said. "We can rest here."

They came clustering out of the houses to look at them, barefoot children with cropped heads and women in drab and dirty homespun. The children spoke a little but for the most part the watching faces were silent. Daisy had the feeling they would run away if she moved toward them.

They went into the low wooden house through a stable at the side, which led in turn to a small room that smelled so strongly of unwashed humanity Daisy nearly gagged.

"Try not to breathe through your nose," she murmured to Flora. There was a bench around two sides of the room and Daisy led Flora to a section that was unoccupied—there were several old women and babies taking up a lot of the room—and helped her to lie flat.

Sweat was breaking out on Flora's head again, and her breathing was still fast. All around the room the old women looked at her, then one, unsmiling, asked a question.

"She is asking if we will take food with them," said Daisy, and Flora groaned. Before she could begin groping for words that were a gracious refusal, a middle-aged woman turned from the huge stove offering a wooden bowl of very small eggs. Daisy looked at Matthew Foulgar, who had followed them in.

"I think we must eat," she said. "I remember my father . . . it would be discourteous to refuse. If you and I eat, Flora can be excused. We will share one so that we do not take too much of their food."

Smiling, nodding with an affability she did not feel, she took an egg, said "*Spasibo*" with as much warmth as she could manage, and received at last a half-smile in return. She gestured toward Flora, shaking her head and placing her hand on her stomach. Cups of brownish liquid were produced and again from somewhere in her past she thought she knew what it might be. "*Kvas,*" she said to Mr. Foulgar. "It's all right, I think. It's fermented beer. It should be harmless."

She stared about, then counted that there were fifteen people in the tiny room, not counting babies. There were the two wooden benches, a table, a crude icon in the corner of the room, some sheepskins on top of the stove, and a kind of bunk over the doorway on which lay a pale thin child whose lusterless eyes stared at them without interest.

She pointed to the child. "Ill?" she asked, but the woman just shrugged her shoulders fatalistically. Whose child was it? Were these refugees or local peasants? They all looked the same, dirty and apathetic.

Her eyes focused suddenly on the walls where several black beetlelike creatures scurried over the wooden planks and she stifled a small cry. They were a new kind of house bug, one she had never seen before. She began to feel her skin crawling with imaginary insects.

"Are you feeling better, Flora? I think we should go."

They helped her back toward the cart, and Daisy tried to arrange the straw-filled sack so that Flora could rest more comfortably, but within ten minutes she was sick again. The journey took on the quality of a nightmare—the flat parched landscape, flies, dust, and the huge glaring white bowl of sky from which there was no protection became the frightening background to the noise of Flora's constant vomiting. It took them eight hours and several more stops before they reached at last the shelter of a pine forest. The driver turned and spoke to her.

"He says it isn't far now, Flora. Just try and bear it a bit longer." She wiped Flora's face with her handkerchief. They were both filthy and there were rings of dust around their eyes and mouths in spite of covering their faces.

"Such pain," murmured Flora. "Such pain . . . never had such pain with travel sickness before. . . ." Her face was burning and tiny beads of sweat shone on her forehead. Daisy longed for the presence of Elizabeth Stubbs, now on her way to Lubimovka in the south.

They came at last out of the forest and saw the village, the usual collection of log huts, but with one or two much larger and more elaborate than their neighbors'. It was apparently a wealthy village and the church with two domes and a tower was surrounded by trees and a low white wall. The big house, when they came to it, looked extraordinary in its setting of steppe land and peasant village. It was a vast white mansion, two stories high, with a water tower and a grand colonnaded porch. As one drew closer one could see the white stucco was peeling and the vegetation in the surrounding garden was dense and overgrown. A broken wall surrounded the garden. The light was fading and as Daisy stepped down from the *tarantas* a cloud of evening midges replaced the flies and swirled around her head. She could feel the bites on her neck and face. Mr. Foulgar came hurrying up from behind.

"We must get Flora inside as quickly as possible," Daisy said through a mouth clogged with dust.

They helped Flora down, and as she stood, supported on each side, the huge door of the mansion opened and two figures came hurrying down the steps. The introductions were hurriedly exchanged, and then with relief Daisy was able to pass Flora into the hands of Dr. Manning. Only much later that night, in a low wooden bed with a straw mattress, did she realize she had been using Flora's Christian name without embarrassment.

Flora had dysentery. It was inexplicable, for neither Mr. Foulgar nor Daisy had contracted it, but somewhere along their journey Flora had been contaminated in some way. Later, during their time at Mogotovo, they all suffered repeatedly from varying forms of dysentery, three of their number had typhus and one diphtheria. Daisy, in spite of the quinine tablets, fell victim to malaria. When, later, a scarlet fever epidemic broke out in the small infirmary attached to the orphanage, they all, by some miracle, managed to remain free, but summer fevers enervated them regularly and colds and influenza struck them all through the long dark winters.

She had thought that she would be put to nursing Flora but she was too valuable for that. Within two days she set out with Matthew Foulgar again in the jolting, bone-shaking *tarantas* to survey the conditions of the refugees in the villages and distribute the first bundles of clothing. They returned in four days, infested with lice and overwhelmed by their first encounters with misery. Mr. Foulgar, not understanding the language, had nonetheless absorbed the despair and was in a state of desperate frustration.

"We had not nearly enough," he cried. "They have nothing . . . nothing. It is unbelievable that people can really have nothing. And their apathy . . . that is dreadful. To see women just sitting on the earth staring at nothing, taking no notice when the children cry. It is difficult to comprehend . . . that anyone could become that apathetic whatever has happened to them."

"No . . ." Daisy said slowly. "No, it isn't difficult to understand, not at all." She had found the trip horrifying because she recognized the people only too well. . . . She could see her mother in the thin dazed women who could no longer cope with life. She could see herself and Ivan in the children with sores around their mouths and not enough clothes to cover them decently. She wanted to run screaming from their misery because she had spent years putting those memories behind her, and now she was planted down in some dreadful nightmare where she was once more part of a terrible poverty that was worse than anything she had known before and yet was somehow overwhelmingly familiar.

As she listened to the refugees, the old men and women who had survived, the mothers whose children had died during the flight across a continent, she recognized the remnants of respectable people reduced to nothing—women who had had farms and Sunday clothes, who had baked bread and set their families at tables of good food and clean linen, now living on the charity of those who had only a little more than they did. And she thought, fighting panic, I must try to be like Sophie. I must remember what Sophie was to us all those years ago, and I must remember how we felt. She tried to explain to Mr. Foulgar.

"It's possessions," she said. "I know it is wrong to value possessions for themselves, but poor people have little else to measure themselves by. They need things."

"What kind of things?" Dr. Manning asked. The others were attentive, trying to understand her, anxious to listen to anything that would help. It was the evening hour, the time after the food had been eaten and the plates scoured. It was the only time they were all able to sit together in a corner of the vast reception hall of the old mansion. Their one oil lamp lit only their small area and the shadows of the huge room rustled with insects and mice.

"Anything . . . so long as it is theirs to keep. A book." Even a book about railway engines. "A handkerchief, a basket, a saucepan. If you have something that belongs to you, then you begin to be someone. You are the owner of a black saucepan. You have an identity. You can begin to see yourself, measure yourself against the people around you. These people don't know who they are anymore because they have no possessions. They are all . . . gray . . . all the same as each other . . . gray."

They were silent and she didn't know if she had made them understand. They were good people, but how could they understand as she understood?

"We can do nothing," Dr. Manning said finally. "We must wait for more clothing to arrive from London. Until then we have nothing we can give them."

The felt boots arrived from Moscow and she went out again, and because they had little that was tangible to give, she tried to give them pieces of herself, tried to listen to their tales of what had happened and what their lives had been before. They had come from a relatively rich farming area, and had been dumped into a community of medieval peasants. The only things they had in common with their hosts were the language and the religion. She listened, and because she was a peasant herself she understood—understood that if you were used to lard and rye bread, one's stomach turned at mutton fat and wheat bread, understood that if your home has been razed to the ground and your man and your children killed by disease and cold, then sometimes it is the tiny differences of everyday life that provide the ultimate despair.

She spent hours sitting on dirt floors, absorbing their sorrows, being bitten by insects, and realizing, too, that their reluctant hosts had their own miseries to bear. Life was hard enough for a

Samarian peasant without having to support sophisticated refugees from the west.

The winter came. There seemed to be just a few short weeks of autumn and then one morning she woke early and saw a light drift of snow blow past the window. When she got out of bed she saw small flurries caught in the September wind. It melted as soon as it touched the ground but the following week a heavier fall came at night and lay on the ground and by the end of October the ground was covered and life, in many ways, became much easier.

The bone-shaking *tarantas* was put away, and the tandems of horses were transferred to sleighs. Now they were able to fly over the ground. It took only five hours for supplies to come out from Buzuluk. The flies, the dust, to a certain extent the fleas and lice, vanished and everything became beautiful, the steppe a great white ocean of undulations that resembled waves. When Robert Tatlock came out with the provisions in October he brought them all sheepskin coats, rather worn, not too clean, but already necessary as the winter began to encroach.

They lived in a curious state of exhaustion, despair and, strangely enough, elation. The elation came from the wonderful white world outside, the brilliant blue skies and trees covered in icicles, the glimpse of an elk in the pine forest. The elation also came, though more rarely, from their feeling of mutual brotherhood. The exhaustion and despair were with them most of the time.

That first winter was the most depressing . . . depressing, and degrading especially for people like Flora who had come from a comfortable middle-class home. The children, rounded up from the cottages in the surrounding villages, nearly all orphaned, some not even knowing who they were, had acquired the habits of wild animals in their roamings across Europe and Turkestan. They urinated and defecated wherever they happened to be, they stole, they fought with each other at mealtimes like snarling cats, on one occasion overturning the table in their efforts to snatch the food from each other.

Daisy, tired and itching badly from the fleabites of her latest overnight sojourn in a peasant hut, encountered Flora in tears outside her bedroom one night. It was a further incongruity of their lives that in the midst of their poverty and depredations the huge derelict mansion was able to provide plenty of bedrooms. It was as ridiculous as the grand drawing rooms with marquetry floors that some of the older children had tried to dig up and burn.

"Are you ill, Flora?"

She shook her head and pointed back to her room, for the moment unable to speak.

"Have they been through your things again and stolen something?"

She pushed past Flora and went into her room. By the side of the bed, on the oiled linoleum, was a pile of excreta and some crumpled paper with which the offender had tried to cleanse himself. Daisy gazed wearily at the offending pile.

"Unpleasant," she said tiredly. "They haven't done it in our rooms before."

"It's not that," Flora said, shaking her head. "It's the paper . . . it's the last letter from home, from my mother. I know it's silly to want to keep it, but . . ."

They had mail from home every six weeks or so, if they were lucky, and even then what came was sparse; many letters and parcels were held up in Petrograd or Moscow. Their letters were infinitely precious—a link with home, a reminder that there were places in the world where the old life still existed. They read and reread their letters many times. When they'd read them to themselves they shared bits with one another. Daisy sought for something comforting to say.

"We've made a great step forward, Flora. At last they're beginning to use paper. They've not used anything until now . . . just gone!"

Flora stared at her, then in despair began to giggle.

"You go and sit in my room for a bit. I'll clean it up."

"No . . . oh no. I mustn't be weak. I must do my share of the unpleasant things."

"You do your share. Let me do this."

Later, when she returned, smelling of the inevitable carbolic, Flora was sitting by the window looking out at the snow.

"I wonder if I was right to come here, Daisy? I don't feel I'm any use. I hate the dirt and . . . I'm so ashamed . . . but often I hate the people too. I know they can't help it, but sometimes I feel they're not *human*. I just don't feel I'm helping any of you. I'm a burden." She put her face down in her hands and began to cry. Daisy, rather impatiently, for she was tired, patted her shoulder.

"We all feel discouraged," she said. "I feel I'm not helping much either. But I felt that all along . . . before we even got here."

"You," said Flora, startled. "Why, you couldn't have felt that!"

"Yes."

"But you're the most useful of all of us . . . speaking Russian, and knowing how to make those terrible stoves work and what food to cook for ninety people and . . . you don't seem to be so bothered by the dirt and the latrines. . . ." She paused, a small frown wrinkling her brow. "You seem to understand these hateful people better than we do. You seem to know what to do for them."

"It's because I'm half-Russian, I expect," Daisy said, embarrassed. "Or perhaps because I've been poor." She stared at Flora and reflected, pityingly, that in fact Flora wasn't a great deal of use. She was sweet and kind and meant well, but constantly she had to be sustained and encouraged. Then, because she felt guilty and mean she said, "I'm not really the most useful. Dr. Manning and Hannah and Elizabeth are the most useful of all. Sometimes I think the only ones who should have come are the medical people."

"Do you think we'll ever go home?" Flora asked quietly. "Will the war ever end?"

The candle by the side of Daisy's bed cast a small circle of light in the middle of the room. It was cold, but not unbearably so for the stoves in the rooms below were kept alight all night. The room was large, grand, designed on stately lines, and the small wooden bed, rough table, and single chair looked incongruous. Daisy thought about going home, back to Fawcett's, to the village, to being "poor Daisy May" again, and then she realized that one thing she would never be ever again was poor Daisy May. If she did go back to Fawcett's things would be different.

"I expect we'll get home one day," she said, comforting as best she could.

"It's snowing again."

Daisy went and stood beside her. Outside a blizzard raged and they could hear the tolling of the church bell in the village.

"That means it's bad," she said. "If anyone is out in this they'll quickly get lost. We're very lucky to be here, inside, in the warm."

"Of *course* we are," said Flora with a deliberate return to optimism. "We must always remember how lucky we are—and I must *try* to be useful."

She rose briskly from Daisy's chair and walked to the door. "I don't think I could manage here without you, Daisy," she said tremulously. "I really don't. But, oh . . . I so long to go home again . . ."

She left the room and Daisy sat for a while, staring out at the whirling snowflakes. Go home? What, and where, was home? Fawcett's? No, she'd been cared for at Fawcett's but it wasn't home. The Owl House, and all the shacks and barns and derelict cottages they'd lived in before the Owl House? The Willoughbys? Yes, perhaps a little. That was the nearest she'd known to a home. But, in spite of their many kindnesses, in spite of Sophie, it wasn't *her* home. She shivered and looked around at the huge bedroom with its molded ceiling and primitive furniture.

"I have no home," she said aloud to herself. "I have no home. But one day I will. One day I shall have a place that is home."

20 FOR OVER TWO YEARS HE HAD BEGGED HER TO RETURN to England, had said that if Heikki wouldn't help her, then he would do his best with the consulate to get her a place on a train going over the border to Finland. For over two years she had stubbornly refused to go, at first because she was enjoying herself, because Petrograd, even in war, was enchanting and entertaining and fun. Later, he had conceded, she had been too ill. But even when she had grown a little stronger, when she could, with a little effort, have withstood the journey, she had refused to go. Since her operation—paid for from the sale of Heikki's diamond earrings and the precious silver cups—she had clung to him, refusing to listen every time he suggested that she go home alone. "Only if you come too!" she cried. "I cannot go on my own. You come, too, Edwin!"

Patiently, repeatedly, he explained that this time he couldn't just drop everything and follow her across the continent. This time, however much she cried and pleaded, he had to stay where he was. She didn't understand. She had spent her life flitting from one occupation, one man, to another, exactly as her mood dictated. If Edwin wasn't prepared to take her back to England, it was because he didn't want to. At one time, when he first knew her, it would have driven him into a frenzy of misery; now he just became angry and when she saw his anger she grew silent and said she would stay with him, she didn't mind, she was happy just to be in the same city, seeing him for a few hours every day. He would look after her, wouldn't he? He had promised he would look after her. . . .

And so they both stayed. Edwin because he had to, and because he had vowed to himself that never again would he run from his duty, and Galina because she was afraid to face life without him. Since the abortion, the operation, the long illness, she had become even more highly strung, given to wildly fluctuating moods of almost hysterical elation, followed by crying and apathetic despair. Once she threatened to slash her wrists if he left her, and he had to stay with her all night, risking trouble when he returned to ship the next morning. Nothing had happened. Things in the city were so serious that often Captain Patterson and Mr. Bathgate and the two deckhands found they were detained in all kinds of ways, the closing of the bridges at unspecified times, leaving one stranded on the wrong island, strikes, sometimes official, sometimes not, when all the trams ceased to run, and even on one occasion an illegal arrest when Captain Patterson was jailed for a day by a suspicious policeman who said his papers were forged. Petrograd had descended into an insane whirlwind of misery, confusion, and the final convulsions of hysterical gaiety.

At some point in February, a strong and unpleasant premonition took hold of him. There was a growing sense of panic in his stomach that anarchy was going to break out. He tried to think back to the February of last year. The bread queues were worse; even in the bitterest wind women waited all night outside the bread shops. Their silent unmoving lines huddled in blankets and old sacks seemed almost menacing in their intensity of misery. There were more strikes, more unpleasant incidents in the streets. One day, right in the Nevsky, he saw a crowd gathered in a circle. Two policemen were hitting at something on the pavement and when he looked over the heads of the crowd he saw it was the unconscious body of a broom hawker. The policemen stopped suddenly and then began to break all the handles of the brooms. When they turned to go, the silent crowd, now about ten deep, did not move. They raised their batons to strike a path through the bodies and from the crowd came a low throaty growl, more animal like than human. The circle, instead of breaking, closed in on the hated police and Edwin suddenly glimpsed fear in their faces before they disappeared from view. The crowd was deadly silent, just a scuffle from the center of the circle and a loud agonized cry from one of the policemen and then the crowd swiftly dispersed, vanished into the shops and side streets. Edwin knew enough not to linger in case of arrest. As quickly as the rest he melted into the Gostiny Dvor, losing himself in the maze of stalls and kiosks. Later, hurrying back to the ship, he couldn't move up the Nevsky for an enormous throng of workers blocking the road right across to the front of the Kazan Cathedral. They were strikers from the Viborg side and their banners mostly proclaimed the one word: BREAD.

Out early on another morning, when the freezing wind across the Baltic had dropped a little and the city was bathed in bright color, he found the body of a young girl lying beside the railings of the Moika, right opposite the Razumovsky Palace. She was wearing felt boots and a coat which had been pulled down decently to cover her body. Her hands were bare and were folded quietly across her breast, as though someone had prepared her for burial. The long dark lashes of her closed eyes were rimed in frost and when he placed a gentle finger on her cheek it was iron-hard. There had been a fresh fall of snow the night before, but there was none on her. She just lay, nestling like a bird in a slight hollow of snow. Poor lassie, he thought to himself, then looked around to see if there was anyone else about and when he saw the road was clear he hurried away. It was dangerous to be caught doing anything, anything at all, even reporting a dead body in the street.

That night, Captain Patterson called them together. Five of them crowded into his cabin.

"I don't have to tell you things are going badly at the front. They are also bad in the city. You know that. You also know our instructions . . . to stay and protect the ship as long as we can. I think it is most unlikely we shall be used for haulage work up and down the Baltic this summer. I don't think the Russian government is any longer capable of organizing civil ships. I also have to say"—he cleared his throat and gave them a long expressionless stare that gave no indication at all of what he was feeling—"I also have to say that I don't know how much longer the embassy or the consulate can protect us. If trouble comes, no one's going to ask what nationality you are before they shoot. However, we

339

must do the best we can. You will carry your passports and permits of residence at all times. I'm also suggesting you carry these." He unlocked the metal chest which fitted beneath his bunk and lifted out a leather bag. He loosened the drawstring and lifted out, somewhat gingerly, a heavy black revolver.

"Do any of you know how to use them?"

"No, sir." The mumble was unanimous.

"Here. I have one for each of you. They are unloaded, but hold them and I will explain the mechanism."

Edwin gazed, mesmerized, at the heavy black weight in his hand. Unbidden, a thought came to his mind of the meeting room at home, of all the commonplace country people in polished boots and Sunday hats, holding Bibles in their hands. What had happened to him?

Captain Patterson's voice droned on. He handed out cartridges, then opened the cashbox from which they were paid.

"I am also giving each of you a substantial sum of money, rubles and also some English half-sovereigns which might be even more valuable than rubles in certain circumstances. You are all trustworthy seamen. This sum is to be kept for emergencies. If we are separated, if you are arrested, if you find yourself stranded, you must use the money as best you can to get yourselves out of trouble. You all have the rudiments of Russian now, and of course I fully intend that we shall remain on the ship and protect her as long as possible. This is a cautionary fund only. I suggest you improvise purses or belts that you can wear next your skin. That's all. You can go now."

They drifted away. It was curious, but although they had been stranded together in Petrograd for over two and a half years, Edwin and the deckhands had never become mates. MacKenzie and Simpson were both Orkney men and spoke to each other in a dialect Edwin had never bothered to try to understand. They were clannish men, not overanxious to become intimate with him and Edwin had welcomed the privacy. He wanted as few people as possible to know of his secret life in Petrograd. In many ways he was more involved with the two officers, particularly Mr. Bathgate, with whom he spoke the common language of engines.

So now, even after the disturbing session in the captain's cabin, they separated as usual, MacKenzie and Simpson to the deckhands' quarters, and Edwin to his solitary bunk beside the galley. Captain Patterson's precautions had only echoed his own presentiments of doom, and he realized that, even as Captain Patterson had tried to protect his crew, so must he do what he could for Galina.

She had lived, since her operation, on the money Heikki had left her, supplemented by help from Edwin. Heikki had been generous—Edwin had been astonished at just how generous— and the bills for the apartment were still paid directly from the bank in Moscow. But food prices had soared in the last year and Galina was extravagant. There were no reserves of money. The next time he was in her apartment he asked her what jewelry she had left. She became brittle, evasive.

"Nothing," she trilled, avoiding his eyes. "You know I have nothing. Everything has been sold . . . for the doctor, for Yelena, for food." Her voice began to grow angry. "You do not know how much everything costs! How much it is just to have the simple things. . . . I have bought nothing for myself, nothing, no dresses, no flowers, no wine. You do not understand how gray my life has become!" Two crystal tears crept softly down her cheeks as she leaned her chin in her hand and stared out of the window at the whirling snow. Although she was pale her hair had regained its lustrous quality. Swept up high on her head it formed a crown over her heart-shaped face. She looked like the snow queen of a fairy tale as she gazed out, her long dark lashes forming shadows on her cheeks. He felt his heart suddenly twist at her beauty, at her ivory sexuality.

"Galina, I am trying to help you," he said. "I want you to have some money, some security in case rioting breaks out, in case you have trouble with the police. You must at least have sufficient for your train fare over the border. You need money for bribes, for buying special papers of exit. I shall try to help you but you have used nearly all the money I have saved. I want to be assured you still have a little . . . a little insurance."

"Nothing. I have nothing," she declaimed, shrugging her shoulders.

"That's not true, Galina. You have your garnets. You were wearing them the other day, and your amber pins and necklace . . ."

"Amber is worthless in Russia," she said impatiently. "In England, when Heikki gave them to me, they were special, but here on the Baltic amber means nothing."

Edwin sighed impatiently. "Just tell me what you have left, Galina. Whatever you have, I shall sell for you . . . for gold if possible. You need to have money. So, what is left? The amber, which is worthless, and what else?"

"Just the garnets," she mumbled, and something about the way she spoke, the furtive manner in which she turned away from him, made a sudden spasm of cold in his stomach. It wasn't as bad as it had been in the old days. Then, jealousy had made him almost sick with despair. This was a milder little twist of anguish, like the dying down of a toothache. He rose from his chair and walked quickly through to the bedroom. The drawer of her boudoir table was locked and there was no key in it. He stood back, lifted his foot, and smashed the lock with one angry blow.

"No! You mustn't. You mustn't!" She threw her arms around his neck and tried to drag him away.

The padded box on the top enclosed the diamonds, the same ones he had taken with his champagne cups to the jeweler's in the Morskaya and sold. Beneath that were the garnets, then the pearls she said she had sold to pay Yelena's wages. He opened all the boxes, all the trinket chests, and one by one he threw the jewels on the floor, not saying anything to her, but glaring into her eyes with accusation at each fresh discovery—the jet and gold collar, the sapphire ring, the gold and diamond fob watch and guard chain, the amethyst bracelets, all the things she had sighed over and told him she had sold.

"Who bought the diamonds back for you?" he said coldly. She covered her face with her hands and sank down onto a chair.

"I suppose it doesn't matter who it was," he said slowly. "I wouldn't know him anyway." The twist of toothache had gone. He supposed it was impossible to go on being hurt just as violently as in the beginning. Now he felt only a terrible disappointment, a weary realization that he would never be able to trust her.

"I had to . . . I had to . . ." she cried. "My things . . . all my lovely things . . . it's all I have left. You don't understand, you never understood how important things are to me. I must have them . . . pretty jewelry and clothes. You"—she suddenly raised her face and glared angrily at him, her black eyes alight with unexpected venom—"you were always so righteous, so *moral*, so proud of being honest and upright and a *Willoughby* . . . always preaching and expecting me to care about the same dull things that you did, always trying to make me feel guilty because I wanted to laugh and have fun. You think I'm not good enough for you!"

"Galina!"

"Yes, yes, that's what you think! Why haven't you touched me since I was ill? You said it didn't matter . . . about the officers . . . but you don't want me anymore! I loved you—the others weren't important—and you pretended to love me, but you've never touched me since you found out about the officers. You think you're so good, so special . . . well, I tell you, Edwin Willoughby, you're dull, and miserable, and you never make me laugh! I hate you!"

Everything she said was true. It was all true, except that he hadn't pretended to love her. He did love her. But all the rest was true and there wasn't anything he could say. He turned on his heel and walked out of the apartment.

He plunged out of the building and began to run along the snowy street toward Znamensky Square. He didn't even know why he was hurrying in that direction but vaguely he was carried that way because a lot of other people were hurrying in that direction too. It was all true, what she had said. He had always been dull, and serious, and pompous. Even when he was young

343

he had been that way, thinking about nothing except railway engines. What a dreary child he must have been. But they'd been happy, a small voice in his head whispered. As a family they'd been happy, until the Barshinskeys came. But Sophie had been the one to make us laugh, another voice said. Sophie was the one who was fun, who was happy and exciting, not he. He and Lillian were alike, dull and stolid and depressingly upright.

He was swept into the square, then couldn't move. A man in a factory worker's cap was shouting slogans from the base of the Alexander statue. Then he heard someone cry, "Cossacks!" and there was a mighty surge backward. He saw some smiling Cossacks walk their horses gently through the crowds. His feet were wet from the snow that had melted under hundreds of milling feet. His brain cleared suddenly and, as he heard the crack of a rifle, simultaneously common sense reasserted itself. The trouble they had all expected for so many months was here.

"It was a Cossack who shot him! It was a soldier, I say!"

"Who have they shot?"

It was impossible to see anything except the surging crowd and glimpses of riders on horseback, but they were not all Cossacks. Some wore the black cloaks and high black hats of the *gardavoys*. He was pushed and swayed from side to side with the overpowering press of humanity. All around was the smell of unwashed bodies. He flexed his back muscles and tried to push back against the crowd.

"Who have they shot?"

But the man had vanished, and then the crowd was vanishing too. Suddenly there was space around him and he ran back toward Ligovskaya, anxious not to be conspicuous in a square where there had been shooting. As he turned into Borovaya Street a truck with two machine guns mounted on it swept past, manned by soldiers. He heard rifle fire in the distance. The street in front of him was suddenly deserted and he dived back into Galina's building. The porter opened the door of his cell three or four inches and peered out.

"What has happened, *Gospodin?*" he whimpered. "What has happened?"

"Shut your door, old man, and know nothing!"

He raced up the stairs and banged on her door. It opened at once and Galina threw herself on his neck.

"Forgive me! Forgive me! I love you, Edwin! I love you. You don't believe me but I do . . ."

He pushed her inside and closed the door. "Now listen, Galina. The trouble has begun. There are soldiers and policemen in the streets and there is shooting. I want you to promise me you won't go out. I will bring you food and anything you need. But you must not go out."

"No, Edwin. I won't." She was suddenly very frightened. Their private quarrels seemed unimportant. "You won't leave me here, will you?"

"I must. I must go back to the ship and see what is happening, what we are to do. But I promise I'll come every day if I can. And if I cannot come myself I'll get a message to you. Is there anyone you could go and stay with?"

"Lizka," she said, white-faced. "I could go and stay with Lizka, I suppose."

"No. That won't do. Lizka is on Vasilievsky Island and there are no trams running. You must stay here. It is dangerous to go out."

They heard, in the distance, the sound of horses, and they both ran to the window. As the icy February afternoon changed to darkness, a troop of mounted police galloped up Borovaya Street, not bothering to slow down when anything crossed their path. A cart that had been left at the side of the road was swept over and crashed into the shuttered window of a chemist's shop.

Edwin put the shutters across the windows and drew the heavy plush curtains to shut out the sound. "I'll stay for a while," he said, and they sat together, not bothering to light the lamps, not bothering to speak.

It was strange, but as well as the fear all around them there was a sense of excitement. The danger, the darkness, had turned them into two different people. He could hear her breathing in the darkness, could smell the mossy scent of the perfume she used. He put his hand out toward her and it brushed against her

345

neck. He allowed his fingers to curl around it. How slender it was, how small, how easy to crush . . .

"Edwin?" The low husky tone of her voice sent a charge of excitement racing through his body. He heard the rustle of her dress, then felt her draw close to him.

"You're beautiful," he said harshly. "You know that I think you're the most beautiful thing I've ever seen."

She laughed softly. It had a sensual, triumphant note to it. A further volley of rifle shots came from outside, a scream, shouting, more shots. She was sweating slightly, he could smell it under her perfume, or maybe it was he who was sweating. Even though he couldn't see her, he could feel her warm exciting body only inches away from him. In the distance there was an explosion and a flash of light in the sky. He placed his mouth over hers and the explosion seemed to be there in the room with them. He'd forgotten what she was like. The petulant, fretful invalid had gone and she was the Galina who had enchanted him, captured him, made him follow her across the world. She was warm, laughing, passionate. She was mysterious, exotic, the way she had always been, could always be. She wound her body around him, the way she had wound her spirit around him. He felt he would kill anyone, or anything, who tried to take her away from him.

He tried to get back to the ship, but there were barricades across the bridges and when he tried to climb down on the ice to walk across the river a policeman fired across his head. He went back to the apartment, and on Sunday tried again. At last, in the afternoon, with the sound of shots reverberating from the Nevsky and from the Kazan Cathedral, he managed to get back to the ship. He arrived just after Mr. Bathgate who, having gone to the embassy, had found himself on the wrong side of the Nevsky.

"It would seem that the army has mutinied," he announced. "They're mounting a searchlight on the spire of the Admiralty to try to stop further insurrection during the night, but the police can't hold the crowds anymore. I think we have to put a guard

346

on the ship now. All the policemen have vanished from the dock and the customs houses are barricaded. The embassy have suggested that if it is possible to do so, we check there every day for news . . . although I don't really think they know what is happening either."

It was almost worse remaining on the ship. Early on Monday morning a crowd of Russian seamen mixed up with soldiers who had torn their regimental badges from their uniforms came surging through the dock gates. They seemed fairly good-tempered and their revolutionary ardor evaporated a little at the eerie sight of the huge, still dock. Every ship along the quay had a silent figure armed with a rifle waiting on the bridge, but there was no firing and, after a few desultory shouts and the waving of some banners, the crowd, motivated by some unanimous but mindless urge, turned and welled back through the gates. Late that afternoon, a glow began to light up the wintry sky somewhere in the region of the law courts. They were guarding the ship, two on and two off, but that night, even though Edwin and Mr. Bathgate should have been sleeping, they spent the night on deck, crouching around a brazier, listening to rifle and machine-gun fire which now came from almost every direction of the city. He began to worry about Galina. He had left her on Sunday afternoon, promising he would return when he could. Now it was Monday night and he knew that, left alone, she was likely to panic, do something stupid like rush out into the streets to look for him. All through Tuesday he agonized about her . . . he should have tried to get her through the streets somehow to Lizka's apartment. On Tuesday night the shooting died down a little and as soon as the sun rose on Wednesday morning he offered to try to get through to the embassy. And without embarrassment or guilt he was able to say, "I should like to try to see my young lady, sir. I want to make sure she is safe."

"All right, Willoughby. Just take great care . . . go around the outskirts of the city as much as possible."

It was definitely quieter, just spasmodic rifle shots and then, incongruously, the distant sound of a military band. The snow had melted over the pavements revealing huge quantities of sodden pamphlets. As he crossed the Fontanka Canal he saw a heap of old clothing near the bridge and then, as he drew closer, realized that the clothes were covered in congealed and frozen blood. A hand jutted out at an unnatural angle. He looked close, once, just to be sure the man was dead, then hurried on.

She was still in the apartment. The shutters and curtains covered the windows even though it was daylight outside, and the gramophone that Heikki had bought her was on the table in the middle of the room. She was busy turning the handle and the strains of a Strauss waltz filled the air. An old woman sat on the sofa clutching a glass of tea.

"This is Madame Dolgurova," she said. "We have been sitting together. She has come from the apartment across the passage."

He breathed a sigh of relief. She was strong again, happy in spite of everything. She turned her face toward him, so that the old lady couldn't see her, and raised her eyebrows in comic distress. Madame Dolgurova stared disapprovingly at him, but bowed stiffly when he greeted her. Obviously she knew who he was, knew that Galina was a whore and he her patron—among others—but the revolution had made such things fall into proportion. No one wanted to sit alone in an apartment listening to the rattle of machine-gun fire and the roar of the mob.

"Do you have enough food?"

"Enough for a few days."

"I'll bring some when I can. It seems quieter today. You mustn't worry if two or three days go by and you don't see me."

"No. It's all right. You mustn't come through the streets if it's dangerous. You must take great care—please don't get hurt, dearest, dearest Edwin."

He felt a sudden glow of warmth because it was the first time, the very first time, she had shown that she cared about his welfare, concerned herself over him.

Because the old lady was there they did not like to embrace. But her dark eyes smiled up at him, promising, loving. The Strauss waltz wound slowly down and she blew him a kiss and hurried away to wind it up again.

Some days the city seemed almost quiet and one could walk all the way from the port to Borovaya Street without any trouble at all. But always there was the uncertainty, the knowledge that at any moment one would hear the crack of a rifle, or see a huge marching throng of people carrying silken banners. Once, after a mass demonstration by the workers of the Putilov factory, he came across a discarded banner lying in the mud and he marveled at how beautiful it was, made of heavy red satin with rich gold braid edging and the inevitable *Khleba* sewn on in black with tiny stitches. Who had done it? Who had spent hours poring over the rich fabric and using their finest needlework? At night bands of soldiers sat around fires at the intersections of the roads. Sometimes they were good-humored and would call out *"Dobraya notch, Tovarich!"* as he passed. At other times he would be stopped and searched, his papers held out uncomprehendingly to the firelight. Once he was forced to drink a glass of vodka, another time he was jostled roughly before being pushed along the road. Rumors abounded. MacKenzie came back to the ship one day announcing that the German fleet was advancing into the Gulf of Finland, and they all sat on deck that night, staring out through the light night toward Kronstadt. One day he heard, from old Madame Dolgurova, that one of the butcher's shops on the Viborg had a huge delivery of meat that was not rationed. He and Galina hurried over there to find a half-mile-long queue which began at the shuttered shop. They waited, like everyone else, for most of the day and then finally drifted away, knowing it had only been another fairy tale. They lived on beans and sausage, and sometimes bread. On the ship they had several tins of food but they opened them sparingly, all of them knowing that the food situation was inevitably going to get worse. Later, they wished they had eaten the food when they had the chance.

The trouble, when it came, was unexpected. He was in the engine room when he heard shouting from the side of the ship. He raced up on deck in time to see two Red soldiers, dirty, disheveled, unbuttoned, advancing on Captain Patterson. One of them held out a paper.

"They've come to arrest me," Captain Patterson said quietly in English. "You take the back one, I'll take the one nearest to me."

He pointed to the ladder going below deck and said in Russian, "The captain's cabin is down there." As the leader passed, pushing the captain to one side, Patterson suddenly seized the rifle and kicked the man violently in the backside. Edwin heard him crashing down the ladder, just as he launched himself on the soldier in the rear. He grappled him around the legs but almost at once the soldier tore himself free and raced toward the gangplank, Edwin pounding after him. He chased him for some way until he saw him disappearing through the gates, then he turned and ran back to the ship. There was no one on deck but just as he got to the gangplank, the Red soldier suddenly erupted from the hatchway and came tumbling over the side.

"Let him go, Willoughby!" shouted the captain, brandishing the rifle in the air. Edwin had just got on board again when six Red soldiers appeared marching down the length of the quay. The captain fired a shot over their heads and they turned and ran back toward the gates. There was silence, only broken by Mr. Bathgate, MacKenzie, and Simpson coming up on deck. The engineer picked up the arrest warrant dropped by the Red soldier.

"It's official," he said. "Issued by the Central Committee of Soviets. The captain and officers of the S.S. *Moscow II* to be arrested for activities against the state. The ship to be confiscated . . ." He screwed up the paper and tossed it over the side. "They'll be back of course. And there's no way we can hold the ship against them."

"We could make sure they can't use the ship, sir."

"I suspect we don't have much time. Can you do it quickly?"

Mr. Bathgate and Edwin looked at each other, then moved toward the hatch.

"I'll collect a small bundle for us both, Sandy."

"Aye."

"What about you, Willoughby? You can come with us and

350

we'll try to get across the border together, or you can throw yourself on the offices of the consulate."

"From all accounts, sir, they're powerless . . . can only just look after themselves. I'll stay ashore with my young lady and we'll try and get out together."

"Aye, well, I think you're right. If they've got wind of our so-called activities against the state, they'll probably line you up beside us and we'll all be shot. And the consulate and the embassy will be watched. MacKenzie . . . Simpson . . . do you want to throw in your lot with us?"

The two deckhands exchanged glances, then MacKenzie said, "Thank you, sir. But we're thinking the smaller parties are the safest. We'll take our chances, the two of us, and get over the border together."

"You may find the consulate of more help to you. . . . Unlike Willoughby you haven't been ferrying British property around the capital and you're probably not on the Red wanted list."

"Aye . . . we'll try there first."

They had lived together, the five of them, for three years and yet, without ceremony or any feeling of sadness, they separated. Mr. Bathgate and Edwin smashed up the valve gear on the main engine. Then they all packed a few essentials and as many tins of food as they could carry. MacKenzie and Simpson had already left when Edwin came on deck.

"You go first, Willoughby. Don't want to leave together . . . too many of us. Good luck now."

"Good luck to you, sir."

It was quiet outside the dock, but as he began to hurry up Bolshoi Prospect a troop of Cossacks suddenly came charging down toward him and he had to dive into the doorway of a coffee shop to avoid them. When he got to the Neva the quays were lined with steamers. Huge crowds of disheveled sailors, their hatbands turned inside out so that the name of their ship could not be read, were lolling both on the decks and on the quays. The paving stones of the embankments were filthy, covered in cigarette ends, leaflets, and the dirt of several weeks. From farther up the Neva, toward the Summer Garden, there was shooting. He was stopped on both sides of the Nicholas Bridge and once over he skirted toward the right, keeping well clear of the Admiralty. Even in the back streets there were bodies on the ground that looked as though they had been dead for several hours. It was July, but the day was cool and overcast; a big ominous gray sky hung over everything. Near the Tsarkoye Selo Station there was a huge crowd of rioters breaking into a building. Most of them were drunk, and although there was shooting it passed aimlessly over his head. As it began to rain some of the looters drifted away, their enthusiasm cooled by the drenching rain. In Borovaya Street there was a battle raging between several soldiers in tattered uniforms and another troop of Cossacks and he had to run several hundred yards to the south before he could cross the street. The *dvornik* didn't answer when he rang the bell, and eventually he had to go around the back of the building and come up through the yard entrance. He shouted through the door to Galina and finally, white-faced, she let him in. She looked small and rather frightened.

"I went to get bread today," she whispered. "Two men snatched it from me. One of them tried to pull me with him. I ran away as fast as I could but they took my purse. Can't I go somewhere else? Couldn't Heikki help me? Shall I go to Moscow and ask Heikki to help me?"

"Moscow is just the same."

"Then what shall I do . . ." Her voice faded away as she caught sight of his bundle. She began to smile, her eyes shone. "Edwin! You've come to stay. . . . You're going to stay with me!"

"That's right . . . until I can get us both out and over the frontier."

"Oh, Edwin!" She was transformed. She rushed about the apartment, undoing his bundle, exclaiming over the tins of food, setting the table with silver and glasses.

"We shall have a party! A celebration, like we did the first time you came. Do you remember?"

"I remember. I remember everything."

She disappeared into her bedroom and he heard boxes being pulled out, doors opened and closed. When she came back she was holding a bottle of champagne and she was wearing a white and silver dress. Heikki's diamonds were in her ears.

She placed the crystal centerpiece on the table and with a chuckle dropped a small spray of artificial apple blossom into it.

"See . . . apple blossom . . . like the first time. Only a small piece but it is apple blossom. Do you remember?"

"I remember." He wondered—idly—who had given her the champagne. He didn't care. It wasn't important anymore. He was going to be with her all the time from now on. As he opened the champagne, the popping of the cork marrying into the sounds of gunfire outside, he realized how happy he was. Life was going to be unbelievably grim from now on, but at last they were together.

21 WHEN SOPHIE RECEIVED THE LETTER FROM IVAN, SAY-
ing that he was coming home on leave, she felt for
the first time in three dreary years that she could
allow hope to blossom in her heart. She had kept
determinedly cheerful ever since Edwin had vanished into the
maw of Russia. As she saw her parents falter, bewildered with
the war, with Edwin's defection, with Daisy May's independence, she had grown increasingly jolly, increasingly confident
that there was nothing to worry about. Sometimes she loathed
just how jolly she had become.

On Wednesdays and Sundays, when she breezed into the
cottage, letting her ma and pa see how good everything was, how
normal and safe and ordinary, how well she was doing in her job,
the mainstay of the Fawcett menage, how well Lillian was doing,
wasn't it wonderful, how brave Edwin was, serving his war in
Russia, and a letter would come soon, she hated the noise of her
screeching voice. Every Wednesday and Sunday she stood outside the back door for a moment and sucked in her breath, swallowing the permanent knot of anxiety that dwelled in her
stomach, fixing her face into a relaxed and happy expression before she stormed in through the door. Every week the questions
were the same.

"We've had no letters, dear. Have you had any letters? We've
had nothing, not from Edwin, not from Daisy."

"Well, of course not, Mother! I told you, I wrote to the central office of the post office, and I wrote to the Foreign Office.
They just can't waste too many lives carrying letters across the
North Sea and into Russia. Bad news will come out fast enough,
they said, through the consulate in Russia. But everyone has to
be patient and understand that letters can only be got through
now and again."

"But it's been such a long time . . ." How strange it was that her mother, her sharp, abrasive, competent mother, should now be so unsure of herself, so hesitant, so clinging to everything Sophie had to offer.

"We've just got to be very grateful that Edwin *is* in Russia, and not in France. Think of the Tyler boys, and poor Frankie Pritchard, and Mr. James, lost at sea. At least we know Edwin is safe and sound in Petrograd."

"But this revolution . . . what's happening to him out here . . . what's happening to Daisy May?"

"Nothing, Mother! If anything had happened, we'd have heard. The revolution is between Russians. They wouldn't dream of hurting English people."

And so it went on, hour after hour, Wednesday after Wednesday, Sunday after Sunday. When she got back to Fawcett's she was so tired she could scarcely stand. And when she did get back, Mrs. Fawcett was invariably waiting for her, complaining, scolding about the shortages and the hardships that war had brought to the household. Sophie took no notice. The war had negated the effect of Mrs. Fawcett and she was no longer terrifying. Sophie ran the house as perfectly as she could with the reduced staff, and Mrs. Fawcett was aware that if she pushed Sophie too hard she would lose her. Nonetheless, like everyone else, she needed to loose her anxieties on someone, and Sophie was that someone.

But when Ivan's letter came Sophie read it alone, read it, and relaxed into a gentle smile that did not have to be forced. Ivan was all right. He was still alive, coming home on leave, and he had written to tell her so. . . .

When she walked home that afternoon, through the hedge-rows bright with wild roses, with the smell of honeysuckle wafting on the sunny air, she realized that for once she wouldn't have to force herself into cheerfulness. The news had restored her optimism, perhaps everything really was going to be all right. Perhaps Edwin and Daisy would be safe in the middle of a revolution.

She walked into the scullery, to the scent of overripe strawberries. Her mother was standing by the sink hulling the fruit and putting them into a preserving pan.

"Your dad's picked all these from Hayward's. Too many. I'll have to jam them. . . . Have you had any letters, Sophie?"

"Yes . . . from Ivan," she added quickly, as she saw the hope in her mother's face. "He's coming home on leave."

"Yes, I know. Lillian had a letter this morning. It came before she went to work."

Just for a second the hope dimmed. But what did it matter if he had written to both of them? What mattered was that he was safe, and coming home.

"Can he stay here, Ma?"

"Well, of course, dear. Where else would he stay?"

How different the war had made everything. The snotty-nosed little boy with torn trousers and a surly manner was welcome now. He was a sergeant and a hero, no longer one of the "bad" Barshinskeys. Ivan had been decorated twice. The village was proud to claim him as one of their sons.

"We thought we'd have a tea for him, up at the Mission," her mother said. "Like we did when Harry Johnson got the Mons Star."

"I suppose so," said Sophie, remembering the misery of the young soldier, who had been unable to cope with a Mission tea party straight out of the trenches. He had reduced them to silence by bursting into tears and running out of the Mission.

"It helps the women," her mother said unexpectedly. "When they can make a fuss of a soldier back from the trenches, they feel their own sons are going to come home."

"Yes . . . yes, I suppose so. And Ivan is a regular soldier. He'd fought before France. It won't be like poor Harry."

"Some of this will do nicely for the tea."

In companionable silence they hulled and stirred, both more relaxed and not worrying quite so much about Edwin and Daisy and Russia. When Lillian and her father came in Sophie felt almost happy.

"Isn't it wonderful that Ivan's got leave?" she said to Lillian.

"Mm." Lillian's voice was cool. She took off her hat and smoothed the thick flaxen braids wound around her head.

"Did he have any special news in your letter?" Sophie asked hungrily.

"No. Just that he was coming home. That dress doesn't fit you at all well, Sophie. You've grown thinner and it's made the hem drop. I'll alter it for you after tea."

They didn't quarrel anymore, not as they had when they were children. Lillian was distant but quite helpful with making over Sophie's clothes. Her "couturier" work in London had changed. Now she was working on officers' uniforms. The regimental tailors couldn't cope anymore. As the young subalterns were killed and others promoted in their place, new uniforms were constantly needed.

"What will you wear to the Mission tea, Sophie?"

"What?"

"The tea . . . for Ivan . . . what will you wear?"

"Oh, I don't know."

"Wear the shantung Mrs. Fawcett gave you. I'll put a lace trim on it, and I've a nice piece of silk in my box at work that will make a new sash." Suddenly Lillian was animated. She always loved getting outfits together and it was the one occasion when she gave generously of her time and attention. "I shall wear the pink lawn I'm making. There was a big piece left after a customer's order. Much better quality than one could buy for oneself." Her voice drifted away on the edge of Sophie's consciousness. She felt suddenly very alone, very aware that she had no one, no one she could talk to about the worries that constantly beset her. She had a sister who was not a sister at all, not the way Daisy May had been. In the middle of a war, Lillian's primary concern was over how she would look at a Mission tea. She felt panic descending on her once more. What if Edwin and Daisy never came back? How would she be able to sustain her mother and father without any help at all?

". . . with the new dipped hem. Sophie! Really, you're not listening at all."

"I'm sure you'll look very nice, Lil. You always do."

"Well, you could look nice, too, if only you tried. The trouble is you just don't *care* what you look like!"

Walking back through Tyler's fields that evening, Sophie reflected that it was probably true. She didn't care all that much. Whatever she did she always looked the same, and it took such a lot of time and trouble to be pretty. She just didn't have that much time.

A week later, when she saw Lillian at Ivan's Mission tea, she wished that, just on this occasion, she had made the time. . . .

She had one afternoon with Ivan that was hers alone. On her Sunday afternoon off Lillian, Ma, and Pa were with them all the time. But on her Wednesday afternoon they went out walking, visiting all the places Ivan had known as a child. They braved the geese that guarded Tyler's farmyard and crossed the water meadows to Sandy Bottom. Bullrushes and kingcups lined the banks and they sat with their backs to the willow, as they had when they were children. Ivan, who had seemed pallid and strained when he arrived, closed his eyes and rested his head against the tree.

"I wish I could end the war for you, Ivan. I can't do anything, but I wish I could."

He didn't open his eyes, just smiled a bit. "Dear Soph," he murmured. "You always were a good sort."

"Is . . . is it terrible?" She knew it was a brash, insensitive thing to ask, but she had to know. She wanted to share everything with him, however bad it was.

"Soph, I just want to forget about it for a few days. It's like . . . like coming back to a dream here. I'm just pretending the dream is real."

His hand was lying on the grass, a very big hand, rough-skinned and the nails were chipped and bitten down. Sophie, daring, gently placed her own hand on it and felt his turn and clasp it. They sat for a long while in the summer silence, a silence that was really the sound of bees and crickets, and the water of

Sandy Bottom trickling slowly through the rushes. After a while she realized he had gone to sleep and she turned and looked at him. Asleep he looked both exotic and vulnerable. The high cheekbones cast shadows on his face and the slant of his eyes was accentuated by a line of dark lashes. His face was totally still, unmoving, and yet she was reminded of the ragged urchin she had fought all those years ago.

"There are two things that help me to get through," he said quietly, still with his eyes closed. "One is that all the men depend on me. I'm a regular, see? And I'm a sergeant, and I've come through without a scratch so far. So all those kids, little snotty-nosed kids like I used to be, they depend on me. Not just for keeping their chins up, but for showing them how to keep dry in the trenches, how to keep the rats off, how to make the most of the bully beef rations, how to keep cheerful. Sometimes I bully them, shout at them, bellow orders. Other times I tell them stories about India . . . helps to take their minds off things. And when they're ill or wounded they know I won't abandon them. So that's one thing that keeps me going."

"What's the other?"

He hesitated. "I dream . . . when I'm lying there with mud trickling down my neck and the guns and the screaming . . . waiting for the order to climb up and advance, I dream."

"What do you dream?"

"All kinds of things . . . beautiful things . . . quiet things. It's all unreal."

She wanted to ask if he thought about her, but she was afraid to in case he said no. And she knew she wasn't beautiful, or quiet, or unreal.

"Do you think about your sister? Daisy May, I mean. I think about her all the time, her, and Edwin, and even a bit about Galina. I think and worry about them all the time." *And I think and worry about you, too,* she wanted to say, but couldn't.

"Sometimes. Not often."

They didn't speak anymore then, just sat holding hands, and when at last he stood up he pulled her to her feet and gazed down at her with a slight smile on his lips. "Dear Soph," he said. "You're such a kind, responsible little thing."

Oh, please think I'm beautiful, or a dream, she thought in anguish. *Please call me* kroshka *or kiss me, or do something to show I'm special.*

"You'll keep writing to me, won't you, Soph? I like to know what's happening to . . . to all of you. I like your letters. Sometimes you make me laugh."

That was special, wasn't it? She could make him laugh. He wanted her to write. That was special.

They wandered home, and Sophie went upstairs to Lillian's room to change for the Mission tea. When she was ready she went straight up to the Mission Hall carrying a basket of bread and butter. She was there, standing right across from Ivan when Lillian came in wearing the pink lawn dress with the new dipped hem. Lillian was twenty-nine years old—practically an old maid —but she looked like a girl of seventeen. She had, from somewhere, acquired a pink lacy hat decked all over with ribbons. She looked clean and fragrant and summery—like a dream. She recognized the look on Ivan's face. She had seen it years before when his father looked at Galina. The dark eyes glowed and the warm confident smile slowly spread across his features. After that she couldn't look anymore. She offered to relieve Mrs. Tyler at the tea urn and she spent the rest of the evening getting hot and sweaty and wet where the urn leaked down the front of her dress. When at last it was time to leave she stepped outside with her father and saw, in the gathering twilight, Ivan and Lillian wandering away together up Cobham's passage. Lillian's hat, looking like a hedge rose from this angle, was tilted right back on her head as she gazed up at Ivan. Even though she was tall she only reached his shoulder. He had one hand under her elbow, gently, carefully, as though she were indeed the fragile flower that she looked. In his other hand he trailed her shawl.

I hope he gets the end of it all mucky, she thought, as her eyes blurred with tears. *That will really upset her, it her shawl gets dirty.*

She felt her father draw her hand through his arm. "You're tired, lassie, very tired. I'm going to walk up to Fawcett's with you now, and you're going straight to bed."

"Oh, Pa!" She couldn't say anymore without disgracing herself. She felt him put his arm around her shoulder and pull her close. "You're my girl," he said, suddenly fierce. "You're my girl, and no one's going to hurt you." She managed to look at him then and saw concern and love and worry and—worse—an unhappy understanding. His tired, strained old face sent a fresh pang through her. She straightened her back and tried to grin.

"I'm fine, Pa, really I am. Just tired, like you said."

When they reached Fawcett's, a silent walk, he suddenly said, "Your ma and me are proud of you, Sophie. We don't know what we'd do without you. You've been a good daughter to us. No one could have a better, kinder girl."

"Thanks, Dad." She could hardly speak without bursting into tears.

As she went indoors she reflected that she was tired of people telling her she was kind. She wished she were unkind, selfish, beautiful, like Lillian, like Galina Barshinskey.

22 EVERY DAY HE SPENT HOURS SITTING IN THE POLICE bureau on Sadovaya, trying to get special exit permits for himself and Galina. Sometimes the bureau was closed, sometimes open, and in charge of a bearded soldier with a red armband. The floor of the bureau was filthy and the soldier in charge repeatedly hawked and spat so that all around his table was a ring of congealed phlegm. On some days one of the new ephemeral officials appeared and examined the rising pile of papers. Every time he came Edwin would watch with rising frustration as the bureaucrat just turned the papers over, one by one, and then reversed the pile. "Tomorrow," he would say, rising to his feet and passing through the crowd in the waiting room.

The consulate couldn't help Galina shortcut the rules. Indeed, they appeared to have little or no power any longer over the turbulent ministry that now ran the city. She had to get the exit permit in the usual way. At the consulate everyone was nervous and not sure to whom to apply for officially approved permits. The government was in a state of constant flux, so were all official procedures. They could help Edwin, they said. His permit of residence was stamped with an embassy seal. Not so Galina's.

Their money was running out. The apartment—miraculously —was still being paid for from the Moscow bank, but the price of food and fuel suddenly soared beyond all reason and he began to grow afraid they might find themselves stranded in this stormy city with no food and no way of getting out. One morning he slipped a twenty-five-ruble note in with Galina's permit of residence and waited until he was called up to the desk. The official turned the permit over, hesitated, turned it back.

"Your exit permit will be issued. Come back tomorrow."

"And the other one? For Barshinskaya?"

The man smoothed the twenty-five-ruble note and without any attempt at secrecy placed it in his top pocket.

"Tomorrow," he said. "The woman must come herself. Tomorrow and we shall see."

He hurried back to the apartment, feeling optimistic for the first time since he had begun to live there. He felt cheerful enough to ignore the unpleasant rumblings of the *dvornik* who, since Edwin had been forced to cut his weekly tip, had ceased to speak directly to him.

"Tomorrow!" he cried as he burst through the door of the apartment. "You are to come to the bureau tomorrow and will receive your permit!" He stopped, noticing that Galina's eyes were red and her shoulders in a disconsolate droop.

"What's wrong?" he asked. Some days she was wonderful, cleaning the apartment, cooking, playing the old gramophone, radiantly happy as though she never wanted to be anything but his wife. On those days he began to believe that if he could only get her back to England and get a job in the turmoil of the war, they would actually be married and live together in a small house and have children and be like everyone else. And then, for a period of time, she would drift away from him, grow elusive, bored. "I am tired of this life . . . surely there is somewhere else we could go to . . . somewhere exciting. It is dull here. I hate it."

She couldn't hurt him the way she used to. He loved her, wanted her, but that adoration, that bedazzled, bewildered fascination had gone forever. But, in a terrible, committed way, his love for her was deeper and more permanent than the old bewitchment had been. She was frail, in spirit as well as body. She was defenseless, in spite of her willful, selfish behavior. She couldn't understand why she had no friends although she said she was lonely. She couldn't understand why Heikki had left her, why Edwin hadn't wanted her after the abortion. Sometimes he wondered what would happen to her when she was old, when the sexuality went and the spritely frailty turned to a stringy middle age, and he knew that he would still love her, even then.

"What's wrong?" he asked again, and she cast herself on his chest in a fresh bout of weeping. "They don't like me," she said. "The people in the building, they don't like me. Madame Dol-

363

gurova . . . she ignored me today, and the *dvornik*, he spat at me when I came in."

"It's because I've cut his tip," said Edwin. "That's all." He deliberately pushed the other thought away. He knew the mood of the city . . . it changed hourly but one thing was certain; anyone who was thought of as wealthy, or bourgeois or privileged, was liable to be plundered. As conditions in the city became worse, more and more outrages were perpetrated on the rich. Until now it had only been the very rich, those who lived in the palaces and the apartments each side of the Nevsky. But as anarchy grew, anyone who had a nice apartment and wore furs and jewels could be at risk.

"I've told you," he said impatiently. "Don't wear your sealskin coat when you go out, nor your earrings. Dress simply, plainly. How can we convince people we are running out of money when you look like . . ." He stopped, because he didn't want to say what she looked like. She didn't look like a seaman's wife, that was plain.

"If I don't look beautiful I shall die," she said simply, and he had a sudden impulse to smack her. It would do no good. He had done it once before, goaded into temper by her foolishness. She had struck him back, then collapsed into weeping, begging his forgiveness. It had made him feel as though he had kicked a dog.

"Tomorrow we go to the bureau and—God willing—you will receive your exit permit. Then we shall try and sell your diamonds again and buy a train ticket. I have just about enough money to buy my own ticket."

"Yes!" she said, her mood changing again. "Yes! We'll sell them and leave this horrible place. I never want to come to Russia again. I wish I had never come. I hate it here."

"And tomorrow, when we go to the bureau, you must dress quietly, like a respectable poor woman, you understand?"

"Of course, Edwin, my darling. Of course. I shall look dowdy and plain, and when we get the permit we will celebrate! We will have a meal in a restaurant! I am sick of cooking these tiresome beans and turnips. We shall have caviar and cutlets of chicken and nesselrode pudding and wine, lots of wine! We will celebrate, shall we?"

"We will celebrate." In the present mood of the city he found it hard to respond to her gaiety. He worried about her constantly, about the trouble she might find herself in if he wasn't there to look after her.

"I shall go to the consulate first thing in the morning," he said. "I'll find out when the trains are expected to leave, and if any other English people will be on it. It is better, safer, to go in parties. And I must find out how far our ticket will take us, and how much money we will need on the other side of the frontier. I must make sure we have enough food and the right papers. You must meet me at the bureau, Galina. Be there early. And do not wear your seal coat, or your diamond earrings."

"I shall be a little mouse." She wrinkled her nose, then pirouetted around the drawing room. He still caught his breath at how lovely she was.

When he arrived at the bureau his heart dropped. "I told you to dress plainly," he hissed, and her lips drooped.

"But I did, Edwin! You told me not to wear the sealskin or the diamonds, so I wore this dull and dreary coat, and the hat and collar because it is so cold."

A black coat, with a sable collar and hat, and expensive leather boots and gloves. And in her ears the garnets which, to one of the new class of working bureaucrats, would probably look like rubies. The soldier with the red armband was already leering at her.

They sat and waited for two hours and finally the policeman came in. He stared hard at Galina on his way to the desk and then began turning over the papers.

"Barshinskaya."

They rose and went forward.

"Nationality?"

"English."

"Why are you called Barshinskaya?"

365

"My father was Russian."

"Are you rich?"

Edwin's heart began to sink.

"No. I have no money."

"You are dressed like a rich man's . . ." Then came a word that Edwin did not know, but he could guess its meaning. The official began to speak quickly, so quickly that Edwin could not understand him. He caught the words "father" and "duty" and several times the word "Russia." Galina paled and shrank back from the desk. The policeman stood and leaned over. His face was twisted with spite and he picked up her permit and threw it at her. Then he turned to Edwin.

"You can go. You can have the exit. Not her. Her father was Russian. She must stay and work for the new state!"

Edwin picked up his own papers with a shaking hand. "You took the money," he said. "I could report you for taking the money."

The man sneered. "Get out," he said. "You can have an exit permit. Not her."

Galina fled from the office and when he got outside she was leaning against the wall.

"He called me a whore," she said. "He said I was a Russian whore trying to trick my way out of Russia. He said my permit of residence was forged, or if it wasn't forged it was given to me by one of my lovers. He said no one with the name Barshinskaya could be English, and that even if what I said was true, I ought to come back and work for Russia."

She was too shocked to cry. Her huge black eyes burned up at him, puzzled, afraid. "What shall we do now, Edwin?"

"I don't know . . . we'll go back to the apartment."

In silence they walked back through the streets. All the leaves had gone from the trees and an icy rain began to fall. The short autumn was over and very soon the snow would come. They would have to begin buying fuel in large quantities.

When they passed the *dvornik* he came out of his door and shouted at them. And this time Edwin recognized the word. It was the same one the policeman had used.

"Does he say that every time you go out?" he asked, staring straight ahead.

"Yes."

"And that is why Madame Dolgurova doesn't speak to you now, why no one in the building speaks to you?"

"I don't know. They used to speak to me when Heikki was here."

And then Heikki left, and the others began to arrive. Not just him, Edwin. Madame Dolgurova had spoken to him . . . just. She had accepted that whatever the menage was, he and Heikki were part of it. It was just, if she chose to think so, respectable. But then the others had come, the officers, the businessmen . . . how many? . . . how often? And then he had moved in. In some districts it would have been passable. In Lizka's apartment block it wouldn't have mattered. That was a riffraff community composed of actors, students, the demimonde. But Borovaya Street was a respectable place inhabited by bourgeois families.

When they got inside the apartment Galina leaned back against the door with her eyes closed. Then she began to unpin the sable hat.

"We must change the apartment," he said. "We must look for a room near Lizka."

"No. Heikki pays for this. If we move we shall have to pay the rent ourselves."

And then her face suddenly cleared. "Of course! Heikki! Heikki will fix my papers for me. He got them when I came in. He will manage it somehow. He is rich and he will be able to bribe the right officials. We shall go to Moscow, to Heikki. I have his address. And it is obvious he is still rich for the apartment is still paid for each month."

"You can't go to Heikki, Galina. You know what trouble you caused. . . . He nearly lost his son, his business, because of you. How can you go to his home and ask him to help you!"

"Then you must go. You must ask him. We will go to Moscow and you will go to see him in his home. Then he can arrange for our exit from Moscow. There will be different policemen there. Heikki will clear our residence in Moscow and get us out."

367

Heikki Rautenberg had said he never wanted to see him again, but there hadn't been a revolution then, or a war. He just wanted to get Galina out of the country before something awful happened to her. All the niceties of good taste and finer feelings didn't seem to matter when there was rioting and killing in the streets. His first priority was to get Galina out before she was lynched.

"All right," he said. "We'll go to Moscow. We can't go back for a train permit, we'll have to take our chance and hope we're not picked up. Pack up everything here and leave."

The Nicholas Station was even filthier than the rest of Petrograd. Hundreds of peasants, factory workers, and soldiers and sailors in unbuttoned uniforms lay stretched out on the floor waiting for trains. The concourse was deep in autumn mud and cigarette ends. Everywhere were the universal leaflets and propaganda sheets trodden into a pulp of gray slime.

It took him two hours to buy the tickets and by that time Galina was near to fainting from standing so long. He watched the blood drain from her face and began to worry that she would not be able to stand the journey. Finally he found a place backing onto a kiosk and he arranged her case and his bag so that she could sit and lean back. When the booking clerk asked for his travel permits he pushed over a five-ruble note and without pausing the man picked it up and pushed the tickets through the window.

It was more than two hours before the Moscow train came into the station from the yards and then the fight to find a place in the carriages began. He knew he had to get her into a seat if she was to survive the journey.

"Put your arms around my waist and don't let go," he bawled to her in English. He had her case in one hand, his bag in the other. He had to hope that she would hold on no matter how much she was pushed. He was strong and big and the last few years had taught him how to fight in crowds. Using the case and bag as weapons he hit and pummeled his way toward the steps.

Once he had a foothold he was able to jam the bag ahead of him and reach back to drag her up.

They found a place in the corridor of what used to be a first class coach. All the seats were taken, and people were already staking places on the floor space between the seats.

"Here. Stay here. I'll make you a seat with the case and then when the train starts I'll try to find someone who'll sell me their seat." She sank onto the case and rested her head back against the carriage wall. She was white and there were tiny trickles of sweat running down her cheeks. "Are you all right?" he asked, and she opened her eyes and tried to smile.

"Soon we shall be in Moscow. Heikki will take care of us."

She didn't realize, he thought, that the journey would take over fifteen hours with innumerable stops along the way. He thought it better she didn't know. If he could bribe someone to give her a seat perhaps she would sleep for the better part of the time.

He had a memory, as the train began to move out of the sheds, of the last time he had been here, seeing Daisy on her way to Buzuluk. Suddenly he saw her little, cheerful round face beneath the Quaker hat, smiling, anxious, composed. He felt a spasm of longing for her, practical, sensible Daisy May, who would have helped him look after Galina, would somehow have been offered a seat because of her very goodness. She would have calmed Galina and helped her to bear the ordeal ahead.

A man in a soldier's coat but civilian trousers finally accepted five rubles for a corner seat. The bribes were eating into his secret fund of money. He dared not think what would happen if Heikki wouldn't help them. He put the case in front of the seat and sat on it himself, taking her legs onto his lap so that she could rest properly. She was wearing the sealskin coat and, even though she was tired and pale, she looked expensive and pampered. One or two of the other passengers glared at her but, as the train jolted on through the failing light people fell into an uneasy dozing. After a while there seemed more room, as though the shaking of the train was settling them down into place. His back ached, and when he looked at Galina his heart ached too. She had never really recovered from her illness. If only he could get her home, get her to stay in the village for a while, with lots of fresh air and good food, then she would be strong again.

He dozed, then woke to find her eyes on his face.

"Will it be much longer, Edwin? I have such a pain."

"Not too long. Try to sleep. I have some water here. Drink it . . ."

She closed her eyes, then began to fidget slightly. They had been traveling for six hours with several stops, when even more people squeezed into the train. Twice she had said she wanted to go to the lavatory and he had been unable to push a way through the corridors for her. If he didn't keep her seat by sitting in it himself it would be taken. The second time she went she was so long he became really frightened, but finally she did come back, looking even paler.

He lifted her legs back onto his lap and put his hands under her knees to support her. Through her coat and skirt he could feel she was burning.

"Do you want to take off your coat?"

"I can't." Her eyes, wide with distress, bored into his, entreating him to understand.

"What's the matter?"

He leaned forward and she whispered, "I'm ill. You know . . . like I was before. Something's gone wrong with me."

The train gave a violent lurch, a sickening crunch, and then there was shouting and shooting from outside. Someone raised the blind to look out and the window was shattered by a rifle shot. Galina screamed, so did another woman in the next carriage. The soldier who had sold his seat tried to push his way along the corridor to the door.

"Keep your heads down!"

They all shrank down, bent double over their legs, and listened to the shooting getting louder and closer.

"Is it the Germans?"

"No . . . the voices are Russian."

"Is it the Bolsheviks? Or Kerensky's armies coming back to Petrograd?"

"Who knows? Be quiet, old man."

The door at the end of the corridor was thrown open and a cold wind blew through the carriages. The soldier who had sold his seat was out, and several after him. There was a loud explosion from the back of the train and all the carriages rocked violently. Everyone was screaming, trying to hold onto something. As the carriage righted itself there was a frantic rush for the door.

"They're blowing up the train! Get out! Get out!"

Cases and bags were abandoned and Edwin was knocked to the floor as the other occupants of the carriage swarmed past him. He reared up and braced his body over Galina's, resting his hands on the carriage wall behind her. From outside came more shooting and screaming as the alighting passengers were picked off by the attackers. There was another explosion from the rear. He bent down to lift Galina, then changed his mind.

"Put your legs up along the seat," he said, gently lifting her. If they were shooting outside he would be a distinct target, getting off the train with a girl in his arms. He crouched down beside her, then began to fumble in his bag for the chamois leather pouch that held the revolver. Another shot came through the carriage window and smashed the light.

"Edwin . . ." her voice whimpered in the darkness.

"I'm here. Don't be afraid. Just lie still."

There was shouting, and shooting, and once a terrible scream from the woods at the side of the track. Then the shooting began to fade away into the distance. One or two passengers, pale and frightened, crept back onto the train.

"Edwin. Can you find something for me? A towel or something."

He rummaged again in the darkness and pulled out a garment of some kind—he thought it was a shirt—and passed it to her. He heard her moving, breathing quickly in short little gasps.

"I don't think I can move, Edwin. I think I'm a little better when I lie flat. I don't think I had better move again."

"That's all right," he said, with a confidence he was far from feeling. "Not everyone will be coming back. You can just lie there until the train starts again."

The shooting finally stopped, the shouting didn't, and when he put his head to the broken window he could hear moaning from those wounded and lying in the mud alongside the track. The train grew quiet as the steam pressure died away. He knew the sounds of a train losing its power.

"I'm going forward to see what's wrong, Galina. I shall not be gone more than a few moments."

"Don't leave me!"

"Only a few moments. You, *Tovarich*, will you make sure my wife is not disturbed? She is very ill. I have bread in my bag. When I return I shall share it with you." As his eyes had grown accustomed to the dark, he had been able to make out that one of the returning passengers was older and dressed in civilian clothes. Perhaps he would be kind.

At the door of the carriage he paused. Except for the moaning of the wounded it was silent outside. He jumped from the carriage and, keeping close to the side of the train, he made his way to the engine. Hanging out of the cabin was a man's arm. Blood dripped onto the ground. Above him, in the cab, a youth stared down, stunned, at the dead man. A single lamp hung from the side of the cabin.

"Who is it?"

"The driver. I don't know what to do. I've only been firing for a short time. I don't think I can drive it. The guard says the coaches at the back are wrecked. He's all right. He's trying to uncouple them." He spoke in short staccato sentences, still shocked. He was very young—too young even for the mass mobilization into the army, and certainly too young to have the responsibility of firing an engine.

Edwin pulled himself up into the cab. In spite of everything, the panic, the confusion, the sick woman lying behind him in the train, he knew a moment's elation at being back on the footplate again. He looked at the regulator, at the brake and reversing mechanism, at the safety valves. It was a four-cylinder engine and the brake was of the cross-cut type and was positioned higher than he was accustomed to, but he thought he could manage.

The regulator was open although the brake was on and the pressure gauge showed there was no steam. The driver must have been killed before he could close it.

"Who put the brakes on, lad? Did you?"

The boy nodded.

"That was well done, but you should have closed the regulator first." He just stared back at him, drained of color in the thin light from the lamp, his narrow, deep-set peasant eyes a blank.

Edwin closed the regulator, trying to get the feel of it. All regulators were different. They were like people, you had to get to know their little habits and idiosyncrasies. This one was loose and old. The entire train was suffering from four years of neglect and underservicing. No proper repair work had been done and all the best maintenance men and crews were at the front. But he could still manage . . .

"Now I want you to get that fire up, lad. I want plenty of steam if we're to get out of here. If you haven't enough wood, I'll get the passengers to collect some along the tracks."

"There's wood enough," he stammered.

"Right. Now, I'm going back to help the guard uncouple the damaged coaches. When I've done that we'll get the wounded back on the train. Then I'll take it to the next station. Which would that be?"

"Tver. We could get to Tver, I think."

"Plenty of steam now."

He dropped from the cab and ran back along the length of the train. The guard, an old man, was wrestling ineffectually with the connecting rods. The rear of the back carriage had suffered from a minor explosion and had sunk right down onto the lines.

"Was anyone hurt in these coaches?"

"There was prisoners . . . under arrest from the government. There's two dead in there. The rest have run off. One must have been bleeding. The back coach was carrying goods."

The couplings were twisted and he had to go to the front of the train again to find a hammer. He looked in briefly to reassure Galina, who was lying flat with her eyes closed. When he got back to the guard he asked him why he hadn't been in the last coach when the explosion occurred.

"I heard the shots and I knew what they was after, the guns and the ammunition in the goods wagon. I come forward as quickly as I could. I wasn't waiting there to be killed."

A couple of soldier passengers came back to help him with the couplings but it took three-quarters of an hour before they could free the train from the wrecked coaches. Then he began to organize the lifting of the wounded. There was much more room in the train now. Many of the passengers seemed to have just melted away into the woods and he was grateful for the space. He put lamps at each end of the wreckage on the line. It was all he could do until they got to a signal station. When he got back to the footplate the pressure valve had risen. He checked the firebox, then opened the regulator and released the brake. The wheels slipped a bit on the wet rails and then, with a sense of deep satisfaction, he felt the train move slowly forward.

"Keep that steam coming now."

He'd thought it might be difficult keeping up pressure on a wood-burning engine, but it seemed, if anything, to be hotter than the coal he had been used to. The boy wasn't a bad fireman either, considering his youth and inexperience.

He drove very slowly. He didn't know the road, and visibility was very bad.

"Have you done this run before?"

"Yes, *Tovarich!*"

"How far are we from Tver?"

"Fourteen, fifteen versts, no more."

"What should I look for? Are there any difficult places?"

"Just before we come into Tver, two rivers, the Tvertsa and the Volga. They are close and there are signals before each river."

"Right!" Without thinking he had spoken in English. He kept forgetting and found himself talking to the boy, and to the engine, the way he had always done. "Come along, old girl, push it a bit more." He realized the lad was staring at him, owl-eyed, and he grinned. "You have to speak to them to make them go," he said in Russian, and the boy looked at him as though he were mad. For ten miles he forgot Galina, forgot the revolution and the war and the problems of getting back home again. For ten miles he coaxed and wheedled the battered old engine along the rails. When they finally drew into Tver, just as dawn was breaking, he leaned out of the cab feeling happier than he had done for years.

The guard came running up from the back and a fury of voices broke out but he ignored them. He drove a spike into the firebox to break up the charcoal and quickly raked out the ash pan and smoke box.

"Pull that wood forward to the front of the tender, lad, ready for the onward journey."

The boy seemed happier too. The madman who had driven the train was both odd and a foreigner, but he spoke with the comforting authority of someone who knew all about engines. When the firebox was in a good enough condition to pass on to the next crew he climbed down from the cab. The guard was explaining in frantic and unintelligible Russian what had happened, and then they all turned to Edwin and began to question him. They were Russian, strangers, but he suddenly felt akin to them. The old camaraderie of the running road was there and he was smitten with a wave of longing, of nostalgia, to belong to a world of men again, men who cleaned and fired and coaxed the great engines into life, who were responsible, and dirty, and vulgar, and sometimes very brave. He wanted to be part of them again. And even as he answered, or tried to answer their questions, he remembered Galina, and with a sense of guilt he made his way back along the train to their coach.

"Are you any better?"

Her eyes were full of tears and she shook her head. "I'm sorry," she whispered, "I don't know why it happened. I'm ill again, like I was before."

He slid his arm around her waist and tried to help her stand.

"There'll be a long delay here," he said. "We'd best break the journey and see if we can find a doctor. If he can fix you up until we get to Moscow, then Heikki will help us."

"Yes." She smiled. "Heikki will help us."

He raised her to her feet and then felt her fall limp in his arms. He looked at her face and at the stain on the seat where she had been lying. He realized, with a sinking heart, that there was no way they could move on to Moscow for several weeks.

23 BY THE TIME THE SECOND WINTER AT MOGOTOVO CAME, the refugee women in the big house had been organized into a kind of cottage industry, making padded coats and woolen stockings that Daisy and Matthew Foulgar were able to distribute in the surrounding villages. They began to go farther afield, trying to cover a wider area of misery with the small bundles that were totally inadequate and yet seemed to bring hope to the underclothed and undernourished women and children. They came at first to tolerate, then to love the native Samarians who were infuriating, apathetic, stubborn, comical, and always, always generous with the little they had. However far afield they went, however many days they traveled from Mogotovo, there was always a house to welcome them, a place on the stove to sleep, and a share of the communal soup pot. They had become more or less immune to the fleas and lice, the colds, the dysentery. Like everyone else in their group they had lost weight during the eighteen months of work and illness. Flora D'Ete, who had been the prettiest of the women at Mogotovo, had faded more quickly than the rest. At the end of their first year, Daisy asked Robert Tatlock if Flora could be sent home.

"She's not strong, not like the rest of us," she said, feeling slightly disloyal to Flora, but worried about her increasing instability. "It's not just physical strength either, everything upsets her, she isn't sleeping and she has bad and violent dreams. I have the room next to her."

But when it was suggested to Flora that she should go home, a stubborn pride made her at first refuse, and by the time she accepted their decision, the breakdown of communications and the precarious traveling conditions following the revolution made it impossible to send her home alone.

The breakdown of communications—no letters, no news,

above all no funds or parcels from home—was virtually the only outward sign they had of the violence that was said to be raging in the cities of the north and west. The officials in Buzuluk were replaced but the new dignitaries of the Soviets appeared, by and large, to be much the same as their predecessors. Certainly they were grateful for the efforts of the group.

The first revolution, the March one, had unsettled some of the older boys at the orphanage. They began to grow rebellious again, wanting to defy once more the men and women who had finally managed to tame them back into ordinary human beings. But as spring came and the ground thawed someone had the bright idea of turning the great garden wilderness into a community farm. The boys responded as peasants always did to the lure of soil of their own and the revolutionary resentment quickly dissolved into sweaty digging.

During that second winter, when they seemed to be isolated by snow from the violence that was said to be raging all around them, Daisy found herself living on two levels of consciousness. Here at Mogotovo she was happy in spite of everything. She was working with people who thought as she did, who liked her, whom she liked. She was part of a team, a valuable part, and her newfound confidence gave her authority and contentment. For hours at a time she forgot about the revolution, the war, her brother Ivan, her friends in England, and Edwin in Petrograd. Her mind was occupied solely with how long the beans and rice would last before new provisions came, with keeping lice under control in the children's rooms, with interpreting in the infirmary, and with the primitive first aid she and Matthew tried to give in the villages. And then, at unexpected, unspecified times, her heart would suddenly lurch with the realization that Edwin was somewhere in Petrograd, in the middle of a bloody revolution, could possibly already be dead. And behind that sickening nightmare dread was the thought of her brother in the trenches, of Sophie and the Willoughbys from whom she hadn't heard for months. What was happening in that other world? Were they all dead? Would there be anything to go back to when this was all over?

She would toss and turn on her narrow bed, wondering how she could possibly have put these people, so dear to her, at the back of her mind, forgetting about them, obliterating them in the snowy wild landscape of a Russian winter. And then Mogotovo, the isolation, the blizzards and rides across the undulating fairy world would close in around her again, lulling her with the drug of endless work which brought its own contentment. When, finally, that other life, the life of Galina and Edwin in Petrograd, blasted itself into her consciousness, it was in such a way that it could no longer be ignored.

They had nearly run out of funds, of food, clothing, medicines, everything. They could get no answer from Moscow or Petrograd. The banks were closed. There was no communication with home. The little group was now totally cut off from its lines of supply. Without help they would soon be refugees themselves. From Buzuluk came the news that someone must try to get to Moscow and Petrograd and contact the Red Cross. Wilfred Little and Anna Haines were chosen and, with food for three weeks packed into rucksacks, they began the long journey to the north.

At the end of February 1918 they were back, with money, and with startling news for Daisy May.

"Your friend . . ." said Wilfred Little. "Your friend Edwin Willoughby who was in Petrograd. He is in Tver. He's working at the station—it's total chaos—anarchy there, you understand —hardly any trains, they all break down, no one to drive them, no one in charge. The most amazing coincidence. He was trying to repair our engine. He recognized our uniforms and asked if we were from Buzuluk. He looked just like a Russian, dressed like a Russian workman, but then none of us look the way we did . . ."

Daisy, who had come up from the kitchens when she heard the commotion of the sleigh arriving, stood frozen with shock in the entrance hall of the house.

"Come now, let us go into the common room. I have a letter for you—although we had trouble finding any paper between us. I'm afraid it is written on the back of a party leaflet. They are both in Tver, your friend and your sister." He paused, stared curiously at Daisy for a moment, and then, kindly, looked away.

She had never told anyone about her sister, never wanted anyone to know. Now it seemed unimportant.

"My sister ran away," she explained. "She was . . . not a good woman. She caused a lot of trouble. But I don't want her killed. Is she . . . are they both all right?"

"They intended to go to Moscow, to get help for exit papers. They set out last September and your sister was taken ill. They had to stop at Tver. They have lodgings in a workman's house on the outskirts of the town. Your friend gets some money for helping in the railyards—although money is little use when you see the food shortages in the cities. We were able to give him a little of our supplies. Your sister is still ill and her permit of residence has run out. Apparently there was some problem with the local officials. Your friend was most kind. He helped us to find a place inside the train—standing room in a goods wagon with a stove, otherwise we might have had to travel on the roof."

Daisy could feel her heart beginning to pound. All the worries, the responsibilities of that other world churned inside her. How could she have forgotten Edwin . . . ?

Wilfred Little's voice penetrated in flashes, details of the journey, of the coincidence of meeting Edwin. She would listen properly to him later, now she just wanted to see the letter.

"Could I have my letter, Wilfred?"

"Here . . . dirty but still legible. We haven't been able to wash since Petrograd."

"Thank you." She smiled at him perfunctorily, and then hurried away up the stairs to her chilled room.

Dear Daisy,
Your friend will tell you of our plight here. I am all right but I desperately need to get Galina home. It grows more and more difficult to survive here and she is ill, certainly not strong enough to stand a train journey in present conditions and I can see no way of getting her an exit visa without us going to Moscow. Dear Daisy, is there anything you can do? The Friends appear to be approved of in all quarters and you seem to have no trouble getting

papers. Is there any way you could get papers for Galina or help us at all. It is not so difficult for me. I think I could probably bribe an official to grant me a visa as my resident's permit has an Embassy stamp and that still seems to count for something, even now.

Trains still run over the border for the evacuation of foreigners. It is just the papers we need, and some help with Galina on the journey. She must sit down all the time. It would be impossible for her to stand several days in a train. I don't know if you can get any answer to me —there is no post—but perhaps another of your people will be visiting Petrograd. You will see my address. We have a room in a railwayman's house. Anything you can do to help, Daisy, anything. I must get Galina out of the country.

Edwin

Written up the side of the paper was a further line

Don't worry about us if you cannot help. I know it is unlikely. I am just following every line of hope. If you are helpless please do not worry. We shall be all right. I'll get her out somehow.

A huge weight of responsibility descended on her. Galina was *her* sister, *her* liability. Indeed, she and Galina were both Russian . . . they should be helping Edwin, the lone stranded Englishman, not the other way around. She would have to do something, but what?

She had to wait until Robert Tatlock came out from Buzuluk before she could explore the possibility of obtaining papers and getting them somehow to Tver. Robert Tatlock was sympathetic but, from two years' experience of dealing with Russian bureaucrats, not overly hopeful.

"Before the revolution we might have been able to do something—perhaps list them as interpreters—but now it would be hopeless. We can do nothing from here. Possibly from Red Cross headquarters in Moscow . . . they might be able to help—would at least tell them the right way to go about it. Is there no way your sister can get to Moscow? We could try telegraphing the American Red Cross there. Some of the telegraphs have been getting through."

"She's ill. She cannot travel. Once they can get an exit permit she can go on an evacuation train. They are said to be easier—places reserved for foreigners going over the border."

"I'm sorry, my dear." His tone was final.

She wrote a letter to Edwin telling him she was trying to think of something, that if he could get to the American Red Cross in Moscow, they might help. She gave Robert Tatlock the letter to post in Buzuluk, knowing the likelihood of its arriving at its destination was remote. Then she went back to her work, trying to tire her ceaseless worries with exhaustion, but now the panacea of Mogotovo ceased to lull her into calm.

Florence Barrow and Miss Ball returned to England in March. Like Flora they had both had more than their share of illnesses and, as the number of children in the house was shrinking—the fighting on the front had ceased and drifting soldiers were appearing like ghosts of better days to claim their children—it was thought they could be spared. Flora, who should have gone with them, was again ill with dysentery. It was a particularly bad bout and destroyed the last of Flora's reserves. Unashamedly weeping, she said she wanted to go home.

"I shall have to wait until another party is ready . . . it will probably be months! Oh, Daisy, I don't think I can bear another summer here . . . the flies . . . those dreadful flies!"

Daisy tried to find some practical comfort to offer but could think of nothing. Feebly she patted Flora's shoulder.

"And we will probably all be regrouped—it's bad enough here, but if I have to go to one of the smaller centers, or into Buzuluk itself—it will be worse! I know it will be worse!"

"What do you mean, Flora? Why are we going to be regrouped?"

"Dr. Rickman told me. Now that the children are being claimed there's no need for an orphanage. We shall be put to other work."

"I see."

Tears flowed down Flora's sallow face. "I don't want you to think I'm running away, Daisy. I did truly want to do God's work with these poor people, but I don't think I can stand anymore."

"Of course you're not running away, Flora."

No. Flora was not running away. She had endured what she was unfit to endure for nearly two years. But if Daisy May Barshinskey went, too, would that be running away? If she went as far as Petrograd with Flora, and then returned to Tver, to Edwin and Galina, would she be running away?

She stared out her window that evening at the melting snow. Soon the mud of spring would be here and transport would come to a stop until the ground was baked hard again in the summer sun. If she wanted to leave in time enough to do any good, she should leave now. But what was right? In her heart she wanted to go at once, make for Tver as quickly as she could and save them, if she could. But what of her friends here? What of the people who depended on her? There was Ksenia here now to act as interpreter, and most of them had learned some simple Russian for themselves. But she was one of the group, she had her own integral part in the efficient little company they had become.

She went to sleep not knowing what she should do. She awoke, knowing there was only one thing she could do, whether or not it was right.

"I thought I never wanted to leave here until our work was finished," she said to Robert Tatlock. "It's been terrible—ugly and tragic—but I have been happy. Now I cannot think of anything but my friend and my sister stranded in Tver. I must try and get to them, help them. If there was still urgent work for me here I would try and forget about them—no, not forget, that would be impossible—but I would try to go on here and not let their situation influence me. I'm sorry if I'm letting you all down.

I'll come back as soon as I can. I'll pay my own expenses. I have a little money saved."

Robert Tatlock smiled at her. "There's no need to come back, Daisy. If you can get home, then do so. I would like to get as many of you as possible home before the frontiers finally close."

"Do you think I'm running away?" she asked, echoing Flora's words.

He sighed. "No one is running away, Daisy, least of all you. You won't have an easy task, getting your sister and friend out. I'd like to forbid you even to try but I know you well enough to guess that would be useless. You're brave but foolish, Daisy. However . . . I suggest that you travel as far as Moscow with Flora. There you can hand her over to the Red Cross and go about your business."

"But I could take her on to Petrograd, and then go back to Tver."

"It would be pointless. There are rumors that the route through Finland is closed because of a war . . . I don't know how true it is. In any event Moscow will be the best place to leave her. When you get there, go first to the consulate, then to the American Red Cross. I cannot see how they can help when your people are in Tver, but the Americans . . . sometimes they can succeed where others cannot. Europe does not seem to intimidate them. They have not had time yet to be spiritually destroyed by this war. Certainly they will help *you*, give you travel passes, vouchers, everything to ease your path. And they will tell you how to get out. If the Finnish border is closed you may have to try another way, through Rumania perhaps, or from Archangel when the ice melts."

"Thank you." The enormity of the undertaking didn't strike her. She was just terribly relieved because he had not made her feel she was running away.

"I wish I could deter you from all this, Daisy," he said, shaking his head. "What you plan to do is dangerous, very dangerous . . . much more so than just staying here. But . . . you have obviously made up your mind. All I can say is, God go with you."

She set out with Flora ten days later. They got a seat between them in a fourth-class carriage for the first part of the journey from Buzuluk, mostly because the guard recognized their badges. Quaker standing was high in Buzuluk. Later they had to change trains and sat on the floor of a goods wagon, sharing their bread and sardines with several Russian soldiers who, at night, hung a blanket from a rope so that the "English nurses" had privacy. She spoke the thick colloquial Russian of a peasant now, entirely confident, not even thinking about it. Flora, who had only mastered the simplest words and phrases, didn't understand the soldiers at all.

She delivered Flora to the Red Cross. Surprisingly their farewell was dispassionate, without tears. They were both tired and dirty and neither of them could really assimilate that this was goodbye. She had already put Flora behind her. She wanted to get to Tver as quickly as possible.

She had stopped in Moscow only briefly on the way out to Buzuluk. It was unfamiliar, dirty, filled with peasants who sat on the edges of curbs and Red soldiers who lounged against the bread shops with rifles in their hands. Everyone looked thin, ill, but, she thought grimly, they were better looking than her peasants in Buzuluk. She had no time for them, no time for Moscow. At the Red Cross she asked how to get to the consulate and, without any problems, arrived there. Her visit was purposeless.

"Nothing can be done from here. If your sister cannot go to the authorities in Tver, then she must come here."

"She cannot. She is ill."

"Why can she not try to get an exit visa in Tver?"

"I don't know. All I know is she cannot."

Back to the American Red Cross, who were kind, encouraging, gave her travel vouchers, currency, food, rail passes, and promised her letters of credit signed by the new Soviet administration if she returned in a few days. She was given a bed in a dormitory while she waited.

Back to the consulate to check again. She was convinced that if only she persevered enough, someone would give her the magic piece of paper. She began the trek daily, the Red Cross, the consulate. Moscow impinged only slightly on her consciousness. It was disorganized but on the whole quiet in a dispirited way. At the Red Cross they told her it was different outside the city where anarchy reigned and gangs of criminal bandits roamed, robbed, and murdered.

"Tver? What of Tver?" she asked.

"There, too, everywhere between here and Petrograd. It was bad here, too, until last week. Trotsky flushed out all the criminal gangs who were terrorizing the city."

Panic rose again. Suppose she was too late? She must try harder, pester them at the consulate, the Red Cross.

On the last day, clutching a bundle of papers that she hoped would protect her wherever she went, a faint gleam of hope was offered by a kindly official at the Red Cross.

"Has it occurred to your English friend, to your sister, that if they were to be married, it might be easier for her to get her exit papers? If, as you say, your friend, the English sailor, can get his papers, then, as his wife, your sister, should find it not too difficult also."

She stood quite still, feeling the color draining from her face. But what did it matter if they were married? Edwin would never leave Galina so they might just as well marry. What did anything matter so long as they got out?

"Married . . . in a church . . . by a Russian priest?"

"That's right. It's still legal—the only legal way at the moment. It might not be easy to find a priest willing to perform the service and issue the certificate. Strictly speaking they should only marry people of the Orthodox faith. And the clergy are nervous at the moment too. The new regime . . . they accuse the church of suppressing the people, of being tools of the Tsar. It will be difficult. But it is a possible way out."

"And then? When I have found a priest and persuaded him to marry them?"

"Then your friend can apply for a joint exit visa for himself and his wife. He can apply in Tver, or you can bring them back here with the marriage certificate and we'll help to get the exits."

Perhaps, if they couldn't get the visa in Tver, between them they could manage to get Galina here to Moscow. With two of them to fight for seats—and she had money for bribes—and she knew how to speak to the soldiers, the peasants . . .

The following day, with papers and money strapped around her waist under her clothes, and a first aid kit packed in her bag, she waited four hours and finally climbed on the train for Tver.

The railway station was to the west of Tver. The room they lived in was in the ground floor apartment of a house on the railway side of the town. The room was tiny and mostly taken up by the iron bedstead. The bedstead came with a mattress but no linen or blankets. Beekov, whose apartment it was, said they had sold all their surplus blankets to buy food and so Edwin had been forced to spend some of their dwindling funds on pillows and blankets.

Beekov and his wife had been kind at first. They responded both to Edwin's skill at bringing in the Petrograd train and to the appeal of the sick woman. Beekov, who had the squat face and deep-set eyes of a northerner, told him where he might find a doctor and had warned him it would cost much money.

Throughout the winter, in spite of the unofficial wage he earned at the railyards, he had to sell off the last of Galina's jewelry. The town was a big one—in better times it had obviously been quite a notable place—and when he tramped into the center he had had no trouble in finding a bazaar with a dealer. But everyone in Russia was selling his jewelry and the price he got was miserable. Galina wept when she learned how little her pretty trinkets had fetched.

He was tired and cold that winter, tired because of working with insufficient food in his belly and worrying about Galina, cold because they had to be careful with the fuel that burned far too quickly in the iron stove. When Galina was well enough to get up he asked Madame Beekova if Galina could sit in her room during the day, to save fuel. Like her husband, she was from the country and she had all the peasant's generosity, even in the

387

misery of the present times. She had welcomed his "wife" and Galina had sat in the Beekov room with the bed and the stove and the icons and the five children. And that was when the Beekovs had begun to be not so kind.

He and Beekov were all right. They worked together in the railyards, shared their daily bread, and spoke sparingly of engines and fuel boxes. It was Madame Beekova who began to change. One night he had come home to find Galina hunched under the blankets of their bed trying to keep warm in the icy room.

"I told you," he said angrily. "I told you to stay with the Beekovs until I come home and light the stove. You're freezing cold! You'll be ill again!"

"I can't go there anymore! I hate it. The children smell and the old woman is nosy and prying. She does nothing but finger my clothes and ask where I got them!"

"Does it matter?"

"Yes! It matters. And today I caught her going out with my sealskin coat. She was wearing it! I won't have it. They are my things and that dirty old woman is not to wear them."

Angrily he stuffed paper and wood into the stove. "That dirty old woman saved your life. She took you in and helped you when you were ill, and she has offered to share her home with you. The least you can do is share your coat in turn. For God's sake! I don't suppose the poor wretch has ever seen anything so pretty in her life. Can't you be a little generous for once?"

"No. No. No! You don't understand! My beautiful coat . . . when I wore it in St. Petersburg everyone looked at me. When I walked into the Astoria all the heads turned, the generals, the princes, everyone looked at me. They thought I was beautiful."

"You are beautiful. What does the coat matter?"

"No! Nothing is beautiful now. I am ugly, old and ugly! My coat—it is all I have. I want to go home. I hate it here. I hate Russia. Oh, how I wish I had never come!"

Goaded by cold and hunger he had been unable to control himself. He had taken her by the shoulders and shaken her so hard her hair had come down.

"You're a spoiled little whore! You will do as I tell you from now on. If you don't, I shall walk out of here and leave you! You understand? Leave you!" He was tired—tired of coping with her foolishness, her vanity.

Suddenly still, she stared up at him, huge luminous eyes shining with fear.

"No."

He began to tremble with rage. Sometimes these days he almost hated her.

"You won't leave me . . ."

He turned away, back to the stove, venting his rage on wood and paper and matches. When it was burning and a little warmth began to shine through the grille and onto his face, he felt her touch his shoulder.

"Forgive me," she whispered. "Forgive me, Edwin. I'll give her the coat if you say so."

She was practically transparent these days. Her skin had a translucent quality and her hands were frail and long on the bedclothes.

"Forgive me," she murmured again, and a small nerve began to twitch at the side of her cheek. "I wish I was like you, Edwin. Kind, loyal, brave. But I'm not. I'm all those things you said, selfish and irresponsible and . . . and a whore, too, although I never thought I was." The huge eyes were full of unshed tears. "I'll never be what you want me to be, Edwin. I'll always be . . . nothing. But I love you. I don't expect you believe me, do you?"

A big tired lump in his throat prevented him from answering. He put his hand over his eyes so that she wouldn't see his misery.

"If it's worth anything to you, Edwin, I do love you." She stretched her hands toward him and then cried piteously, "Oh, Edwin, please don't be angry with me! I'm so afraid when you're angry. You're the only one I've got in the whole world."

The lump in his throat broke in a croak of anguish and he pulled her into his arms, buried his face in her hair, trying not to grip her too hard, trying not to hurt her. God, dear God, how was he going to get her out of here! How was he ever going to get them out of this terrible insane world and back to England?

"Edwin, please don't cry! I'll go back to the other room tomorrow. I'll be good, I promise."

They curled up in the bed together, warm at last, taking spurious comfort, false security from the warmth and darkness, feeling a little peace in the dreadful Russian night, but only a little.

She had gone back to Madame Beekova's room, but since that time things had become steadily worse. Madame Beekova didn't speak to either of them now, and then one day Beekov said Edwin should give them money toward the wood for their room as "the woman" shared the warmth.

He knew they weren't married, else why were their papers in different names? He could read, yes, and he had seen the papers when Edwin took them to the Soviet bureau to have them stamped.

At the bureau the problems were the same as in Petrograd.

"Why is the woman, Barshinskaya, not here herself?"

"She is ill."

"Why are you renewing her permit? What is this woman to you?"

"My mistress." He had long ago given up being embarrassed. Mostly the officials didn't really care about their immoral status. They were far more interested in Galina's passport.

"This woman is a Russian. She has a Russian name. Her permit is not stamped the same as yours. I do not think she is British at all. This passport is forged. She is a capitalist spy."

"No. She is English. She is very sick and must go home."

"She must come here. I do not stamp her permit until she comes here for questioning."

Every week he lived in terror that someone would come to the room and demand to see her. There were so many officials of different rank, different status, all intent on proving their authority, each one conflicting with the last.

When the spring came she grew stronger and, hating the apartment, began to walk a little outside. She still, even though she was ill, looked elegant and beautiful and he knew it was only a matter of time before someone questioned her.

At night now it was dangerous to go out. They ceased to work late shifts at the railyards because of the bandits, the criminals let out of the jails who, in the guise of Bolsheviks and Red Guards, plundered anyone they found out after dark. Every morning there were corpses in the streets and no one dared to stand in the bread queues until it was light. Even then it wasn't always safe and one morning a gang of thugs held the bread line at gunpoint while they were robbed.

At the end of April, when he went to the bureau, there was a different official there, a mean, small man, with two front teeth that stuck out, giving him the look of a ferret. His breath stank and there was a wet-looking abscess just below his left ear. The usual interrogation began.

"Who is this woman? Why do you carry her permit? Why is it different from yours? Why has it not been renewed?"

He gave the usual answers. He stood a good twelve inches higher than the ferret who had to stare up at him. When he told him Galina was his mistress he could feel the man's body quiver with resentment.

"You are a foul capitalist, a foreigner, corrupting our Russian womenfolk, undermining the decency of the Soviet state!"

"She is not Russian. She is British."

"You lie! All foreigners are liars and cheats. The British have betrayed us. They have used the Russian people to fight their capitalist war, and now you try to steal our women! I do not believe your papers. They are false. You are to be questioned!" He shouted at the guards who stood outside and when they hurried in he said, "Arrest this man."

Strangely he felt no fear, only total astonishment. For months he had been terrified that something like this might happen to Galina, but never envisaged it as happening to him.

"You can't do this," he said reasonably, almost amused. "You can't do this to me. I have a British passport and a special permit stamped by the embassy in Petrograd."

He noticed that the abscess on the ferret's neck had suddenly broken and was seeping all down his neck. He was fascinated by it and couldn't stop staring. At the same moment the ferret suddenly leaned forward and smacked him across the face. It didn't hurt but he was shocked, even more so when the two guards gripped his arms and forced them behind his back.

"You can't do this," he shouted, no longer amused. They pushed and pummeled him down a long wooden passage and out across a yard. A low stone building, the old police station, stood on the other side. He was pushed into a cell and the metal door locked behind him. There was no furniture in the cell, no chair, no bench, only a noxious bucket in the corner which had not been emptied after the last inmate. He stood leaning against the door, and slowly a murderous rage overtook him. After all he had survived, to be subdued by an evil little official with a bursting abscess. He fought an urge to scream and pound on the door of the cell. How dare they, how dare they do this to him? He beat his fist against the wall and heard, from the other side, an eerie moan. It stopped him in his tracks. It was the moan of a man sick, or in pain, or in despair. As he stared at the wall from where the sound had come he saw small, pitted holes, and underneath the holes a black smear. He followed the smear down the wall to the floor. For the first time an icy chill began to creep around his heart. He had never really been afraid before, not during all the rioting in Petrograd, or in the ambush on the train, or during the anarchy of the streets at the present time. But here . . . here he was helpless, he couldn't fight back. He was shut in a stone box at the mercy of an unbalanced bureaucrat whom he knew he couldn't bribe. He suddenly remembered all the stories he had heard, of people shot in their cells without trial, of foreigners beaten to death just because they were foreigners. I don't want to die in here, he thought in a silent scream. I don't mind dying, but out in the open, please! In a blow-back from a boiler or out on the footplate, or even shot down in the streets, but not here, in this dark, stinking little cave. Please, God, please let me die out in the open!

He fought hard to keep control, retaining just enough self-respect not to allow himself to descend into hysterics. He forced his mind into calm waters. He thought of home. He took his fevered mind walking across Tyler's meadow to the river. He had Sophie on one side, Daisy May on the other. They walked step by step, past the haystack, over the stile, through the lane and across the track to the water meadows. He could see their faces if he concentrated hard. Two nice, lovely, ordinary English faces . . .

As it was beginning to get dark they came for him. The ferret and the two guards entered the cell and the ferret stood against the pitted wall while one of the guards held him and the other hit him with a piece of chain. At intervals the ferret would stop the guard and shout, "You must confess that your papers are forged, that the woman's papers are forged!" but Edwin knew it wouldn't make any difference if he did confess. He felt one of his teeth break and spat it out onto the floor and he wanted to cry for mercy but wouldn't because he knew that was what the ferret was waiting for.

They stopped at last. It had seemed hours but he supposed it couldn't have been all that long because it still wasn't completely dark. He leaned against the wall. He was determined not to fall down because he knew the ferret wanted that too.

"Get out!" said the ferret.

He stared at the open door. The guards were waiting, one on each side.

"Get out. You will return tomorrow. So that you do return I shall keep your passport and permit. You will return every day until I decide to renew your permit. And the woman . . . I shall not return her papers either. She must come herself. Tomorrow."

He still couldn't understand. The pain in his ribs was so bad he couldn't understand.

"Get out!"

One of the guards pulled him forward by the shoulder and he

screamed as pain from his chest shot through him. They pushed him back across the yard, into the long passage and through the office. The official sitting there was the old one, the one before the ferret. He shook his head from side to side in a disapproving way. "You should not have attacked my colleague, Englishman. It is forbidden to use physical violence against a member of the Soviet. Now we cannot give you your papers because you are dangerous, a threat to the revolution. You were lucky we did not shoot you."

He looked faintly amused. He swung his chair on its back legs, then reached into a drawer of the desk and handed Edwin a piece of rag. "Please do not drip blood on the floor of the bureau."

Edwin turned very slowly and walked toward the door. Outside he shuddered and drew a deep breath which hurt his lungs. He didn't know how he was going to get home but he began to walk, and after a while the cool air made him feel a little better. It was dark and behind him in the town he could hear the usual nightly shooting, the screech of tires, shouting. It did not affect him. He just concentrated on getting home.

When he walked into the room, Galina wasn't there and he went over to the bucket and poured some water into the tin bowl. He didn't want to frighten her more than she was going to have to be frightened. He gritted his jaw and began to wash the blood from his face, rinsing his mouth and spitting the blood back into the bucket.

"Edwin?" She had come in from the Beekovs' room and was whispering. She was already afraid. "Edwin. They came for me today . . . two Red Guards. I was out. They told Madame Beekova they had my papers and that they were forged. They said they were coming back for me."

He turned around and faced her. It hurt to move quickly but he didn't want her to know how bad he was.

"Edwin!" She put her fists up to her mouth and stared at him, fear magnetizing her eyes so that they seemed to fill her face.

"It's all right, Galina. I had a bit of a fight, that's all. I got into an argument at the bureau and had a fight."

"Your face is all cut! And your eye . . . your eye is covered in blood."

"I had a fight, that's all."

Behind Galina, Madame Beekova appeared.

"You must leave here," she whispered. They were all whispering, as though the ferret and his guards were listening outside the door. "I wanted to help you . . . the woman so ill. But you have brought us bad luck. The police were here and they asked why I took you into my house. You must leave, leave before they come back. I will give you food but you must go."

"We can't go, Madame Beekova. We have no papers. They will not give us our papers."

"You cannot stay here."

"Edwin! I'm so afraid. What shall I do if they come for me?"

He suddenly saw her in the cell, in the cell with the ferret and the two guards. He began to feel sick.

"Excuse me one moment," he said, and went outside the door, and around to the side of the house. He put his hand against the wall and began to vomit. After a while he felt better. He could taste blood in his mouth and throat but he thought he was probably all right.

As he went back to the door Beekov came out. "I am sorry, friend, but my wife is right. You must leave. The times are too difficult. I have many children. I do not want trouble."

"We have no papers. They have kept our papers. Where can we go?"

"I have spoken to my sister's husband. He works for the steamship company. There is a steam tug leaving early at dawn . . . they leave early because they do not want the people to know they are moving grain down the river. If you can pay you can travel without papers."

"Where does the tug go?"

"Down the Volga, to Kortcheva, Uglich, probably down to Nizhni Novgorod if the cargoes change. You can get off anywhere you like. From Savelovo a railway runs to Moscow . . . sometimes."

Priorities were different now. He had been waiting until she was strong enough to stand the journey to Moscow. Now they couldn't wait any longer. Somehow—when he didn't feel so ill he would work out how—he would have to get her to Moscow where the consulate was. Lost papers, confiscated papers were perhaps easier to deal with than out-of-date ones. He would worry about it later, when he felt better, when he had got her away from the ferret.

"Beekov, my friend, I have only a little money, but I have also a necklace belonging to my wife. Do you think your sister's husband will take the necklace and let us travel with the grain?"

"You must ask."

"One other thing. My wife cannot walk into town. It is too far. And I am ill just at present too."

"What . . . ?" Beekov hadn't seen him in the light yet. Edwin moved and let the gleam from the window fall on his face.

"Eeeh!"

"The police . . . the officials at the bureau. My wife does not know what they did. I do not want her to know."

"Eeeh! You must leave at once! It is not safe . . . they will come for me too. I should not have taken you in. They will punish me!"

"We will leave tonight. But we must ride as far as the town."

"I do not know . . . what can I do? Perhaps Alexander Alexandrovich? He has a cart, a donkey."

"I will pay him. I still have a little money."

"Go inside."

He braced himself and walked back into the house. Galina was frenziedly throwing her clothes into a bag. Madame Beekova watched, expressionless, as all the garments she had touched and stroked disappeared into the valise.

"Give her something," he muttered to Galina.

"What?"

"Give her something. A skirt or a petticoat or a scarf, something."

"No. These things are all I have left now you have taken my jewels."

"Give her something. If she decides to tell them where we've gone they'll come after us."

She paused, quite still over the valise, then one by one touched the things, hesitating over first one piece, then another. She finally, reluctantly, extracted a worn but silken shirtwaist. Sullenly she held it out to Madame Beekova, whose expressionless face suddenly wreathed into moons of smiles. Effusive thanks burst from her lips.

He went to the back of the stove and rooted about for the small package there. He had been forced to hide it, not only from the Beekovs but also from Galina. Inside was the revolver, the pearl necklace, and the last of his money. Outside he heard the rumble of wheels.

"Here," Beekov said. "Alexander Alexandrovich will take you to the edge of the town. No farther. It is too dangerous. You must walk from there. My sister's husband is Alex Sergeitch Androv. He is in charge of the tow. He will be at the landing stage just before dawn. You must be there by then and you will have to walk there from the edge of the town."

He sensed there was no point in asking for more. He must save his strength for getting Galina to the landing stage.

They crept out of the house and Beekov lifted Galina into the cart. Slowly Edwin hauled himself up, every movement making an agonizing spear shaft through his chest. The cart began to move.

"Goodbye, Englishman. May the good God attend you."

"Thank you, my friend. Thank you many times."

It was a long way into the town. He wondered how, earlier, he had managed to walk so far with his pain-racked body. They seemed to be trundling along the road, rutting in and out of the tramlines for a long time and once or twice he nearly drifted off into confused sleep. Galina was quite still beside him.

He listened as they drew close to the town. It was quiet. The gangs of anarchists and robbers seemed mercifully silent. The cart stopped.

"I will go no farther, *Gospodin*. It is dangerous enough. From here you must walk."

He pressed money into the man's hands, and clambered down. Alexander Alexandrovich lifted Galina onto the road, then put the valise on the ground. In a few seconds the rumble of the cart vanished back along the road and they were on their own. He lifted the valise on his good side, the side that did not hurt so much.

"I can't help you, Galina. You can walk to the landing stage, can't you?"

"I'll try. Do you have my valise?"

Slowly they began to stumble toward the square. There was shouting in the distance and a rifle shot on the far side of the river. Perhaps they were going to be lucky. Perhaps all the trouble and looting was on the other side of the river tonight. But he didn't think so . . . he could feel tension . . . something all around them. He began to sweat, tried to walk faster.

"How much farther, Edwin? How much farther?"

"Ssh."

They passed the law courts and were out of the square, were in the road leading to the landing stage. He could feel eyes staring at him, could sense the presence of the ferret.

It wasn't the ferret. There was a burst of murderous laughter behind them, pounding feet; a rifle shot went over his head.

"Run, Galina! Run!"

He dropped the valise, grabbed her by the arm and forced both her and himself along the road to the landing stage. They were screaming and shouting behind him. They were drunk, he could hear that from their voices, violently, bestially drunk.

"Run!"

Another rifle shot just as they reached the landing stage. The gate was up and dimly, in the night, he could see the shape of a barge moored in close to the bank. He pushed her through the landing gates, down the steps and along the bank. From the steam tug came a rifle shot in return. Someone was guarding the grain.

A fresh burst of fire broke out behind them, but it receded as

398

the defenders of the grain shot back. He dropped down onto the barge and reached up for Galina. She fell, fainting, into his arms.

"You are the Englishman?"

"Androv?"

"You have the money?"

"I have a necklace. Real pearls. You can have that." He felt the man hesitate, and a fresh burst of shooting broke out on the bank behind him. "I have a revolver, too, with ammunition. I will give you that." He'd have given the man anything to get away from the savages on the bank. With a grunt, Androv motioned them to the back of the barge.

"There are sacks there, enough to make you a good soft bed. And the night is warm. Very soon we shall leave."

He dragged Galina over the sacks and dropped to the deck. She was breathing heavily and he felt only relief that somehow he had managed to get them both here. There were other figures around the tow, some with rifles. Spasmodic shots lit them as they fired haphazardly up onto the bank.

"Edwin?"

"It's all right. We're safe now. We can rest. We shall be moving very soon."

"Edwin."

"Try and sleep now."

The shooting died away and he lay, fighting receding waves of pain, dozing at times when it lessened, listening at the bad times to the noise of the barge making ready to move off. There was a gentle lulling motion and he realized they were out in the center of the river. There was light in the sky, the light that comes just before the dawn.

"Dear Edwin. You are hurt. I shall put my arms around you."

As her frail hands went around his shoulders he reached out his arms and wrapped them about her. His right hand moved in something sticky, warm.

"Edwin. You shouldn't have dropped my valise. I have nothing now."

He took his hand away and looked at it. Blood. It was coming from somewhere beneath her left shoulder blade.

"Edwin. Look over there, on the bank . . . apple blossom . . . do you remember . . ."

The sun came up and he stared at her lying in his arms. She was dead.

24

SHE ARRIVED AT TVER TWO DAYS AFTER EDWIN LEFT. She walked from the railway station carrying her bag because a tram had been derailed in the early morning and all transport had ceased. She was tired but, as she neared the edge of the town, a sense of elation made fresh energy and excitement pump her aching legs along the road. She had the address written on a piece of paper but the paper was unnecessary. She knew the address by heart and, as though the fates had recognized that her journey had been hard enough, she found the house without difficulty. She knocked, several times, and finally the door was answered by a peasant woman holding a child in her arms.

Daisy smiled. "My sister, Galina Barshinskaya, is staying here, with her husband, the Englishman. I have come to see them."

"*Nyet*," said the woman, fear in her face. She tried to shut the door. Daisy put her hand on it, her heart beginning to thump.

"An Englishman, tall." She raised her hand in the air to Edwin's height. "Tall, thin, gray eyes, and my sister who is ill . . . Barshinskaya . . ."

"Not here," said the woman tonelessly. "Gone."

"Gone? Gone where? Why did they go?"

"There was trouble. They have gone. We want no more trouble."

"No, wait, please!" Daisy pushed her bag forward so that the woman could not close the door. "I must find them. Where are they?"

"Gone. I do not want trouble. You must speak to my husband. He is not here."

She wanted to scream but controlled herself. "May I wait for him?"

"Not here. Come back this evening. I do not want trouble."

The bag was pushed back and the door closed. She was suddenly aware that she was hungry and wanted to go to the lavatory but she didn't dare move too far away. She put her bag against the wall of the house and sat on it. She was suddenly angry. To have come all this way, to have been prepared to encourage Edwin and Galina to marry, to help them to Moscow, and after all this to be thwarted by a frightened woman who would give her no explanation. Suddenly she stood and banged on the door again, banged and banged when no one came, and continued to hammer away, knowing that she would not give up until the door was opened. Eventually it was, and the woman stood there again, a mixture of fear and fury.

"I have traveled all the way from Samara in the south to find my sister," Daisy said, white-faced with rage. "I am not leaving until I hear everything you have to tell me. If you don't want trouble with the police you had better allow me to come in and speak with you. Otherwise I shall stay here all day and make a noise at your door."

The woman didn't answer and Daisy stepped forward and began to pound again on the open door.

"Sssh . . ." and when Daisy paid no attention she suddenly took hold of her arm and pulled her inside. They stood staring at each other.

"Now, tell me about my sister and the Englishman."

"They left. Two days ago. On a grain tow down the river. There was some trouble. The man was beaten by the police. They had no papers . . . they were taken away by the police and so they had to leave quickly. My husband found a place for them on one of the tows."

"Where did they go? How far down the river?"

"Who knows . . ." The woman shrugged. She seemed to have totally recovered from her fear and was now just disinterested. It didn't puzzle Daisy too much. She had seen the same swift turn of temperament too many times in her own peasants at Mogotovo.

"Where does the tow go to?"

402

"In the old days . . . to Ruybinsk. But now there is no time-table. Sometimes they change their cargo at the first stop and continue down the Volga, even as far as Nizhni Novgorod, farther than that, who knows? Many people give orders these days."

"The name of the steamship?"

"It has no name. It was the *Nicholas*." She crossed herself. "But the name has been painted out, my brother says."

"Your brother?"

"He works for the steamship company. He was in charge of the grain tugs. He arranged for them to travel on one of the barges."

"Your brother's name?"

"Alex Sergeitch Androv. But he will be gone for the summer. He will be on the river until the ice comes."

"Which way to the river?"

"You must take a tram to Catherine Square."

"There are no trams."

"Then you must walk." She gestured back to the main road that led from the station to the town.

"Good," said Daisy, picking up her bag. "God be with you."

"God be with you."

All animosity gone, they touched hands and Daisy turned back to the road. Russia was a huge country, the Volga was thousands of miles long, but she was going to find him.

Throughout the rest of May, and through June she plied a route up and down the Volga, as far as Nizhni Novgorod. At every official stop she disembarked to ask questions of everyone at the landing stage. Sometimes the steamers and barges went on without her, and she would follow false leads for a couple of days before returning to the river and seeking a passage on another tow. She tried to think with Edwin's mind and she felt sure that probably what he would do would be to go ashore at a town that had a railway line running to Moscow. Inevitably these towns were the bigger ones, market cities some of them, huge thoroughfares full of people, of beggars, renegade soldiers, and bands of Bolsheviks roaming the streets. Always she began by asking the steamship officials, "An Englishman who speaks Russian but badly. Very tall, taller than a Russian and thin. And a girl, very beautiful, a Russian but unlike a Russian, black hair, more like a gypsy than a Russian. On a boat once called the *Nicholas*, pulling a grain tow." After the quay captains she would go to the police station and, by some miracle, she was never kept in prison overnight or lost her papers. Daisy May, unlike her sister, aroused neither passion, lust, nor envy in the hearts of the men she met. After the police stations she would try the hotels and boarding-houses, then the *isvoshtchik*, although they were her last resort. She thought it unlikely Edwin would have enough money left to take cabs. Twice she got free passages on the tows by offering to cook for the crews. The food was bad. There was little but turnips and unhulled grain taken straight from the cargo sacks. But she was used to cooking for refugees in Samara and she did the best she could, making a kind of Russian fish pie with turnips and whatever they caught from the river.

One night, at a river village beyond Kineshma, she got a bed in a one-story house on the riverbank, a filthy house with a felt pallet on the floor for a bed. She sat with her back to the wall all night which was just as well as, in the early hours of the morning, two men broke into her room. She wasn't surprised. She had expected it to happen before and she had prepared herself. She had a kitchen knife sharpened to a fine point and, although it made her feel quite sick, she dug it hard into a shoulder and when the man screamed she picked up her bundle and ran. She spent the rest of the night huddled down low on the bank of the river where no one could find her.

Just once or twice she stopped to wonder why she wasn't frightened. Constantly she saw terrible things happening around her, shooting, and villages burning, set alight by bands of rioting soldiers and, what was far worse, the new Soviet officials arresting people, coming on board the steamers and examining papers and then, apparently at random, taking passengers away. But she never once felt fear. She had no room for fear—only room for constant anxiety, wondering what was happening to Galina and Edwin, hoping she would be able to find them before something terrible happened to them. She discovered that if she wasn't careful she would be caught in the middle of a war. The quay captain at Yaroslavl told her an army was approaching from the north and that if she went any farther downriver she might find herself cut off. She ignored him and went on. There was shooting and arson all along the Volga and it made no difference if they were gangs of looters or a rebel army.

Several times she was laughed at, not unkindly, but with the hopelessness of the long-suffering Russians. Many times she was told she was mad—to look for two lost souls in the middle of a revolution. Nah! It is no good, she was told. Forget them, they are dead, you will never find them, go home. But she knew she would find them, she wasn't going home until she did, and off she would get at the next scheduled stop to begin her questions again.

At Nizhni Novgorod she faltered for the first time. It was a big city and she hunted and searched for four days. Back at the river landing stage there was a map of the Volga pinned up on the wall and she saw, with a sinking heart, how far she had come, but how much farther she had still to go. Her finger followed the river down and then she saw it pass through Samara and the horrifying thought struck her—supposing Edwin had decided to try and get to her. Supposing he had followed the enormous waterway right down to Samara and was now trying to get across country to the wastes of Buzuluk! While she had been going north, he had been traveling south!

She slept that night on board, curled up on some sacks on deck and, before her tired and fevered imagination, the map of Russia spread out—the huge land, the huge river with its interminable low sandy banks stretching out into the hazy distance. Where were they? How could she find them? Supposing they were already home? Had they, by some miracle, got out and were safe back in England while she was lost in the great wasteland maw of the central plains of Russia? Her heart began to pound and, for the first time since beginning her voyage, she was afraid. She sat up and looked out at the banks. One or two lights were flickering in the town. There was the usual distant shouting and rifle fire which was now nothing more than the common background noise every night, but here on the river the night was quiet, just the lapping of the water against the landing stage and the odd cry of a snipe. The huge bowl of the night sky was starstudded and she gazed up, her panic slowly subsiding and in its place a growing conviction that she would find them. She drifted off to sleep and when she woke some miracle of intuition had happened. She knew they hadn't gone on to Samara. She knew that wherever they were it was somewhere between Nizhni Novgorod and Tver. She had missed them this time, but tomorrow she would change boats and work her way back upriver, making more inquiries, asking more people. Someone, somewhere, would know how to find them.

In July she was back in Tver, tired, thinner, her store of money depleted, but convinced that there was still something she could do, something that the Beekovs could tell her that she had missed before. The trams were running from the square and she was able to get a ride to the junction near the Beekovs' house. The woman was kinder this time and asked her to come in. She sat in their back room and, with gratitude, accepted a glass of very weak tea. She was deeply touched. Tea was scarce and very expensive.

"This is good." She closed her eyes and let the warm fragrant liquid revive her. "I did not find them."

"No." The woman suddenly evaded her eyes, turning away and picking up a small child from the floor.

"Has your brother ever returned? Have you had any message from him?"

"He has come back one time." There was something furtive, no, not furtive, sympathetic, about Madame Beekova. Daisy's heart began to thump again.

"What did he say? Where are they? I have searched every

village and town along the river as far as Nizhni Novgorod. They are not there. Where did he take them?"

"There was trouble." Her wide, impassive peasant face was immobile, but Daisy could see her eyes. She had bad news. That was why the tea had been offered. Something terrible had happened. She breathed deeply, forcing herself to be calm. She must not collapse in front of this woman.

"Please tell me," she said in a tight little voice.

"There was trouble getting onto the tow—shooting. The woman was killed."

"And the man?"

"He was hurt. Not by the shooting. By the police—before he went."

He wasn't dead. Edwin wasn't dead. He was wounded, ill perhaps, but he wasn't dead. She could still do something. But she mustn't cry or become panicked. She must organize herself, organize this woman.

"Where are they now? Where is the Englishman now? What did they do with my sister?"

"It was bad, you understand. My brother said it was very bad. They did not want the authorities to know they had foreigners on the tow, especially a dead one. My brother hid them, him and the body of your sister, and then they put them ashore, at an unscheduled stop, a village just before Myshkin."

Daisy closed her eyes. Myshkin. She had searched there of course. No distance at all downriver—at least no distance compared with the journey she had made.

"Does he, your brother, know what happened to the Englishman?"

"He was hurt, but not too bad. He was able to carry the body. My brother was good. He took no money for the journey. There was a necklace . . . he gave it back to the Englishman. He had misfortune enough, my brother said. He did not want to add to his sorrow."

"That was very good of your brother," Daisy said quietly, and she began to rummage in her pocket.

"That is all right." Madame Beekova put out her hand to restrain Daisy. "I do not want anything. You are a good woman. Not like her, your sister. You are good. And your face is Russian."

Daisy finished her tea, savoring the last few drops, knowing she wouldn't have anymore for a long time.

"You have been kind, very kind. Now I must find a boat to take me to Myshkin and, if it is not too far, I will walk to the village."

"If you tell them you are a friend of Alex Sergeitch Androv, it may be they will take you on to the village and stop the boat for you. You must find a place on one of the smaller boats. The river will be dropping and there will be no proper landing stage for a big boat."

"Yes. I see. Thank you."

"God go with you."

"And with you."

She trudged back to the tram depot. Her heart felt as though it were going to burst but she had to keep calm. There was much to do. Later, later she would think about Galina dying. Now she must get to Edwin, in case he was ill. She must get to him and then work out how to get him home.

They tried to stop her from going. The steamers were only going a short distance downriver. There was a battle raging at Yaroslavl, just beyond Myshkin. It had been captured by the rebels. It was not safe on the river.

She waited, buying a space on the floor of a house in the poor quarter. She had to save her money in order to get them out.

The boats began to go down again. Another battle, another war, Yaroslavl was clear, the Bolsheviks had taken it and the waterways were partially open again.

Three days later, a bargehand lowered her into the muddy waters of the Volga. It came to just below her waist and she was able to wade to the bank, keeping her bundle held high out of the water. She dried her legs on her shawl, wrung out her skirts, put her boots back on, and began to walk toward the village.

408

The village priest had found him, lying on the tangled grass beside her body. The old man had come weaving through the rustling birch trees and had placed his hand on Edwin's shoulder. Startled, he had opened his eyes.

"She is dead, my son. The woman is dead."

"Yes."

"Can you stand?"

He was a fat old man in a rusty coat. He bent with difficulty and tried to help Edwin to his feet. "Come with me."

"I can't leave her. She couldn't bear to be alone. She was afraid of being alone."

"She is not alone, my son. The Holy Virgin will guard over her."

He fought back a hysterical guffaw. Galina and the Holy Virgin . . . The pain in his chest exploded into a huge, all-enveloping pain that spun around the body on the ground. She was dead. That greedy, lovable, deceitful, helpless wanton was dead.

"Oh, God! Why did she die like that!"

"Come, my son. I shall take you to a kind woman in the village. I think you are ill."

Surprisingly the old man seemed strong when Edwin leaned upon him. They stumbled through the trees and Edwin noticed, in a disjointed way, a little white and gold church. He gestured behind him.

"Her body . . . the church . . . here." He took his arm away from the priest's shoulder and, swaying, fumbled in the pocket of his coat. "Here, take this, it was hers. You must see to her . . . everything properly done . . . she didn't like poor things, cheap things. It must all be done well . . . a nice dress to bury . . ." He choked suddenly, remembering all the times he had scolded her for extravagance. The priest took the pearls in his hand and sighed.

"It will all be done . . . as best it can be. But these days we have to manage with the little we have. Come now."

Behind the church the village stretched out on its two crossed roads. The house nearest to the church was slightly bigger than the others and the priest tapped on the window. "Yelena Nicolaevna! Yelena Nicolaevna!"

He felt so distanced from all around him, so tired, so very tired of himself and his life, that he scarcely noticed when he was taken inside and placed on a blanket on the dirt floor.

They were kind to him, very kind considering he had no money and no papers. It was a poor village, something of a backwater for which he was, in time, to be grateful. Apart from a roving band of looters earlier in the year, and the intermittent calls of the Soviet officials to requisition food, the revolution seemed almost to have passed them by. It was such a poor and insignificant village, and had always been so, that no one could be bothered with them. There was, so they were told, a battle raging between the Bolsheviks and Savinkov's Russians not far to the north around Yaroslavl, but no sound of it ever reached them. The tiny village, no more than the church and a handful of houses, appeared to remain inviolate while battles, looting, and arson exploded all around.

Most of the time he was in an apathetic dream that was enhanced by the landscape in which he found himself. The village seemed to float between the green water meadows and the huge light of the sky. For the first time he experienced the sensation of Russia's vast, sprawling sky, the flat meadows and plains and waterways that went on forever. Everything was wild, untidy, even familiar things like the kingcups in the streams were slightly different, the coltsfoot was bigger, the clover was wilder, even the bees were of a different shape to the bees at home. This alien world, so enormous, so forgotten, made him realize the utter impossibility of ever getting home again. It was hopeless. It had always been hopeless. One could not fight a vast tangled green world like this, it was too big. One could only bow to the inevitability of village life.

When his ribs and shoulder healed he went out into the fields and worked as hard as he could. Yelena Nicolaevna's man had not come back from the war. She had a young brother, two sons, an old *baba*, an assortment of girl babies, but no man of her own. He found that it helped to become a mindless work machine. Somehow he must pay his debt to these people, but also by endless physical labor he was able to turn himself into the non-thinking automaton he longed to be. He mended the arm of the village draw well which had been broken for several months. He salted the fish for the winter, thinned acres and acres of turnips and radish seedlings, hoed potatoes, reroofed several leaking houses, and carried back large bales of hay on his back for the winter feed. He spoke little and, in time, they came to accept him as an eccentric foreigner, quite harmless, a good worker with a kindly way of looking after animals and children, but not quite right in the head.

Once, on a July evening, when a flight of wild geese lifted through the evening sky, a sudden pang of homesickness assailed him, a memory of that summer years ago when the Barshinskeys had come, the summer of the swifts and the wild geese. He had a terrible longing to be home again, home with his own people in his own village. The pain was so real for a moment that he had to run back to Yelena Nicolaevna's house and wait inside, in the now familiar but unevoking atmosphere of cabbage soup and sweat, unwashed bodies, onions, and charcoal from the stove. He didn't ever want to feel strongly about anything, ever again.

His salvation—if so it could be called—came on an August Sunday when he had taken a sack of wheat to the priest's house. He left the grain and then, because he heard singing from the church as he passed, he stepped inside and was immediately stunned into glory. He had never been inside a Russian church in all his time in Russia. He had been raised a strict puritanical nonconformist and the corrugated meeting house in the village was the right home, he had always thought, for God. This over-whelming spectacle of gold filigree and baroque ornamentation, painted walls, ceiling, and a priest transformed in robes of gold and silver, reduced him to naïve awe. Wild, plaintive chanting filled the small but exotically beautiful church, such a tragic sound, as though wrenching the agony out of the human soul.

He looked around at the faces he knew in the village, brown,

411

lined, roughened faces lifted up to the priest's steps as he held the Host in his hand. He felt the raw emotion of the people, the music, the beauty suddenly enter his soul and he understood. This heartbreaking, huge, tragic country, which had taken Galina from him and reduced him to a stateless beggar, offered *this* as compensation. This was how they managed to live. This was how, from now on, he must live. Days, years, of apathetic misery and toil and then brief moments of ecstasy, of a vision beyond himself. He suddenly understood Galina and her will-o'-the-wisp moods that had infuriated him so much. Life had to be lived at extremes, of either glory or abject misery. There was nothing in between. This would be his life from now on.

When he left the church he sought out her grave. The misery of her was still there, but now he felt he was joined to her emotional intensity. However much the misery of her death reduced him, there would be moments of glory too. Now he was as Russian as she. He would live here and die here, surrendering himself to the apathy and toil of village life. It was easier to surrender than to try to salvage the man he had once been.

He returned to the church long after everyone else had left, when the old man was going around putting out the candles. And even then the spirit of glory was still present in the church.

"You must go now, my son."

The priest reached out and made the sign of the cross on his forehead and Edwin felt peace descend into his heart.

"You are in God's hands. Surrender yourself to his will."

It was so easy to do, such a relief to be able to relinquish self-will and personal endeavor. Now he could give up and not try anymore.

He stepped out of the church into the midday sun. The hugeness of the sky, the never-ending landscape didn't oppress him. He was just a mindless blob in the universe. He walked slowly through the birch trees toward the river, seeing, as though in a vision, that everything, including himself, was in its place, the unvarying landscape, the wide dusty tracks of the village street, the small figure of a peasant woman trudging toward him from the riverbank.

He watched, without interest, as the figure drew near, noticing vaguely that her skirt was soaking wet and clinging to her legs. She had a blue kerchief over her head and a large bundle clutched in her hand. The face was typical of those he saw every day, high cheekbones, narrow deep-set gray eyes in a sunburned face, a face that was overwhelmingly familiar.

"Edwin!" said the woman, in English. "Is that you, Edwin?"

And with a feeling of shocked resentment, a jarring into a world and life he no longer wanted to remember, he saw that the face belonged to Daisy May Barshinskey.

25 SOPHIE HADN'T REALIZED, UNTIL SHE RECEIVED THE telegram from the War Office, that Ivan, in the absence of his sister, had named her next of kin. She didn't have time to reflect upon it until later. She was too busy fighting the sickening drop in her stomach at the sight of the yellow envelope. It had come many times to the village in the last four years, but never, until now, to her.

It was addressed to her at home, but everyone in the village, including the post boy, knew that she worked up at Fawcett's and so he had pedaled up to the White House. There was a code in the village that telegrams from the War Office had to be delivered at once.

She leaned against the mantelpiece in the kitchen, holding the horrible envelope in her hand, trying hard to control her breathing and the pounding of her heart.

"Don't let him be killed, God. Please don't let Ivan be killed!"

She opened it and the words jiggled themselves into place and began to make sense. Wounded. Shipped from a field hospital in France back to the military hospital at Redhill. Informing her as next of kin. Inquiries to be made direct from hospital, address . . .

It didn't say seriously wounded, did it? Just wounded. She began to undo her apron. If she hurried she'd be in time for the 10:20 over to Redhill.

She was putting her arms into her coat as she swung through the baize door in search of Mrs. Fawcett.

"Sorry, ma'am. Ivan Barshinskey, wounded at Redhill. I have to go over now."

"What . . ."

"Mrs. Collier will give you and the master your lunch. There's some cold fowl left from last night, and I've made potato

414

salad and soup." She hadn't made any soup but she knew she could trust Colley to open a tin and add some stock and a bit of sherry and cream. They'd never know the difference.

"Really, Willoughby . . ." began Mrs. Fawcett pettishly.

"I'll be back well in time for dinner, ma'am. Everything's done. You've no need to fret yourself."

"Yes, but . . ."

"And I know you'd want to do your bit, Mrs. Fawcett, ma'am, going to visit our brave boys, even if you have to make personal sacrifices, like getting your own tea. . . . It's all for our brave boys, isn't it?"

"Well, yes. I suppose if you put it like . . ."

"All right, then. I must go else I'll miss my train. Thank you so much, Mrs. Fawcett."

She hurried back to the kitchen, instinct, even in these revolutionary times prohibiting the use of the main entrance, then dashed out through the kitchen garden and began to run across the station fields.

Wounded. Not dead. But how wounded? Supposing he was blind? Or had lost a leg. It didn't matter. She'd work to keep him going until Daisy came back, and then the two of them could get him sorted out somehow. In a way she almost hoped it would be a leg, not blindness, but a leg. Then he needn't ever go back to the front.

She arrived at the hospital out of visiting hours, but found a sympathetic staff nurse in charge of the ward who was prepared to make an exception in her case.

"I don't think Sister would allow it," she said, somewhat frigidly. "But in view of the distance you've come. . . . And of course, he is something of a celebrity here . . ." Her frigidity melted a little and a gracious smile wafted across her face.

"We offered him a room on his own—in view of his status—but no, he preferred to remain in the ward with the men."

"What status?" breathed Sophie. "Do you mean he's badly hurt? Is he blind?"

"Certainly not. He has a very bad leg wound, but the surgeon thinks he may be able to save it. And he has had a bad attack of pleurisy."

She opened the glass doors of the ward and sailed full ahead, a galleon of starched sails.

"Sergeant-Major Brown, a visitor for you."

Ivan looked up and smiled. He was half sitting, and there was a big cradle arrangement over his leg. His face—she nearly cried out but managed not to. It wasn't cut or battered or scarred. But it seemed black, as though all the dirt and dust of the trenches had grimed into his skin forever. And out of this dark, tired face his eyes burned in two glittering nightmarish pits.

"Ivan! I was so worried. I came as soon as I heard." It suddenly seemed natural to bend down and kiss his cheek. She couldn't remember about modesty or anything like that. She just loved him. She wanted to cry she loved him so much.

"Soph, I knew you'd come. I knew you would." There was something wrong with his speech, a kind of halting quality, as though he had to search for the words and push them out. He didn't smile, but those two burning eyes devoured her face.

"Ivan, what happened? What's wrong with you? Are you all right?"

"Leg. Smashed below the knee and still got shrapnel in the thigh. Digging some more out tomorrow. They thought I'd got gangrene but I hadn't. Doctor here says he can save the leg. Had pleurisy too. Better now." He was holding her hand, very tightly, so tightly in fact that he was hurting her fingers.

"How bad is your leg?" she asked slowly. "I mean, is it damaged forever? Will you have to go back to the front?"

The blackened face didn't answer. Impassively he stared, then to her horror his head began to shake. It went into a juddering movement, like she'd seen on very old men when they were nearly senile.

"Ivan," she whispered, and then, "Shall I get the nurse?" but the hand holding hers only pressed harder and she remained where she was until the shaking began to die away.

"It's the pleurisy," he said, and she answered, "Yes, of

416

course," and all the time she was wondering what awful, terrible thing had happened to him. Some instinct made her realize she mustn't talk about the front, or his injuries, or anything about what had happened to him. Blindly she began to prattle, forcing back tears, trying to sound sane and amusing, like a jolly sort of sister, full of fun and chatter. She spoke about walking out on Mrs. Fawcett as soon as she got the telegram, and about her mother and father and everyone in the village. She spoke of Lillian and her heart gave a fresh twist of anguish when suddenly, at the sound of Lillian's name, she saw his face soften, the hard black lines in his jaw and around his eyes untense and he reached out—she could feel him reaching out—of his nightmare to hold on to Lillian's name.

"Does she know I'm back in England?" he asked. "Does she know I'm here at Redhill?"

"No. Not yet. I just came as soon as I got the telegram. She'll be in London today. I'll tell her this evening." She swallowed her own pain and said in a strong firm voice. "I know she'll be in to see you just as soon as she can."

Some of the blackness seemed to leave his eyes. "Will you bring her next time you come, Sophie? Could you bring her on Sunday? I know you can't keep taking time off and neither can she, but Sunday afternoon is visiting time. You could bring her then."

Bring her, she thought bitterly. Why should Lillian who was older than she have to be brought to hospital as though she were a delicate, helpless creature, unable to cope with trains and hospital wards. But, "Yes, I'll bring her on Sunday, Ivan. I promise."

She chattered on, sitting there by the bed, stroking his hand although neither of them seemed to notice what she was doing. And because every time she said Lillian's name he seemed to relax, to escape from the rigor holding his body, she found she was talking about her all the time, dredging up anything she could think of about Lillian, hating her, loving him, treasuring this moment when she had him to herself. The staff nurse came back eventually and said she had to go and she was grateful. She didn't know how much longer she could have gone on. She kissed him goodbye and as her face was close to his she heard him whisper, "Soph, I can't take much more," and then he closed his eyes and when he opened them it was as though he hadn't spoken. "So you and Lillian will be along on Sunday, then?" he said.

She walked from the ward. The other figures, other men in beds, were a hazy blur to her. Men with bandages over their faces and pulleys on their legs, and arms covered in white. She couldn't really see any of them properly. When they were outside the ward doors the staff nurse smiled at her quite kindly.

"I'm so pleased he's had a family visitor," she said. "We've had a great many visitors from his regiment to see him of course. The colonel came himself to tell him the news."

"News?"

"Of his decoration. He's been awarded the Victoria Cross. For outstanding gallantry. Didn't he tell you himself?"

"No."

"Sergeant-Major Brown is a very modest man. But then all the real heroes are, aren't they?"

She left the hospital, her heart a churning mixture of love and pride, and pain because her love was not needed. All the way home she thought of the pale, scrubby little boy who could hardly read or write, and who had become Sergeant-Major Brown, M.C., V.C. And all the way home she heard that whispered "I can't take much more," and she was afraid for him.

On Sunday she "took" Lillian. She saw his face as they walked up the ward. His eyes were fixed on Lillian and a smile spread over his face. Lillian looked like a flower as she walked between the beds. Every man in the ward stared at her as she wafted past, tall, graceful, her face glowing and animated as she went to visit her V.C. hero. Sophie could see it was doing Ivan so much good that, after ten minutes, she went outside and left them together, making plans for the future when Lillian would become the wife of Company Sergeant-Major Brown, M.C., V.C.

Daisy had known it wasn't going to be easy getting Edwin out of Russia. His papers had been confiscated and he was English. The two factors combined to make his position on a journey highly dangerous. Rumors, even in the backwater village where she found him, were beginning to circulate . . . that the Little Father of all the Russians was dead . . . that the English and the Germans had become allies and were going to invade Russia . . . that the Bolsheviks were shooting peasants . . . that the Bolsheviks were saving the lives of peasants threatened by bandits. She had known it was going to be difficult. But she hadn't ever thought that her greatest difficulty in getting him out would be Edwin himself. He refused to go.

"I'm finished, Daisy," he said tonelessly. "I can't do anything or go anywhere. I'm finished." He was quite calm, but it was as though he were incapable of emotion or passion ever again.

"But you can't stay here, Edwin. You're English. You've got a home and a family . . . and if you stay here, sooner or later you'll be arrested. All foreigners will be arrested. You'll be shot. Don't you see!" Anger made her shout. To come all this way, and be blocked by his passivity.

"So be it."

"Oh, Edwin! Don't be so . . . so Russian! I've spent two years fighting people who couldn't be bothered to . . . to *exert* themselves. What's the matter with you? Just because . . . because *she's* dead . . . there's other people, your parents and Sophie"—and me, she wanted to cry. What about me?

He smiled vaguely and looked up from the straw he was baling. "Daisy, everything you say is true and right. But don't you understand? I'm finished. I don't care what happens to me . . . I can't even care about them at home anymore. I'm too tired to fight for myself, and I'm not worth anyone else fighting for."

"Yes, you are," she said fiercely, but he only shook his head.

"Daisy, I never liked myself very much when I left home and ran after Galina. All the time I despised myself—and when war broke out I despised myself even more. But I felt . . ." He choked

419

suddenly, then shook his head. "I felt if I could just be true to the one thing I had set myself, then I wouldn't be so bad. If I could look after her, get her back to England, I wouldn't be such a . . . such a despicable weak fool. But I failed in that too." He carefully tied twine around a bundle of straw and forked it up onto the top of Yelena Nicolaevna's winter storage space. "I'm not worth saving, Daisy. Your sister and I were two of a kind . . . useless, wasteful, selfish people. Leave us here together."

"But you're being selfish now!" she screamed, but he only nodded his head.

"Yes. But I can't do anything else. I'm finished."

She wanted to shake him, beat him over the head, kick and punch him into action but, infuriatingly, he was beyond her. When her wrath against him died away it left a virulent hatred for her dead sister. A destroyer in life, her power stretched out from the grave to emasculate Edwin.

She stayed. She realized that, in some way, he was in a place, a state of mind, where she could not touch him, but she refused to give up. She bedded down on Yelena Nicolaevna's floor and went out every day into the fields with the other women. She had lived in Russia, with peasants, long enough to become one of them. These northern peasants had a slightly higher level of life than her own poor people in Samara, but still she understood them, knew how to speak and be one of them. She helped Yelena Nicolaevna to dig a hole in the floor of the hut and bury a sack of grain. She had with her the carefully preserved first aid bag, all the way from Buzuluk, and when the children began to get summer boils and abscesses she went around the village lancing and sterilizing as best she could. The village had no doctor and, according to hearsay, neither did Myshkin. The doctor there had been shot on charges of spying. She found she was able to do things herself that, in Mogotovo, she had only assisted with, sewing up a gashed foot with coarse needle and thread, setting a broken wrist in rough homemade splints. The villagers accepted her, even liked her as one of themselves. Edwin they called "the idiot." It was kindly meant but he was not one of them as she was. He noticed her, vaguely, on the periphery of his shocked abstraction; noticed the sturdy little peasant girl who was so familiar, so much a part of his old life, before this one. Sometimes, when he could be bothered to think at all, he was vaguely surprised at the way timid, downtrodden Daisy May had turned into a tough little woman—it was a surprise that quickly drifted away into fatalism.

He lived for the moments in the beautiful baroque church, when the pagan sound of the music lifted him into an ether where he no longer existed. She came with him and stood with the other women, scarf over her head, waiting, waiting, as they all waited. As Russia itself waited. He sensed she was angry with him, but her anger barely touched the surface of his consciousness.

The weather began to turn colder, the leaves began to drift from the trees when one day she came hurrying to him on the banks of the river. He was gutting fish, ready to salt down for the winter months when he saw her, and saw her angry, tearful face.

"It's too late now!" she cried. "You've made us wait, and now we'll never get out. We'll be lucky if we can just stay here and not be noticed. We'll never get away from here now." She cuffed her arm across her face, wiping her eyes and nose at the same time. He felt a faint flutter of interest. Why was Daisy crying?

"What's the matter?"

"Something awful has happened in Moscow. Mitya Gregorovitch has just come back from Myshkin. Someone has tried to kill the Bolshevik leader. He is very ill and they are arresting all foreigners. Hundreds of people are being thrown into prison and killed. We shall never get out now . . . never."

"But did you want to go back to England, Daisy?" he asked, puzzled.

"Of course!" she screamed at him. "Of course I want to go home. But I can't go without you. We've got to go together. And now we'll never get out, never, never!"

At last a vague awakening of responsibility began to stir in him. Daisy May, Galina's sister. He had told her in Petrograd that she shouldn't have come, that she was a naïve child and

421

wouldn't be able to cope with the dangers of Russia in war. In the event she had coped, better than he. But now she was as lost as he was.

"Why didn't you go, Daisy? You've got papers. You could have gone."

"Not without you," she shouted. "I'm not going without you. I came to Russia because of you, and I've spent since March trying to get papers for you and Galina, trying to find you both. I've been up and down the Volga, on steamboats and tugs, looking for you, hoping to get you out. I'm not going without you. *Do you understand?*"

And suddenly he did. Suddenly he realized the enormity of what she had done, the sheer strength and courage of her. And he realized, too, as he looked at her weather-stained, angry small face, that the misfortune he brought to others still wasn't finished. Daisy was here, trapped in this village, because of him. He had failed with her sister, now it looked as though he was going to destroy her too.

"Daisy," he said, "you shouldn't have stayed. Your papers . . . you've got everything you need to get out. I'll walk with you to Myshkin and we'll put you on a boat back to Tver. You can get out . . . I'm sure you can still get out. The Quakers . . . they are friends of Russia. They won't hurt you."

"It's too late! Don't you listen when I tell you? They've tried to murder Lenin and if he dies we won't any of us stand a chance. We won't anyhow. Gregorovitch says they are arresting people, even in Myshkin—a little town like Myshkin. It won't be long before they get to us!"

He stared at her, comprehension of their position dawning at last. He was horrified at himself, at his indulgent self-absorption. What had happened to him? He had been raised to believe that women should be protected, sheltered. He'd let her sister die, wasn't one of them enough?

"Oh, God, Daisy! What have I done?"

"You've done nothing, that's the trouble," she hurled at him, and the sight of her, diminutive, stocky, brave little Daisy, spitting abuse at him, awoke all the old affection he had had for her and for his family, the normal feelings of affection and fondness that obsession had driven from his soul. He remembered how brave she had been as a child, how brave she still was. He owed her something. It was because of him she was here.

"Daisy, I'll get you out somehow. We'll find a way. I'll come with you as far as I can without papers, then send you on your way. There must be some of your people still in Russia. Didn't you say they had some base in Moscow? If I could get you to Moscow someone would surely look after you . . . the Red Cross, or the consulate, or someone."

"They won't be any safer than we are. They're shooting people in Moscow—anyone who is foreign or suspicious is likely to be arrested. There's no one to help us now, Edwin. We've left it too late." She was quieter. The situation was still hopeless but she felt a sense of growing security because Edwin had suddenly become Edwin again. The "idiot" had vanished. He was more like the Edwin of childhood.

He was silent for a moment. "All right. We'll stay here, very quietly, for the time being. We're all right here. They like you. They think of you as a Russian and they tolerate me. An extra man in this village is useful and I'm strong. We'll just sit tight and quiet and wait out the arrests. The minute things become settled we'll move on, not back to Tver, we'll go downriver, somewhere we can get a train to Moscow."

"You've got no papers."

"Neither have half the people who crowd the trains. I'll steal some if necessary. I'll get you to Moscow somehow, Daisy. Trust me. I'll get you home somehow."

He had made that promise before and failed. This time he'd keep his word.

26 AT THE END OF SEPTEMBER IVAN RETURNED FROM hospital to spend two weeks' convalescent leave in the village. Then he had to report to a medical board who would decide if he was fit enough to return to France.

He seemed happy, relaxed. Sophie watched him carefully but could see no signs of nervousness or shaking. Whatever had troubled him had been cured by the magic presence of Lillian.

She had never looked so beautiful. On her hand was a small rosette of diamonds, on her arm the handsome hero who had brought fame to the village. A reporter came down from London and she had her picture in the newspaper—"Beautiful Bride for V.C. War Hero." It was that article that told them all exactly what Ivan had done to win his medal. His company had been cut off from their lines with three officers killed and two seriously wounded. Ivan had led the company back through the enemy to their own lines, and then he had gone back, not once, but twice, for the two wounded officers. He had then re-formed the company and broken the enemy defense, restoring his men to their original positions. Sophie felt sick when she read it. All she could see was his terrible ague when he was in hospital, that and the dark pitted eyes.

Lillian was possessive with Ivan. She wanted to take him everywhere, be seen with him by all her friends and the people she worked with. Sophie, in her moments off from work, was amazed at the sight of Ivan making the social rounds, being taken from house to house, exhibited like a wild beast on a leash. When his last day came Lillian couldn't see him off. She had gone with him to the medical board and heard he was well enough to go back into action. But she was working in London when he actually left. The night before she had cried, gracefully and beautifully, and Ivan had comforted her and begged her not to weep. The next day Sophie walked across the fields with him to the station, not knowing what to say, a welter of emotions that she could only just conceal.

It was one of the last golden days of summer, with a high hazy sky and a kind of ripe somnolence in the air. The station fields were lined with blackberries and sloes and, where the crab-apples leaned over the ditch, three scrubby village children were filling sacks.

"Do you like the village now?" she asked. "It was such an unhappy place for you when you were a boy. I never thought you'd come back."

"All the family I've got are here."

They both fell silent, thinking of Daisy, Galina, Edwin. The war had reduced everything to a full stop. At some time everything would start again and either the others would come home, or they would be told of their deaths. Until then they had placed them in a limbo world.

They waited on the station platform, not speaking, looking out at Mr. Braithwaite's cows grazing along the lines. Then they heard the signal drop.

"Sophie . . ."

"Ivan . . . don't worry, " she said breathlessly. "We'll still all be here. Just like we are now. None of us will change. It will all be just like it is now, ready for you to come back. Quiet and peaceful."

He suddenly reached out and grabbed her in his arms. He gripped her so tightly she was reminded of that first day in hospital, when he had hurt her hand. She could feel him beginning to shake again.

"We'll be here," she squeaked. "All of us, waiting for you, thinking of you . . . and there's Lillian . . . she'll be waiting for you. . . ."

He buried his face in her hair, just for the briefest of seconds, but she knew it wasn't anything to do with affection for her. He was saying goodbye to the peace, trying to stop himself from being afraid. Then he pulled away and smiled, just the way his father had done.

" 'Bye, Soph," he said, cuffing her gently on the chin with his fist. He turned and threw his kitbag up into the train. His face, as the train drew out of the station, had the black look again, with dark pitted eyes.

Lillian began an orgy of dressmaking—for her bottom drawer. The kitchen was covered in bolts of cambric, lawn, insertions, and threadwork. More was needed than just an ordinary village bride's requirements. Lillian was going to be a soldier's wife, traveling from station to station, probably even going to India when the war was over. There would be social engagements on company stations. A sergeant-major's wife would have a position, a status to maintain. There would be mess gatherings and bazaars and sales of work which she would be expected to organize. Every time Sophie went home Lillian and her mother were discussing the various merits of wool versus face cloth for a really good company dress, or how sensible it would be to invest in warm clothes when a first posting might take them to a warm clime.

Sophie watched and listened and screamed inside herself. *What are you doing thinking about clothes when he might not even come back, when the war might not end for years? How can you care about clothes! What about him, out there. Can't you think about him instead of sewing petticoats?* Sometimes she hated them. At other times she was honest enough to realize that at least the bustle of Lillian's trousseau helped her mother not to think about Edwin so much.

She lost weight again and her skin took on a sallow gray look. One night Lillian held up a length of royal blue wool crepe against Sophie's face.

"You look dreadful, Sophie," she said, not unkindly. "I'd thought of this for your bridesmaid dress—I got it at trade discount from Mace's—but this color doesn't do anything for you."

"Bridesmaid?"

"Of course, Sophie," said her mother. "You didn't think Lillian would ask anyone else, did you?"

"If we're to get married on Ivan's next leave, I ought to be starting your dress, Sophie. There's not that much . . ." Her voice receded from Sophie's consciousness. She concentrated on keeping her face free from expression. Bridesmaid. She couldn't do it. She couldn't bear to do it. She opened her eyes and saw her father watching her.

"I should leave all that, Lillian love," he said. "Leave the bridesmaid thing and do your own. We'll see later about Sophie."

She thanked him silently, trying not to let them see the incipient tears. Two mighty swallows, and a disciplined, deliberate image of the rabbit she had to skin when she got back to Fawcett's that night, pulled her back in control again. She had discovered, some time ago, that when she was unhappy and worried, it helped her not to cry if she thought of nasty, sordid jobs that had to be done.

The war seemed to have drifted into a tired and interminable period. No one believed, after four years, that it would be over by Christmas. There had been too many Christmases. There were too many faces gone. Each night she prayed that Ivan would not do anything again like rescuing wounded officers. He had survived four years of the trenches. His luck could not last forever.

Two weeks after his departure, Lillian received the briefest of letters from one of the women's voluntary hospital units. Ivan was back in a field hospital with pleurisy again. And God must have heard Sophie's prayers for he was still there, five days later, when the armistice was declared.

Unannounced, he turned up in the village on more sick leave at the beginning of December. Sophie saw him first as she was coming home for her afternoon off. He was standing in the yard, staring through the window at Lillian, just the way he had when he'd first come back from India, staring at her framed in the light.

When he came into the scullery she could see he was thinner, tireder, and even though the war was over, she could sense the awful tightness in him. There was a chatter of welcome, a flurry of rearrangement of bedrooms (so that Ivan would not be sleeping in the room next to Lillian), and the best tea service came out. It was their own little armistice. A chance to rejoice and forget that Edwin and Daisy had still not come home.

Ma put on a festival tea; the rest of the cold lamb with home pickled walnuts and a tin of fruit salad. She was mortified because it was the middle of the week and there was only slab cake left. Under the warmth of the welcome Sophie could feel Ivan relaxing, could feel the tenseness subsiding a little.

They sat around the table, Lillian prattling on about the wedding and how soon they could call the banns.

"There won't be any difficulty getting leave now," he said slowly. "I'll have to go back of course, go back to clear up, but when that's done . . . that'll be the end of it."

They were all silent for a moment and then he said, "I'm not going on with it. I can't take anymore. I'm coming out."

"What do you mean, Ivan?" Lillian's pretty white forehead wrinkled up.

"The army. I've had enough. I'm coming out."

"Oh!"

Sophie watched Lillian's face and saw the dream of lording it over the ladies of the sergeants' mess fade from her visions.

"What will you do?"

He rubbed his hand tiredly across his eyes. "I don't know yet. I just know I don't want to stay in the army anymore. I can't."

"But you've done so well, Ivan! A sergeant-major and a V.C. and all that. If you stayed on you'd be important. You're a hero."

He gave a derisive laugh. "Hero! What does that mean? Everyone was a hero except for the generals. They stayed back behind the lines. Just because I got a medal doesn't mean I'm a hero. They were all heroes, every one of them. Just for sticking it out they were heroes."

His voice was loud, rough. There was an uncomfortable pause and then Ma stood up, the teapot in her hand.

"I'd better start clearing this lot away," she said. "I expect you two will want to go for a walk."

"But what can you do, Ivan, if you don't stay in the army?" asked Lillian coldly, ignoring her mother. "You've done nothing but the army since you left here. You don't know anything else."

"I can learn. I could turn my hand to anything when I was a boy. My father was supposed to be the best cowman in the county. You said that, didn't you, Mr. Willoughby?"

"That's right, lad, but . . ."

"I'll do that, if someone will have me." He was nearly shouting now. "I'll work with animals and growing things for a change. That's what I want—to work with living things instead of corpses!"

"Come outside for a moment, Ivan." Sophie touched his hand very gently and tried to pull him to his feet.

"You can't be a cowman!" said Lillian, her face as flushed as his. "You can't possibly be just a cowman."

"Lillian," warned her mother. "Don't be so rude to your father."

"That's different!" She turned a red face toward her mother for a moment. "Pa never had a chance to be anything else. But Ivan has. Ivan's a war hero and a regular soldier. He'll be respected. He'll be someone. He'll go all over the world and retire with a good pension. He could do something else then if he wanted, after he's retired with a pension. We could start a business together, anything. He can't be just a cowman!"

"Why don't you two young folk go in the parlor and sort it out between you," Pa said very quietly. "This is not for us to listen to, lassie. This is private between you."

"I can't stay on in the army. I can't be a soldier anymore. Don't you understand?" Sophie saw him put his hands underneath the hanging tablecloth. The cloth began to shake.

"No, I don't. I don't understand at all." Two large pearl-sized tears dropped from Lillian's eyes and crept softly down her cheeks. "You said you loved me. You said you'd do anything for me. You just wanted to look after me for the rest of my life. That's what you said."

"It's true. I do," he said hoarsely.

"Then how can you!" she sobbed. "I can't be married to a cowman, a farm laborer. What would everyone say . . ."

The shocked silence permeated even Lillian's misery. "I didn't

429

mean it like that," she mumbled. "It's just that . . . everything was going to be so wonderful."

"It could still be wonderful," he said. His face had drained of color. Its whiteness emphasized the dark lines under his eyes and down the sides of his nose and mouth.

"I really do think you'd both better go into the parlor," said Mother sadly, and finally Lillian rose and with sudden icy calm led the way out of the room. In silence Sophie and her mother cleared the table and did the washing up. They could hear their voices in the front parlor, Lillian's calm now, very controlled, and Ivan's deep rumble, occurring only spasmodically. When Sophie and her ma went back into the kitchen Sophie realized how sad her father was too. He sat, staring into the range; his shoulders were slumped and his face weary.

"I was ashamed," he said simply. "I was so ashamed of my girl."

She went to him and bent her head to his, just resting her cheek against his face. He seemed such a tired old man now.

"Pa, dear," she sighed. "Oh, I do wish Edwin would come home soon," and then when she saw his further dejection she cursed herself for her thoughtlessness.

They heard the front door open and close—no one ever used the front door—and then Lillian came back into the room.

"There's no need to look at me like that," she said coolly. "Nothing's been decided. We shall leave things as they are for a while. He can't leave the army yet anyway."

"Where's he gone?"

"He didn't say. He just left by the front door. I expect he'll be back when he's got over his temper. He always did have a terrible temper, even when he was a child. Look how he attacked his father that time . . ."

Sophie suddenly choked and flung open the back door. "I hate you, Lillian!" she cried. "I really hate you!" and then she began to run up the lane, trying to find him in the crisp cold night. When she came to where Tyler's alley branched off from the road she plunged up it, hoping he would have gone that way and not through Cobham's passage. She found him. He was leaning over the stile at the top of Tyler's fields, right where the water pump was. She tried to control her breathing, tried to stop her distress showing. She leaned on the stile beside him, forcing herself to speak calmly.

"You all right, Ivan?"

He didn't answer. She could sense the rage, the misery boiling in him.

"I'm sure it will come out fine," she chattered nervously. "She's just excited because you've come home unexpectedly."

"I can't go back! She doesn't understand . . . I can't be a soldier anymore."

"I know."

"I'm sick of death and fighting!"

"Yes."

"Oh, Sophie!" He suddenly put his head down into his hands, covering his eyes, gripping his fingers tightly into his face. "It's not just the killing . . . not just that. I'm afraid. I got a V.C. I'm a hero, and none of them know how afraid I am. I can't fight anymore. I'm afraid."

She put her arm around his shoulders and screwed her face up tight to stop herself from crying. He lifted his head. In the moonlight his face looked awful, dark and twisted.

"Did you wonder how I got pleurisy again? Nobody asked, did they? Well, I'll tell you. I'd only been back in the trenches one day when I got a shrapnel wound. They sent me to the field hospital and left me there for one night. When it was dark I got out of bed and soaked my pajamas in cold water. Then I put them on again and stood outside the tent all night. That's how I got pleurisy again."

"That's not so bad," she said huskily. "You never shirked before. You wouldn't have been made a sergeant if you'd shirked."

"I'm not afraid of being killed, or injured. I'm afraid of . . . all those corpses . . . all those men I ordered up over the top . . . all the boys, young boys, like I used to be, they all trusted me, trusted me to look after them. They're nearly all dead now. My fault."

"Not your fault," she crooned. "Not your fault."

"That's why I can't do it anymore. I can't give orders anymore. I can't tell them, those boys, silly young fools, to go forward . . . and get blown to bits . . ."

"Leave the army. The war's over now. No one will blame you for leaving now."

He turned his face toward her and she was reminded of the miserable small boy who had come to say goodbye to her after his mother had died.

"She'll blame me. I'll lose her, won't I? I always wanted her, even when I hated her. She was everything we were not—everything that you Willoughbys meant. She was clean and beautiful and she smelled nice—I used to hate that when I was a kid—the fact that we smelled, even when we washed we smelled of poverty. And she had . . . something . . . the way she walked. She knew she was better than any of the rest of us. She walked like a princess."

"Maybe it'll all come right, Ivan. Give her a chance to get used to the idea."

"She won't get used to it. I'm one of the dirty Barshinskeys, the tinker's child. I'm not good enough for a Willoughby."

"You are! You are! You're too good for her!"

He seized her roughly by the shoulder and shook her quite savagely. "Nothing really changes, does it? The sergeant's stripes and the V.C. . . . they don't really cover up the fact that I'm a dirty little Barshinskey with a drunken father. You'll none of you forget that, will you?"

"It doesn't matter. It doesn't matter!"

"I wish I could forget about you all!" he shouted. "I wish I could put you away, and not care about the Willoughbys. You've dogged me all my life!"

"Ivan!" He was shaking her, pushing her, and she was suddenly afraid of his great strength. She tried to knock his arm from her shoulder and her slight gesture of aggression seemed to flame him into madness.

432

"You never let go of us, any of you," he bellowed hatefully. "You were always there, teasing, promising us things we could never have, sneering at us because we were the dirty Barshinskeys."

She tore herself away from his huge hands and began to run away from him, but he caught her by the arm and jerked her back.

"It's time we showed you," he shouted. "Time we paid you back . . ."

He threw her onto the ground and then was suddenly there beside her. He took hold of her hair with one hand and yanked her head right back onto the grass. His leg was pinning her down and then she felt him wrenching at her coat buttons and she knew what was going to happen. He was like a mad bull, like the bull that had injured her father, but she also knew that he wouldn't be sane again, wouldn't be healed until he had hurt someone. Her struggles at first were instinctive, the age-old reaction of a woman to protect herself from violation. And then she suddenly realized it was Ivan whom she loved, and when at last he let go of her arms she wound them around his neck and pulled him closer.

He was rough. He hurt her. There was one moment when his great hands were on her throat and she was afraid he was going to kill her. Then it was over and she was conscious of the hard ground beneath her and of her torn clothes letting in the freezing air to her body. He lay slumped over her for moment, quite still, and then he began to sob.

"Oh, God! What have I done!"

"It's all right. I'm all right."

"Sophie. What have I done to you! Oh, God, what have I done."

"Nothing. It's all right. Truly it's all right." She was trembling. She couldn't stop and she was suddenly terribly cold. He sat up and pulled her into the shelter of his body, trying to straighten her clothes and wrap her coat around her. The buttons had all been wrenched off.

"Oh, Sophie. Poor little Sophie!"

His tenderness was almost too much. It was worse than his

433

attack. She put her arms up around his neck again and pressed her face into his shoulder. It will probably never happen again, she thought, that I can be this close to him. She tried to record every sensation, every feeling of the warmth and strength of his body in her mind for the future.

"It was her," he said. "It was her I wanted to hurt. Not you."

"Don't, Ivan. Don't say anymore, please."

"It was her . . . and the war . . . I'm not sane, not normal. I've been killing things, men, people, for too long."

"I know, Ivan. There's nothing to be sorry about. We'll never mention it again. Just help me up. Help me back to Fawcett's. I won't go home again. I'll go straight to my room at Fawcett's."

He helped her to stand, and turned his back when she tried to make her torn clothes tidy. Her legs were shaking and he put his arm around her waist and nearly carried her along. When they got to Fawcett's he opened the kitchen door and led her gently inside.

"You must go now, Ivan. Don't think about it. Don't worry about it. I promise you I'm all right. I understand. I understand, truly I do."

His eyes scoured her face. She knew a brief bitter moment when she thought how wonderful it would be if he suddenly said he loved her, but, wryly, she knew that love was not born of a savage sexual encounter.

"You are my dear, dear friend," she said. "And you will always be my dear, dear friend."

She shut the door then. She could take no more. She limped up the stairs, washed, and changed back into uniform ready to come down and prepare the supper.

She learned later that he had gone back to the cottage just to collect his kit, then he had caught the last train to London, saying he wouldn't be back anymore.

27 THE SNOW FELL AND THAT AUTUMN AND WINTER IT was particularly heavy. The village was cut off from the outside world and, apart from a sleigh driven by a Red Guard from Myshkin, no one came. The Red Guard wanted food and, sullenly, the villagers watched as he took their grain and potatoes and gave them useless pieces of paper in return. When he came, Daisy and Edwin blurred into the background of the family. They were just two more bodies in the overcrowded home of Yelena Nicolaevna.

Daisy had her clothes from Buzuluk. She had carried them all over Russia with her, even in the summer when her bundle had been heavy. She had the thick sheepskin coat and a pair of *valenki*. She was prepared. But Edwin had lost his clothes running from the mob in Tver. He had ordinary leather boots that were nearly worn through and which were no use in the thick snow. The leather froze hard in just a few moments and when he took them off the skin tore from his feet. He had a heavy seaman's jacket that he had worn all through his winter in Tver, but it wasn't really warm enough for the desolate countryside of the northern Volga regions. They shared the sheepskin coat between them, and Daisy begged rags from all over the village, useless worn pieces of old homespun that she packed, together with straw, between two layers of cloth cut from her shawl. She shaped them into socks and then tied them onto Edwin's feet for the winter. They didn't notice the smell of Yelena Nicolaevna's room anymore for that smell had become their own.

Yelena Nicolaevna was a kind, good woman. In the summer they had earned their food by working in the fields but in the winter nobody went outside and they were just two extra mouths to feed. For a while Edwin went to the river each day and smashed through the ice to try to fish. But as it got colder the fish seemed to vanish and finally the ice was too thick to penetrate.

They tried to eat less, knowing they had no money to spare to offer for their food, but Yelena Nicolaevna would shake her head, and say "tck, tck" in a disapproving way when they took only small portions from the communal soup pot. Hers was an affluent home and there were bowls for everyone rather than just the one pot with several spoons. She would scoop up more of the turnip and potato stew and they were too hungry to refuse. The years of poor food and long hours of work in bad conditions had begun to affect Daisy's health. She had been in Russia for two and a half years, constantly exposed to disease and dirt and, over the last eighteen months, with less and less to eat. She caught bad feverish colds, one after the other. The crowded home of Yelena Nicolaevna did nothing to help.

At night they slept on the bunk over the doorway, near to the stove but not on it. The top was tightly packed with the *baba* and the children and Yelena Nicolaevna and there was no room for them. It got cold on the shelf in the early hours of the morning and they kept the sheepskin coat and the seaman's jacket on top of them.

In January the snow was piled so thick over the barn it was impossible to get out of the door, and Edwin unsealed the upper window, climbed out and began to move the great mountain of snow that sloped down from the roof. He gazed out across the landscape. The river had vanished. It was just a part of the great snowfield that stretched all around them. To the north was the fir forest and, as he looked, he saw a two-horse sleigh skimming toward them. The tinkling of the horse bells sounded brittle in the morning air. He felt a stirring of unease. Rumors had leaked through of mass killings of foreigners in the cities, of secret arrests, of banning anyone from leaving the country. Each rumor seemed to lessen their hopes of escape, but the Russian winter had spread its apathetic anodyne over them. They knew they would have to do something, but not yet.

The sleigh drew closer. There was one man, other than the driver. Both had cartridge belts strapped over their greatcoats and his heart sank. They looked like policemen or commissars. The sleigh shot past Yelena Nicolaevna's house and stopped before the church. Hastily he climbed back through the barn window and went into the main room of the house.

"Policeman," he said quietly to Daisy. "Stopped at the priest's house. We can't get out without them seeing us. And they have a sleigh. They can follow our tracks."

"Lie on top of the stove," she said. "Pretend to sleep and perhaps they will not speak to you. I sound like a peasant but you do not."

She went back to her baking, taking loaves from the oven, and then the door was thrust open and the two men came in. Daisy gave a little involuntary scream and some of the bread slid from the pallet onto the floor. She made a great pretense of scolding and picking up the loaves and, when she turned to face the men she had regained her self-control.

"There are foreigners in this house. Spies. Who are they?"

Yelena Nicolaevna gave a frightened cry and gathered her children around her skirts. She looked at Daisy with a terrified face. Daisy was no longer one of them. Daisy put down the bread pallet.

"I am a foreigner," she said. "But I am not a spy."

"Who else?"

Edwin slid down from the top of the stove and came to stand with his arm around Daisy.

"Papers."

Daisy lifted her skirt and took the wallet from her pocket. Silently she handed them over and the smaller of the two men rifled through all the passes and permits she had been given in Moscow.

"My friend has had his papers stolen. He was attacked on the river and robbed, then he was thrown into the water and left for dead. This kind woman gave him shelter." Edwin noticed she had deliberately thickened her accent into the country dialect of the local peasants.

"You are English? You are both English?"

"Yes."

437

"I think you are spies. You will come with me."

The other man, the driver of the sleigh, unslung the rifle from his shoulder.

"Outside!"

They just had time to shrug into their coats before they were pushed out of the door. The rifle was jammed into the back of Edwin's neck and they were propelled in the direction of the church, not inside, but around the back, toward the churchyard. A spasm of ice moved in Edwin's stomach. They were going to be shot.

"Please look at my papers again," said Daisy, very calmly. "I am a member of the Friends' Voluntary Relief Unit. You have heard of us perhaps. We have been looking after refugees in the south. My papers are signed by the Soviet Commissar for Social Security in Moscow. I have travel permits from him, and my passport has a special extension granted by him. My people, the Friends of Russia, are helping the poor. They are friends of the Bolshevik revolution. I beg that you will look at my papers. The Soviet Commissar in Moscow took a special interest in me."

Edwin felt the rifle removed from his neck, and slowly, slowly, he turned. The smaller of the men, the more dangerous he sensed, was staring at Daisy with a cold impersonal intensity. He took the wallet from his pocket and clumsily, with gloved hands, he leafed through it again. A multitude of stamps and signatures held his attention.

"You will come to Rostov with us," he pointed to Daisy. "We shall see what the authorities there say. Your case will be heard in the Soviet court. Him"—he pointed to Edwin—"shoot him."

"No!" Daisy's cry rang loudly in the cold, brittle air. "No! He is also from the Friends' Voluntary Relief Unit. His papers were exactly the same as mine. The Soviet Commissar in Moscow sent me to this village to find him and bring him to Moscow. He said he was very important to the relief work. My friend is a very important person in England. When he gets to Moscow his signature will mean that a special food consignment can be released and brought into the country. And money too. He has special access to money that is to be used to bring milk and grain to Moscow!"

She screamed in a brisk babble of Russian that Edwin could not begin to understand. She pointed to her papers, to Edwin. She sounded quick and authoritative. He heard names—Chincherin—dropped into her flood of official rhetoric. He could sense that the senior man was hesitating and Daisy must have sensed it too. Her manner changed. She became imperious, threatening. The commissar put the papers back into the pocket of his greatcoat.

"We will take him to Rostov," he said. "You will both be tried in Rostov before the Soviet court. You"—he pointed to Edwin— "I think you are a spy."

Edwin felt a flicker of hope. Now it was only he who was a spy. They seemed to have accepted that Daisy was not. If Daisy could only be released he would be happy.

"Tie his hands and feet and make them both lie on the floor of the sleigh," the policeman said, and the driver pushed them both toward the waiting horses.

Edwin crouched at the bottom of the sleigh and the driver pushed him over, then tied his ankles together, and his hands behind his back. Daisy, white-faced, sat beside him, squashed into the narrow foot space. On the seat behind them sat the policeman with the barrel of the rifle pointing directly at their heads. The driver cracked his whip and the sleigh rolled down the slope of the snow and sped over the frozen river. He tried to recall what little geography he had of the local terrain. Rostov, he thought, was about sixty miles away. It would take them between five and six hours to get there.

His brain was remarkably clear and he felt no fear. Undoubtedly they would execute him in Rostov. But what of Daisy? Even if they decided to take her to Moscow to check her story, even if some of the Quakers were still there, at some point they would discover she had lied about him. She had condemned herself by shielding him. Daisy was not going to die, he was determined on that. Even if he had to attack the two men with his hands bound, she was not going to die. He felt a surging sense of purpose race through his veins. He only had to wait and plan. At some point in the journey they would stop. There would be some point where he could strike out.

The subtemperature permeated through his seaman's jacket and Daisy moved closer to him. His hands, in padded gloves, were beginning to lose all feeling. The twine that circled his wrist was cutting off circulation and he began to move his fingers, flexing them to and fro to prevent frostbite. Daisy sat up and removed her coat. The policeman jabbed her in the shoulder with his rifle.

"Sit. Do not move unless I give permission."

"My friend's coat is thin. I wish to wrap mine around both of us."

The rifle followed her every movement as she fitted herself around Edwin's back, like a spoon, and pulled the coat over her shoulders, around him as far as it would go, tying the sleeves across his chest. He knew what she was going to do and could hardly believe the policeman wouldn't think of it. They lay quite still, pretended to go to sleep and prayed the policeman wouldn't use his common sense. One hour passed, two, reactions became blurred, the alertness of the policeman settled into frozen endurance.

He adjusted his hands without moving his arms or any part of his body. Three hours passed, hours when they both held their bodies rigid, trying not to show by a muscle that Daisy's fingers were picking away at the twine. He twisted his wrists. He could move his hands now, slide them from one side to the other. Then he felt the pressure ease. The twine was just held loosely around his hands. One pull and he would be free.

"I want to go to the lavatory."

"Wait, Englishman."

"I cannot wait."

He grunted to his companion and the sleigh began to lose speed. When it stopped the policeman prodded him with the rifle. Daisy moved out of the way, wriggling around so that she was in front of him. He kept quite still.

"Stand up slowly and face out to the snow. I will undo your hands and will shoot you if you do anything but urinate."

He poised himself on frozen, bended knees. If only he wasn't so cold, his limbs iced into rigidity. He flexed his leg muscles and blotted out cold and stiffness from his brain. Then, with a surge of determination he leaped to his feet, catching the rifle under the barrel with his shoulder. It exploded into the air, and as the policeman tilted back he hurled himself forward, snatching his hands free and gripping the guard around the throat. The horses, startled by the rifle shot, bolted and the driver tried to draw back on the reins and spin around with his rifle at the same time.

"Keep down, Daisy! Keep down!"

Somehow, by a superhuman effort, he spun the policeman's body right around so that it was between him and the driver. The man was clawing at his face. He was strong, much stronger than Edwin, and it was only the surprise of the attack that had given Edwin the advantage. He brought his knee up hard in the man's groin, desperation making the blow effective even through the thick layers of clothing and as the policeman doubled over, his hands dropping from Edwin's face, Edwin pulled the twine, still hanging from his wrists, around the man's neck. He tightened it, straining and pulling with his frozen hands, knowing he was killing a man, intending to kill, determined to kill so that he could save Daisy.

The sleigh was hurtling over the snow, the driver swaying and rolling from side to side, still trying to turn with his rifle and keep his balance.

"*Stoi . . . stoi!*"

He couldn't allow himself to think of anything but keeping the twine tight. The back of the policeman's neck went purple. He was vaguely glad he didn't have to look at his face. Dimly he was aware that Daisy was standing up but he didn't have the breath to shout at her again. From the corner of his eye he saw her grasp the barrel of the driver's rifle, and push it violently into his stomach. He lurched, fired—a shot that went harmlessly into the air—and tumbled off the box into the snow.

Suddenly the body beneath his hands slumped. He held the

441

twine a moment longer in case it was a trick and then, trembling with the exertion, let it fall to the floor of the sleigh. Daisy was clinging to the swaying front seat and Edwin pulled himself over the dead policeman, up onto the box, and seized the reins of the bolting horses. He didn't want them to stop. Behind him in the snow was the driver with a rifle and he wanted to get as far away from him as possible. In the distance he could see a line of forest and slowly he turned the horses until they were racing toward the trees. He felt Daisy picking at the twine around his ankles. After half an hour they began to slow and finally, when they were in the forest, Edwin hauled on them to stop. They were sweating hard. So was he.

They pulled out the body of the guard, trying not to look at his bloated, blackened face.

"Take his coat, Edwin. It's got no badges or anything on and it's thick. And the hat too. There's nothing to show they belong to Red Guards."

He pulled them off, turning the body face down in the snow, feeling easier when they couldn't see him anymore. He felt inside the pocket of the coat, took Daisy's wallet of papers and handed them to her. Then he began to hunt through the rest of the papers. The identification pass had a photograph of the dead man. He wasn't a bit like Edwin.

"It's too risky," said Daisy. "If you take the photograph off you still can't pass as a policeman, not with your accent. You must leave them."

"There's money here. That's good. We can use it for bribes. Perhaps I can steal some more ordinary papers later on."

"What shall we do now?"

"Carry on to Rostov if we can. The railway line runs from there to Moscow. If we can force our way onto a train without a travel permit, we should be able to get to Moscow. And from there . . . well . . . we'll see . . ."

He put on the dead man's hat and coat, then scooped out a depression in the snow with the rifle and rolled the body into it. Carefully they piled up snow so that no one could see what was underneath.

442

"How do we know which way is Rostov?"

He looked up into the sky, at the sinking sun. "It's southeast from the village. We've been coming southeast ever since we left. We'll carry on in that direction and hope we hit something before night comes." They didn't say, although they both knew, that if they didn't find shelter before the sun went down they might just as well have been shot.

Half an hour out of the forest they hit the railway line running across the snowfield. They turned right, for the east was where Moscow was, however many miles away, and as darkness fell over the white landscape they saw the lights of a town in the distance. It was Rostov.

They begged shelter that night from a poor house on the outskirts of the town. Experience had taught them both that poor people were more likely to be hospitable than the people in the towns. They had abandoned the sleigh outside Rostov, turning the horses loose to be stolen by whoever was lucky enough to find them first. The following morning they began their three-day wait at the station for the Moscow train. The crowd grew bigger and bigger. Typhus had broken out in the town and those who could manage to do so were anxious to leave before the epidemic spread. When the train finally did come in Edwin managed to push Daisy into a freight car and then found a place for himself clinging to the steps outside. He had a warm coat now and, with luck, his hands would last long enough to allow him to hold on. Within a few hours, as the bodies in the freight car shook down, he was able to squeeze in beside her. He had purchased a ticket for each of them, Daisy's with her travel permit, and his own with a bribe from the policeman's wallet. Half the people who clung on to the footplate and lay on the roof of the train hadn't purchased a ticket at all, but he was anxious not to court more trouble than they already had.

Later, when he thought about it, he wondered why the journey with Daisy didn't remind him of another railway journey, his last journey with Galina, his frail loving wanton who lay in a village graveyard far to the north. But he never once thought back. He was consumed with two anxieties—that the guards would not make trouble because he had no papers or travel permit, and that Daisy's weakened constitution would survive the journey. He never once thought of Galina, nor of the man he had murdered in the snow.

When the guards did come on board, Daisy was feverish. Another of her interminable colds racked her body and her thin face was flushed. A constant film of sweat lay over her forehead. She tried to sit up, ready to help him with the guard's queries but it was unnecessary. The conditions in the freight car were foul. They had been there for forty-eight hours and the corner of the car had been used as a lavatory. The day before a passenger had died and they had had to push the body out of the car. The guard coughed at the stench and spat out of the door. Edwin handed him a bundle of papers, all Daisy's.

"Where are you from?" the guard asked without looking at them.

"Rostov. They have typhus there. My wife is ill."

The guard looked at Daisy's sweating face and pushed the papers back. He jumped from the car and slammed the metal door shut.

They reached Moscow the following morning. Hardly any transport was running, and the snow hadn't been cleared from the streets for several days. Long depressing queues of women outside the bread shops reminded Edwin of Petrograd before the revolution. Nothing seemed to have changed. Everything was just as bad as it had been.

Daisy rallied as she realized just how far they had managed to come on their journey. Over the last few days Edwin had watched her health and spirit dwindle away. She had used the last of her strength to knock the policeman from the sleigh but now Moscow, sordid and cold and filthy, but known to her, restored her hope.

"We'll go to the consulate," she said briskly. "They were very helpful before and they told me they would help if only I could get you here. They'll manage something, in spite of your lost papers. They'll help us."

They had to walk from the Yaroslavl Station, a long walk with the icy wind blowing in their faces, but Daisy appeared to grow stronger and more confident with every step. It was for this she had come to Russia, searched the villages of the Volga, and stayed with Edwin until he recovered from his malaise. This was what she had set out to do, save him, and get him home to England. When they reached the center of the city and she began to recognize where she was, her steps quickened. It was as though the British Consulate were home. And then she stopped.

"It's there," she said, bewildered.

A barricaded door and a soldier lounging across it. There was something about the look of the place. A truck drove up and a soldier jumped down and joined his comrade. Then they moved the barricade and let three men and a woman—Russian men and a Russian woman—in through the door. The soldiers saw Edwin and Daisy watching; one of them gestured toward Edwin, and Daisy pulled him back around the corner.

"Something's gone wrong," she faltered. "The consulate isn't there anymore. They must have moved."

"Who can you ask? Who else do you know in Moscow?"

"The Red Cross. We'll go to the Red Cross. I know where they are and they'll help us. They might not be able to get you papers, but they'll tell us where the consulate is."

They began to walk again. Daisy was tired. She leaned against him and wasn't moving so quickly. They were both hungry and thirsty but Daisy was too frightened to stay in one place in case someone asked to see their papers.

There were guards outside the Red Cross building as well. A large placard pasted on outside called on the Russians to fight against Allied Intervention and White Generals. Daisy, quite softly and gently, began to cry.

"I don't know what to do anymore. I thought I could get you out. I don't know where to go anymore . . ."

He felt a sudden and unexpected surge of protective power

sweep over him. She'd fought like a terrier to find him and persuade him to leave. She had become a stubborn, strong, tough
little creature that he hardly recognized as the Daisy of his childhood. He'd not really had time to stop and think why she had
done what she had. He couldn't pretend it was to save Galina,
and he didn't really *want* to think too much about why she should
have saved him. But she was tired and ill and he felt a lump come
up in his throat with pity for her. It was up to him now. She had
accomplished the impossible. Now it was up to him to save her.

"There's one place else we can go. There's just one person
who might still be here in Moscow, and who would help us." He
put his arm around her and led her away from the center of the
city, back toward the railway station. He remembered seeing a
wooden building down a side street, a cheap workingmen's café
where they probably would be all right providing they didn't stay
too long. For half a ruble they got two mugs of thin soup and a
slab of black bread. He watched Daisy cup her hands around the
mug, hugging the warmth to her chest.

"When you feel a little better, Daisy," he said, "I want you to
ask the woman serving the soup how to get to the Stretenskaya
district." She sniffed and nodded, too tired even to ask what he
was going to do.

The address of Heikki Rautenberg was burned into his soul.
He had learned it by heart when he and Galina had run in panic
from Petrograd. Everything about Heikki Rautenberg had stayed
with him from those days. . . . "I do not want to see you, ever
again."

The words meant nothing now. There had been a war and a
revolution since then. Values were different. Now it was more
important to find food and a place to sleep, to stay alive, out of
prison, get papers, go home.

They found the apartment in the middle of the afternoon.
The entrance was blocked by snow and refuse that had not been
collected for several weeks. Once, he supposed, the apartment
had looked elegant. Now it was scruffy and pockmarked with
rifle fire. They climbed the stairs from the courtyard and peered

at the doors. He sent up a silent prayer that this time someone would be there. At least there were no armed guards standing outside.

The door was opened a couple of inches and a voice said, "What do you want?"

"I wish to speak to Comrade Rautenberg. I am a friend. From Petrograd."

The door opened a little farther and he found himself staring into the face of a thin, sad, old man, an old man who bore only a faint resemblance to the jolly carouser of his London days.

"Heikki? Is it you?"

He smiled nervously and opened the door wider. In a timid way he actually seemed pleased to see him. "Ah . . . my friend . . . many times I have thought, where are you? What has happened? So many friends gone . . . so many dead . . . the war, the arrests."

"This is . . . Galina's sister. I have to tell you"—he stared at a spot above Heikki's head—"she's dead . . . Galina . . . last summer, dead."

Heikki didn't answer. He led them into the room. Once it had been an elegant room, there was still a carpet on the floor, but the furniture consisted of a cheap wooden table, three chairs, and a bed in the corner. Shutters over the window closed out the darkening day and the fresh snow that was falling.

"So many dead," he sighed. "So many . . . my wife, also my son. We had no food. Last summer was very bad in Moscow—no food, no medicine, everything was taken. My son caught diphtheria and I could find no doctor to come. Then my wife caught it from the boy. I have this room now. The rest of the apartment is taken by three families from the tenth district. It does not worry me anymore. I have nothing now and it is good not to be alone. They are not bad people."

He had a shawl around his shoulders. There was a stove in the corner but only a few sticks burned in it.

"We are in trouble. We have been to the British Consulate and to the Red Cross. We need help to get home again. I have no

447

papers and must apply for a new passport. Where have they gone, all the officials? All the people who could help us?"

"Gone. Left the city. It became dangerous for them. The French and English are now hated enemies of the revolution. They were lucky not to be killed."

"Is there no one who could help us?"

"The Danish Red Cross is still here. And I heard, the other day, that Holmbo, the Norwegian Consul, remains."

Edwin let the breath escape from his body. He had begun to feel the nightmare was all-encompassing, that there was no way out for them. "The Danish Red Cross . . . they would help her. . . ." He gestured toward Daisy, on a chair at the table. "If I can just get her home I'll be satisfied. It is probably impossible for me now. But her . . . I want her to get out."

Daisy had slumped over the table, her head pillowed on her arms. She was asleep.

"So," said Heikki, looking at her. "This one, so unlike the sister . . . not pretty, no?"

No, she wasn't pretty. She would never be pretty—not the way Galina was. But she was ill, and brave. She was worth saving. . . .

"Can we stay here tonight? It is too late to go to the Danish Red Cross now. And she is tired, very tired. We have walked a long way across the city today."

They put her on Heikki's bed in the corner. They passed the night themselves sitting at the table, dozing and talking intermittently of old times. The memories of Galina hurt them both and, as they spoke of her, Edwin realized he would never be cured. However long he lived, the memory of her would cause him pain and longing. The candle on the table burned low and, bit by bit, Edwin told what had happened to her, the betrayals, the deceits, the frailty, the fear. She came alive and sat with them at the table. When the morning came and the candle had guttered out it was as though he had buried her afresh.

The old man took them to the Danish Red Cross the next day. He seemed pleased to be involved in people's lives again. He had always been generous. With money, with hospitality, with presents—especially with Galina he had been generous. Now he had nothing to give but his time and guidance around the nightmare city.

The Red Cross representative, once he saw Daisy's papers and heard who she was, greeted her warmly and with respect. Edwin was surprised. He hadn't realized that Daisy's work, her reputation, or at least the reputation of the Friends' Unit, was so highly revered.

"So many of you good people stranded, isolated," the man said, shaking Daisy warmly by the hand. "We have not heard from Buzuluk for many months now. Some of them set out toward Vladivostok, but God knows what has happened. The war with the Czechs broke out right along the Trans-Siberian Railway lines. We can only pray they have survived. Two of your people are here, in Moscow. They have been running a children's refugee home at Znemenka."

"Who?" The old Daisy was back. Though weakened and ill, she was suddenly in charge of things again, fighting, confident.

"Theodore Rigg and Esther White. They are staying with the Tolstoys who have offered them shelter until they can find means of leaving. You will be welcome there, I am sure."

She smiled, hesitated, and looked at Edwin. "I think it best I stay with my friend. Mr. Rautenberg will let us remain with him, yes?"

Heikki nodded several times.

"This is my friend, Edwin Willoughby. It is difficult for him. His papers were confiscated by the police in Tver. Last April. Somehow he has managed to survive without them but we must try and get new ones for him so that he can get out."

The Danish representative turned to Edwin, his face sober. When he spoke to Edwin he was very slightly patronizing. Edwin realized that beside Daisy he was considered a helpless refugee and he began to wonder if the Red Cross man was right. Compared with Daisy he was of little value.

"It is not going to be easy getting new papers. The Friends now, that might be different. They have a good record and, even

449

now, when the English are so hated, the Friends are made welcome. For you, my friend, things are going to be very difficult."

"If you can just get Daisy out of Russia . . ."

"No!"

The room was quiet. The Dane stared at Daisy, astonished.

"I only go with him. If he doesn't go, then I shall remain here and help him."

"It will be impossible. I do not know anyone who could help . . ."

Daisy, two bright spots of color burning on her cheeks said, "Before . . . when I was in Moscow before, they told me . . . they said if a man had papers and a woman married him, it might help."

"That is true. It might help."

She cleared her throat. "Would it work the other way around? If the woman has papers, and is a Friend, highly thought of, respected, would it help the man?"

Nobody answered.

"I have papers," said Daisy. "I have papers, and I am one of the Friends. If we were to be married, it would be easier, wouldn't it? He could apply as my husband. It would be much easier."

The Red Cross man's face was impassive. "It would probably help. If you could find a priest who would issue a marriage certificate *before* the young man has his papers, it would at least prove a beginning. He would exist on a marriage certificate at least."

"Then that's what we'll do," said Daisy. "We'll find a priest."

Later, back in Heikki's room, he tried to speak to her but she wouldn't listen. She put her hands over her ears every time he tried to discuss it and suddenly it seemed futile, churlish, mean to do anything but agree. They both wanted to go home. That was all they wanted. And a small voice within him knew why she was doing it. For the same reason that she had come to Russia risking her life to search for him. She was trying to pretend it was all a matter of expedience, but he knew why she was doing it.

In the end it was Heikki who found a priest. For most of the money remaining from the strangled policeman, the priest was prepared to marry them, in spite of Edwin's lack of registration. The church was small, and inside the building the paintings, the icons, the screen, and brass rails were, surprisingly, still intact. The revolution had not yet touched the church. Perhaps it never would. The priest was plump and venal and Edwin thought, with sadness, of the kindly man in the village who had buried Galina and tried to give him peace.

Nonetheless, when the service was over, he turned to look at Daisy beside him and saw the secret happiness in her eyes, happiness and longing, and a desperate pleading for him not to smash her happiness.

He could do nothing else but lean forward and kiss her on the lips. "Dear Daisy," he said softly, "my wife."

He got his papers. The two Quakers, the Danish Red Cross official, and Daisy finally got him a provisional passport issued by the Soviet government. It took three days. He thought, with bitterness, of the months he had spent trying to get exit papers for Galina, of the months and the nightmare journey to Tver and the battered face and broken ribs he had taken, all to try and get her papers. And to emphasize the final irony they heard of a train due to leave almost at once for the Finnish border—probably the last train before the frontier closed.

On February 10, 1919, the special train carrying the last French residents of the city steamed out of Moscow with the three Quaker Friends and Edwin on board. The last thing he saw was the lonely figure of Heikki Rautenberg standing on the platform. A part of his life had finished forever.

Two days later they walked across the small bridge spanning the river at Byelo-Ostrov. They were in Finland. They were free.

Part Three

Sophie, Again

28 IT STUNNED US ALL WHEN EDWIN AND DAISY MAY CAME back, married. I think my mother, in spite of her affection for Daisy, in spite of her overwhelming relief that Edwin was alive, regretted the marriage. Daisy was, after all, a Barshinskey. Edwin could have done better for himself.

It never ceased to surprise me how the war didn't really alter people's attitudes. So many people dead and injured. You would have thought that nothing mattered anymore except that some *had* come home, but no, it was plain that Ma was disappointed. And then, bit by bit, it began to come out, the full story of what Daisy had done. Everyone but me was surprised. I'd remembered her fighting the Jefford set that first day in the playground. I remembered her silent independence, her strength, and above all that she had loved Edwin since she was eleven years old. I could believe the whole story—and more that they probably hadn't told.

I'd never seen Daisy so happy. She was ill when she first came home, seriously undernourished, and for a while they thought she might have caught tuberculosis. But with all her frailty and her bad cough she had a radiance about her, a glow that was nothing to do with her feverish sweats. She kept talking about Edwin, My Husband, as though she had to keep saying it to assure herself. Of course, they weren't properly married according to us, and there was a quick marriage meeting up at the Mission Hall to make it all legal. Edwin did it for peace and quiet at home. He wasn't part of the meeting anymore, it was plain to see that, and very soon he joined the Quakers with Daisy.

He was changed, my brother, totally and irrevocably changed. He was quiet and responsible and much, much older than his years. He was kind and gentle with Daisy, sitting up

455

with her at nights when her chest was bad, reading aloud to keep her quiet, bathing her face with lavender water and making her hot drinks when the rest of the house was asleep. They had the middle bedroom, the one that he had had as a boy. There was no way they could set up on their own for the time being. They had heavy debts to pay. The Danish Red Cross had loaned them their train fare to Finland, and the British Consulate had paid for their passage from there. Edwin went to work on Mr. Hayward's farm and in the evenings and on weekends he worked at the garage which had opened up in the village for the new motorcar trade. He never stopped working to pay back the debts, and what with the work, and looking after Daisy at nights, I suppose his quietness, his . . . silence was understandable. One day it came to me who he was like. I'd never noticed it before. He was exactly like my pa. It must have been there all the time but it had taken the war and Daisy to turn him into the kind, gentle, fair man that my father had always been.

He never spoke about Galina, other than to say she was dead, and I never spoke of her either. It's better to let certain things lie fallow, cover them up with weeks and years of ordinary, everyday happenings until they are buried firmly in the past. Whatever had happened in Russia, whatever remained of Galina in my brother's mind and heart, it didn't affect Daisy's happiness and that was good enough for me.

She wrote to Ivan of course, and I wondered what would happen. There had been an exchange of letters between him and Lillian, and then Lillian had announced that she had broken the engagement off. Father made her send back Ivan's ring. I *think* she would have done so anyway, but Pa didn't give her time to consider the matter. It was packed up and sent by registered post to Ivan in the Army of Occupation in Germany. Lillian was very bitter, very proud. She felt she had lost face in the village and very soon she announced that she was going to work for the London couturier all the time and intended to live in London. Ma was very upset but Lillian was adamant. She wasn't going to remain in the village and have people pointing her out as the girl who had broken her engagement. Whenever she spoke of Ivan she was scathing and scornful and it was plain she considered it all his fault. It never occurred to her that she could have married him if she had been content to be a cowman's wife. Poor Lillian. She never learned.

She astounded us all two years later by buying out Miss Clark from her dressmaking business and coming back to the village in a flourish of triumph. She had saved the money over the years without telling any of us. Of course, she'd got good wages in the war, making officers' uniforms, but even so it was a remarkable achievement and she had done what she set out to do, show the village she was better than they were. Once she had become the owner of Willoughby and Clark, Modes and Haute Couture, she apparently never had any regrets for what might have been. She had fulfilled her long-desired ambition. She was a Someone. She left the meeting and joined the church, and eventually changed all her friends, too, becoming part of the circle that included the shopowners and the schoolteachers and the organist. I often thought how mean she was not to have offered to help Daisy and Edwin with their debts when they came home, but I suppose it would have broken her heart not to have come back to the village to "show us all."

Ivan did come home at last. Daisy was all he had left in the world, and even the embarrassment of the broken engagement couldn't keep him from that. I kept away from home every time he came to visit Daisy. It was better that way.

It had been bad for me, after he'd gone away that time. For quite a while I couldn't see anything in life that was hopeful. All my childish dreams, my ambitions, had come to nothing. I'd longed to travel, do exciting things, meet people outside the village. I'd wanted to be a missionary, a nurse, a soldier's wife. Instead here I was at twenty-eight, housekeeper at Fawcett's where I'd worked since I was fifteen. Everyone else had done something with their lives, gone to Russia, or got a V.C., or gone to live and work in London, and here was I still looking after Ma and Pa, unable to get away.

Things improved. They always do if you hold on long enough and don't talk about them too much. Edwin was home. Daisy was happy, and now it was up to me what I did with my life. Edwin and Daisy would look after Ma and Pa, and now it was my turn to try my luck in the outside world. If Daisy could do it, so could I.

I only knew domestic service, of course, but housekeeper at twenty-eight wasn't bad, and I went up to London and registered with an employment agency. They seemed impressed with my qualifications and I told them exactly what I wanted.

I had to wait for six months before the right post came up, and when it did it was exactly what I wanted. The depressing past began to slide away. Things were going to happen. I went up to London again to see the gentleman I would be working for, and I got the position. But I still didn't say anything at home. I wasn't sure what I was waiting for but then, one day, I knew. I walked into the kitchen on my afternoon off and found Ivan there. He'd come to see Daisy without telling anyone.

Daisy was getting better and was up every afternoon. He was sitting with her in the front parlor. The plush curtains were drawn across the window to stop the sun from fading the rug, and because of that I couldn't see his face clearly. And, thank goodness, presumably he couldn't see mine.

"Ivan."

"Sophie."

There was a pause and we carefully didn't look at each other.

"How are you?"

"Very well. And Daisy's getting better too."

We both turned back to Daisy, deeply relieved. The first moment was over. It would be all right from now on.

We finally sat around the tea table, all of us, slightly strained, but observing the conventions with proper formality. Ivan was there as Daisy's brother, not Lillian's ex-fiancé.

And as we sat around the table I knew this was the moment to break my news. It would make it plain to everyone, especially Ivan, that I was going to begin a new life.

"I have some news. It will probably come as a surprise, but I hope you won't mind. It's very good news really."

Everyone stopped eating and looked at me.

"I'm leaving Fawcett's at the end of the year. I haven't told Mrs. Fawcett yet; there's plenty of time for her to get someone else and I'll have time to train her."

Mother looked shocked. "Where are you going, Sophie?" She still felt it was up to her to guide my employment. Well, now she had to learn.

"I'm going to Africa."

"What!"

"To Africa. Kimberley. As housekeeper to the manager of one of the diamond mines. He has an invalid wife who cannot run her household. It's a very big house and there is a huge staff. It will be much bigger than Fawcett's, and I'm told there is a great deal of entertaining and social life. It will be very exciting."

"But, Sophie!" breathed Mother. "The servants will all be black!"

"That's right. It will make a change."

"Well!" Mother fiddled with the teapot, her cup, the jam dish, the way she always did when she was flustered.

"Why didn't you say anything before?"

"I wanted to be sure I had the position," I lied.

"I don't know what to think, what to say . . ."

"Are you sure it's what you want, lassie?"

"Yes, Pa." I didn't look Pa in the eye. He knew me too well. He was the only one who did know me really. The only one who had ever suspected I wasn't happy.

"Then you must go, lassie. If that's what you want, you must go."

The table suddenly exploded into a loud babble of conversation, Mother, Edwin, and Daisy all talking at once. And across the table I found myself looking straight into Ivan's face.

"I've made a dreadful mistake," he said loudly, cutting right across the babble. "Please excuse me."

He got up from the table, took my hand, and led me from the

room. We went up the garden, through the copse and over the stile. Then we walked, very quickly, up the field to the pump.

"I think we'd better be married, Sophie. I take it you won't mind being married to a cowman?"

"I'm going to Africa, Ivan. You don't have to feel anything . . . any guilt, or responsibility . . . because of that night. I understand everything."

"No, you don't. I don't myself. I just know that when you said you were going to Africa I wanted to stop you. I don't really know if I love you. I just know you've always been there when I needed you. I haven't seen you for long stretches, but I always knew you were there. I can't imagine my life without you."

"You've got a cheek, Ivan Barshinskey!" I wished he hadn't said that, about not knowing whether he loved me or not. "You breeze back here, Lillian's jilted fiancé, and tell me to upset all my plans and marry you. You don't love me, and you haven't got a job."

"That's right," he said calmly. "That's exactly right."

I felt so hurt I could hardly speak. "Well, you go and jump at yourself! I've had just about enough from you."

"You're going to have a lot more. Several years of me. I just know, Sophie, that I would be mad not to marry you. I know you so well. You're like Daisy. . . . You're loyal, and kind, and generous. And you're passionate about the people you love. And you love me."

"But you don't love me. And what about Lillian . . ." I was really angry now. "Your *dream!* Your beautiful dream who was so different from the rest of us!"

"Oh, Sophie! Don't be jealous of Lillian. She was a dream . . . a wonderful Willoughby dream for a dirty little Barshinskey kid. You're not a dream, but you're still a Willoughby. I'll never be cured of the Willoughbys. I'll have to marry one of them, and you're the only one that'll have me."

He was grinning. He was big and wide and he had a thatch of black Barshinskey curls over black Barshinskey eyes. It was Mr. Barshinskey, but this one wasn't a drunkard or a wild, unhappy foreigner in a strange land. He'd never call me *kroshka*, but still he was a Barshinskey. He was right. The Barshinskeys had to marry the Willoughbys, and the Willoughbys had to marry the Barshinskeys.

"All right," I said.

"What?"

"All right. I'll marry you. It will be very embarrassing for you after being engaged to Lillian."

"Oh yes, and that reminds me." He fumbled in the pocket of his uniform. "I was planning to try and sell this when I got back to London. But you may as well have it."

It was Lillian's engagement ring. Alas, rings that fitted those delicate Cobham fingers wouldn't fit on my stubby Willoughby paws.

"Oh well," he said. "I'd better sell it after all and buy you a bigger one."

And that's what he did.

Did we lose out, Daisy and I? We'd both married the men we loved—their second choice. It was Daisy who made me change my mind so swiftly. She'd taken Edwin on any terms, and she was happy. She had scoured a continent in the midst of war and revolution to find him and bring him home. She didn't care about anything except that she was married to him. It was enough for her, and if it was enough for her, then surely it should be enough for me also.

I think, in time, I ceased to be Ivan's second choice. He did what he said he would do. He became cowman at Hayward's, eventually head cowman and, over the years, the best cowman in the county. He lived in the same village as Lillian, part of the same family. He observed and watched her as only Ivan could do, and I saw his dream fade. One day, many years later, when I was older and stouter, he looked at me and said, "Sophie, my dear. What a very narrow escape I had. My life would have been quite dreadful if I'd married Lillian." And that was the nearest he ever came to saying he loved me.

461

I never told him of the thing that happened soon after we were married. I never told him because even now, after all these years when he had become a soldier, a hero, a husband, I wasn't sure if he had forgiven his father for those childhood years of misery and humiliation.

I'd gone with Mother to a family funeral over the border into West Sussex. It was a fair distance and we didn't often travel that way. After the burial, crowded into a cottage parlor for the funeral tea, I overheard the words that suddenly sent me reeling back, shocked, breathless, into the golden summer of the Barshinskeys.

". . . strange, a foreigner, but 'ee's wonderful with the cattle, Jack says. Just come out of nowhere, with this concertina thing, plays it real lovely 'ee do. Jack couldn't say 'is name so we call 'im Bill . . ."

"Barshinskey," I said. "Was that his name? Barshinskey? A big man with a great head of black hair and a black beard?"

The two women looked from each other to me as though I was mad. Then one said, "Could 'ave been that name I suppose. We couldn't get it properly. But 'ee didn't 'ave black hair. An oldish man 'ee is, with a big white beard. But, yes, 'ee's big. And plays the concertina real lovely—all kinds of foreign tunes. Two summers 'ee's come back and worked with the cows. Don't know where 'ee goes in winter. Offered 'im a regular job on the farm but says 'ee don't like being tied down. The children, they love 'im. Tells them all kinds of tales about Russia, 'ee does. They really love 'im. 'Ee's a sort of a tramp really. . . ."

I could have found out. I could have asked more questions, even traveled to their village—it was further over yet another border into Hampshire—and seen for myself, but suddenly I didn't want to know. I didn't want to see Mr. Barshinskey with white hair and a concertina instead of a fiddle. I didn't want to know he was a sad old tramp. If I didn't see him I could think of him as he was, just a bit older, still wild, free, living his life the way he wanted. Bewitching children with his dreams, making them long for things they wouldn't, couldn't, ever have. And perhaps, too, I didn't want him to see me, to see his *kroshka* grown up. So I came back home and I never said anything either to Ivan or Daisy May. Their lives, their security, had been bought at too high a price for me to disrupt them with a rumor from two counties away.

Daisy still continued to surprise us. She grew strong and well again, and they finally managed to pay all their debts. And then, in 1922, when the famine broke out in Russia, she and Edwin went back to Buzuluk with the Friends' Relief Unit. It stunned us all. It was ironical that Daisy, who had never wanted to leave the village, traveled halfway around the world on two separate occasions, and I, who had longed for adventure and the excitement of the outside world, remained in the village for my whole life, daughter of a cowman, wife of a cowman, and finally mother of one.

They came back in 1924 when Daisy got typhus and after that there was no question of their doing relief work ever again. Daisy's health never really recovered.

Edwin reapplied to join the railway, and he finally ended up taking over Mr. Watkins's old post as the stationmaster of our little village.

Sometimes I wondered if he was happy. Unlike Ivan he never had a chance to see his dream fade and turn sour. It remained shrouded in the mists and distances of northern Russia, a part of his youth that would never return. And even though I had hated Galina, I had to admit that her magic was real, not like Lillian's. But he was a good husband and, I think, in the end, his dream returned. When their one child, a girl, was born, her eyes were gray like Daisy's, like Edwin's. But everything else was just like that gypsy girl who had danced into the village years before.

They called her Galina.

Bibliography

(All titles published in London)

Baedeker's Russia 1914. First published 1914 by George Allen & Unwin. Reissued by David & Charles, 1971.

Blake, George. *The Ben Line.* Thomas Nelson, 1956.

Burtt, Joseph. *Relief Work in Russia.* Friends' War Victims Relief Committee, 1916.

Catchpool, E. St. John. *Candles in the Darkness.* Bannisdale Press, 1966.

Friends' House Reports of War Victims Relief Committee, 1915, 1916, 1917, 1918.
  The Friend, 11 August 1916.
  Friends' Quarterly Examiner, Vol. 51, 1917.

Graham, Stephen. *Undiscovered Russia.* John Lane, 1912.

Grigg, A. E. *Country Railway Men.* Calypus Books, 1982.

Jackman, Michael. *Thirty Years at Bricklayer's Arms.* David & Charles, 1976.

Lockhart, Bruce. *Memoirs of a British Agent.* Macmillan, 1974.

Miller, Wright. *Russians as People.* Phoenix House, Ltd., 1960.

Murray's Handbooks—Russia, Poland & Finland. John Murray, 1888.

Pares, Bernard. *My Russian Memoirs.* Jonathan Cape, Ltd., 1931.

Robien, Louis de. *Diary of a Diplomat in Russia.* Michael Joseph, 1969.

Salisbury, Harrison E. *Black Night, White Snow.* Cassell, 1978.

———. *Russia in Revolution 1900–1930.* Andre Deutsch, 1978.

Scott, Richenda C. *Quakers in Russia.* Michael Joseph, 1964.

Strong, A. L. *The Unchanging Russia.* Friends' War Victims Relief Committee, 1918.

Wilson, Francesca M. *In the Margin of Chaos.* John Murray, 1944.

Wood, Ruth Kedgie. *The Tourist's Russia.* Andrew Melrose, 1912.

Printed in Canada